Knife Edge

Knife Edge

Douglas Reeman

arrow books

Published by Arrow in 2006

1 3 5 7 9 10 8 6 4 2

Copyright © Bolitho Maritime Productions

Douglas Reeman has asserted his right under the Copyright, Designs and
Patents Act, 1988 to be identified as the author of this work

First published in the United Kingdom in 2004 by William Heinemann
The Random House Group Limited
20 Vauxhall Bridge Road, London, SW1V 2SA

Random House Australia (Pty) Limited
20 Alfred Street, Milsons Point, Sydney
New South Wales 2061, Australia

Random House New Zealand Limited
18 Poland Road, Glenfield, Auckland 10, New Zealand

Random House (Pty) Limited
Isle of Houghton, Corner Boundary Road & Carse O'Gowrie,
Houghton, 2198, South Africa

The Random House Group Limited Reg. No. 954009
www.randomhouse.co.uk

A CIP catalogue record for this book is available from the British Library

Papers used by Random House
are natural, recyclable products made from wood grown in
sustainable forests. The manufacturing processes conform to
the environmental regulations of the country of origin

ISBN 0 994 3629 9

Typeset by SX Composing DTP, Rayleigh, Essex
Printed and bound in Great Britain by
Bookmarque Ltd, Croydon, Surrey

For you, Kim, with all my love.
I couldn't have done it without you.

The author wishes to acknowledge the friendship
and support of Sir James Hann, C.B.E.,
fellow sailor and kindred spirit.

"Guard these Colours well and remember that, whatever the problem, a Royal Marine Commando is always expected to achieve the impossible."

H.R.H. the Duke of Edinburgh, presenting Colours to the Commandos in Malta, 29th November 1952

1970

LEARNING

CHAPTER ONE

"Are there any further bids, gentlemen?" The auctioneer's gavel hovered momentarily above the table. "Thank *you*, Mr. Roberts." It sounded loud after the sudden stillness. The end of a long two days. It was over, until the next time.

John Masterman, senior partner of the company which bore his name, closed the leather folder around his papers and a well-thumbed catalogue. He felt tired. Drained, perhaps more than usual, but would not admit it. The faded lettering on the folder said it all. *Masterman International Valuers and Auctioneers. Established 1802.*

He glanced through the nearest window. It was only noon, but it looked like dusk in the dull grey light. The new year of 1970 was just three weeks old, and it felt like it, he thought. He was sixty and then some, and his junior partners, especially, often hinted that he should think about retiring. He half smiled. *And do what?*

The big room was emptying. A lot of the faces he knew; some were strangers, hoping for a rare bargain, or here out of curiosity. His assistants were removing the last item, an old campaign chest from the Crimean period, while outside, lining the drive, the vans awaited instructions. Like undertakers . . . A few dealers were already collecting in little groups, taking their own bids now that the main event was over.

3

He touched the date on the leather folder. *1802*. Just a few weeks ago he had been at another auction in another fine old house. There had been some plates from the Horatia Service made by Chamberlains of Worcester and commissioned by Lord Nelson at that same time, three years before the little admiral had fallen at Trafalgar. They had gone under the hammer for far more than he would have dreamed possible.

He looked at the lines of tall trees, stark and leafless against the surrounding fields. Would they, like this old house, be destroyed when the new road came through?

Hawks Hill was heavy with memories, overlaid with them, like some of the paintings and furniture which had changed hands here today. Originally a fortified Tudor farmhouse, it had been bought and enlarged by old Major-General Samuel Blackwood, described as 'the last soldier'. After him, all the other Blackwoods had entered the Corps of Royal Marines.

But like so many country houses, it had outlived its time in a modern world of austerity and recovery. During the Great War it had been used as a hospital for officers blinded in the hell of Flanders and the Somme. During the last war it had served in a similar capacity, while the estate had been worked by the Women's Land Army and Italian prisoners of war, the only men of military age available. Twenty miles north of Portsmouth, and some seven miles from Winchester, it had remained almost isolated but for the nearby village of Alresford.

Masterman thought suddenly of Lieutenant-Colonel Michael Blackwood. He had been due to retire from the Corps; perhaps in some ways he had been coming to terms with it, if not accepting it completely. He had intended to convert the old stable block into a smaller but more practical home for the Blackwood family. Masterman

4

looked at the walls, the pale rectangles where so many pictures had marked the years, the triumphs and the tragedies.

Some of the vans were moving off now; cars too, probably down to the local pub.

He wondered where Joanna, the colonel's wife, was at this moment. One last appointment, they had told Michael Blackwood. To visit two separate bases where the Royal Marines, his commandos, were carrying out peacekeeping duties, in Cyprus and in Northern Ireland. Blackwood had been in a lot of tight corners since the war, Korea, Suez, Aden, but as one marine had said, he had the touch. The lads looked to him when the going got rough.

It had happened the day he had been due to leave Cyprus and return to England. A booby-trapped car, they said later. Both he and his driver had been killed instantly.

It was a new kind of warfare. He frowned, angry with himself. It was plain murder. What must Joanna Blackwood be thinking today? They had a son, Ross, and a daughter. Ross was in the Corps, carrying on the tradition.

"I can clear up, Mr. Masterman." It was his assistant. New and eager, waiting for him to leave.

"I'll just hang on until . . ." He stared past the remaining handful of dealers, and his clerk, checking the invoices.

A young man was standing by one of the makeshift benches where a pile of silver frames were awaiting collection. They had been marked down to a jeweller and silversmith in Winchester, a man who often appeared at estate auctions.

Masterman said, "Sorry, but that lot's all taken." The young man had picked up one of the frames and was holding it. A stranger, yet somehow familiar. *I must be getting past it.* "The buyer is over there by the fireplace.

5

You could make him an offer." He reached out. "You have good taste, anyway. That's an Asprey frame, as I recall."

But the young man held on to the frame and shook his head. "I don't give a damn about that. It's the photo. I wanted to . . ." He broke off, but did not resist as Masterman took the frame from his grip. Despair, anger, defiance, it was all of those.

He thought the photograph had probably been taken in this very room, by the window. The same trees were in the background, recognizable, but in leaf. The subject was in WRNS uniform, her cap with its Royal Marine Globe and Laurel badge perched on her knee.

It was like opening a door, or hearing something shouted on the wind.

"Diane Blackwood, the colonel's sister. Lovely girl, I understand. Never married . . . died in a car accident just after the war. I believe it nearly finished her brother."

"I know." The eyes were watching him steadily as Masterman unfastened the frame, and removed the photograph.

"I told them to make sure these were all empty." He hesitated. "Did you know her?" Ridiculous; he was too young. How could he have known her?

The other man said nothing. Instead, he pulled a wallet from inside his raincoat and opened it with care, taking out a photograph, which he held up, still without comment. It was worn and carefully repaired, as if some one had tried to rip it in half, but the same photo. The girl named Diane, who had never married.

Like studying documents, or going through some one's effects before a sale; it was vague one moment, vividly clear the next.

There had been a scandal of some kind; the family had closed ranks. Like the Corps.

Masterman said, "Take the picture. It's between us, right?"

Their eyes met, and he was surprised that he had not realized before, or seen it immediately. The same features in some of the paintings . . . or the face of the man who had been killed by a terrorist bomb in Cyprus.

He held out his hand.

"If there's any way I can help . . ."

He got no further.

"You just did, sir." The mouth smiled, but it barely reached the eyes. The handshake was hard. "I'll not forget."

Then he was gone, and Masterman stood gazing at the empty frame, trying to remember every moment.

His new assistant asked brightly, "Some one from the past, sir?"

Masterman bit back a sharp retort, and said, "From the future, I suspect."

The morning was bitterly cold, and yet the sky was surprisingly clear after overnight rain. A washed-out blue, enough to chill your bones to the marrow.

Lieutenant Ross Blackwood raised himself very slightly on his elbows, teeth gritted against the pain of loose stones, his uniform denims clinging to his legs. Cold, wet, impatient. He should be used to it by now. He was not.

Why did the army, and for that matter his Corps, the Royal Marines, choose such godforsaken places for their training exercises? He covered his mouth with one hand while he took stock of the immediate area. On the edge of Dartmoor, this was now a waste of fallen buildings, walls starred with rifle and machine-gun fire or scattered by every kind of lethal device. Even in the hands of skilled marksmen and eager instructors, the bullets were often too close for comfort. Or over confidence.

There had been a small, private flying club here once. Taken over and enlarged for a fighter squadron during the last war, it had become derelict in the uneasy years following Germany's surrender. There was a village of some kind, too. Now only crumbling shells where men had tended the land and children had played at being soldiers.

When he moved his hand he saw the breath from his lips, like steam. The instinctive warning . . . He lifted his binoculars, small and powerful, and scanned the nearest cottages, eyeless ruins, shelled, burned and stripped by the countless drills and exercises this wasteland had seen.

He thought of the previous week. Or had it been longer? Hawks Hill, the gaping strangers, the expressionless auctioneer, and the silent exchange of signals. Money changing hands, deals settled. Like conspirators. Vandals.

He tensed. A shadow, dead leaves moving in the bitter air? It was Boyes, his sergeant. Too experienced to make mistakes on an exercise; he had seen and done too much of the real thing. A true Royal Marine. His mind lingered on the old house, as it had once been, and the life he had grown up to accept. *His* life. His future. Sergeant Boyes had served with his father, and had been at the memorial service. With many others, young and old, some wearing their medals, from campaigns he could only imagine.

Hawks Hill . . . Soon it would be demolished. Where, then, would go all the memories and ghosts?

He pictured his mother, strong and beautiful amidst the sadness and the well-intentioned sympathy, which must have torn her apart.

Afterwards they had walked through the echoing house together, past the bare walls and the packing cases, and some officials from the local council, already making notes.

She had stood looking up at the one remaining portrait in

8

the empty study, where, as a boy, Ross had first discovered an old photo album with some of the faded prints of the Great War. Groups of officers, sitting cross-legged and self-conscious, at some Corps function or other. Others, grim-faced in steel helmets; and one print of a battlefield, craters brimming with rain and mud. No trees. Nothing. Somebody, perhaps his grandfather, had written beneath that torn landscape, *Where no birds sing*. Ross had never forgotten it.

His mother had slipped her hand through his arm and said quietly, "Your father would be so proud of you, Ross."

As she had done, he had looked at the portrait. She was taking it to her friend's house in London, while she was getting her bearings. What would she do without him? *Your father would be so proud of you.* That was almost the worst part. Thinking back, he must always have been in awe of his father. *The colonel.* Out of reach.

He lowered the glasses and wiped the lenses with a piece of tissue. Even that was wet.

Ross had just returned from Northern Ireland when the news of his father's murder had broken.

He had had it all prepared. In his thoughts, he had heard himself coming out with it.

His father was leaving the Corps, with pride and with honour. There was no point in pretending, making any more excuses.

Your father would have been so proud of you.

How would his father have taken it? Reacted to being told that his only son was going to quit the Corps? Break with tradition. The last of the Blackwoods.

He watched the cottage on the end of the row. Empty windows, a fragment of tattered curtain still clinging to a splintered frame. Where people must have seen the enemy bombers, and the tiny fighters cutting the sky with their

9

vapour trails as they went after them. The high hopes and the setbacks. Korea, Suez, Cyprus and Malaya, and the Royal Marines were always there, often when it was already too late. The end of empire, some called it.

But men died because of it. And women, too.

Tough veterans had seen it all and made light of it. In the Corps, like the navy, the response was always the same. Maybe it had to be.

If you can't take a joke, you shouldn't have joined!

What had changed him? He heard a far-off crackle of machine-gun fire, blanks or otherwise. He often wondered how many men had been killed in bleak places like this one, by accident, by ammunition that was intended to make it a little too real.

He remembered the street in Belfast. Almost peaceful after the initial hostility. Backing up the local police, facing the threats and the bricks from the back of the crowd. And the petrol bombs. And there had been kindness too, like a bridge.

The police had cleared the street; hot drinks and some doorstep-like sandwiches had appeared. The marines had relaxed.

There had been a young marine named Jack, new to the commandos, who was always being ragged by his comrades because of his strong Birmingham accent.

He had been the only one to see the danger, but had not recognized it.

"Th' kids'll be comin' back soon, sir. My grandad used to play one of them things. He'd never leave it lyin' about to be nicked!"

The 'thing' was a barrel organ. Ross could see it now. Outside a boarded-up shop, with two ragged puppets propped on the top as if waiting for an audience.

Before any one could do anything Jack from Brum, as

they had nicknamed him, had crossed the street to have a closer look.

Ross could not recall the explosion. More of a sensation than a sound. Like a shock, and a blinding white flash.

He twisted round on one elbow, his nerves like hot wires. But it was only Sergeant Boyes. A big man, who could move like a cat when necessary.

He said casually, "There's one of 'em in that second window. Not as smart as he thinks. Saw the sun flash on somethin' – lookin' at his watch, most likely."

He might have been watching me.

Was that what Boyes was thinking? Wondering about his lieutenant, doubting him? He had been there too, that day in the street in Belfast, when the carefully set booby-trap had exploded. Where children would have come to play.

There had been nothing left of the young marine to bury.

He heard himself say, "Use the grenade. We'll move in now!" Like some one else.

He saw Boyes nod. Approval, relief, who could say?

He loosened his holster and rose slowly on to his knees.

"Now!"

The stun grenade exploded, and some of his men were already converging on the row of ruined cottages. Whistles blew, and an officer had appeared waving a flag. The exercise was over. The pros and cons would be debated later.

Ross realized that he had half drawn his pistol, although he did not remember doing so.

Like that day when the bomb had exploded. The police had said that no one else had been killed or injured. Not like some they had faced.

All Ross recalled was that they had caught the man responsible, and somebody had been gripping his own

11

wrist, Boyes or one of the others, he was never certain. Like now, today, on a piece of Devon moorland, the gun in his hand.

I would have killed him. I wanted to.

He thought of his mother's hand on his arm in that deserted study at Hawks Hill, sharing the moment. And the portrait of his father.

Proud? I wonder.

Lieutenant-Colonel Leslie De Lisle glanced at the cup of tea on the desk where a well-meaning orderly had placed it, and frowned. Something stronger would have been more welcome. He half listened to the regular tramp of boots, the occasional bark of commands, a tannoy speaker calling some one's name. It was sometimes hard to remember what it had been like in those far-off days.

He was suddenly on his feet at one of the big windows that overlooked the barracks square. A grey January forenoon, the square still shining from the last rainfall.

He shivered despite his usual self-control. Winter in Plymouth: Stonehouse Barracks. Less than a week ago he had been sweltering in Singapore.

He opened the window very slightly and braced himself against the keen air. As assistant to the Chief of Special Operations he was far removed from the mysteries facing those marching ranks of Royal Marines, raw recruits for the most part. *As we all were.*

"At the halt . . . On th' right . . . *foooorm . . . squad!*" It could have been the same sergeant.

He saw some other marines marching easily past the square, their green berets marking them out as commandos. The recruits would be watching them with envy and perhaps awe, dreaming of the day when they, too, might number among the elite.

De Lisle turned away as another bellow of commands snapped them back to reality.

He caught sight of his reflection in the glass. Self-contained, austere, with the neat moustache favoured by many senior officers in the Corps. A splash of colour on his uniform; *for gallantry*, the citations had said. Not a cloth-carrier like some he had known. And still knew.

It would be strange to be leaving his H.Q. and his personal staff. Away from the steady stream of signals from all over the world, wherever Royal Marines were keeping the peace and being first in the field in the bush wars, and against terrorism wherever it appeared.

He smiled. And away from the General. Some one else had already been appointed to take the weight.

His wife had been less understanding.

"Why you, Leslie? You'd be retired in a few more years! Why throw it all away?"

They had been married for twenty years. Was that all it meant?

He glanced at the painting opposite the commandant's desk. Royal Marines manning the International gun at Peking, during the Boxer Rebellion. It would never be like that again. He touched his moustache with his knuckle. There had been a De Lisle during the embassy seige. He looked at his watch. A Blackwood, too.

There were voices outside the door. Right on time. But then, this was Stonehouse.

De Lisle made a point of knowing as much as possible about every addition to the various sections of Special Operations.

A name or some family connection, *The Old Pals Act,* as the General had been heard to call it, was never enough. Courage, leadership, self-dependence, were only a part of it.

The Blackwood name was well known in the Corps, and De Lisle had been working with Ross Blackwood's father just before he had been killed in Cyprus. A strong man, professionally and ethically, and a good friend. The combination was not always possible in their trade.

The door opened and closed, and they faced each other. De Lisle held out his hand. He disliked formality; sanctimonious bullshit, his old colour sergeant called it.

"Sit down – this won't take long. Ross, isn't it?"

They studied each other across the borrowed desk, the marching feet and hoarse voices like a soundtrack in the background.

De Lisle had always learned everything he could before this kind of interview, and had trained himself to distinguish fact from surmise, and truth from intuition. For once, he could admit surprise. Ross Blackwood was twenty-five years old, by only two months. His record was good, and his commanding officers well satisfied with his progress. He was patient but firm with his subordinates, and wary of some of the older N.C.O.s. And an excellent shot with a rifle on the range. Not that it counted for much in these days of rapid fire, when the gun could too easily take over from a nervous marksman.

But it was not the youthful, eager face he had been expecting.

The eyes were level, grey-blue, and almost cold, the colour of the sea. Outwardly he seemed very calm, almost relaxed. Detached, as if they were meeting by accident.

De Lisle said abruptly, "I was very sorry to hear about your father, of course. We all were. A fine man. A first class Royal Marine."

Yes, the family likeness was there, in the eyes most of all, steady, giving nothing away. Yet.

Strange that he had never got used to the new Lovat

14

uniform, although some six years had passed since it had been adopted by the Corps, as something between the familiar battledress and the formal blues. De Lisle had been at the ceremonial parade at Buckingham Palace when Her Majesty the Queen had carried out the inspection held to mark the Tercentenary of the Corps, the first occasion on which the new uniform had been worn. Six years ago. It felt like yesterday.

"This is short notice, but then, it usually is. Most of the details are still top secret. Have to be. If the press got wind of it . . ."

He looked briefly at the window as a bugle cut through all the other sounds. *Stand Easy*. A break from the drills and the sarcastic comments of the N.C.O.s. A mug of pusser's tea.

"It's a comparatively small operation, maybe a waste of time." He made up his mind, could almost feel it click into place, like a rifle bolt ramming a round up the breech. "You were trained to work with the Special Boat Section, right? It'll be a bit like that. Hong Kong. To begin with . . ." He swore under his breath as the telephone came to life. *"Yes? This is De Lisle! I told you I was not to be disturbed!"* A pause. "Oh, I see, sir. Well, in that case . . ."

Ross Blackwood made himself relax, muscle by muscle. Hong Kong. He had been there briefly when completing his training in a frigate. What had he expected? Northern Ireland again, perhaps that same street. The barrel organ. A man he had scarcely got to know, blown apart. No warning. No reason.

He looked directly at the officer across the desk. Who had known his father, and came of the same tradition. De Lisle's father had gone through the war, had been in Penang when the Japanese had surrendered. *Just as my father had marched into Germany at the end of it all*. Wars with

15

meaning and purpose. Something to show for all the pain and the sweat. To be proud of.

Hong Kong, then. And afterwards?

He glanced at the medal ribbons on the lieutenant-colonel's breast. The D.S.O., and the Croix de Guerre, probably from the ill-fated Suez campaign, when their so-called allies had turned their backs.

De Lisle was saying nothing, and was listening intently. The 'sir' explained a lot. It was probably the general, his old boss.

He was reminded suddenly of Hawks Hill, and his mother. Always so strong, stronger than any of them in her quiet way. She had never spoken to him about her own war service, or how she had been captured by the French police while on a mission during the German occupation. An old family friend had told him, but not until a few years back. Captured and tortured, he had said.

What would she do now?

De Lisle was saying, "Yes, I agree, sir. It will be *my* decision, I am aware of that." He put down the telephone with great care, as if the general could still hear him.

He said, "Tradition is something hard to explain, let alone describe. But it's important, some would say vital. It's what we are. What we do. Your father said that to me once in rather a tight corner, as I recall." He turned up his lips in a humourless smile, and his eyes were hard. "What d' you say? Can I put you down as a volunteer?"

Ross Blackwood thought of the portrait in the old study, his mother's hand on his arm. There was still time. There would be no shortage of volunteers, even for Northern Ireland.

"How soon, sir?" Like hearing somebody else again. One of those portraits . . .

De Lisle stood up and peered at his watch.

16

"What I expected." Then he did smile, and it was genuine. "Hoped." He looked at the telephone. "Two weeks. Intelligence will give you your orders. Major Houston is running this show. He'll liven things up."

The mood changed. "Remember. Top secret." He added casually, "Your sister is a journalist, I understand?"

He did not elaborate, but thrust out his hand and strode to the door.

Ross Blackwood picked up his green beret from a chair and stared at it.

It was decided. Choice had never really entered into it.

De Lisle had mentioned a Major Houston, who would be in direct charge of things. The name rang no bells, but that would soon change.

Ross Blackwood had been in the Corps long enough to know and appreciate the importance of security, and secrecy also.

He pulled on his beret and smiled faintly at his reflection in the window, which was once more spotted with rain.

Your sister is a journalist, I understand?

A reporter, anyway. Susanna, Sue as she preferred, was probably already contemplating a change. Twenty years old, restless and headstrong, she was always full of surprises. He sometimes thought he hardly knew his sister at all. Maybe that was it. The Corps and its family traditions had fashioned their lives, and had somehow come between them.

Like the time she had been seen and recognized on television, taking part in a students' anti-nuclear march in London. She had made no apologies, even to their mother. "Some one's got to do it," had been her only comment.

But she had been in tears at her father's memorial service.

He wondered what De Lisle would have said had he

known that the young Lieutenant Blackwood he had selected for special service had been on the point of resigning?

Somewhere a bugle sounded, and the marching feet resumed.

He walked out into the grey light, facing it. Accepting it.

Now back to Hawks Hill, perhaps for the last time.

Two marines in green berets threw up smart salutes as they marched past him. Their eyes met, with that familarity they all took for granted.

If you can't take a joke . . .

Sergeant Boyes was waiting for him outside the guard room, although he made every effort to make it appear coincidental.

"All done, sir?"

"I'm getting a bit of leave."

Boyes, despite his fifteen years in the Corps, ten as a commando, was unable to keep it up.

"Got my orders too, sir! Hong Kong or bust!"

So much for top secret. But it was like that in the Corps. 'The family'. And De Lisle would know that better than most.

He said, "I'm glad. I hope we don't regret it."

They fell into step and headed for the transport section. He looked back only once.

It was too late now.

He stood in a pool of light beside the iron bed while he checked the neat piles of kit and personal belongings. Some he would keep with him, some would be flown on ahead. A proper flight this time, not some slow passage in a Royal Fleet Auxiliary ship or, worse, a commandeered merchant-man. Fast: no time for doubts.

It had been a short course, a 'crash course' as some joker

18

had called it, to learn the workings of a small underwater limpet mine. The weapon had originated in Russia, and had made its appearance in several trouble spots in Borneo and Malaya. A toy compared with some he had seen, but deadly in the right hands.

Now it was over, and the Royal Marines N.C.O.s and some petty officers who had taken part had gone on leave. He looked along the rank of beds and cupboards. *Gone home.*

This was his home, or had been for the last few weeks. A makeshift extension to H.M.S. *Vernon*, the torpedo and mine establishment across Portsmouth Harbour. Here on the Gosport side, it seemed almost deserted by comparison.

It would be dark by now, and tomorrow was Saturday. He ticked it off in his mind. A run ashore, maybe meet a familiar face in some pub or other. Drink too much. Or sit in the mess with the duty N.C.O.s and watch the TV, play snooker, or drink beer in the NAAFI, while the manager kept one eye on the clock.

He should be used to the gaps. He was twenty-five years old and had served seven of them in the Corps. *Should be used to it.*

He sat down on the edge of the bed and pulled his suitcase up beside him. He was still not sure why he had gone to the old house. It was only twenty miles from here, but he had been to Portsmouth several times, to Eastney Barracks at Southsea, or to attend one course or another. And he had never been to see Hawks Hill before.

The high-ceilinged rooms, the gesticulating bidders and the regular click of the auctioneer's gavel: he had walked through and past them. Like being invisible. One of the ghosts.

The news of Lieutenant-Colonel Blackwood's murder by EOKA terrorists in Cyprus had gone through the Corps like lightning. Even those who had never laid eyes on him, or served with him in any capacity, had felt it. *Personal.*

He had often imagined the house, wondered about it, and the generations of people who had lived there. In reality, it had been hard to come to terms with the litter and the jostling strangers.

He opened the case and held the photograph in his hands directly under the light.

He recalled the auctioneer's sudden kindness, his interest, maybe, in the revival of the story. The old scandal.

He touched the photograph very gently. He could hear one of the messmen whistling tunelessly, and the muffled beat of music from his radio. What would he think if he looked in and saw him? And a lot of others along the way?

And he had been in that room where the photo had been taken. When she had been a 'Maren', as they were nicknamed in the Corps. The same Globe and Laurel.

And she had died in a car crash, just as her brother had been killed in Cyprus. Years apart, their lives divided.

In the same room. Perhaps where she had made love to . . .

He heard feet on the stairway, and slid the photograph into the case again, his face the professional mask.

It was a corporal from the signals section, whom he knew vaguely by sight.

"Glad I caught you, Sergeant." He thrust out a piece of signal pad, his eyes moving quickly across the neat pile of kit and luggage. "Flight's been brought forward one day."

"Thanks. I was half expecting something like that." He waited. "Anything else?" Like a guard going up. A defence.

"The colour sergeant wants to stand you a drink in his mess. Tell Sergeant Blackwood I won't take no for an answer, he says!"

"Tell him I'll be there. And thanks."

He heard the door slam shut, the boots descending the stairs.

He touched the suitcase again. He was ready.

No longer alone.

CHAPTER TWO

Major Keith Houston swivelled his buttocks around a corner of the desk and folded his arms as he looked at each face individually.

"Essentially, gentlemen, this is to be a combined operation. The navy certainly, and to some extent local police forces when necessary." He plucked his shirt away from his chest and added, "The army will have the lion's share, but we can deal with that when we have to. You will be in command of some ninety Royal Marines, many of whom are specialists, and have seen a lot of service in the Far East. Not exactly a major force, but properly handled it should suffice." He ticked off the points he had already mentioned on his strong fingers. "Stop-and-search, and a swift response in any trouble spot. Illegal immigrants are a real pain. They can also develop into something far worse, and dangerous."

Ross Blackwood eased his back away from the chair and felt his shirt sticking to his skin. A mere three days ago, he had been walking in the rain with his sister on a typical January day. It seemed like a dream now. Beyond the half-shuttered windows was the full expanse of Hong Kong harbour, the many anchored vessels and other, moving craft shimmering and distorted in haze, as he had seen this morning, with Kowloon on the other side of the water, the dockyard, and beyond them the New Territories. No hotter than an English summer, but the air was heavy and humid, clinging.

He found Major Houston an interesting character. He recalled De Lisle's curt comment. *He'll liven things up.* Heavily built, but surprisingly quick on his feet. A face dominated by a broken nose, a memento from his time as a keen rugby player. Ross had already learned that he had played for his old school, the Combined Services team, and, of course, the Corps. A man who took a lot of exercise and expected his subordinates to follow his example. Squash, jogging: it was said that he would be back in the front line of a rugby scrum at the drop of a hat.

Their first meeting had been brief. *Knew your father pretty well. It's a different enemy we're facing now, I'm afraid.*

Houston had turned to stare at the map that covered most of one wall.

"Most of the boats used for illegal immigrants, smuggling and, yes, sabotage, are faster than our own. But that follows, doesn't it?"

Some one chuckled. The barriers were coming down.

But Ross was looking at the major's broad back. His shirt was dark with sweat, as if he had been lying on wet grass. Exercise and fitness were a necessity for this powerful, restless man.

Houston was saying, "Big area to cover, but you are here to wait, then hit the buggers hard!" Just as swiftly, he relaxed again. "By the way, the captain of *Tamar* is giving a little reception tonight. To make you welcome, is the excuse." He grinned. "So be there. That's an order."

The meeting was over. There would be another tomorrow at Naval Operations.

H.M.S. *Tamar* was the navy's base here, named after an

old trooper which had been the first depot ship in Hong Kong. She had been sunk to avoid capture when the Japanese had marched into the colony in '41.

Ross looked around at his companions, two lieutenants, and an acting-captain he had met once on a battle course in Scotland, whose name was Irwin. The others were on Houston's staff, and obviously enjoying it.

Through the nearest window he saw the bat-like sail of a junk, the low hull still invisible in heat haze. Timeless, and strangely moving.

"Gets to you, doesn't it?"

Ross had not even heard him shift from his perch on the desk.

Close to, it was like seeing another person entirely. Not the battered 'old China hand', the ex-rugby forward, but the true professional, a man probably still in his early thirties.

Houston said, "Results, that's what we want. There'll be a general election at home this year, if I'm not mistaken." He tapped the side of his broken nose. "*Results*, right?"

He strode away, calling somebody's name.

Ross put on his beret, and looked again for the junk. But it had vanished.

There was a hand on his shoulder. "Time for a gin and something, eh?"

But all Ross heard was the voice in the commandant's office over the sound of marching feet.

He'll liven things up!

Ross Blackwood stepped into the outer office and waited as another lieutenant finished his telephone conversation, stabbing the air with a cigarette while he emphasized something about transport.

All the other rooms he had passed had been empty and in darkness. But not this one. He could hear Major Houston's voice in the adjoining office where they had been only this morning, and he had seen the junk standing above the haze. The captain of H.M.S. *Tamar* and his wardroom had laid on a typical naval welcome for the newcomers. It was hard to keep a tally of the drinks, which was not unusual; you turned your head and your glass had been refilled. There had been women there, too, some officers' wives. Others . . . he tried to remember the introductions.

The duty officer slammed down the telephone and stubbed out his cigarette.

"Go right in, old boy. The Boss is expecting you." He was already pulling out another cigarette.

"Does he always work as late as this?"

The lieutenant shrugged. "He never sleeps."

The office was in darkness but for one small lamp on the desk, a decanter and some glasses beside it. An old-fashioned bladed fan was revolving slowly, directly overhead, but the air was still and very warm.

"Come over here. Look at that view."

The panorama across the harbour was indeed impressive, and bustling despite the lateness of the hour. Hundreds of lights were reflected or moving across the black water; it seemed impossible that some would not collide or become entangled with darker shapes at their moorings. Here and there he could see the sharper edge of a larger, swifter vessel, heading perhaps for the open waters of the South China Sea, or taking its chances amidst the traffic toward Kowloon. The haze had dissipated, and the night was clear.

Turning back to the room, he saw that Houston's shirt was hanging open, his scarlet mess jacket on the back of a chair.

Houston asked, "Good party at *Tamar*?" He did not wait for an answer. "I've been wined an' dined by the army." He

25

paused. "Do their best, I suppose. But we have to think of the future. Co-operation, and all that, eh?"

He leaned on the sill. "Ferry's running late. This'll be the last one 'til morning."

Ross watched the red and green navigation lights, like bright eyes on the water, the sudden surge of froth and foam as the ferry's skipper manoeuvred alongside the pier. The Star Ferry ran back and forth across Victoria Harbour all day, every day, as frequent and familiar as a bus.

He felt Houston's eyes on him and sensed, suddenly, that something was wrong. He had not been called here merely to admire the view.

"Everybody judges us, Blackwood. Waiting to criticize. Looking out for a mistake, a blunder somewhere along the line. But I don't tolerate mistakes, not if they can be slammed on the head before they get in the way. *My* way."

He turned abruptly and strode to the desk, his watch glinting in the lamplight as he tilted the decanter over two glasses.

"Drink this."

Ross sipped it and nearly choked. It was neat; Scotch, brandy, it might have been anything.

Houston seemed to have no problem with his. When he put the glass down, it was empty.

"I want you to be quite open with me. No rank, no bullshit. And I'll be straight with you. Good or bad, *right?*"

"Right, sir."

"Heard about it as soon as I got back from the barracks. Another flight came into Kai Tak, the last of our contingent. N.C.O.s, specialists – they were delayed somewhere." One hand fanned at the air as if he were impatient with himself. "Sergeant Steve Blackwood – ever heard of him?"

"I knew of a corporal . . ." He got no further.

"Well, he's a sergeant now, and a bloody useful one to

all accounts." He tried to lighten it. "Have to be, lumbered with a name like that in this bloody regiment!" But it did not work. "This assignment could come to nothing. We've all seen that kind of cock-up before. But it may be the start of something big, too bloody big for old scores and recriminations. I wouldn't stand for it."

Ross looked past him, at the lights, the darkened ferry, the garish signs across the water, a police boat slowing down beside another, anonymous craft.

But all he could see was his father's face.

It would have been easier if he had told him about it. The rumour and the resentment had all been a part of growing up. Even his mother had avoided the subject; maybe she had been made to carry the brunt of it, so that he and his sister would be spared.

It was common enough in wartime. Two people thrown together, and perhaps the love had been genuine. Who could judge them, or condemn?

"I knew some of it, and guessed the rest. I never knew Diane, who was my aunt. She died in a car smash before I was born. I never got the whole story, nor wanted to, I suspect. But her child lived, and he was a Blackwood in every sense. I suppose this had to happen."

Houston nodded. "De Lisle should have known. Probably did, if I've got his measure. *The Corps comes first. Now and always.* Should be his family motto!" He swung round suddenly, a silhouette against the harbour and its constant movement and life.

"Family and tradition have always been strong in the Corps, I don't have to tell you that. But to me, trust and loyalty are paramount. You've not been in action yet, but the time will come, probably sooner than we think."

Ross said, "I was in Northern Ireland, sir."

The big hand sliced the air again. "Rules and attitudes,

27

usually directed by those who've never heard a shot fired in anger. Call 'em what you will, patriots, freedom-fighters or religious fanatics, but when I'm on the wrong end of a gun, that man is an enemy!"

"I know that, sir."

"Good." He walked to the decanter again but apparently changed his mind. "You've heard it said often enough. An officer is only as good as his sergeants. True or not, I'll not risk men's lives because of some rift, family or otherwise. Do I make myself clear?"

"I think I was expecting it, sir."

Houston grinned. "Three years ago, I think it was, when we were pulling out of Aden, my life was saved by a sergeant I had always hated. It was mutual. But I'm here because of him. So think about it, if and when the time comes."

"I won't let you down, sir."

"I know that. Otherwise I'd have you on the next plane out of Kai Tak. Now be off with you. See you in Operations tomorrow."

Ross paused in the doorway and looked back. Houston was still framed against the harbour lights.

"Well?" He did not turn.

"The sergeant who saved your life, sir."

Houston gave a shrug. "Met him some months later. Offered to shake his hand. He refused, the bastard. Reassuring, I thought!"

Ross walked through the outer office, where a different officer was on the telephone and did not look up.

It had been a long day.

Sergeant Ted Boyes reached out to grip a handrail as the deck lifted suddenly and plunged across another vessel's wake. The harbour launch was one of many serving both the Royal Navy and the Hong Kong authorities, always busy regardless of time and weather and showing all the signs of it. The hull and the thick, protective rubbing strake around it were scarred and scraped from many clashes with jetty and quayside, and more especially going alongside other vessels in total darkness. There were clusters of motor tyres kept handy for the worst of such encounters. Boyes had heard one seaman describe Hong Kong as the world's final resting place for old tyres. It was easy enough to see why. Harbour craft like this one, junks and sampans, and even the bigger coasters were similarly adorned.

Boyes shaded his eyes from the reflected glare to watch a motorized junk passing slowly abeam. The deck was loaded with crates, and nets full of vegetables, and two small Chinese children were playing with a mangy-looking dog by the tiller. Like hundreds, even thousands of others, the junk's skipper and his family no doubt lived aboard and would moor alongside other such craft. The boat people were taken for granted.

He looked over at the chief petty officer in command of the launch. A face like tanned leather, against which his neatly trimmed beard looked almost white by comparison. They had not spoken much, except when they had passed a rakish destroyer which had entered harbour the previous day. Gleaming paintwork, and awnings spread so tautly you could have walked on them. The chief petty officer had given a casual salute as the destroyer's shadow had passed across them, and the officer of the day had returned it while one of his gangway staff leaned over the guardrail as if making sure the launch did not steer too close to the paintwork.

Boyes had remarked, "That's the real Andrew, Chief."

"They can have it."

"My first ship was a cruiser, Chief. One of the last big

eight-inch-gun jobs. Everything at the double, pipes for this and bugles for that. Our O.C. Royal Marines' biggest worry was stopping his guard of honour poking their bayonets through the awnings when they presented arms for some V.I.P. or other!"

The bearded C.P.O. had unwound a little after that.

"What's your officer like? Usual young tyrant, is he?"

Boyes looked at the quivering deck grating and pictured Lieutenant Blackwood below in the cabin space, probably trying to get through to the formidable Major Houston on the R/T, if it was working. They had been here for a week, and nothing had happened. The commandos had been instructed to keep as low a profile as possible. One section had been posted to Government House on guard duty, as if it was all normal routine. As well it might be.

"He'll do me, Chief. Takes life a bit seriously, that's all. Still feeling his way. But he's straight, no flannel."

"I expect you'll all be shovin' off soon. Not enough action for your lot."

He broke off as one of his ratings clambered into the small, box-like bridge. Like all the others aboard, he was Chinese, and his black eyes watched the Chief's mouth intently as he fired some questions at him.

He said, "Got to pick up a marker buoy before we go back. The harbour master wants it for some reason. Be getting dark by then." He did not even glance at his watch or the sky. Another old China hand; he was part of the place. He belonged, perhaps without knowing or remembering why or how, and would stay on when his time was up.

Not enough action for your lot. Maybe that said it all. He thought of the streets he had walked, the colour and the sound. Chinese schoolgirls running barefoot through the rain, holding their shoes and socks under cover, laughing and chattering, not a care in the world. The young businessman and his girlfriend teasing a bony cat, which was being watched protectively from the back door of a restaurant by an old man in shorts and singlet. Another standing in a crowded, nearly perpendicular lane reading the financial pages while a curbside tailor measured his other arm. Boyes had heard you could get a suit made to measure, and have it delivered all within twenty-four hours. He thought of southwest London, Battersea, where he had first drawn breath. What would they say about that?

He heard Blackwood's voice and turned as he spoke to the Chief and one of his young sailors.

It was not an act with him. Not like some he had known and served under.

He was reminded of Blackwood's father. You could see the likeness. The eyes, and the occasional smile. But beyond that . . .

"Anything happening, Sergeant?"

"Busy as usual, sir. A minor collision, two fishermen, but I think they settled it before the police came on the scene."

Ross Blackwood shaded his eyes as the launch altered course to starboard, where two derelict freighters were anchored, perhaps waiting for the breaker's yard. Ship-building was a growing industry here, diesel-driven steel coasters side by side with junks which were still being constructed as they had for centuries, of Chinese fir and hardwood from 'Big Brother' over on the mainland.

Boyes watched him. Without the familiar green beret, his shirt unfastened and the dark, unruly hair blowing in the offshore breeze, it was a surprise. Like stumbling on a secret, seeing some one he had not seen before.

He gauged the moment, like a gunlayer observing the fall of shot.

"Not like Ulster, is it, sir?"

"Not here, it isn't." He swung round as the deck swayed over again. "But given a chance . . ."

Boyes thought he might have gone too far. "I didn't mean it like that, sir."

"I know you didn't. You, of all people. It's just me. Going over things again. Not knowing what we're getting into . . ." He shrugged. "Forget it."

It was darker already, like a great shadow creeping out from the land, but the taller buildings on the high ground were still edged with gold. There were tiny lights, a car ashore, or another small boat moving in the shallows. But the diesels were still thumping away, and the bearded chief petty officer seemed unconcerned.

So why had Houston sent small parties of his company on these local tours, with the police, the harbour patrols, or sightseeing like this? To prevent boredom, and its inevitable consequences, which ended at the defaulters' table? Even with a well-trained and disciplined force, there were always the lurking dangers of unrest.

He had felt it just now. His own unreasonable outburst at Boyes' comment on Ulster. That day, that mean street. The pistol in his hand. *I wanted to kill him.* Boyes remembered it. Was he wondering what might happen the next time? Would his officer crack up?

The Chief called something, and a handful of his men were laying out some kind of tackle for the marker buoy. Just another job for them.

The Chief remarked, "'Nother fifteen minutes, sir. Wait for this one to pass, then I'll move in and pick up the buoy." He paused, studying the young officer's profile, and saw the sergeant give an almost imperceptible nod. "I've got some Tiger beer in the fridge, sir."

Ross did not hear him. "That junk, Chief. Do you know her?"

"Very well, sir. A regular." He cocked his head. The officer was making conversation. Maybe because he had dared to suggest cracking a beer or two with him.

He relented slightly.

"Johnny Cheung. Owns a couple of trading boats. Been around for years. Works amongst the islands mostly – never afraid of hard work, that one."

Boyes said, "Rather him than me, picking his way through all this lot in the dark."

The Chief beckoned to one of his seamen and smiled. "Johnny Cheung wants to be snug alongside in good time for Chinese New Year. High jinks all round, that'll mean!"

Ross felt the engines settle down into a steady growl, slowing down as the ghostly junk idled past. He had seen the New Year decorations being prepared when he had made his way to the harbour master's jetty. Flowering plants and decorated branches, banners, and platforms where people could stand and watch the promised fireworks display over the harbour.

The Chief was standing close beside the helmsman, gesturing, and pointing across the port bow. Boyes was looking astern toward Victoria, the panorama of lights and flickering advertisements which never seemed to be extinguished.

He studied the junk again, hearing the measured beat of engines. Slow and careful. The Chief's friend Johnny Cheung would have to be on full alert, no matter how long he had been trading here. Chinese New Year. It made De Lisle's sense of urgency seem even more misplaced.

He pulled out his handkerchief and dabbed the corner of his eye. Smut from the engines, or something in the air. He dabbed his eye again and then froze. Like being numb, unable to focus his sight, or his mind.

33

He held his breath and stared into the shadows, the vague hint of movement in the black water alongside.

The junk's high poop was almost directly abeam; he could just make out the pale shape of an upended boat, and a faint pinprick of light, probably the old-fashioned standard compass.

He tried again. There was something hanging below the poop, reaching down into the water, fabric, but loose, not sailcloth or a displaced awning. And it was moving, lengthening, tugging in the backwash from one of the screws.

He felt the helm going over, knew the Chief was saying something to one of the hands. But he could not move. For just a few seconds there was enough light left for him to see that the trailing thing was coloured, shining on and below the choppy water like blood.

"Chief! Belay that order! Put her alongside the junk!"

The Chief was beside him now, and he heard Boyes exclaim, "Must be some of 'is cargo, sir! Some tailor's going to be cheesed off about this!"

Ross unclenched his fists, slowly, his eyes never leaving the other vessel's fading shadow.

"Go alongside, Chief. *Now*." He moved across the grating, holding on to the image in his mind.

The Chief had said something about R/T contact with the harbour police. It meant nothing.

"Do you have any weapons aboard?"

Feet thudded on the deck planking, voices hissed orders and silenced questions. The Chief said, "I've a Smith and Wesson in the cabin, sir."

"Get it." He looked at Boyes' figure, pale against the dark backdrop.

The Chief was back, handing his revolver to Boyes without a word.

Ross said, "When you're ready, Chief." He gripped the handrail. So tightly that he felt as if he might never let go. What was it? Instinct, fear, or some unspoken warning?

It was now.

"Hard a-starboard! Fenders out port side! Hold on, lads!"

The old launch seemed to come alive across the narrowing arrowhead of surging, trapped water. Small, blurred pictures stood out in the enclosing darkness. Seamen clinging to anything that was fixed down, one man seizing a boathook and pointing it at the looming shape as the boat squealed alongside, the motor tyres taking the full impact even as the engines went full astern, and then stopped.

It was as if all other sounds had been blotted out, the harbour and its lights beyond reach, meaningless.

Ross jumped from the launch and found himself clinging to wire rigging, broken strands tearing his skin, one of his feet kicking out to avoid being crushed as the two hulls sidled and groaned together again.

He heard the sudden roar of high-powered engines, felt the junk shudder to the burst of power, and knew that another craft had been tied alongside, biding its time, invisible to the launch . . . until what?

But all he could hear was the scream. Close enough to feel it. Like a tortured animal caught in a trap.

It stopped just as abruptly. But he could still hear it.

He was on the deck, unfamiliar objects catching his feet. There was the compass light, the tiller moving aimlessly, abandoned. His chest was aching, as if his lungs would burst, and he could feel blood on his hands, and on his face where he had tried to push the hair out of his eyes.

He heard the clink of metal and Boyes' hard breathing close beside him, his voice harsh but steady.

"I'll cover you, sir! I think the bastards have done a runner!"

The deck lurched again as the two hulls came together in a deep trough. But others were following, and a grapnel clattered over the junk's bulwark before gripping and taking the strain. A light flashed from a low door beneath the poop as it swung open and shut to the sickening movement.

He knew some one had grabbed the tiller, and that the junk's engines had taken on an even beat. He heard the Chief shouting to his men; the sound of the high-powered boat had gone, as if he had imagined it. But the scream still scraped at his mind, like a memory. A threat.

He reached the door even as it swung open again. A heavy torch was rolling from side to side with the motion, its beam picking out items of scattered clothing, and a splash of scarlet where the inboard end of the material had snared on the edge of a square port.

The torch rolled across the deck again and Ross swung on his heel, his arms outstretched like a wrestler caught off balance.

Only seconds, but it was as if time had lost all meaning. Like the scream. A pair of eyes were fixed and staring directly at him, into his face, until the beam swung over again, cutting off the stare. The door creaked again and he tried to lick his lips, to recover his wits, yell out to Ted Boyes.

But he could not move. Not shock, not fear. Like something in the past. The instructor's voice on a battle course he had done. Even that would not register, only the voice. *Not the time to relax and pat yourself on the back, Mister Blackwood! It's now!*

He sensed it, and his body braced, poised for the blow, the agonizing thrust of a blade. Even as he turned he felt the arm around his head, rough clothing scraping his skin, his throat. He let his knee take the strain, then as he swung round he drove his elbow into the other man's belly. They were on the deck, the flashlight's beam following them like a spectator as he found a wrist and twisted it with all his strength, turning his attacker on to his face, sitting astride him, hearing him gasp with pain as his arm almost broke under the pressure.

That same voice from the past. Like a madness. *Remember, Mister Blackwood, it's him or you! Give it all you've got!*

He heard the knife bounce across the deck, saw it reflecting the flashlight's beam. But the light was steady now, gripped in somebody's hand.

He saw the pistol cocked and steady as Boyes pressed it into the man's skull.

"Just move, matey, and they'll have to scrape your brains off the carpet!"

The small cabin space was suddenly full of people. The man who had tried to knife him was being dragged away, with a few blows and kicks as he was moved. The Chief was here too, watching Boyes help Ross to a chair. It could have been anything.

"You took a bit of a chance just then." He beckoned to one of his men. "Sir?"

Ross touched his face and neck. Feeling the grip, the pure hate. Some one was covering up the corpse, hiding the staring, accusing eyes. The one who had risked everything to warn them, and had paid for it in that last scream.

The Chief said, "That's Johnny Cheung's son. He was training him to take over the business one day."

He reached out to take a mug from the hovering seaman. "Drink this."

It was not Tiger beer, and Ross thought of Houston's casual warnings. The unseen dangers.

37

He heard the whine of sirens. The harbour police were here; routine would take over now.

Boyes also had a mug in his hand. In the other he was still holding the Chief's Smith and Wesson, dangling it by its trigger guard like a toy.

He raised his mug.

"'Ere we go then, sir! Kung Hei Fat Choy!"

Happy New Year.

CHAPTER THREE

"This is a bloody cheerful spot to be spending the New Year, I don't think!"

Ross Blackwood glanced at his companion and smiled. Acting-Captain John Irwin had never been slow to speak his mind. And he was no longer 'acting'; his promotion had just been confirmed in orders. It was almost impossible to guess his feelings. Alert, restless, hardly ever still, except when the situation demanded it. A man who had been taught the hard way how to survive, how to win.

When they had been on a training course together, a refresher, the brass termed it, he had got to know Irwin reasonably well. Better than most, it seemed. He had been in the Royal Marines since boyhood. His mother had been killed during one of the last hit-and-run air raids in the war, and his father had moved to Deal to become a school caretaker. A day hardly passed there when you did not see the Royals, recruits as well as old sweats, parading or drilling for one ceremony or another. Coming up through the ranks was a rough passage at the best of times, and Irwin had made it. At the spearhead of the Port Said invasion, and in the thick of the bloody fighting in Borneo and Malaya, he had earned his third pip the hardest way imaginable.

In his thirties, lean and straight-backed, as if

everything superfluous in body and manner had been honed away, he was old for his rank, and often abrupt, even impatient, with subordinates. A man you would follow to hell and back.

But know him? That was something else.

Ross looked around the box-like room, everything brilliant white and antiseptically new. It was a miniature medical clinic adjoining the naval sick quarters, but so isolated that it could have been part of a prison. An orderly had accompanied them from the main reception centre, saying nothing until they had reached the door to this room.

Irwin had remarked, "He'd look more at home with a bunch of keys at his belt!"

He touched the bandage and dressing around his right hand. Even that was like part of a dream. He winced. Nightmare, more like. He must have been asked the same things over and over again. Shown pencilled diagrams, photographs, while in his mind he had held the unreal memory of the staring, accusing eyes in the flashlight's glare, the feel and smell of his attacker. The pain. Houston had been at every interview, interrogation would be a better description, but he had said surprisingly little, except to fire a brief question or jot down a note. The police had been there, and Ross had made a full statement to one senior officer who had asked several questions about the actual boarding of the junk, the state of the cargo, if any, and the man who had died trying to signal for help.

And the New Year celebrations continued. A part of life. The grand fireworks display, dragon dancers, jugglers, and flowers everywhere. He would have to stop making comparisons with England in winter. Or Hawks Hill . . .

"Must be off, old chap." Irwin was looking at the door. "You've got the doctor coming to see you. Then a senior copper to bring your statement. Otherwise . . ."

Otherwise. That said it all. Irwin was not one to celebrate his confirmed promotion, probably his last in the Corps, with others still in the mess because of duty, or merely because they were broke. He would do it alone. Or with some one who would never become too close.

He said, "You've bloody earned it, John." He thrust out his hand. Tomorrow it would be *sir*. This was now.

Irwin grinned. "Other hand, Ross." They both looked at the bandages.

One policeman had commented that it was probably just some private feud. *All blow over before you know it.* Another had said, "There are more we never hear of until they're washed up with their throats cut." And so on.

The door closed. He sat on one of the hard, white-painted chairs and loosened his shirt in the air conditioning.

He felt his back rub against the other dressing. Always a reminder, if he needed it. *All blow over before you know it.* It must have happened in those few seconds of desperate madness, the knife twisting from his attacker's hand, glinting briefly in the beam of the flashlight. And he had felt nothing. He recalled the bearded chief petty officer opening a first aid box and saying, "'Nother inch, sir, and you'd have known all about it!"

Sergeant Ted Boyes, who had been interrogated separately, had exploded, "I should've given the little bastard the one up the spout at the time!"

He did not hear the door open or close, and looked up, half startled. Like guilt.

She was tall, and, like the room, all in white. It was not a uniform but an open-necked shirt or blouse, and white slacks. Her face and arms were so deeply tanned that for a moment he thought she was a local woman; in the overhead lights her hair was almost black.

She held out one hand.

"Don't get up, please. I'm sorry I'm a bit late. You know how it is."

Ross was already on his feet. Beautiful, striking, with high cheekbones, and level dark eyes meeting his.

She smiled.

"You'll know me if we meet again, Lieutenant."

"I'm sorry. I was expecting . . ."

"I know. It happens. Especially in this place."

Something in her voice. Not so much an accent as a lilt. Like one of Sue's friends. Welsh, he thought.

She was saying, "I help out here sometimes. Keeps me occupied. I used to be a nurse." The smile was warm, unaffected. "Bit like being a copper, isn't it? You never really stop being one."

They both turned as a telephone jangled noisily.

She said, "Bloody hell," then tugged open a drawer to reveal the instrument.

Ross watched her, as if she were another part of this feverish dream.

She said, "No, I can't. I *told* you."

He could just hear the other voice, male, insistent. Perhaps she was going to a party, too. With a table light behind her, he could see the outline of her body, her breast beneath the shirt as she laughed shortly at something the caller had said.

"Oh, all right. But only a minute. I mean it!"

She looked at him across the room. "Won't be long. Get your shirt off. Toilet's through there if you need it."

He sat down again and obediently began to unbutton his shirt. *Matter of fact. In charge.* He saw his reflection in a mirror and smiled. What had he expected?

He heard her voice, then that of a man. The caller.

She was laughing, then she said, "That's *enough*, Andy. You know what I told you."

42

Ross felt the air conditioning like cool breath on his bare shoulders, and saw the door swing inward a few inches under the sudden pressure. She stood with her back turned in the outer room, which was more of a hanging space for hospital clothing. It was enough to reveal that the caller was a naval officer, a lieutenant-commander, the red cloth between his gold rings showing him to be a doctor, probably a surgeon, with that rank.

"You've had too much to drink, Andy. That's you all over, isn't it?" Very calm. Unworried.

Ross saw the man's hand circle her waist, and in the corridor light the gap between her shirt and slacks, the tanned skin shining.

She said, "All right, for New Year, then." They were kissing, and the hand was now hidden under the white shirt.

Ross stood up and collided with the chair, and swore.

The door clicked shut and she stood looking at him, her face composed, the suggestion of a smile on her lips. Her shirt was back in position, but her breathing was a little less than calm.

"Coming to my rescue, Lieutenant? No need. New Year is an excuse for anything, as you'll discover if you stay here long enough." She was taking out a pair of surgical gloves. "I wasn't laughing at you. I saw it in your face just now. It's rare enough these days. I was touched."

He could not see the expression in her eyes as she gripped his hand and held it under the light. "That was the first thing I learned in hospital. If they know you're a nurse, they think you're anybody's." The scissors clipped away at the dressing, her fingers very steady, and strong.

He heard himself ask, "What hospital?"

"Eventually, Homerton." The eyes flicked up. "I see you've no idea where that is." She laid a piece of stained dressing on the tray. "It's in London. The East End."

She moved behind him, one hand on his shoulder, and he felt her hair brush his skin.

"This will sting a little."

The plaster tugged for a second and he knew she was dusting the long, fine wound with something on a wad of cotton.

"You can put your shirt back on now. You've got a visitor coming soon . . . You must be fed up with it, after all you've had to go through."

Snap, snap. The two gloves were in a bin. The moment was over.

He saw her fingers buttoning his shirt.

"Here. Let me."

She stood back and unfastened the top of her shirt, and he saw the fine chain around her neck. On it was suspended a plain gold ring.

She said, "Gets in the way sometimes in this job." She moved her head slightly. "That's the lift coming up. Your next visitor."

There was a brief silence.

"Thank you for what you tried to do, for what you thought. It was only New Year, you see." And smiled. "I know *your* name." She looked at the door. "Mine's Glynis." Then she faced him again, her eyes very steady. "New Year, Ross. Remember?"

He did not recall moving. It seemed so natural, so right. As if there was no control.

She was tall; their mouths were almost level.

He kissed her, and could feel her body against his.

She twisted her face round, her lips parted. "No, Ross, a proper kiss!"

There was a tap at the door; the same orderly was there, and this time he was actually carrying some keys.

She turned away from the cupboard, although Ross had

44

not felt her move. In his mind she was still pressed against him, her tongue seeking his.

She was saying, "Here he is, Lieutenant."

One of the faces he had seen at the meetings. A senior police officer. The questions . . .

"I don't have to introduce you, do I? This is Chief Inspector Diamond. My husband."

Major Keith Houston was warming to his subject.

"The results have been far better than I dared to hope." He put a paperweight on one corner of a map as the overhead fan suddenly speeded up and scattered some of his papers. "Thanks to you and your swift, if unorthodox, handling of the situation." He looked directly at Ross. "And how are the cuts and bruises? All fixed?"

He did not wait for an answer; he rarely seemed to. "The Big White Chief is pleased. 'Operation Ratcatcher', he's christened it!"

Ross tried to relax. It was the same spacious office, with its maps and files full of signals. The same wide window, the midday sun on the harbour gleaming like copper. Alive and full of movement: coasters and ancient tramp steamers, a small cruise ship moored on the Kowloon side, vessels loading and unloading. As he had first seen it, and yet so different. Now.

Captain John Irwin sat in another chair, engrossed in some notes, and comparing them with something he had just written.

No sign of fatigue or excitement. Yesterday had been his big night out. How could he switch off so easily?

Houston was saying, "The chap you caught, Ross, was known to the police both here and in Singapore. A link they've been looking for. I expect Chief Inspector Diamond told you." And smiled, almost triumphantly. "I can see from your face, he did not. A close one, is Jock Diamond!"

Ross could see him in his mind. Tall, well built, kept himself in good condition. Tanned features, but not a man who stayed too long in the sun. And a permanent frown of which he was probably unaware. Steady grey eyes which revealed nothing, and missed nothing, either, watching him at the meetings, and when he had signed the witness statements. She had been there too, legs crossed, reading a paperback. But when he had touched on the more personal side, the Royal Marines, the Blackwood family, even his father's death in Cyprus, Ross had seen that her eyes were unmoving, the paperback a pretence.

She had been wearing the ring he had seen hanging on the chain. *Gets in the way sometimes in this job.* So casually said, but did it have another meaning?

Diamond's face had given no hint. The tipsy naval doctor named Andy, his hand fumbling with her shirt. New Year, then . . .

Did he know, or suspect? Did he care?

Only yesterday. Ross had thought of little else. *No, Ross, a proper kiss.* It was pointless to search for comparisons or excuses. The young girls at the various service events. The regattas and open days, *bags of swank an' swagger*, as Sergeant Boyes would have said. But always keeping up appearances. A game which was never serious, unless you were asking for trouble. And some did.

But this was quite different. She was not some young flirtatious girl, out for a laugh and nothing else. He could see her name as if it was written in fire before him. Glynis. Who came from Wales, and who had been a nurse in London. Her smile as she had said, *the East End.* As if it were another world. And it was, too.

She was a real woman, and some one else's. Beyond him in every way.

He heard her voice again. Testing him? Mocking his interest? *They think you're anybody's.* Was she?

He realized with a start that Houston had asked him something.

"Sir?"

"Sorry if I'm putting you to sleep!" The mood changed just as quickly. "You will remain on call. This is a top secret operation, a raid, if you like. Acting on information received. Boat action. Not a word to any one. If you fart in Victoria, they pick it up in the Peninsula Hotel. The Big White Chief will be overseeing every move. Remember that."

Three weeks ago: Lieutenant-Colonel De Lisle, the rain-spattered windows, the tramping feet on the square at Stonehouse . . .

The Big White Chief had only just returned from Singapore. *Operation Ratcatcher.* He must have known then what was coming.

He could feel the thin wound on his back, the touch of her fingers, which the surgical gloves had not disguised.

She would laugh if she knew. *They think you're anybody's.*

There was going to be a raid. Old hat to men like Irwin and Boyes, but no room for mistakes. The scar should act as a reminder.

Houston was showing Irwin a new squash racquet, swiping at the humid air. Irwin was nodding at some remark, but Ross knew his mind was elsewhere.

Tomorrow, or the next day, they might be in some sort of action. Bandits, smugglers, rebels, it made no difference.

Houston's words again. *When I'm on the wrong end of a gun, that man is an enemy!*

Despite his father, the Corps, De Lisle, even Houston, the decision had been his, but now that moment was behind him. He had the lives of others to consider. Men who had no choice but to follow and trust him.

He found himself gazing at a newspaper cutting pinned on Houston's bulletin board. It was a photo some alert reporter had snapped of the Duke of Edinburgh, the Corps' Captain-General, turning to stare at a marine in his guard of honour who apparently had dropped his rifle in the middle of the ceremony. Somebody had scrawled underneath, *If you can't take a joke, sir!*

Ross breathed out slowly.

It was the only way to look at it.

Sergeant Ted Boyes stood at the end of the jetty watching three marines handing down bundles of personal gear and some anonymous crates to the crew of a harbour launch alongside, while he picked at his teeth with a matchstick to rid them of the remains of a massive bacon sandwich.

It was dusk, and the water was already alive with navigation lights, and the occasional winking buoy.

He could hear the traffic behind him, the constant movement. To any casual passer-by the marines and the harbour launch would look like just another working party. This time, it was not. The assorted bundles being loaded into the launch were weapons, ammunition, the tools of the trade. You stopped asking 'why' and 'what for'. Otherwise you were in the wrong job.

It was almost time to pick up the others. Twenty in all. Not an army, but enough, if the brass had got their sums right.

The launch was moving stern first away from the jetty, the bowman raising his boathook in mock salute to the marines above him.

It looked like a twin of that other hard-worked launch he and Blackwood had boarded. About the same time of day, too, glaring lights switching on along the waterfront and the high buildings inland.

Boyes had been in plenty of tight corners before, but that had been different. The unexpected roar of engines as the hidden boat had sped away into the darkness, the scream, the desperate encounter in the cabin . . .

He had seen Blackwood only twice since the interrogations by Naval Operations and the harbour police. The last time had been near the sick quarters when he had seen him talking to the woman. A real smasher, older than the lieutenant. *Nearer my age.* He grinned. She had certainly had all Blackwood's attention. Lucky lad!

"'Eads up, Sarge. Mister Follow-my-example is comin'!"

It was the sarcastic nickname given to one of the three lieutenants who had been flown out from England. Lieutenant Alan Piggott was young, about Blackwood's age, Boyes thought, very fair and good-looking, and he knew it. From another old service family, Royal Marine and naval, he always displayed a tremendous self-confidence and was quick to show his impatience with any one who did not measure up to his standards. Those who had served with him before usually had to admit that Blondie Piggott was usually right, and efficient in every-thing he did, which only made it worse.

Boyes spat the matchstick into the water, where it joined other floating rubbish, and braced himself. Officers sometimes had to be carried by their senior N.C.O.s, but always obeyed.

There was nothing in Q.R.s to say you had to like them.

"Ah, there you are, Sergeant. All done here? Those marines don't appear to be busy."

"All stowed, sir. The launch has just shoved off."

49

Even in the fading light Boyes could see the fine profile, the rakish way he wore his green beret. Like everything he did.

"Everything checked to your satisfaction?" Boyes thought, *it's too bloody late now if somebody's forgotten something.* But he answered, "As ordered, sir. Do we know the final destination yet, sir?"

"The marines will be told nearer the time, right?"

Boyes relaxed slightly. So Piggott did not know, either. It was that important.

Somebody called, "Some more are comin', Sarge," and added self-consciously, "Sir!"

There were three of them, a sergeant and two corporals.

Boyes said, "Demolition party, sir. Come across from Kowloon," and said abruptly to his opposite number, "I'm Boyes. This is Lieutenant Piggott."

He looked at the officer. "We can move off now, sir."

Piggott was regarding the other sergeant.

"Then you must be Sergeant Blackwood." He seemed to rock back on his heels, a little mannerism Boyes had already noticed. "A pretty famous name in the Corps, or has been. Something to live up to. But on this mission we put all personal odds and ends to one side."

Boyes waited, and was not disappointed.

Piggott said, "Just follow my example, right?"

"Boat comin'!"

Boyes watched Piggott's pale outline move to the opposite side of the jetty, and said, "Welcome aboard. Steve, isn't it?" They shook hands, and there was a brief, unspoken question.

Boyes said, "He's got a lot to learn, but . . ."

The other sergeant's teeth were white in a broad smile.

"Yeah. *But.* Says it all. And thanks. We're going to get along fine."

Boyes nudged his arm. "Sure thing. Just follow my example!"

The others turned as they both laughed. It couldn't be all that dicey.

A boat surged alongside, a smaller, faster version this time, and the marines clambered into it. Lieutenant Blondie Piggott, correctly, entered last. Operation Ratcatcher could now begin.

"There she is! Starboard bow!" The seaman's oilskinned arm showed briefly above the choppy water as the helm went over, and the motor's pitch eased for the first time since they had climbed aboard. It had begun to rain, too, warm and refreshing against the skin, but making the lights along the shore seem far away, alien.

Ross Blackwood took a firmer grip as the coxwain swung the little craft on to a different course. There were only three men in the boat's crew, shining occasionally like wet seals as the tiller swung this way and that, and prior to this nobody had said a word. They knew their jobs, and any attempt at conversation was pointless anyway. He could feel Irwin pressed beside him, bouncing up and down with the hull's lively motion, twisting around from time to time to peer astern, but otherwise keeping to himself.

A dark, wet night; it could have been anywhere, but suddenly, rising over them like a grey breakwater, was the ship. No challenges or flashing signals, no fuss at all. One moment they had the black waters to themselves, dashing it seemed into nowhere, and now she was here. H.M.S. *Taunton*, one of the TON class, so called because every ship's name ended in 'ton', had been originally designed and built as a small coastal minesweeper. Dozens had been constructed during and in the wake of the Korean War, with every kind of non-magnetic material to lessen the chance of disaster. As some wag had said at Naval Operations, they must have fast been running out of 'tons' when the last vessels were launched. Now they had changed roles, and most had been relisted as patrol vessels, ideal for this part of the world.

They were almost alongside, and Ross saw the *Taunton*'s brightly painted pendant number, *P1095*, passing just above his shoulder. A new life for a veteran ship. She must be at least fourteen years old by now. Launched at the famous yard at Cowes on the Isle of Wight, which had been the birthplace of so many wooden vessels, motor torpedo boats, rescue launches, and sweepers. Now they were back to building luxury yachts for those who could afford them; and there were a growing number who could. He had been serving in Ulster when the great new liner *Queen Elizabeth II*, 'QE2' as she was already affectionately known, had made her maiden crossing to the States. The year his father had been killed in Cyprus, and a young marine had died in a mean Belfast suburb. It still made no sense.

The boat squealed against the grey side, and somebody jumped down to fix the hoisting gear. Wasting no time.

Figures loomed out of the rainy dimness, a hand reached down to grasp his elbow as he climbed a short ladder and on to the deck.

A voice murmured, "Welcome aboard, sir."

Another called, "Take up the slack! Stand by to hoist away!"

Irwin said, "They've done this sort of thing a few times before, by the look of it."

"This way, sir!"

Somewhere a bell clanged, and Ross felt the wet deck shiver into life. They were moving, even as the boat was being hoisted and manhandled into position abaft the squat funnel. It was strangely exciting, like going back, and yet somehow new. The hot air and smell of diesel, the whirr of fans, even the sluice of sea and spray drifting from the bows. Under way . . .

Taunton, like her many sisters, was a far cry from frigate or destroyer. Less than four hundred tons, and some hundred and fifty feet in length, with only two Bofors guns as her main armament, she was exactly right for her new role, and with a company of thirty, including her four officers, she was the last of her kind.

Taunton's commanding officer appeared for a few seconds. A quick handshake, a voice in the darkness. "All your people are below. One's in the sickbay, I'm afraid. Fell down a ladder when he came over the side. Thought it best to keep him aboard. No sense in wasting time, or drawing attention to my ship."

Somebody murmured in his ear and he said, "Time to chat later when we're clear of the channel." Only a lieutenant, but *Taunton*'s captain. And proud of it.

They groped and stumbled after their guide. And then, suddenly, there was light, the ship's sounds and smells crowding around them.

The commanding officer's cabin was cramped and neat, with a bunk and a desk, and a battery of telephones. There was a framed photograph above the desk, the glass of which was cracked. The little TON craft could be very lively in a storm, not to mention a typhoon.

As one of the Operations staff had commented, "The old TONS roll on wet grass!" He had served in one himself. A 'small ship man'. It was always there.

Their guide proved to be a midshipman, the youngest member of this small wardroom.

Curiously, Ross looked at the photograph, and recognized the lieutenant now up there on his crowded little bridge, feeling his way clear of all other shipping. He was standing with his bride outside a church doorway.

The deck tilted steeply and the engine vibration became more insistent.

Irwin said, "Cracking it on a bit. What can she do?"

The midshipman smiled, and it made him look like the schoolboy he had so recently been. "She can manage fifteen knots, sir." The smile broadened. "With a following wind, that is!"

He pointed to a file of signals.

"The C.O. left these for you, sir." He looked at Ross. "I've got some food laid on."

He left the cabin, his foot lifting automatically over a coaming, in time with the lowering of his head as he ducked through the door.

Irwin said, "Fifteen knots. Jesus Christ, we should have taken the Star Ferry, *with a following wind*!" He unfastened his coat. "Well, let's get on with it."

Then he leaned back against a pile of folded lifejackets, his eyes very calm again. Like some one else looking out.

"I'll go through it first with you, Ross. Then we'll get the others into the picture."

Ross thought of the other lieutenant who had taken a different route to join the *Taunton*. Debonair, very sure of himself.

"What about Piggott?" He had almost called him 'Blondie'.

Irwin shrugged. "Far as I'm concerned, you're second in command. My decision, O.K.?"

There was a tap at the door and it swung inboard without waiting for permission. It was a petty officer in a grubby boiler suit, an empty mug in one hand.

"Sorry to trouble you, gents." He looked directly at Ross. "One of your chaps is askin' for you."

54

The door closed and Irwin said, "Very matey lot, aren't they?" It seemed to amuse him. "I'll leave you on your own. Ten minutes?"

The door opened again, and there was a brief blare of music, probably from the main messdeck, which would be more crammed than ever with the marines aboard. A voice yelled, "Turn that bloody row off, for Gawd's sake!"

There was silence again but for the everpresent shipboard noises, and the occasional sluice of the sea against the hull.

They faced each other across the small cabin, lieutenant and sergeant.

"Sergeant Blackwood, sir. I thought I should report to you, and not wait until the briefing tomorrow." He swallowed, but did not remove his gaze.

Ross said, "You must be a mind-reader. I was thinking of making my number, too. But I expected you might have your head down."

Steve Blackwood looked past him. "In this ship, sir? Not likely."

Ross gestured to the other chair. "Well, I'm glad you came. It can't have been easy." It was not what he wanted to say at all. Like strangers. Or enemies. "I've often thought about this moment. After all the years, the uncertainties. As it was, I almost didn't get assigned to this mission. I bloody nearly put in my papers."

"Resigned? Leave the Royals? Why the hell—"

Ross reclipped a deadlight over one of the scuttles. He had not noticed it rattling before.

"Sit down, will you?" He turned abruptly and thrust out his hand. "Look, we've met. That's what matters." Just a momentary flicker, a hesitation. He had been about to refuse. Like Houston's old sergeant, who had saved his life.

But the handshake was strong. Like the man. His cousin.

"I went to the house. When all . . . well, what were they, salesmen? When they were there. I'd heard about the Colonel, of course, everybody had. And I knew about Hawks Hill. I just wanted to be there. To be sure." He broke off, as if unable to put it into words.

"I wish I'd known."

The eyes challenged him again, searching for something.

Ross thought of Irwin. "We're in this together." He smiled unconsciously. "This is like part of a bad film, isn't it?"

"We'll not let you down." The slightest pause. "Sir."

"I'm the one who should be saying that." There were feet on a ladder, voices: Irwin and perhaps the *Taunton*'s skipper. It had to be now.

He saw the surprise on the other man's face, the features like and unlike his own.

"This is as good a time as any. At least, I hope it is."

He took a piece of folded velvet from his pocket and laid it carefully on the desk. It was the old, much polished badge, the Globe and Laurel. The one in the photograph.

"This is for you. It was your mother's."

The door was open and Irwin was inside the cabin, his hair almost brushing some pipes that ran across the deckhead, his eyes full of questions. Two of *Taunton*'s officers were close behind him.

"All done, then?"

Ross could remember exactly, as if it had been this morning, when his sister had given him the square of velvet. *Just in case you meet up with him.* It was probably the worst thing he could have done.

He looked at the desk. The piece of velvet still lay there, but the badge had gone.

It was not over. Maybe it was only just beginning.

56

Taunton's commanding officer had lit a cigarette, and the other officer was filling his pipe. Some coffee or tea had appeared, and some one had laid out a chart on top of the bunk.

Ross heard himself answer, "Ready when you are, sir."

Something fell heavily on the deck above and feet thudded across the wet planking in response.

The wind was getting up; he could feel it. But all he could think about was the stranger walking alone through Hawks Hill, perhaps thinking of what might have been, or, for only a few moments, being a part of it all.

He moved closer to the chart, another voice speaking in his mind.

It's what we are. What we do.

He glanced at his hand and the scars where the broken wire stay had ripped the skin. They were healing well, and he was surprised to see that the hand was completely steady. Relaxed. Like seeing some one else.

It was true, then. He *was* ready.

CHAPTER FOUR

Ross Blackwood raised himself carefully on his elbows and waited for his breathing to recover. He felt the hard, uneven ground digging into his body; it was like being on another exercise, except that this was the real thing. He could still feel the tossing discomfort of the little boat which had brought their party ashore in darkness, minds dazed by the sickening motion and a continuous rain.

He peered at the sky. The rain had stopped, and even the sounds of sea and wind were silent, as if a giant door had been slammed.

He pictured the chart and the hand-drawn maps, which they had studied and discussed until every one had run out of questions. Or choices. There were none left.

In total darkness, *Taunton* had closed with this island and waited offshore while the marines and their weapons were landed, at any second expecting an alarm, or a challenge, even a burst of gunfire. They could have had the place to themselves. Some one had found breath enough, after scrambling through the shallows and flopping down to cover the rest of the landing party, to suggest they might find themselves completely alone when daylight found them.

Ross did not pull down his glove to look at his watch. It would be dawn within the hour. But the sky was still hidden in cloud; not even a star had shown itself since they had cast off from *Taunton*, no margin between land and sky.

Hard to accept that so much had happened in so short a time. The marines had crowded into the ship's main messdeck while Irwin and *Taunton*'s skipper explained the layout and the approaches to this gaunt little island, Raven's, one of many scattered across the South China Sea. Barren and uninhabited for the most part, except by fishermen or local craft sheltering from bad weather, they were not a safe or wise refuge if the wind rose to storm force. This island took its English name not from a bird but the master of a passenger vessel which had caught fire and been driven aground in the twenties. The master, one Daniel Raven, had used every trick and no little courage to save nearly all his passengers. He had died shortly afterwards, but his name lived on.

Ross wiped his mouth with the glove. The intelligence which had brought them here must have been good. *Taunton*'s skipper was the last person he could imagine who would want to share Raven's fate.

Only today, while the hands were being piped to breakfast, they had passed another patrol vessel, *Yelverton*, *Taunton*'s exact twin to all but those who served in either. A brief blink of signals, no alteration of course to exchange greetings or gossip; it had been an ordinary crossing of patrol areas, had any one been watching.

He thought of the faces around him as Irwin had listed the risks. Young and eager for the most part. No sign of anxiety, or the fear he would recognize. Only the more experienced showed any uncertainty, and there had been a question or two, a few nods in confirmation.

Even the marine who had fallen and injured his leg had been present, ignoring the jokes thrown in his direction by his mates, and openly distraught at the prospect of being left behind.

So where do I stand? He had seen Steve Blackwood pointing out something on one of the maps.

Irwin had said, "Of course, you were in the Malayan flare-up before, weren't you? Well, we don't want that happening again just yet. Big Brother over the border would see it as open provocation, and the United Nations would say we were still trying to cling to the days of Empire!"

The sergeant had said, "We had a few battalions of Gurkhas to back us up at the time."

He must have been as young then as some of the marines around him now.

So where do I stand?

He screwed up his eyes and opened them again very slowly.

It was still no lighter. Or was it?

He tried to imagine what it would look like. Bare rock, and some narrow crevasses, a central spread of water, hardly worthy of the name of anchorage, and several channels that led eventually to the open sea. As if the island had once been one great boulder which had dropped from heaven and splintered into pieces.

The channels were deep enough for small craft in favourable conditions.

Taunton's skipper had said, "If the time and tide were wrong, you could wade across some of those without getting your knees wet!"

Taunton drew six clear feet of water. He would be very aware of that.

He felt his stomach rumble. He had been too tense to eat any of the huge meal the galley had provided.

"All in position, sir." A whisper, but he might have

shouted it. Ross saw the gleam of teeth in the camouflaged face. One of the two corporals.

"Thanks, Laker. Still quiet everywhere."

The corporal wriggled closer, one hand protecting his submachine-gun from the ground and its loose pebbles. They had all waded ashore with every strap, buckle and clip firmly taped to prevent any unnecessary sound or accidental shot.

"Cap'n Irwin's on a little recce with Sarn't Boyes." He chuckled. "Rather them than me, sir!"

All those drills and exercises. Backing up the police and dodging bricks. And seeing some one die to no good purpose.

But these men, who will look to me, will have to face far worse.

He imagined he could feel the wound on his back. But it was nothing.

I was lucky. Next time . . .

Another voice from the past. An old W.O.2 instructor somewhere.

"In this mob, Mister Blackwood, we don't rely on luck. It's skill wot saves yer bacon!"

"'Ere comes your dawn, sir!"

He reached out and touched the corporal's arm, but did not see his surprise.

"So be it, then!"

Sergeant Steve Blackwood eased his back against a slab of rock and arranged a pack between his legs where he could reach it without changing his position. The rock was surprisingly smooth, as if it had been hand-made. Wind and weather: it must have lain here for generations.

The sky was still overcast, but within hours this island would be like a furnace. Nothing seemed to grow here, he thought; no wonder it was avoided. It was getting lighter, and he imagined he could see one of the channels which had been marked on the map and described by a ship's officer at the conference. Out there, like something black and solid, was the sea. Amongst the fallen rocks you couldn't even hear it. But it never left you. Instinct, experience, call it what you like. It was there.

He heard a clink of metal, probably somebody taking a sip from his water flask, despite all the warnings. There was always one. When the sun came up, he'd know all about it.

It might all be a waste of time and effort. He had known a few setbacks in his time. Then it came, when you were least expecting it.

Three officers, two sergeants, two corporals and some ten marines. All different; only the uniform was the same. The injured man in *Taunton*'s sick bay was no doubt looking forward to another gargantuan breakfast in comfort. But he would not be allowed to forget it.

He touched his pocket and tried to feel the badge, which he had wrapped in a handkerchief. He should have left it on board for safekeeping.

Then he thought, *if anything happened, who'd care anyway?*

He remembered the moment exactly. The badge on the desk, in the cabin with the cracked wedding picture. His feelings: cheated, betrayed, humiliated, it was none of them. Like the photograph some one had neglected to remove from its silver frame prior to the auction at Hawks Hill.

He peered at his hand, upturned on the pack. He could see the shape of it, the grit and blood left there when he had thrown himself from the boat. It *was* lighter. *Taunton* would be standing well offshore, but when the sun broke the horizon she would stand out for all to see. If there was anybody . . .

He thought of the lieutenant, Ross Blackwood. What had he expected? Every one else claimed to see the likeness, but it had not been like looking into a mirror. To others, maybe. But they were strangers.

He watched the pale hint of dawn, like something spilling over the sea's edge. This was always the best moment of the day, no matter which sea or ocean it was. Not like those other times, the jungle becoming wild and alive with cries and squeals, and furtive movements, while your hair stood on end, and it was all you could do to keep the safety catch on. Irwin had touched on it at the conference, but most of them did not fully understand. An enemy disguised and invisible, who struck without mercy at security forces and civilians alike. Screams in the night. Only an arm's length away; human, not animal. It had taken him a long time to put it behind him. He had learned a lot by working alongside the Gurkhas, tough, hardy little soldiers who acted first and asked questions later.

Some one was coming up the rough track below him. Every man was in position. It could only be the other lieutenant, Piggott.

He could hear his breathing. The climb from the waterside; on edge; nervous? He did not know him well enough to judge. Seemed efficient, and ready to jump on anybody who did not measure up to a certain standard. His mouth moved in a faint smile. *His standard.* He certainly did not try to be popular, like some.

"All alert, Sergeant?" He squatted down on his haunches, his head and shoulders pale against the sea's backdrop. "I'm beginning to think we're on a fools' errand."

Blackwood waited. It was a question, not an observation.

"I mean, who would come to a hole like this?"

"They used to bring old vessels here for scrapping, breaking up, then sell any useful gear to fishermen and the like."

"Really?"

Blackwood tensed. They had all heard Captain Irwin and *Taunton*'s C.O. discussing the background of Raven's Island. Piggott had been all ears at the time. Was this pretence of ignorance a guise to cover something else?

"Good place to shelter if you were shifting smuggled gear from one boat to another, sir."

Piggott said calmly, "Just what I thought." He broke off as a marine appeared by the slab of rock. "What is it, Ellis?"

"I'm Cooper, sir."

"And *I'm waiting*!"

"We heard some sounds, sir." His guard was up. "Like bells." He made a gesture, and his hand was clear against the sky. "Rattling, like."

Blackwood felt his resentment, and said quietly, "Like they hang on goats, sir."

Piggott almost laughed aloud. "For Pete's sake! *Goats!*"

He was on his feet, his hair almost white above his stained features, against the colourless sky.

"I'd keep down, sir. The light's directly behind you." He let his words sink in. "Better safe than . . ."

"Oh, not you, too, Sergeant!" But he sat down again.

Steve Blackwood forced himself to unwind a little. He had been going to say, *better safe than dead.*

He edged forward again and felt his knee crack. It was cramp. He looked down the slope and saw the narrow channel below, when minutes earlier there had been only darkness. He tried again. Piggott's impatience and irritation were doing nothing to help . . . He stiffened. He had heard it, too. As the marine had described it, a rattling sound.

"Go and tell Mr. Blackwood." He saw the marine lurch to his feet. "Nice and easy. No panic."

Piggott said abruptly, "Taking sides, Sergeant?"

He checked himself. "We don't know where Captain Irwin is, sir. And Mr. Blackwood is second in command."

"On the ridge, sir!"

He glanced at the sky, the growing light, and carefully eased his binoculars from their case. A risk, but they had to know. He could still hear the tinkling noise. He licked his lips: bone dry. Then he raised the glasses. If Piggott said a single word . . . He pictured the marine who had whispered the warning . . . His name *was* Ellis. Young, keen-eyed. Good record. So why the bullshit?

He held the glasses absolutely still. The ridge, one of several, was directly ahead, the nearest channel appearing around its lowest edge like a ribbon of black glass. Unmoving as yet. But in a few more minutes . . .

Just a small movement, like a shadow. The sound came from the same direction. Then Ellis said softly, with surprise and disbelief, "Not goats, Sarge!"

Piggott snapped, "Do I have to guess?"

Steve Blackwood panned the glasses slightly from side to side, but the tiny, magnified image remained fixed in his mind.

He said, "Children. Two, maybe three. Coming down the slope from the ridge." His voice was unemotional.

Who were they? Where had they come from? He could feel Piggott fuming. Perhaps he was right after all.

The sea was much brighter, pale green and shark-blue, the current visible now in the light. The ridge remained hard and dark against the dawn. He tried again, holding his breath. Two small children walking hand in hand, girls or boys he could not tell. A slightly older child, a girl with long, black hair, walked just behind them. Something glinted in her hand and he heard the sound again. Like a necklace of seashells. He had seen them in the bazaars. Toys, or indeed for goats, to help their owners find them in a hurry.

Piggott stood up and said, "I'll soon put a bloody stop to this nonsense. You can think what you damn well like!"

He threw his leg over the loose rocks and swung down toward the steep slope.

A shift of light, tension, instinct; there was no room for thought.

He shouted, "Get *down*, man!"

It was all he could do to hold the glasses steady, fixed on the two children. Not laughing or playing but staring ahead. Small, frightened faces. *Staring at me.* And not holding hands. Their wrists were tied together.

He heard the binoculars hit the ground, then he was up and over the same rocks, leaping and almost falling as he burst from cover.

He saw a marine staring at him, another dragging back the cocking lever of his automatic rifle. Piggott, taken by surprise, had half turned, lost his balance and sprawled headlong among some boulders.

None of it seemed important. He saw the two children, their mouths open in unheard screams, pulling away from each other but trapped by the lashing around their wrists. Of the girl with the shells there was no sign.

There were flashing lights, but not reflected sun. He heard the sudden rattle of gunfire, felt invisible fingers clutching at his clothing as he charged down the slope. Part of his brain recorded that the bullets had ripped past him only inches away.

He threw himself down, his arms around the children so that they all rolled gasping into a narrow gulley.

He heard a voice yell, "*Open fire!*" and imagined he heard the rapid fire directly overhead.

The voice had been his own.

A marine flopped down beside him, pausing to fire two shots while another ran past, reloading as he ducked halfway down the slope. There was no sign of Piggott.

Steve Blackwood waited for his breathing to steady, and realized that he had been hugging the children, and that they were quite still, their dark eyes staring up at him, too terrified to move.

"Near thing, Sarge." It was Ellis. "How did you know?"

"Saw something like it once before." He tried to moisten his lips; they felt like leather. "Used some kids to flush out any opposition. Nearly worked, too."

Ellis rolled on his side, his eyes on the ridge, still dark against the first rays of sunlight. "The whole bloody island will know by now!" Surprisingly, he grinned. "Good thing you're around, Sarge!"

The channel was alive, still partly in shadow, but the rest was moving. You would get more than your knees wet in it now . . . "Crawl back and get my pack. And go easy with it." He was watching the water. "If it's going to happen, it'll be soon."

Ellis muttered, "Here comes Blondie."

One of the children whimpered.

"Never mind, chummy, soon be over." It seemed to work.

Piggott was on his knees beside the gully.

"How many were there, d' you think?"

"Two or three. All it needs."

"I would have bagged one of them if I hadn't tripped." It was a question again.

Ellis was coming back, his features clearly visible in the frail sunlight.

"Captain Irwin should have got the message by now. He'll know what to do." *Why am I telling him this? It's all bluff.* Piggott was shit-scared. "Watch over the kids."

Piggott said sharply, "I don't see why . . ."

"'Cause it's not their bloody war, *sir*!"

The rest was drowned by the sudden roar of engines.

"Quiet as a bloody grave now the damage is done!"

Captain John Irwin crouched on his knees with his back to the sea, one hand cupped behind each ear as he listened for the slightest sound, apparently oblivious to the stone and sharp fragments littering the track. "Like a bull in a damned china shop."

The sporadic burst of firing had stopped, as if it had never happened. You could almost feel the silence. Physical.

"Did Sergeant Boyes check our section at this end?" He was quite calm again, almost offhand.

Ross Blackwood replied, "I checked them myself, sir. Standing to."

"Information was good. We were just a bit too late. They'll make a run for it very soon. Not much that *Taunton* can do now, even *with* a following wind." He stood up lightly, without any apparent effort. "Unless your namesake keeps his head." He stared at the sky. "Corporal Laker, keep two men and cover the ridge." He must have sensed the corporal's doubt. "Man, you could hold up an army from this point!"

Then, to Ross, "Could be wrong. In which case . . ." He did not finish.

Ross fell into step beside him and knew that the others had fanned out across the treacherous, rubble-strewn slope, weapons at the ready, berets tugged over their eyes against any glare from the water.

He had seen some of the old and broken wrecks that littered the sheltered water beneath the ridge. It was hard to believe that they had once been seaworthy, for local trading and fishing. Left to rot, abandoned except by lawbreakers and faceless men in search of power.

He glanced at Irwin's lean profile. He could see the stubble on his stained features, some holes ripped in his camouflage clothing, but no evidence of fatigue or disappointment. He almost fell as Irwin's hand reached out and gripped him like a trap.

"*Listen.* They're on the move, the bastards!"

Ross had heard nothing, and then it was above, below, all around them. The mounting roar of engines, swelling and shaking as if it was coming from the nearest channel. He tried to clear his mind of everything but the impending action, but all he could hear was the sound of the fast launch as it had cast off from the junk's side and vanished into the night. Only the scream had remained.

"At the double, lads! *Move it!*" Irwin was already running toward the channel, his shouts now drowned by the sound of engines.

And all at once it was there, black and shapeless, and in the uncertain light it seemed to fill the channel, a great wash spilling and boiling over the stony banks, changing colour as the land fell aside like a huge gateway. Beyond it was the widening expanse of the sea, where only hours earlier they had waded ashore.

Whoever was on the helm had the skill, and the nerve to match it. One misjudgment, a wrong twist on the rudders, and it would be disaster. As it was, they were pounding into open water.

Ross exclaimed, *"Lost them!"* He felt himself trembling, with anger, defeat, disappointment. He knew he was shaking his fist, and barely recognized the sudden flash of tracer, rising and then curving down toward the edge of the land.

Irwin was shouting at him, punching his arm, pointing. *"It's them!"*

Two figures, one kneeling by some rocks, his beret catching the strengthening sun, the automatic rifle bucking into his shoulder with each carefully aimed shot. The second figure was half submerged, wading into deeper water, into nowhere, staring at the fast-moving boat and the mounting bow wave which must certainly sweep him away, into oblivion.

The launch was turning slightly, leaning over, the hull gleaming, almost gold now, light glinting on a low cockpit.

The wading figure had stopped, the sea up to his chest, one hand raised as if he was waving. The second figure stood upright by the rocks, then very slowly pitched forward on to his face. He did not move even as the broken bow wave swept across him, and tossed him aside like a rag doll.

The man in the water had fallen, and was being swept into the shadows. Perhaps he was also dead.

Sergeant Boyes was here, his face almost touching, eyes and mouth wide, yelling, the words making no sense.

"He done it, sir!" He was shaking Ross's arm. "Lobbed one of his toys right into them!"

It was not much of an explosion. More like a cough, a sensation. Like the barrel organ in Belfast . . . But there was a growing plume of black smoke, covering the little channel, rising and spreading so that even the sun was blotted out.

Ross imagined that he felt the launch hit the last spur of rock, the screws churning and thrashing impotently as the hull began to turn turtle, striking the bottom again. And again.

They were all running, wading into the shallows,

ducking as something exploded and hurled pieces of the hull above and among them.

"Easy now. Easy." Ross dashed the spray and smoke from his eyes and shielded the sodden figure while they dragged and carried him to safety.

He was on his knees; held his hand and watched him fighting back. Some one said, "Nothing broken by the looks of it, sir."

Another was saying,"The mad, brave bastard!"

He had known it was Steve Blackwood as soon as he had seen him wading toward the launch. Somebody had produced a clean handkerchief. Ross took it and dabbed away the stains and the vomit around his mouth.

He realized then that his eyes were open, staring up at him, grappling with shock, memory, recognition.

He whispered, "Where's young Ellis?"

Irwin was here, and gave a quick shake of the head.

"He was covering me. Wouldn't have made it otherwise."

His head fell back again. Irwin said, "You did well." He looked around and saw some marines coming down the opposite slope. One was carrying a child in his arms, another was leading a second child by the hand. It was unreal. "You all did."

He looked toward the launch, lying half submerged, with only a few wisps of smoke still rising from the battered hull, the twin screws motionless.

He said, "A job for the divers. They should get the evidence everybody was so mad about."

He glanced at the dead marine's body, covered by a strip of canvas.

"At a price."

He was able to say it without emotion or anger. That could wait.

Ross stared at the open sea. It had changed colour yet again. Some of the marines were moving along the water's edge; most of them looked at Ellis's body as they passed. One paused as if he was going to reach down and touch it, but another pulled him away.

Ross turned; some one had patted his shoulder as he went down the slope. It could have been any one of them.

He saw Piggott for the first time. Some of the marines parted to let him through. He could have been invisible.

Something made him shade his eyes and look toward the sea again. And there was *Taunton*, sharp and pale against the horizon, as if she had never moved, the tiny, diamond-bright wink of her signal lamp as close as the hand patting his shoulder.

She was probably calling up her sister ship, invisible around the next headland.

He made to get up, and felt a hand grasp his.

No words. There were none left to offer.

CHAPTER FIVE

The door was labelled *Reading Room*, probably, Ross thought, because nobody had been able to think of another use for it. He opened the door and glanced quickly around. It was, as he had hoped, deserted. There was the usual clutter of magazines and newspapers, some well out of date, but *The South China Morning Post* was fresh, and apparently unread.

He sat down and put his drink beside him on a brass-topped oriental table. There were books on one side of the room, mostly official, and some on local navigation and pilotage, a photo of the Queen above an imitation fireplace, opposite one of the Duke of Edinburgh wearing the uniform of Captain-General, Royal Marines. There was also a television set, mercifully disconnected.

He leaned back in the deep armchair and tried to empty his mind. He should have been exhausted, but he was fully alert; even if he closed his eyes, the pictures remained.

Taunton had entered harbour this morning, alongside for a change, her ship's company fallen in fore and aft, with a minimum of piped and shouted commands. Two armed police launches kept close by in case of too many sight-seers. Ross could not recall sleeping at all. Despite the hour, Houston had been on the jetty to meet them, while two ambulances hovered discreetly in the background.

73

The marines had assembled on the jetty in silence, weary, and visibly surprised when *Taunton*'s commanding officer had walked down the brow to shake hands with each one of them.

Then Captain Irwin had called his men to attention, and marched over to Houston to throw up a salute which would not have been out of place at Stonehouse Barracks or Whale Island.

Ross had felt it, the invisible thing which had taken over. Pride, habit, sheer bloody-mindedness. Torn and dishevelled, eyes red with strain, they had marched past the dock workers and gaping commuters heading for the Star Ferry, not a man out of step.

Sergeant Steve Blackwood and the marine who had been injured on the first night aboard *Taunton* had gone ahead in one ambulance. The other had waited before taking Marine Ellis's body to the mortuary.

It was only a short march, but accompanied by contrasts so sharp that it would be hard to forget a single one of them. A blind beggar reaching out with his bowl as the marines tramped past. Some children, up early in readiness for school, marching beside them, beaming and waving, unaware of the silent tension in these men, the inability to accept what they had seen and done in a few days of peacetime.

Ross had chosen his moment well. The wardroom bar was almost empty. Officers who had not gone 'ashore' to enjoy Hong Kong's sleepless night life were at dinner. One officer had been checking mess bills with the chief steward, but when he had seen Ross he had wanted to talk. And to listen.

He reached for his drink. The glass was empty. He could taste the brandy and ginger ale of the Horse's Neck, but could not remember drinking it. He pulled the folded letter from his pocket. It had been in the rack, waiting for his return. A far cry from Operation Ratcatcher.

It was from his mother. Reading it again now in this featureless room, he could feel her hand on his arm, hear her voice. She mentioned only briefly her new but temporary home, an apartment on the Thames at Richmond. If she was full of regrets at leaving Hawks Hill, she kept it to herself. She wrote of it only in passing. *The old house is being pulled down next month.* The rest of her letter had been about Susanna. She had begun a new job with some up-and-coming magazine called *Focus.* His sister had spoken of it on his last day in England; it was run and largely owned by a man often seen on television.

As usual, he had felt protective toward her, and asked about her views on her new employer. *I'll have a go at it. And I'm not lying on my back in exchange, if that's what you're suggesting.*

She was always trying to shock him, so that their roles sometimes seemed reversed. He touched his lip with the letter. And she did shock him, quite easily.

His mother touched on the Corps only once. *I am so proud of you, Ross. I know what it costs you.*

He thought of the grubby hand on his while the pieces of burning launch had scattered around them. Steve Blackwood was in the sick quarters, where it was thought he had a couple of cracked ribs. *She might as well know. I'll tell her in my next letter.*

And there was the other letter. His conversation with Houston on their return to the base had been forthright. Like the man.

"The young fellow, Ellis. I think a letter from you to his people would be the right thing. The official version will come soon enough, but yours would mean something. In time, anyway."

I lost my father. You lost your son.

Some one was coming. He shifted slightly in the chair, unconsciously, as if to hide.

But it was a steward.

"Phone call, sir."

"I'm not expecting . . ." He quelled the irritation. "Sorry. Not your fault."

The steward picked up the empty glass and smiled. "We were sayin' in the galley, after what you lot did—" He stopped. "I'll show you where the phone is, sir."

He had seen the signs.

It would be just like Houston to call a meeting to clear up some point about the mission. *He never sleeps.*

Another steward was arranging a tray for somebody, but did not look up. Not that it mattered. Even the best-kept secret was soon common knowledge in Hong Kong.

Another picture. The marines had been marching through the gates when a line of cooks had left the kitchens to greet them. All in white hats and aprons, one of them waving a saucepan over his head.

Ross heard later that the cooks had been waiting for them, even before *Taunton* had signalled her approach.

He pressed the telephone to his ear.

"Blackwood."

"I was afraid you'd be fast asleep."

Ross straightened. Even on the line he could hear the slight lilt in her voice.

"No. I'm awake." He glanced at the steward bending over his tray. "Sorry. I suppose I'm being a bit stupid." He hesitated. Her husband would take over. Another statement. But surely not today. Tonight . . .

She said, "I just wanted to know that you were O.K. I can't spell it out over the line. Not in this place."

"I'm fine. Really. Tidying things up. I don't know why

I'm not out on my feet." There was a pause, and he thought he heard her breathing. "What about you? Not working too hard, I hope?"

"I saw the ambulance. I found out about things. But I had to talk to *you*." There was a slight sound. "I'm not making any sense either, am I?"

"I'm sorry you were worried. You of all people."

For a moment he thought she had hung up, or that an operator really was tapping the line. Security . . .

But she said, "I'd like to have a drink with you. I think we both deserve it, don't you?" Very calm. Like the time she had cursed the naval doctor for calling her on New Year's night.

"Here? In the mess?" He was making a fool of himself. He noticed that the steward's hands were motionless over the cutlery.

"No. Here. You'll be in good company." She added quickly, "Just a short way from you, Java House, off Ice House Street. Get a taxi."

Then the line did go dead.

He put down the phone. *Leave it right there.* More faces. Questions. The chief inspector might be planning a private interrogation all of his own.

He heard voices, and some noisy laughter. Dinner was over, and the bar was open again.

A prowling taxi pulled up immediately.

"Ice House Street."

The driver reached out and closed the door for him.

He beamed. "I got brother near here, sir. He sell fine leather goods. He will open shop for you right now. Any time!"

He saw the look on Ross's face and shrugged.

"O.K., sir. Ice House Street!"

*

The taxi driver was in no hurry, taking his time, perhaps in case Ross changed his mind about his brother's shop. Nevertheless, the journey only seemed to take a few minutes. There were plenty of people about, and Ross had seen stalls still open, and little barrows where food was being sold to passers-by, chopsticks busy like knitting needles.

By contrast, this street off the main road was stark and glaring. The whole place was a blaze of light, brighter than day, with huge, gas-fired arc lamps everywhere. Men were working above and below street level, and a new building was already taking shape above the debris of one or more just demolished.

Ross stood beside the taxi and saw a large mechanical digger rumbling into the glare through a cloud of dust, to tip another pile of bricks and rubble into a waiting truck. It sounded like an avalanche. For anybody who lived around here, sleep would be a rare commodity.

The driver watched as Ross tugged out his wallet. He said cheerfully, "Building! All time building!" and waved at the night sky. "Very soon you not see the harbour from here!"

He pointed across the street. "Java House, sir."

A square, unpretentious apartment house, soon to be dwarfed or replaced by the other new buildings beside and beyond it. He took the notes and the tip and then produced an engraved business card, presenting it with both hands in true Chinese fashion.

"You need me, sir, you call any time!"

Ross crossed the road. At a guess he could have walked here easily; the blaze of arc lights would have led the way.

A workman was tending a brazier on a pathway. Two policemen were nearby, drinking tea. Ross could feel their eyes as he pushed open the double doors and found himself in a spacious entrance hall.

A porter was sitting at a desk, wearing headphones, nodding in time to some unheard music.

He lifted one from his ear and listened, his eye on Ross's lips, then he gestured to a lift and replaced the headphone.

There was a letter rack, and a list of names. A few ranks, naval and military, some officials, and the name 'Diamond'. Second floor.

He stepped into the lift, suddenly unsure. He should have written the letter to the dead marine's parents, or simply gone to bed. Was it that he was afraid of sleep? What it might bring?

The lift started with a violent jerk, and through a trap door in the ceiling he could see the cables beginning to move. He plucked at his shirt. Clammy. The taxi driver had said something about a storm coming.

He straightened the shirt. It was not the storm.

Four doors, two on either side, a plain carpet along the centre. An empty vase on a lacquered table. There was some old ribbon in the bottom of it, left over from Chinese New Year. How long ago was it?

Go now. Make your excuses. Blame it on fatigue.

He pressed the door bell.

Then she was there. Pleasure, surprise, anxiety.

"Ross, you *were* fast! You must have dropped everything you were doing . . ." She waited for him to enter, then held her head to one side. "Welcome, anyway! So good to see you!" He kissed her cheek, aware of her uncertainty. She was dressed all in white, like that other time, but completely different. Silk, he thought, so that her arms looked even darker. She grasped his hand and led him through to a large room, which he guessed opened on to one of the long balconies he had seen from the street.

She said, "I was expecting you to be in uniform. I don't know why. It's nice to see you like this. More human."

She was on edge, nervous. Perhaps something had happened.

"Where is everybody?"

"Jock . . . my husband . . . had to fly out very suddenly."

She moved to a Chinese table where some wine was standing in a misted ice bucket. There were only two glasses.

"Didn't I tell you? It was something urgent." She faced him again. "Still, I did say you'd be in good company." She smiled and held out her arms. "I'm it!" She smiled and the arms slipped around his neck. "I was so worried about you, Ross. You've no idea."

"Pour us a drink, will you?" The smile remained, but he could sense the difference. Regretting the impulse? Already seeking an escape.

She said, "Sorry it's so stuffy. All those lights, and that bloody noise outside – you can hardly think straight."

She gestured to the glasses and Ross poured. It was champagne. He saw that she was sitting on one of the big sofas, a cushion cuddled in her lap.

"Here's to you, Ross. I worried a lot. The rumours, the ambulance on the dockside . . ." She moved her shoulders. "You know."

He sat beside her, careful not to touch her. *You should not be here. You should not have come.*

"I spoke to one of your sergeants, the one with your name, and his friend Boyes. Ted Boyes? He was visiting him in the sick quarters." She nodded, a lock of dark hair falling across one cheek. "Steve is fine, by the way. They both said how good you were, 'on the job', as they put it."

"They did all the work."

She ran her finger around the top of her glass until it squeaked.

"A lot of people are going to thank God you came out of it all right." Her eyes were very steady, like her voice. "Tell me about yourself, Ross. You must have some one special, waiting and fretting about you. What's she like?"

"She's a very lovely girl, who has no idea what she can do to a man with just a glance. I have no right even to think of her the way I do."

She looked down at her glass. "Of course you do. She's the one who's lucky."

He took her hand.

"Her name's Glynis, by the way."

The champagne glass rolled away, unheeded.

"Me? A girl? I can give you a few years, I bet!" She clung to his arm, half laughing, half sobbing. "You've ruined my make-up! I went to so much trouble—"

She watched him toss away the cushion and lay fully against him, her head on his shoulder.

"Your injury, how is it?"

He could not see the eyes, hidden by her hair.

"It's fine." He felt her tense as he touched the front of her blouse, and carefully unfastened the buttons until her breast lay in his hand. "*Now*, it is."

Her body was stiff, unmoving, only her breathing fast across his face. Shock, fear, anger?

Her skin was like the silk which had slid from the sofa. She took his wrist with both hands and pinned it against her.

How long they lay like that he could not imagine. Minutes, seconds . . . Even the distant street sounds seemed to stop.

Then he felt her face turn against his, their lips almost brushing.

"Kiss me, Ross."

A proper one.

He felt her fingers tighten as she forced his hand, deliberately, still further, into her body.

She might have cried out, but her words were muffled.

"*Now*, Ross. Do it now . . ."

At least two partitions had been removed to make this room large enough for the conference. Officers from Operations and Communications, uniforms from all three services including two R.A.F. 'wingless wonders' from the Met Office, mingled with others in civilian clothes, police or intelligence people it was impossible to know.

Major Houston stood by the table, his fingertips lightly pressing some files, his eyes on the seated figures, waiting for every one to settle down.

By his side, but obviously removed from him in spirit, was the visitor, Lieutenant-Colonel Leslie De Lisle, his neatly cut hair shining beneath the overhead lights. He seemed calm and relaxed, his trim Lovat uniform looking as if it had just been cleaned and pressed. Like its owner. There was no evidence from his appearance that he had been attending meetings at various high levels for several hours, and flying in directly from Singapore before that for good measure.

Ross, sitting by a partly opened window, recalled their last meeting on that bitter January day in Plymouth, the sound of marching feet a background to the conversation. De Lisle was exactly as he remembered him, even to the studied informality. The meeting had begun with brief but friendly introductions, De Lisle nodding or smiling in the direction of each face as Houston rattled off names. Some De Lisle addressed like old friends. If any were complete strangers, he gave no sign of it, a diplomatic skill many would envy. The general must have been sorry to lose him.

Houston had uncovered a powerful assault rifle, gleaming like new; a curved box-magazine was lying beside it.

"Familiar to some of you, no doubt, gentlemen, and frequently used with deadly effect by rebels and terrorists for some years. This one, with others, was salvaged from the launch which was destroyed in Operation Ratcatcher. Originally, the Russian Kalashnikov AK47, but there have been several versions since they appeared in Vietnam. Copies mostly, Chinese, Polish, you name it. More recently they've shown up in Malaysia and Borneo." He glanced at Captain Irwin. "I can see *you* haven't forgotten!"

Ross looked at De Lisle, whose fingers remained interlaced, unmoving.

Houston had picked up the weapon; it looked like a toy in his big hands.

"Now they're reappearing in larger numbers, but this time we are not completely in the dark."

There was a murmur, and Ross saw Piggott lean forward in his chair, with either approval or self-satisfaction.

When they had all gathered round to welcome De Lisle, Piggott had been one of the first to step forward and thrust out his hand. *My father asked me to give you his warmest greetings if we met, sir.*

De Lisle had made some vague comment and moved along the line of waiting figures. Missing nothing. Giving nothing.

Houston looked fastidiously down at his tunic, where the gun had left a greasy stain. He said, "Your artificers are getting slack, Arthur!"

They all laughed, as he had intended.

Ross caught sight of Chief Inspector Diamond, who was seated with another man in civilian clothes; he was wearing a pale grey, lightweight suit, obviously hand-made, which fitted him perfectly. He had come into the room with De Lisle, perhaps straight from the airport, perhaps after returning to Java House to change and clean up. He showed little sign of fatigue. Their eyes had met only once, and there had been a curt tilt of the head. Recognition, nothing more.

What did I expect? He had left the apartment yesterday morning. Was that all it was? Like a wild dream, which ended only when he was standing in the street again, the noise and machinery just stirring into life.

He had slept some of the time since; he must have done. It was impossible to clarify it. Once they had gone to the windows and drawn the curtains. There had been silence outside, and only a couple of arc lights were still burning.

They had drunk more champagne, doubtless warm, although he had neither noticed nor remembered, and they had made love again. She had pretended to resist, had struggled, teased him with hands, lips, words. It had been almost dawn when they had finally broken apart.

She had helped him pull himself together, had even loaned him a razor.

"I use it for my legs, but it's better than nothing."

Laughing, anxious that he should not be late back to his quarters. And the last touch, the moment of parting. It was still a dream. She had been cleaning some lipstick off his shirt when he had noticed that her bedroom was separate from her husband's.

She had seen his eyes, but had merely shrugged bare shoulders.

He gazed at Jock Diamond once more. What kind of man was he? Did he suspect anything? Did he care?

He had seen a bag of what looked like expensive golf clubs in the other bedroom. She had tossed her head.

"Don't get him talking about golf, Ross. You'd be at it all day!"

Was that all it meant to her?

He realized that De Lisle was on his feet, and that there was complete silence.

"It has been a slow, painstaking operation. Illegal immigrants, piracy, and gun running have often been regarded, and dealt with, as matters quite independent of one another. Now we know that the central themes of rebellion, and the many uses of terrorism to support it, are, if you like, a plan of battle.

"With the gradual diminishing of Empire, and the establishment of individual states within the Commonwealth, we now see the next, if not the last, challenge."

For a moment his eyes moved to Ross.

"Small pieces of a puzzle, and many have suffered because of it." He looked at the weapon on the table. "A gun never wears out or becomes completely useless. In the First World War, many of our soldiers who survived the trenches said that eventually they came home with the same rifles they had first been issued. The lucky ones, that is."

He paused to look around the faces. Like an actor, Ross thought, with a captive audience.

De Lisle said quietly, "One name, gentlemen. Remember it well. Richard Suan." His eyes rested now on Captain Irwin. "I can see that you know it, John?"

Irwin was half on his feet. "But he's *dead*, sir. It was confirmed. I remember . . ."

De Lisle said, "Older now, John, but very much alive!"

He pointed at the files beside the gun.

"Read and remember. Richard Suan. Once a lawyer, a promising politician, and a dedicated rebel and terrorist. You name it, Richard Suan was there. So this will be, must be, a combined operation. Trust and secrecy must go hand in hand. It will be soon. Later may be *too* late. I can assure you, gentlemen, our part is vital." He sat down and several officers began to applaud.

Ross felt Piggott slide into the chair beside him, still clapping his hands.

"That's more like it, eh?" He was unusually flushed.

The files were being separated and distributed; they were to be collected before the meeting was dismissed.

Irwin stood behind them, a sheet of paper in his hands.

"I thought – *prayed* – we'd seen the last of him." No emotion. No anger.

Ross said, "A combined operation?"

He did not see Irwin's expression. "That means somebody's really scared. At last!"

Everybody was talking at once, and men were crossing and recrossing the room to ask questions or share an opinion.

Ross tried to stay apart, clear his mind. This was no mere skirmish, no test of nerves.

He heard Houston's boisterous laugh, saw him put his hand on Diamond's shoulder. Was that an act, too? *Chalk and cheese.*

He had telephoned her this morning. There had been no reply. She was probably at the sick quarters, or avoiding him, perhaps only now fully aware of what they had done.

He realized that Houston was beside him.

"Did you do that letter to young Ellis's people?"

"This morning, sir."

"Good. Good show." He had not even heard him.

Acting a part? Or did he not really care?

He thought of the small room where they had first met. Her warmth toward him after his anger at the drunken naval doctor. Like some one telling him, helping him come to terms . . .

"See you in the mess, Ross?" It could have been anybody.

Diamond was in deep conversation with another suited man.

Don't get him talking about golf.

He thought of the faces in the dawn light, the sound of shots, the unknown hand patting his shoulder. Men who would be depending on him, because it was all they knew, and they had no choice anyway.

And neither do you.

Sergeant Steve Blackwood heard the persistent drumming of rain against the shutters, the sluice of overflowing gutters. The expected storm had arrived.

It was mid-afternoon but the day looked dark outside, what he could see of it. Inside this new wing of the sick quarters all the lights were dazzling against the white paint and shining glass.

He hated hospitals, large or small, the way every one else knew exactly where to go, which direction to take. *You* were always invisible.

"Sorry to keep you waiting." A sick berth attendant in a white coat had appeared around a screen, with what looked like a chamber pot covered by a towel. "You can go right in. Number Twenty-two." As an afterthought. "Not too long now."

That was also the same.

The door was unmarked but for a number. There was no bell, either, so he pushed it open. At first he thought he had taken the wrong route. It was more like a cupboard, with racks of what appeared to be medical or surgical gowns, hanging like motionless ghosts.

He saw another door and a bigger room, brightly lit, with a large mirror on the far wall.

He heard a woman's voice and saw her leg swinging up and down, the movement, like her tone, impatient, possibly even angry.

The door opened wider and he saw her sitting on a bed, with a telephone to her ear.

He said, "I'm sorry, Miss Diamond. I was told to come on through."

She put down the telephone and pushed some hair from her eyes.

"Hello, Sergeant. Can't you keep away from this place?" It was the smile he remembered, but it had not come easily to her. "Take a seat." She uncrossed her legs and moved to another chair.

She had on a pale blue dress, unlike the semi-uniform shirt and slacks she had been wearing when she had visited him after *Taunton* brought them back to Hong Kong. And the legs were very nice . . .

She seemed more composed now. "It's *Mrs.* Diamond, by the way." She held up her hand so that he could see a ring. "But Glynis will do."

Funny he had not noticed the ring before. The 'hands off' signal.

He said, "Just wanted to thank you for your kindness." He moved his shoulder experimentally. "All O.K., nothing broken after all. I was lucky, I guess."

"You all were." She smiled. "I heard your Major Houston was here as well. He's a fierce character and no mistake."

"Oh, he's not so bad. The bark and the bite. You know." He saw her start as some one dropped some glasses in the corridor. She was very on edge.

He thought of Houston's visit. Always bustling on to somewhere else, but no flannel. Straight to the point. "You're being put up for a medal, Sergeant Blackwood.

Captain Irwin came to see me about it. Can't say, of course, but you deserve a gong for what you did."

He already knew who had made the suggestion: the lieutenant who had helped pull him from the water after the world had exploded, and had held his hand while he was waiting for assistance. He had still been able to look out for the two little Chinese kids who had almost been cut down by gunfire.

And the woman sitting opposite him cared about that same man. Ross Blackwood.

"I'll be shoving off then ... er ... Glynis. Nice knowing you."

She was on her feet, very calm again. Too calm.

She said softly, "Something big is going to happen, isn't it? You don't have to spell it out. I can see it for myself."

In the hard light the ring gleamed like a challenge.

He said, "It had to come. That's all I can say. All I know."

The telephone rang and she snatched it up, and put one hand over the mouthpiece.

"Come and see me again if you can." She blew him a kiss. "I'll be thinking of you."

He opened the door. She was already far away. It was hopeless, and maybe dangerous. A married woman with an influential husband ... it had been doomed right from the start.

No more leave. It's on. Clear your mind. No mistakes.

But as he closed the door he heard her voice.

"It's me, darling. I knew you'd call. I just want to be near ..."

He walked past the racks of gowns. Like ghosts.

All he could feel was envy.

CHAPTER SIX

Two days after De Lisle's conference, final orders were received. Overnight, a ship had entered harbour and moored amongst the regular naval occupants. *Avondale* was a moderate-sized merchantman, or had been, but now she flew the blue ensign of the Royal Fleet Auxiliary. She was no stranger to Hong Kong, and like others of her breed was used to many roles, humping fuel and stores, naval or military equipment, and personnel.

Two big landing craft carried sixty Royal Marines of the Special Operations Unit out to the *Avondale* without fuss or excitement. They were just another cargo.

De Lisle was about to fly out again, but had decided to call the officers of Operation Ratcatcher together for a last, informal meeting. It was held in one of the sumptuous suites of the Mandarin Hotel, facing the harbour, and only a few minutes' walk from naval headquarters. Ross Blackwood had seen the hotel several times from a distance; next to the Peninsula on the Kowloon side, it was said to be the best in the world. He had wondered idly about the people who stayed there, passing through Hong Kong, or perhaps just visiting for some special occasion. He had never imagined himself inside.

He mingled with officers of De Lisle's own staff, Houston and Irwin, some of *Tamar*'s wardroom, and others he recognized from other conferences. A table had been prepared and featured platters of exotic foods, several kinds of wine, and fresh flowers; it was more like a celebration than the eve of something which might backfire in all their faces.

There were a few women, the wives of some senior officers. *Doing the right thing.* He saw Piggott button-holing Irwin in a corner, making a point by pounding one fist into the other. Irwin appeared to be listening, but his eyes were on the suite's balcony, from which he would have seen the one-funnelled *Avondale*, hemmed in by harbour craft and sampans.

Ross had been expecting it, but he had tried to contain the feelings, wanting and dreading together.

He heard Chief Inspector Diamond's voice first, and somebody else greeting him. "How are you, Jock, you old rascal! Heard you showed 'em a thing or two at the club!"

She was a pace behind him, smiling at some one, but her eyes were on Ross, across and past everybody else.

A sleeveless dress, a flower, perhaps an orchid, pinned in her hair. She looked lovely. And unreachable.

Houston said, "'Course, you two know each other." He grinned at her. "You heard how young Ross here refused to budge until he had reunited a couple of local kids with their family? Wouldn't damned well move!"

She was close now, holding out her hand. "I *did* hear." She squeezed his fingers for a second, then dropped the hand to her shoulderbag.

He said quietly, "I'm so glad you came." He did not use her name. *Like playing a part.* The dark eyes were very level, but where the shoulder strap of her bag tugged at her dress he could see, or imagine, her heart beating. Like his own.

A tray of wine thrust between them and a smiling waiter insisted, "All French, all good!"

She said, "I saw the ship. They told me about it." She touched the glass with her lips, but the wine did not move.

Houston had returned. His glass was empty.

"I hear your husband's packing the job in when this lot's over and done with. Back to the police in the U.K., is it?"

Ross saw the pain in her eyes, and she hesitated as if to brush something off her arm.

"No. His time is up in the Branch, although they offered him an extension."

Houston was staring around the room. "Should think so, too, after all the work he's put in with the local force and Intelligence."

She said, "He's been offered an appointment with a big security firm in London." But she was speaking to Ross.

Some one passed a folded paper, obviously torn from a pad, to Houston, which he opened around his glass.

He said, "From *Avondale*. All our lads have embarked." He refolded the paper. "I'll tell De Lisle."

Ross heard Diamond's voice. He was coming over.

He said quietly, "I am so *sorry*. I wanted . . ."

Diamond touched his arm.

"Well, at least we know what to expect, eh?" He put down his glass and frowned at something. "Just a moment."

Ross saw that a thin silk bra strap had slipped from beneath her dress and fallen around her arm. Like the one on the floor after they had made love.

Diamond tucked the strap out of sight.

"That's more like it." He retrieved his drink and wagged it at Ross. "You're a young chap, everything waiting for you. When you find a nice wife, do what I did. Marry one a lot younger than yourself!" He laughed. "Keeps you young, you see?" He glanced at his watch. "Come along, Glynis, we'd better mingle for a bit."

He took her arm and together they walked toward another group of guests.

Ross watched her shoulders, the angle of her head. She did not look back. She did not need to.

Houston had returned.

"De Lisle wants a chat with you, Ross. I think he's going to vanish shortly."

Ross felt the big hand on his shoulder, its suggestion of restraint.

"A word in your ear, my son. When you're entering a mine field, tread *very* carefully!"

Ross looked across the room. Just for a moment he saw her face, before some one moved and it was lost to him.

She had put two fingers to her lips, like a kiss. Reaching out.

He saw Houston watching, waiting for him.

The mine field was still there.

Sergeant Ted Boyes sat comfortably on a rolled canvas canopy with his back against a wash-deck locker and contemplated the spread of another sunset. The sky was already patched with deep shadow, and a few early stars to mark the horizon from the sea. Around and beneath him the R.F.A. *Avondale* trembled to the engines' regular beat, and the air was warm from fans or ventilators. Nearly five days since they had slipped their moorings in Hong Kong, on and on at a regular twelve knots, or so he had gathered from the brains up on the bridge.

He watched a cluster of gulls wheeling and screaming around the ship's quarter. Always ready: one of the cooks had just pitched a bucket of gash over the side. Their presence showed that the land was close.

It was strange that during their entire time at sea, they had sighted so few ships of any size. Perhaps the captain had taken extra care to avoid any such encounter. The radar was always on the lookout, and at a guess the radio in constant control.

Sixty Royal Marines, commandos, needed a lot of attention. As Major Houston had said from the outset, *keep 'em fit, and keep 'em busy!* They had tried to do just that. Arms drills and inspections, self-defence and unarmed combat, and every kind of physical exercise. Nobody was excluded, and usually Houston himself was in the forefront.

Boyes gazed at the fading horizon. Singapore. He could see it as if it was in print. Houston had spoken to the whole unit as soon as the ship had cleared harbour. Until then, the 'combined operation' had been just another rumour.

Boyes had thought about it, but he was past surprise at this stage of his life. For some it was not so simple. Tempers had flared and a few scuffles had broken out, nothing bad enough to warrant the defaulters' table. Not yet, anyway. The sergeants, all experienced N.C.O.s, had made sure of that. Others had settled down to write letters to family or girlfriends, to be left with the ship when eventually they disembarked. Homesickness was a constant companion, no matter what the hard cases claimed to the contrary.

He had gone through it enough times. He half smiled. Even for his own home in southwest London, Battersea, a council flat close to the busy Clapham Junction station, where the vibration of the express trains thundering over the points and bridges had made the cups and saucers rattle in his mother's kitchen cupboard. Or in the summer when the windows were open, noise or no noise, and you could smell the pong from the candle factory in York Road. Or having a jar with the lads at the pub . . .

He felt some one beside him, near the guardrails.

"Hello, Steve." He patted the rolled canvas. "Park your arse down here." Sergeant Blackwood sat beside him, a cigarette cupped in one palm. "Nearly there, eh?"

Boyes glanced at the dark profile. Probably seen more close action than any of them, except Captain Irwin, or Houston. Was he bitter? Did he deeply resent still being an N.C.O. when his was such a well-known name?

Only once had he come straight out with it. "Both my parents were Blackwoods, Ted. I was wrong side of the blanket, though."

"Tomorrow, I'd say." He grinned. "The latest buzz from the galley says so."

Boyes tested the ground. "I hear you've been put up for a gong. Bloody good show, after what you did."

"Won't help young Ellis."

"Could happen to any one of us, you know that. If it's got your number on it . . ." He shrugged. "It goes with the job!"

Feet thudded overhead on what passed for *Avondale*'s boat deck, and somebody laughed. *Follow my example.*

Steve Blackwood said quietly, "Now if it had been Blondie Piggott . . ." He did not need to say any more.

Boyes watched the cigarette glow in the cupped hand. During the rough stuff that morning, unarmed combat which usually got out of hand, several marines had jumped on Piggott, the one chance you got to thump an officer without any comeback. That made it worse. Piggott was more than a match for any attacker. It was time to change the subject.

He said, "My Mr. Blackwood's certainly got his eye on the Diamond girl. Bit of all right, if you ask me."

"You think so?"

"Well, I'd rather be on her than guard duty!"

He glanced down as he felt something put into his hand. It was a flask. Steve Blackwood said, "Have a wet with me. May be the last chance before we get busy."

It was neat brandy. Boyes wiped the flask with his sleeve and returned it.

"Thanks, Steve. Good stuff." Perhaps just what he had needed. That, and the friendship. "Any thoughts about this coming job?"

The cigarette glowed in one final, deep drag.

"Yeah. Remember, shoot *first!*"

The transfer of the sixty-strong commando unit took place at sea in less than ideal conditions. Following the tail-end of a tropical storm, there was a deep swell running, and the air was clammy and lifeless.

The marines lined *Avondale*'s side and upperworks to watch the two vessels manoeuvring, all fenders rigged to lessen any impact upon going alongside. For once, most of them had little to say. Surprise, disbelief, in some cases a hint of shock described their feelings.

The amphibious patrol vessel of the Singapore Navy was old in design and years. Houston had already given a rough outline of her service, but even he must have been taken aback.

She had begun life as a tank landing craft in the U.S. Navy, and had been commissioned in 1944, just in time for the closing campaigns of World War Two: Korea and Vietnam had seen her employed in other support roles, and last year she had been transferred, with several of her aging sisters, to the new navy of Singapore. In various guises, from training to anti-terrorist and piracy patrols, she had survived when most of her breed had long gone to the breaker's yard.

She was named *Vigilant*, and according to the records

she mounted two forty millimetre guns, and, to every one's surprise, a solitary howitzer, for 'local bombardment work'.

Houston watched the heaving lines going across and murmured, "Talk about Ancient and Modern."

Irwin nodded. "No wonder De Lisle went by air!"

Ross Blackwood felt the deck shudder as both hulls ground against the fenders. The *Vigilant*'s box-like deck was crammed with assorted gear, two-man canoes, camouflage netting, lifting tackles, lengths of timber and sacks of fuel, presumably for the galley. But Singapore had survived and prospered, where many others had gone under.

Irwin had described the kind of obstacles which could be regularly encountered in the area they would be covering. "A spanking new frigate wouldn't last a dog watch. Fast rivers one minute, hard aground the next. *Vigilant* might have the edge on the newcomers."

Houston rubbed his battered nose. "If you say so, John. Give the word, then. No slip-ups."

Watched by *Avondale*'s seamen and greeted with wide grins by the Singaporean hands, the marines clambered down the nets and across the narrow strip of trapped water.

Ross paused to recover his balance and gripped a rail below the squat bridge structure at the after end of the hull. It had been newly painted, but through the last coat he could see the builder's name plate. *Chicago Bridge & Iron Co., 1944.*

Some one said, "Must 'ave 'ad sails in them days!"

Others laughed. Ross felt his stomach muscles unclench. They were on their way.

The *Vigilant*'s captain raised a casual hand to them from the bridge and then called to his deck party. The lines were snaking free, fenders already splashing inboard, the strip of choppy water suddenly a widening arrowhead.

"Get your men below as soon as possible!"

Ross turned at the voice. The speaker wore a loose army waterproof coat, without insignia of rank or regiment, and was carrying what looked like a bush hat, again with no badge.

This was the liaison officer. The mark of Commonwealth. He thought of Houston's summing up at their first meeting. He was not disappointed.

"They know what to do, *sir*. This is a commando unit."

The other man did not even blink. A narrow, sharp-featured face, with a neat military moustache: he might just as well have been wearing a red coat and bearskin.

"Mannering. Major, Welsh Guards." No change of expression, nor did he offer his hand.

Houston grinned pugnaciously.

"At your service, sir!"

"Er, yes. Well, there's a signal for you. Urgent."

The *Vigilant* was moving again, shaking to the thrust of her twin screws. Ross looked abeam. There was a smudge on the horizon. Land, but it could have been anywhere.

He saw the liaison officer striding ahead, followed by Houston's athletic figure. Welsh Guards. Maybe the mission was off, superseded by something else. But all he could hear was the lilt in her voice, something Mannering would probably not even recognize.

Piggott joined him by the bridge ladder. "Bit of a bloody mess, isn't it? No wonder the Yanks gave it away!"

Ross said nothing. You could usually get along with your opposite numbers, if you had to. And Piggott had a good record; De Lisle would have made sure of that. But, unlike some officers, he did not even try to be popular.

He would brush it off. Steve had saved his life that day on Raven's Island. Piggott had turned his back.

Houston clattered down the ladder, beckoning to Irwin.

"The plan has changed." He was thinking aloud. Seeing it. "We're making a different landing for the first section."

Irwin regarded him without expression, as if nothing could surprise him.

"Not the rubber plantation, sir?"

Houston had removed his beret, perhaps without knowing it, and was screwing it up in his hand.

"It's been attacked. Bombs, flamethrowers, the lot. The owner, his family, any one who wasn't fast enough on his feet got the chop. Oh, it's started all right!"

Ross saw the sea rising and falling beyond the flapping ensign, but felt nothing, was removed from it. Letting fragments fall into place, like the arrows on the maps and charts, the cold statistics of life and death. The man who owned the plantation and other valuable property was an important government official, a future Malaysian leader. He corrected himself mentally. Who *had* owned the plantation. Irwin would understand only too well. It was history repeating itself.

"I want to speak to all N.C.O.s." Houston looked at his watch. "In half an hour. You too, of course." He replaced his beret, in charge again. "Tomorrow, next day at the latest, otherwise we'll lose 'em. And *that* I don't intend to happen!"

He shaded his eyes to stare up at the bridge. "Half an hour, then, chaps."

Ross walked to the guardrails and watched *Vigilant*'s sluggish bow wave rolling past.

Houston was angry. As if it had become personal, a challenge.

The jungle on one side, the sea on the other. He had

heard Boyes remark, "You could lose a bloody regiment in there!"

Tomorrow. Next day at the latest. The luxurious suite at the Mandarin seemed like a year ago. As if it had never happened, except for the kiss across the room. The last time he had seen her. Did Houston remember that, he wondered, or the warning remark about the mine field? Further and further astern, with every turn of those screws. She would soon forget. She would have to. *But can you?*

"Coming, Ross? Better not keep the boss waiting."

The waiting was over, too.

She walked slowly across the room, her bare feet soundless on the carpet. She pulled the curtains partly open, bracing herself for the arc lights and the endless din of construction. Some of the lights were on, but most of the street below was in darkness. There were still a few cars crossing the intersection, and some reflected glare of advertising signs shone back at her from the empty windows opposite Java House.

She closed the curtains and walked through to her own room, one hand brushing the sofa where they had come together. Ecstasy, joy, madness. She had believed that she could deal with it, cope with any aftermath.

She was seated at her dressing table although she did not recall moving. She stared at herself. In white silk pyjamas. *All in white*; she could hear him saying it. She shook her head and saw the lock of dark hair fall across her forehead. No, she could not deal with it.

She put her hand inside her jacket and touched her breast, as he had done.

Not *he*. His name. *Speak his name.* She watched her lips move. *Ross.* She took off her watch and laid it on a bedside table. She did not look at it; she did not have to. It was Thursday night. Club night. He would be getting into the lift in about ten minutes, after he had checked his change from the taxi driver.

Hard to remember how it had all started, what had changed things. She recalled Ross's face when she had mentioned the hospital at Homerton, in the East End of London. Another world. And he cared, because he could not share it with her. Where she had first met Duncan, or 'Jock' as he liked to be known. A C.I.D. officer in those days, he had come to the hospital to question a man who had been injured in a pub brawl. He had just been divorced, and she had been getting over an affair with a young doctor.

They think you're anybody's! Perhaps they had needed each other at that moment in time. Jock had done well in the force, C.I.D. to Special Branch, and on to more confidential work with various embassies. Now he was a chief inspector, looked up to by every one. Almost . . . And finally, Hong Kong.

How could it have happened? A bright young officer in the Royal Marines, from a well-known service family. Out of the mould, many would say. She pushed her hair from her forehead, remembering. Nothing rough or brutish. And not taken for granted. Used.

She had held him, guided him, given herself as she could never recall having done before.

Now he was gone. It was not like a war, *the* war. This was something that would appear on TV and the front page for a few days, and then be forgotten, except by those who waited for the dreaded telegram. Like the marine who had been met by an ambulance when the others had returned. *And I called Ross to ask him to come here. That night.*

She ran her palm along her bare arm. It had been like a dam bursting.

And at the hotel, when Jock had mentioned marrying a

woman younger than himself. Proud, boasting? Or was it a threat?

Where was Ross now? At sea, or on some other worthless island? Who would care?

It happens, they all said. It made no sense.

She felt her spine go rigid. Like that night when she had heard the door bell, and he had been standing there. No uniform. So young. So unsure. So eager.

But it was the lift. Right on time.

Club night. As if she could see it happening, like a spectator.

But she was not a spectator. He would pour himself a drink. A large one, and glance at the newspaper, always laid out by the table. Where she had prepared the champagne. And then . . .

Suppose I refuse? Tell him the truth? Or just pretend. Many did; she heard enough stories about it.

Her heart was pounding. She heard him call out, "Home, dear!"

They would be going back to England soon, London, the new appointment.

She heard him swear as he dropped something on a tray. There would always be *club night*, wherever it was.

She felt the door open, saw his shadow reach across the lamplight.

"Ah, there you are, my dear!"

Hands on her shoulders, unsteady but insistent.

He would probably hurt her, and tomorrow remember nothing.

She felt something tear, and heard him swear again. The smell of whisky.

Ross, I love you.

The pain.

*

102

Captain John Irwin paused in his slow stride, one foot motionless in mid-air, and breathed out, counting the seconds. The brief movement which had caught his eye had been a lizard of some kind, or a snake. Probably on full alert. *Like the rest of us.*

He peered up at the trees, trailing lianas, and so closely entwined that the sky was hidden. It had been about two hours since they had jumped into the shallows from *Vigilant*'s low hull and waded ashore. It had started raining almost immediately, the sound of the downpour shutting out the old landing craft's engines as she headed once more into deeper water. Something you never got used to: the sensation of being entirely alone, cut off from familiar faces and sounds.

Two hours. The rebels, terrorists, or however they saw themselves, could be miles away by now. He tightened his jaw. That would be too simple, a solution to everything. It was rarely that easy. He imagined the men at his back, and in the loose arrowhead formations they had planned and practised so many times. In the training exercises they had tried to simulate every sort of threat and disaster.

But nothing like a squealing wild pig, which had burst through the undergrowth and charged toward two crouching marines. A nasty moment, but nobody shouted, and the sense of danger and need for stealth remained paramount.

Sergeant Bolton was somewhere on his left. An experienced N.C.O. who had served in several trouble spots, he was known to his friends as 'Rimshot'. He had begun his service with the Corps as a boy musician in one of the divisional bands. Off duty, he had joined up with a local jazz band, and his dexterity with the wire rhythm brushes and the snare drum had brought him a lot of admiration at two or three dance clubs. Unfortunately, he had been seen by a senior officer, who had reported the matter. Defiantly, Bolton had applied to transfer to the commandos, where he had taken to the sometimes brutal training without apparent regret. The nickname 'Rimshot' had followed him.

Sergeant Ted Boyes was close behind him with a squad acting as rearguard. Another veteran, some one you never had to nag or remind. A true commando, and it still amused Irwin that such a heavily built body could move with the stealth of the lizard he had almost crushed. Good with the marines, experienced or green, but try and take advantage of him and you'd think a cliff had fallen on you.

He saw the lieutenant and a corporal pressed against some fallen trees. There was no time to linger. This was the most dangerous moment: officers and N.C.O.s all together. It only took a short squeeze on the trigger.

They passed, Ross giving a mere nod, but keeping his eyes on the rough, partly overgrown track, where plantation workers had once hacked a path. Rain was dripping from a gap in the jungle canopy overhead; he saw it bouncing on Ross's shoulder, splashing his face. He ignored it. Another irritation which could change into a trap for the unwary, or the over confident.

Irwin tested a piece of rotten wood with his boot, and saw the immediate swarm of large black termites from beneath it. When he looked back, Ross and the corporal had vanished. Ross seemed to have changed so much in the short time since they had met. A far, far cry from those other times on some training course or other. Scotland? Somewhere . . . *Matured.* Even that was not the word he wanted. Young, with a full career ahead of him. If he lived long enough. And with the Blackwood family name . . .

He peered at his watch. Timed to the second. Each small section would stop. Right now, just as they discussed. It was the only way to avoid the risk of some solitary person getting separated, lost, wandering alone.

He thought of Ross again. Might end up a half-colonel like his late father, if he kept his nose clean and stayed out of trouble.

And what about you? As if somebody had spoken to him aloud. He glanced at the sergeant, 'Rimshot', squatting nearby, one leg folded beneath him like a spring. He was apparently watching a procession of ants winding its way over a piece of stone, but one hand was resting on his light machine-gun.

It was a question that often bothered Irwin. He had been lucky to gain a commission, let alone get three pips on his shoulder. But later on, what then? He would not rise any higher with so many cuts in the armed forces, penny-pinching by the politicians who were always ready enough to throw lives away if they made a mess of things in Parliament. At best he might end up in the recruiting section, or talking to all those eager young faces at various Royal Marines cadet corps units. Telling them what they were missing if they didn't sign on. If he had got married, things might have been different. But she had tired of all the waiting, the 'brush fire wars' as the newspapers called them, and she had married a petty officer in naval stores at Portsmouth. He was retired now and they ran a little pub down there, not a stone's throw from the barracks. Two kids as well.

Rimshot Bolton lifted his wrist and tapped it where his watch would be under his tunic.

Irwin nodded abruptly. This was not like him. Dreaming like some dozy recruit.

He rolled over and was on his feet in seconds. Not even out of breath. He glanced at the sergeant and was about to grin, but it was like being stricken, his mouth stiff, unmoving.

A marine stood between two trees, viciously spiked rattans, one hand reaching out as if for support, the other pointing directly at Irwin and the crouching sergeant. Except that Rimshot Bolton was now kneeling and perfectly balanced, the gun firm in his grip.

He said softly, "It's Davis, sir."

Irwin said nothing. Marine Davis was one of the rear party, the tailenders. But how did Bolton know?

He had turned toward the voice, still reaching out, head turning from side to side but seeing nothing, trying to speak, choking on his blood.

The insane question repeated itself. How did Bolton recognize him? He had no face.

Bolton moved swiftly.

"Here, Taff! I've got you, lad!"

But he had fallen.

Irwin dragged out his whistle. Warnings flashed through his mind. Caution, experience, discipline were suddenly meaningless, the very things which had brought this poor butchered creature back to the only hope he had left. Too late.

The whistle shattered the silence, joined instantly by unseen birds as they burst away through the dripping trees overhead.

Like a madness, a fury that drove all else aside.

Us or them!

He heard feet crashing through the undergrowth, caught the glint of steel.

He ducked around a tree and felt his finger squeeze the trigger and the gun jerk in his hands, heard a sharp scream, and ran on with the others pounding behind him.

Not an exercise this time. It was in deadly earnest.

Us or them.

CHAPTER SEVEN

Major Keith Houston pressed both hands on his map across the top of a steel locker on *Vigilant*'s bridge and studied every pencilled calculation, although he felt he knew them by heart. He had been politely offered the use of the chart room but had declined. The apparent calm of the place went against his mood of uncertainty; he might even have called it doubt. The occasional helm orders, the distorted voices from the upper bridge, were like a pretence. When he raised his eyes he saw the reality, an endless panorama of green, broken only by a strip of beach, or an outthrust prong of headland. Like something solid. Any map or chart told a different story: tiny creeks and larger, hidden stretches of water, winding tracks through the thicker areas of jungle, deserted now if Richard Suan's rebels were still around.

He weighed it in his mind. Intelligence, realistic information, or simply guesswork? He should be used to that.

He looked over at the two senior N.C.O.s. Colour Sergeant Brannigan was an old sweat by any standards, with a reputation for complete reliability. A lot of service in the Far East; the sort of man who obeyed without question. A type of marine who was slowly disappearing. And Blackwood, who was watching the distant shoreline, outwardly relaxed but eyes always alert, perhaps measuring the value of the whole operation. Houston had seen him rub his side a few times. The bruises, the reminders, were still there. He stopped if he thought he was being watched. A first class N.C.O., but one you would never know. Unless he wished it.

He glanced at the lieutenant. Piggott was reading from a little notebook, his lower lip set in a pout. Neat, clean, efficient. Not even a webbing strap twisted or out of place. No wonder the marines loathed his guts. He simply could not be faulted.

And the others. Some he knew by sight, others not at all. It was like that in his Hong Kong detachment. Marines came and left, by air or in crawling troopers, according to need and urgency. Not like the top commando brigades, where you even knew their nicknames and hobbies. The 'family'. He saw Norman, his Marine Officer's Attendant, who was leaning back against an unyielding stanchion, apparently asleep. Servant, orderly, and more than once a bodyguard, nothing ever seemed to shake Alf Norman.

His time would be up soon. Houston shied away from the thought. This was not the moment for regrets.

He watched the land again, a vast hotch-potch of islands, large and small. Names written in blood, so often at each other's throats, *and at ours*. Borneo, Sarawak, Sumatra, Malaysia and Singapore. Law and order had not come easily. From the South China Sea to the Malacca Strait, piracy, smuggling, and revolution had made all the political bridges hard to build, and harder to maintain. He heard feet on the ladder, sharp and precise, like the man. The liaison officer. He wondered what drew men like him to these outlandish appointments. Houston had worked with and alongside the Brigade of Guards several times during his service. There were none wilder when the chips were down.

"You'll be going ashore soon now, Major." It was not a question.

Houston kept his eyes on the land. "When we're ready. My people are on their toes. They have two days' rations, no more. So it's got to be right."

"Of course. But *Vigilant*'s captain is under the strictest orders, too. The Singapore-Malaysia Agreement, Section Eight, restricted waters, and so forth."

Houston saw Sergeant Blackwood get to his feet, hands checking his pouches and pockets. His ammunition. He knew.

Major Mannering said, "Your Colonel De Lisle understood this agreement from the beginning."

Houston answered sharply, "Well, *my* Colonel De Lisle isn't bloody well here, is he?"

M.O.A. Norman stepped casually between them and picked up the map case. It could have been an accident. He might even have given an imperceptible shake of the head.

He made his point. The threatened storm had passed.

You should be a bloody general, he thought.

He said, "My compliments to the captain. We are ready. And that is *my* decision."

Steve Blackwood had heard some of it and guessed the rest. He looked at the land. Two miles off, no more. He could already smell it, feel it, mistrust it. Would Boyes remember what he had said? And the other part: *ask questions afterwards*.

The rudders were turning, the land slowly swinging across the blunt bows. He thought suddenly of the grand old house, Hawks Hill, which was probably already being demolished to make way for more 'progress'. One large painting had caught his eye, a battle scene somewhere, the uniforms all scarlet, muskets and fixed bayonets thrusting through the smoke.

And one young officer, sword raised, waving to his men to follow him. The painting had been listed in the catalogue as *The Royal Marines Will Advance!*

He watched the land, dipping with the swell.

The young officer's face could have been Ross Blackwood's. He checked his webbing pouches unconsciously.

It could be now.

His fingers encountered a packet of cigarettes. Time for a last smoke before things got hectic, or ground to a full stop. Coming to terms with it . . . It took them all in different ways. Age, experience, willpower. Like drink; he could take it or leave it. He had seen what it had done to others. He glanced at the burly colour sergeant, Brannigan, a strong presence to have nearby, a man without fear. He tapped open the packet. *And without imagination.* That was his strength. All talking had stopped now, and the landing party waited in silence, watching the shore spreading out slowly on either bow, like arms opening to receive them.

Deliberately he straightened his back, assessed himself. There was no fear. He put a cigarette into his mouth and felt for his lighter.

Houston turned and saw it. A last cigarette . . . He shaded his eyes against shafts of weak sunlight reflected from the narrowing strip of water. The sky was clearing again, the decks steaming very slightly in the humid air.

How long was it since he had drawn on a cigarette? Ten years now, at least. He had tried to switch to a pipe; his wife had said it suited him. But then, as now, he was too restless, too eager to be on the move. Always scraping and poking, filling and refilling. His friends had claimed that he used more matches than tobacco. Fitness was a challenge, a battle. He could feel his shirt clinging to his skin. He was losing the fight.

He saw Blackwood looking at him. Heard him ask, "Care for one, sir?"

Houston said, "I think I will. Thanks."

He coughed and watched the smoke in the sunlight.

Where was his wife right now, he wondered. She had been having an affair. Rather more than that. He brushed some ash from his sleeve. *I was a fine one to throw blame at her.*

He felt the deck shudder. *Vigilant*'s captain was cutting it fine. What would Section Eight have to say if they ended up hard aground?

He dropped the cigarette into a sand-filled bucket and readjusted his holster.

"Take stations for landing!" He saw faces turning toward him as the marines hurried past. A decision had been made. Like something from the schoolroom of long ago: *theirs not to reason why . . .*

He closed his mind. The water was warm, up and around his waist, his boots sliding and then gripping as they waded up the beach.

Darting, crouching figures fanned out on either side, weapons at the ready, staring at the jungle, the sun at their backs.

Norman was with him, breathing hard and fast, ready to prove as always that he could still keep pace with the best of them. One man slipped and fell, another paused to drag him to his feet. Just a few seconds, a quick exchange of grins, then charging on together again.

How many times . . . Houston wanted to call out but his breath failed him. All the exercise, the knocks and bruises of the rugby scrum had been wasted. Just when he needed it. Then came the pain, with the force of an explosion. When he tried to draw breath again there was only a groan. Inhuman. The sun had gone suddenly. Another storm . . .

But his reeling mind told him that men were stooping over him, shutting out the light. And there was blood, choking him, blotting out all but the sound of his agony. Two hands gripped one of his. It was Alf Norman. *I must say something to make him smile.*

Sergeant Steve Blackwood swung round, his eyes on the trees, the gun moving only slightly while the first marines reached cover and vanished.

Quietly he said, "Leave him, Alf. Keep with the others."

He remembered Houston's voice when he had snapped to the liaison officer, *that is my decision.* Before he had taken that last cigarette. One bullet. That was all it took. He heard a volley of shots shattering the stillness, and only then did he turn to look at the sprawled figure on the wet sand.

He had seen a lot of men die, in different circumstances. He thought he was hardened to it. It was not as if he had known Houston well. He heard some one shouting, the lieutenant, he thought. Piggott, who might have died that day on the island, and would have been no loss to anybody.

He looked at the familiar, battered face, frozen at the second of impact, and was deeply moved.

He shouted aloud, "And for *what?*" It was like a private epitaph.

Then he strode up the last stretch of beach, surprised that he could feel so calm again. As if something was already decided. Final.

"Coming, *sir!*"

He found Piggott with some of the others inside the first barrier of trees. In his mind he could picture the remaining section, crouching and tense, weapons covering all likely openings for an attack. He saw Norman staring back at the beach, still unable to grasp the abruptness of death. The Boss had been his friend . . .

112

Colour Sergeant Brannigan gestured with his sub-machine-gun.

"Up there, Steve. If the bastard had held his fire, we'd never have spotted him."

Blackwood peered up the nearest tree, the blood-spattered bark, then a pair of legs dangling from a crude harness, a long-range rifle still tied to the dead man's wrist. An old ruse: even if you managed to mark down a hidden sniper, the corpse would remain out of sight and give no hint of success or failure, or the possibility of more attacks. Something learned from the Japs during that other war.

Piggott exclaimed, "We must call up the ship. Let them know what's happened. Get word to Captain Irwin." He seemed to be faltering, unable to accept what had happened. He swung on the colour sergeant. "What do *you* think?"

Brannigan was staring at the dangling rifle. "How did he know, sir?"

Steve Blackwood said sharply, "If Houston had been stark naked, any one would have picked him out as the leader! That sniper couldn't resist it, man! And it was his one big mistake, don't you see that? It's all we've got to act on."

Piggott stared at him. "Without orders? What the hell are you saying?"

"We got our orders, *sir*. There is nobody else. It's up to us to close the trap, and finish what we were sent to do."

Piggott looked toward the beach, still unable to grasp the brutal change of circumstance.

Brannigan said slowly, "That's true, sir." His big hands came together. "We've got them between our two landing parties, just like the major said."

Norman stepped closer and held out Houston's map

case. He did not look at Piggott, but said harshly, "Yours now, sir."

Piggott looked around, perhaps expecting more shots. Even the trees were still, as if they, too, were listening.

He opened the map case and stared into it.

"Captain Irwin's men should all be in position now." He looked up and stared at Blackwood, directly for the first time. "Have *you* anything to say?"

"There'll be boats of some sort. They'll have planned an escape route. Probably rendezvous with a local coaster – it's happened before."

Piggott licked his lips.

"Yes, of course. You're the old campaigner."

Blackwood felt the anger run through him like fire, but saw the look on Brannigan's face. *No imagination.* He would never let you down, though.

"We can head for the river." He knew Piggott's eyes were following his finger across the map. "There's an old mission there, and Captain Irwin's section should be on the high ground just above it."

Piggott closed the map. "Suppose you're mistaken?"

He glanced at the trees, but only birds broke the heavy stillness.

"Not my decision, sir."

Piggott called, "Warn the others, Sergeant!" As he went past he reached out and gripped Blackwood's sleeve. "I'll not forget your insolence."

Blackwood loosened the webbing pouch across his shoulder.

"I'm banking on it, sir!"

The other marines were ready to move, Brannigan and his corporals making a last check of weapons and equipment. Glad, relieved even, to be under orders once more.

One final look down the shelving white beach. The

elderly *Vigilant* had already vanished, waiting somewhere to pick up the pieces. The solitary shape near the tide line was still there, surrounded by blood and boot marks, where men had paused to grapple with the curt simplicity of death.

It would be good-bye to the medal which had been proposed. *So what?* He turned on his heel and faced the jungle again. No turning back. Not now.

Ross Blackwood lay flat on his stomach, his chin resting on his forearm. For a moment he had been tempted to shift on to his side, but the pressure of the pistol wedged against his hip jarred him back to reality.

He felt the ground under his fingers, dry now despite rain during the day. It was difficult to gauge the time, or how long it had taken to work their way up and on to the ridge. It was completely dark, without stars; there was nothing to give any hint of their progress. Pitch black, and yet he knew the sea was somewhere down ahead of them. In an hour or so it would be visible. Like the maps, and the discussions . . .

They had caught and shot the murdered marine's attacker. They had heard other shots as well, that morning, when the second group had been landed on the opposite side of the narrow river, but nothing since. As if the whole place was now deserted. He touched his watch, but did not need it. Pointless now; it was beyond his control.

Captain Irwin was somewhere along the ridge, checking each section, letting them all know he was wide awake. Strange to think of him as a young marine, as young as Davis, the one who had been killed. Out in this same territory when a full-scale guerilla war had been raging. The Royal Marines had been in the thick of it then. The knife edge, one senior officer had called them. When the legendary general Sir Gerald Templer had been in overall command, a violent man in deed and language to all accounts, feared by politicians of all shades and loved by the men he commanded. As one ex-submariner had described him, *he was not content to be the eye of the periscope. He was the torpedo in person!*

Irwin knew all about that. And he had not forgotten the terrorist named Richard Suan, whom many had thought dead, a bloody memory.

He flinched as Sergeant Ted Boyes slithered down beside him. *I should have heard him coming.*

"All quiet?" Something to say.

Boyes fumbled with his coat and handed him something. "Have a bit of nutty, sir."

It was a piece of chocolate, half melted, but the best he had ever tasted.

Boyes said, "Takin' too long. Be dawn soon, an' there's more bloody rain about. I can smell it."

"Major Houston will want to be sure before . . ."

Boyes repeated, "Too long."

"What about Davis?"

"Covered 'im as best we could. Nice lad."

Like a door shutting. Perhaps the only way.

Boyes said, "We'll not get another chance to catch these buggers if they get past us this time. They'll know we're right on top of 'em." He peered over some dead branches as if he could already see beyond the ridge. "A quick getaway, right up their street!"

An anonymous voice murmured, "Cap'n's comin', sir."

Ross moved again; his body was getting stiff. He could still feel the scar on his back. Remembered her hands, strong, but gentle.

Irwin joined them and sat down with his arms around his knees. It sounded as if he had been running, but his voice was steady.

116

"Change of plan, Ross." He spoke to the anonymous voice. "Fetch Sergeant Bolton." There was a slight sharpness to his tone. "Fast as you like, eh?"

Ross waited, the chocolate still sweet on his tongue.

Irwin said, "Houston's bought it, I'm afraid. Sniper on the beach when they came ashore. The only casualty."

Ross stared at his outline, unable to see his face.

"So this is what we'll do. The old mission is the obvious hiding place, and maybe the only suitable bolt-hole for Richard Suan's raiders."

Boyes said, "If it really is 'im, sir."

Ross tried to swallow, but his throat was too dry. What they had come to do. What they had all expected. From the day when he had heard Houston describing it in the office overlooking Kowloon. Even before that . . .

All he could think of was Houston lying dead somewhere, like the youngster who had lost his face.

Irwin's eyes were on him; he could feel them.

"So you see, Ross, it's up to us, right?"

That time in the hotel suite. Houston taking his arm, and gently warning him about Glynis, and the mine field.

"I'm ready, sir." What he had trained for, lived for, all his adult life. Discipline and trust. But all he could recognize was anger, and the desire for revenge.

"Good."

Boyes half turned.

"'Ere comes Rimsh – er, Sarn't Bolton, sir!"

Ross heard himself say, "What about Sergeant Blackwood, sir?" Like the voice of a total stranger, detached, almost casual.

"Coming to that. He'll be needed down by the river. I've sent word. Piggott can cope with his sector."

Irwin was on his feet again, looking at the sky.

"We are dealing with dedicated and ruthless terrorists. I

want them killed, captured or made harmless. I do not want to lose or throw lives away for no good purpose. Tell your men."

As the others moved away, he reached out and touched Ross's arm.

"The Boss is dead. We won't let him down."

The words were quietly spoken. But later, as Ross watched the ragged trees taking shape along the lower ridge, they reverberated in his mind like thunder.

Waiting . . . waiting . . . He peered at the nearest trees and wondered if they had become clearer, or if his eyes had grown used to the dark, the overcast sky. He wanted to yawn, but suppressed it by force. The old hands always said that yawning was a first sign of fear.

He heard the sharp clink of metal, followed immediately by an obscene curse. He twisted round and saw one of the marines unfastening an entrenching tool from his belt. He saw Ross looking at him and showed his teeth in a grin, stark against his camouflaged face.

Ross touched his chin and felt the bristles. How long since the last shave? Or until the next?

He stared at his hand, amazed that he had not noticed. The dawn had come upon them. One minute blackness, and now . . .

He said quietly, "Not long, Godwin," and saw his acknowledgment. *Probably as surprised as I am that I remembered his name.*

What must we look like? Stained faces, dirty clothing, red-rimmed eyes. Leeches. Insect bites. A far cry from the barrack square, the stamp of feet and the terse shouts of command.

He looked around. The ridge here was sparsely covered with trees, an overgrown, bypassed piece of land. Not a place worth dying for. But many had, over the years. He heard Irwin scramble down beside him. He, more than anybody here today, would be remembering, seeing it as it was. Reliving it.

Irwin said, "We can move up now." He gazed along the ridge, watching an occasional shadow as the nearest section crawled slowly toward the vague margin between sky and land.

More light now, so that individual slabs of rock and rotting vegetation took shape around them. And so strangely silent, only the sounds of cicada and distant water.

And the smell . . . like a greeting, or a warning. The sea.

He recalled reading an account of the fall of Singapore in the very early years of his service. One fragment had always remained in his mind. A Royal Marine had described his feelings when the garrison had surrendered to the Japanese. The nearest land still unoccupied or uncontrolled by the enemy had been Batavia, about six hundred miles away. *Not another Dunkirk*, he had written, *with the white cliffs just across the English Channel, but six hundred bloody miles.*

I just thought, get me to the sea, and somehow I'll get back with the lads.

He had succeeded.

He heard Irwin exhale softly. "And there it is, Ross. Not much changed, as I recall."

Ross rested his binoculars on a slab of rock and waited for the image to settle.

The mission was larger than he had expected. Square and solid, more like a fort than a place of worship, a beachhead for some creed. Starkly white in the rapidly growing light, it had become part of a trading estate, then both prison and stronghold for the occupying Japanese army. Fought over repeatedly, while the local people suffered and endured the ebb and flow of war, and waited for independence and freedom.

He thought of the man called Richard Suan, and others like him, who knew only how to destroy and subvert.

Irwin was saying, "Some of the place is built on piles. Unreliable in the rainy season. Why they made the bridge to give access to the shore. You could hold off a whole bloody army if you had to."

Ross rubbed his eye with one knuckle. Clearer now, the white walls stained with mildew at closer quarters. The slow-moving river was littered with leaves and fallen debris from the recent storms.

He shifted the glasses away from the water and the open sea. More jungle. You could lose a regiment in there.

He felt Irwin touch his sleeve, but he said nothing.

Ross lowered the glasses and stared at the crude, timbered bridge. A shadow, like part of the structure itself, moved suddenly, only a few paces, the first daylight bringing it to life. A man with some kind of cape draped over his shoulders. The light strengthened. He had a shape now, pale against the muted greens of the jungle. Ross did not need binoculars to recognize the rifle he carried in one hand.

"Richard Suan won't be short of men. Not when his own skin's at risk." Calm, almost matter-of-fact. "We'll keep them off the bridge when the time comes to blow it."

Ross nodded, remembering his cousin and the exploding launch. The burning fragments, and the pain in his hands as they had dragged each other to safety.

Irwin said gently, "The only way, as I see it. We can hold off any attempt to shift the buggers by boat."

Ross felt his throat tightening in a yawn. "They may have more of their men already here."

"Doubt it. Any case, Ross, we don't have a lot of choice."

He could almost hear Houston's voice. *Any one on the other end of a gun is the enemy.*

He said, "I'd like to tackle the bridge, sir."

For a moment he thought Irwin had not heard, or was ignoring him.

Then he said, "You don't have the required skill or training with explosives, unlike your namesake. Otherwise . . ." He paused. "Besides which, if anything happens to me, you'll be in command here." He could have been smiling. "There's a thought, eh?"

Sergeant Boyes was here. "In position, sir."

Irwin looked at the dull sky and then at the back of his hand. The rain had started. "Bloody hell."

Boyes said, "Just like you said, sir."

They might have been discussing a cricket match. *Rain stopped play.*

"More of 'em on the bridge, sir!"

Irwin was up and running.

"Start the attack! At 'em, lads!"

There was no more time. Not even for fear.

The outburst of machine-gun fire and the crash of heavy bullets slashing through trees sounded so close and concentrated that for a few seconds Steve Blackwood imagined they had already been seen, and were pinned down. Somehow he had managed to keep his balance, waist deep in the river, both hands gripping the camouflaged canoe as his mind grappled with their chances.

He focused his thoughts: experience over alarm, even panic. It was cross-fire, some from the opposite side of the river, Captain Irwin's section, and the rest from Colour

Sergeant Brannigan's carefully sited guns, which he had left behind minutes or half an hour ago; he had lost track of time. He had heard shots hitting the rickety bridge where some of the terrorists had been seen, so confident that they had done little to conceal themselves, and he had heard faint screams when eventually the firing ceased. Just like Irwin, he thought. Never waste ammunition simply to impress somebody.

His companion, who was stooping even lower in the sluggish water, straightened up carefully. "All done, then?" It was Corporal Laker. He was even able to grin.

"Better get moving." Blackwood stared at the sky. No sun yet, but the sudden, heavy rainfall was easing, the water smoothing in its wake, reflections and shadows shaping the lie of the land. The bridge, and beyond it the fort-like mission, splinters on the woodwork from the gunfire, and star-shaped scars where bullets had smashed away the plaster and paint from the walls. Something still moved on the bridge, kicking the air, and dying as he watched.

Laker was testing the lashing around the canoe. There was some camouflage netting as well, which, added to a few broken branches of bamboo, might just do the trick. Not good to think too much about the explosive charges inside. If things went wrong, they would not feel much. There would be nothing left.

Blackwood climbed carefully into the canoe. There seemed to be only a few inches of freeboard. *Enough. Has to be.*

He saw something pale on the water, like a feeble torch beam. The clouds were moving fast. It was the first ray of sunlight.

More shooting, from his left. That was one of Brannigan's gunners.

Keep it a bit higher, old son. Aloud he said, "Ready?

Now or never." He gestured with his paddle. There was a narrow strip of mud. Several clumps of flotsam and fallen branches had already become marooned there. The storms had been some use after all.

Laker was in the little hull, legs braced, his paddle already testing the flow alongside.

"What about leeches, Sarge?"

"Don't worry. The cobras'll probably get you first."

Laker grinned again. "Thanks. See you in . . ." and broke off in disbelief. "What the hell!"

Blackwood exclaimed, "Christ! You could have got your head blown off, *sir!*"

Piggott was standing in the water a few feet away.

"So could *you*, Sergeant!"

There were a few more, single shots. Marksmen, marines or otherwise, it was not possible to tell.

Piggott seemed oblivious to them.

He said, "They might see this *thing*." He gestured at the canoe and its crude camouflage. "Before you get within range. Had you thought of that?"

Blackwood shot a quick glance at the sky. Brighter still. What was the point? Was Blondie Piggott going off his rocker?

At any second now . . . .

His mouth was like dust. What did it matter, anyway? He felt himself shrug. So Piggott was right again.

He said, "Hop aboard, sir. I'm afraid it's not what you're used to!"

Piggott clambered across the rear of the canoe and raised the paddle.

"Watch your stroke. Not too much movement!"

Corporal Laker pushed a waterlogged branch aside, muttering, "Just follow my example, boys!"

There were more shots, stray or haphazard, cutting down

more leaves or cracking angrily inland. None hit the water nearby, and Blackwood could feel the canoe already moving faster, carried clear of the shallows and past the first sandbar.

Piggott snapped, "*Back* paddle, Corporal! We'll broach to if you don't watch out!"

Irwin's men were firing now, timed to the second. Anybody remaining on the bridge would be an easy target. *Crack crack crack.* Larger pieces of wood were being blasted from the bridge. It looked almost as old as the mission. Blackwood thought suddenly of Houston, all the planning, the quick-fire exchange of ideas and doubts. *And for what?* He saw the bridge rising to meet them, the upper span in bright sunlight as if it alone had been painted.

"Are you ready?" Piggott was leaning right over, his face wet with sweat or spray. "No slip-ups, right?" He looked wild.

Blackwood wanted to yell at him. To ram the paddle into his stupid face. But somehow his mind remained in command. Each stroke of the paddle. Start the timer . . . Loosen the grapnel. Ready to drive right under the centre span. Laker could make fast. Be ready to get the hell out of it.

Piggott was calling out again. If only . . .

It was like being kicked with a hob-nailed boot, in the shoulder or his waist, but all sensation was leaving him. He saw Laker twisting round in his cockpit. He was holding two paddles, and yet Blackwood could not remember letting go of his. Piggott was shouting, but his voice was coming like an echo, or from far away.

The canoe swung against the scarred timber, pivoting hard over until the grapnel brought it under control. There was water everywhere, sluicing over the camouflage netting, and around his legs.

Piggott was clambering past him, shouting, his mouth like a hole in his smeared face.

It was like fighting something. Holding on. Telling yourself that it was not enough.

He realized that Piggott was above him, climbing straight up, toward the sky and the sun-painted span, still shouting but not looking back.

Blackwood pulled himself on to the lowest span, his mind reeling as the pain drove into him like the tip of a furnace bar.

He held the pack in position, and sensed that Laker was reaching up to help him. But he was not an expert. It would be unfair. Dangerous . . . He shook himself again, and the pain helped clear his mind. The timer was in his hand; he stared at it. So slippery, although he had kept it in his special pocket until this final moment. It was blood.

Shots came from somewhere; he knew they were hitting the woodwork only a few feet away. *At any second now . . .*

Laker was somehow pressed against him, their faces nearly touching. He was shouting or sobbing; it was all blurred. But where the hell was Piggott?

The canoe seemed to be moving again, but he was staring up at the sky. There was a solitary bang, loud and very near, followed by complete silence. Even the sporadic small arms fire had ceased.

Misfire. I failed.

The canoe was being held steady, and he knew that Laker was covering him, shielding him.

Soon he would stand away and leave him. Like those others. Houston.

His arm was bare, one hand dragging in the water. He tried to pull away as something pricked the skin. There was no pain now. Nothing.

It was impossible, but he could hear men's voices.

They were cheering. The sudden crash of the explosion went unheard.

Lieutenant-Colonel Leslie De Lisle crossed to one of the wide office windows and pried the slats of the sun blind apart with his fingers. He winced as reflected light lanced up from the harbour; he could feel the heat of the sun through the glass. And it was still only March. Back in England you could see your breath as you walked. Greatcoat and gloves weather.

He seemed to have been constantly climbing in and out of aircraft. Here in Hong Kong, then Singapore. Meetings, some familiar faces, some strangers. Decisions.

He looked at the big fleet destroyer below, awnings spread, ensign lifting lazily in an offshore breeze. Busy police boats cruising nearby to keep the sightseers at a distance. Beyond her, a wisp of oily smoke drifting around her bridge, was the old Singapore patrol vessel, the *Vigilant*, which had played her part in Operation Ratcatcher. Getting ready to sail. Another mission, perhaps?

He turned his back on the window and looked around the office, the maps and plans folded away, so quiet now without Houston's larger than life presence. Irwin would stay on in Hong Kong until . . . He would never fill Houston's shoes, no matter what might have been suggested.

He paused and rubbed his spine. Too many flights, too little sleep. He was feeling it now.

Only March. He glanced at the squash racquet which was still propped in a corner. He could see it all in his mind, as if he had been there.

He looked at the clock. Why had he come? Some one else could have done it.

He strode to the window again and opened the blinds

fully. *Taunton* and *Yelverton* were moored side by side. They had made a fine sight when they had entered harbour, flags flying, some cheers from old ships greeting friends. No ambulances this time; the casualties had been put ashore at Singapore. Mercifully few, as if that made any difference. Two officers and three marines killed. Twelve wounded.

Just a flea bite, as the old sweats would say. He turned, hearing the door before it opened. It was a lieutenant he did not recognize.

"Yes?"

The lieutenant cleared his throat. He was frightened of De Lisle, and De Lisle knew it.

"Mr. Blackwood is here, sir."

"Well, don't keep him waiting, man!"

He fled.

It was unfair. But . . . It was only two months ago. Stonehouse Barracks . . . He strode to meet him and thrust out his hand.

"Good to see you, Ross!" And he meant it.

Ross sat in the offered chair and looked around the office, acutely aware of Houston's absence.

De Lisle was saying, "I'll get us a drink in a minute. It's all dead around here." He spread his hands. "Sorry, not a good choice of words."

Ross rubbed his eyes, but the fatigue was still more mental than physical. For days he had still seen it, the white mission building, the darting figures, gun flashes in the jungle's dimness. Men bleeding, wounded. Calling out.

And the final image; awake or asleep, it was always waiting. The crudely camouflaged canoe, breaking cover and striking out for the bridge. Bullets splashing nearby, return fire from Brannigan's gunners, and his own below the bridge.

He had not seen who had been hit, but instinct told him it was Steve Blackwood. He had watched helplessly with Ted Boyes, Irwin and the others while the canoe had lurched amongst the wooden piles, and while shots had slammed around them Steve had somehow managed to secure the charges.

And then the solitary figure had appeared on the bridge, firing into the defenders, falling but struggling up again to ram another clip into his gun, firing again until that, too, was empty. He was hit several times; they could see the blood even without binoculars. Dying even as his attackers had started to push forward.

Voices had yelled, "They've done it!"

The canoe had reappeared, only one paddle being used. But all eyes were on the lone, bloodied figure on the bridge. Rolling on to his side, teeth bared in agony or determination, his uninjured arm curving back, a live grenade in his hand. Even at that distance the sound was lethal. Then, only the canoe was moving.

Ross had managed to see Steve at the hospital before he had been taken elsewhere. The bullet had passed through his body. He would live. They had clasped hands, like that other time, oblivious to the nurses and orderly confusion around them.

All Steve could say was, "Piggott, of all people! The bravest thing I've ever seen! Without him . . ."

He did not need to spell it out.

Ross was suddenly on his feet, the response instant and automatic as the screech of a ship's siren filled the room.

De Lisle said, "It's all right, Ross. It's *Vigilant* getting under way."

Ross sank down again. The same sound he had heard when the old landing craft had suddenly appeared, filling the river, its ancient howitzer lobbing a shell directly into the mission. It was done, the 'combined operation' Major Keith Houston had always wanted.

The door was open, and in the other room a marine was putting some glasses on the desk. Through the windows beyond, he could see the Mandarin, as he had seen it when he had stepped ashore from the destroyer's motor boat. Where he had last spoken to her.

A messenger had been waiting for him, determined that he and no one else should receive the note.

Dearest Ross. I thank God you are safe and out of danger. I am on my way to England as you read this. My husband Jock was taken ill unexpectedly. And I am a nurse. Take care, dear Ross.

She did not finish it, but signed only her name.

De Lisle said, "Here, get this down you."

They touched glasses, and De Lisle asked with studied casualness, "So. What do you think you got out of all this, eh?"

Ross walked to the windows and saw a junk moving past, slowly, through the haze.

"I think I grew up."

He imagined he could hear her laugh.

1980

LEADING

CHAPTER EIGHT

Ross Blackwood felt the seat belt tighten across his chest as the car braked hard behind a large builder's lorry, but only for a few seconds before they were swinging out and over-hauling it, even as another car came speeding toward them.

He looked over at his sister as she blew some hair out of her eyes, gauging the next stretch of road. She was driving too fast, and enjoying it.

He loosened the seat belt and tried to unwind a little, put his thoughts in order. He felt like a complete outsider.

Sue had met him at the station, right on time, as she had promised. He glanced around yet again. A sleek, cream-coloured convertible, brand new by the look of it, and by the smell of the leather upholstery. A Mercedes, and expensive. She was doing well. But a stranger to him.

He shaded his eyes as the sun lanced off the gleaming bonnet and said, "What happened to old Follett's garden centre? Have they pulled that down as well?"

She took one hand off the wheel and rubbed finger and thumb together.

"Money, Ross. Don't they teach you about these things in the Corps?"

She had nice hands, well-shaped and strong. She wore no rings of any sort. The last time they had been in touch . . . *Stop right there.* It had not worked out.

She had not changed. Still confident, quick-minded, perhaps a little harder. Unsettled. He felt the brakes again.

"Are we there already?"

Her mouth softened slightly in a smile. The Sue he remembered.

"The cops keep watch on this piece of road. Just past the garage."

Sure enough, he saw the aerial and blue light showing above a clump of ragged bushes.

She added, "I've already got one endorsement. No sense in spoiling things!"

He consciously relaxed his hands in his lap. The skin was very tanned. All those miles. Faces. Challenges. And now he was back in a world he had almost forgotten. Like the bus they had just overtaken: packed with children, balloons trailing from the windows, grinning faces, an adult trying to pour drinks, others waving to this car as it flashed past.

She had said, "School holidays. Glad when they're over!"

It was July, nearly August, 1980. A week or so ago he had been in Hong Kong yet again, with the Raiding Squadron for duties against illegal immigrants. Before that, in the New Hebrides. Then Cyprus, and of course Plymouth. His life seemed like a film in motion, playing at different speeds.

He glanced over at his sister once more. Unbelievably, she was thirty years old.

"Get ready, Ross. We turn off in a few minutes."

He asked suddenly, "What made Mother come back to Hawks Hill, after everything that happened? The memories . . ."

She shrugged. "*Because* of the memories, I guess."

She flashed a thumbs-up to another car which was giving

way to her as she turned. "Still got a lot of friends in this area, you know. A lot of women have to sit around and put up with things!"

He watched the road, a little anxiously. All concrete and high-slung lighting. "Not you, Sue."

She blew another piece of hair from her eyes. "Too right. *Not me!*"

A modern-looking pub with a large, empty car park. Where the hell had that come from? The familiar lines of trees were all gone. On one side of the road was a white-painted motel. *The Blackwood Arms.* How had they managed that?

She braked again and steered toward a pair of opened gates. The old farm, at least, had been by-passed by progress.

Another set of gates, and a painted sign that read, *Hawks Hill Livery Stables. Accommodation Available.*

The car had stopped. She was looking at him, one hand on the key in the ignition.

"Stop thinking 'it's not how it used to be'. It's ten years since you made your decision and went off to be a hero." She reached out and seized his hand, the first time they had touched since the station. "Since I took that job with *Focus*, remember?"

Two girls in riding kit were crossing a cobbled yard, leading horses. One of the girls waved.

She said, "Yes, this place is different, but it's alive. What Joanna needs, don't you see?"

Ross nodded, but turned as if to look at the old house, which had been a beginning and sometimes an end. There was only the road now, and the steady flow of traffic.

His sister was taking out the one case he had brought with him. *Until the next time.*

"Here she comes now. Don't forget what I said."

He heard his mother's step on the cobbles, the catch in her voice as she called his name.

She was in his arms, hugging him, laughing as he always remembered, close to tears. The same old straw hat hanging from one shoulder, like those other visits. A week, a few days, in some one else's flat or house. This, at least, was her own.

Her hair was darker, where it had been grey the last time. It suited her.

She dabbed her eyes with her knuckles.

"You're early. I must look a mess." She leaned back in his arms. "I was expecting to see you in uniform!" She pulled away. "I have to deal with somebody."

Ross watched her hurry into the shadow of the house, glad she could not see his face. You were never ready when it happened. *I was expecting to see you in uniform.* When he had gone to visit Glynis, and they had become lovers. He had never forgotten. How could he?

He had even gone back to that same street in Hong Kong. Pointless, painful, but he had gone. Even more like a dream. The apartment building, Java House, had vanished. In its place was yet another tower block, hiding the harbour . . . *I was expecting to see you in uniform.*

Everything had been different. Like the Raiding Squadron. No longer a casual, hit-or-miss operation. Every marine was armed and ready. *Us or them.*

He looked at the last of the trees, where the developers and their machinery had come to a halt. A part of England still. That other, secret war only rarely hit the front pages. *Nothing to do with us.*

Did people really forget so easily? Less than a year ago it had struck at the Corps and the whole country. Earl Mountbatten of Burma, the Colonel Commandant of the Royal Marines, had been brutally assassinated by the IRA while holidaying with his family in Ireland. It should never have happened. Poor security, over confidence, some called it arrogance; but the stark fact remained.

Ross heard Joanna's voice again. Just as her husband had been killed in Cyprus ten years before. War was still a fact of life, although now it was called terrorism.

"How long this time, Ross?" Her hand was linked through his arm, their shadows joining across the cobbles.

"I have to go to London – next week, I think. The M.o.D. or something."

"Are you worried about it?" She was looking at him; he could feel her eyes. "Things are so uncertain these days."

Tell her. Promotion is almost at a standstill. Cutting down. Always cutting down. And there was to be yet another government White Paper on the subject of the country's defences. It could only get worse.

In two months' time he would be thirty-five years old. About the same age as Major Keith Houston when he had been killed on that Malaysian beach. Probably the same age as Captain John Irwin when he had been told at Hong Kong that he was no longer required for active duty. It had been his whole life, all he had ever wanted. Needed. They had found his body in one of the workshops at *Tamar*, a pistol still jammed between his teeth.

De Lisle had retired as a full colonel. It did not seem as if he had been given much choice, either.

Another training appointment, perhaps? Eager faces, commandos in the making. The drills, and the aches and pains of mock combat, at Lympstone, or one of those godforsaken camps in Scotland.

Don't wait to see who's following you, lad! Move your bloody self! Stay in the lead if you want that green beret, my son!

They stopped by the pond. It had once been near the

137

edge of a moat dating from Tudor times. You could hear the traffic, in particular the heavy lorries, quite easily from here.

She squeezed his arm. "You've never let *them* down. And I know what it cost you." She looked at the sky. "We'll ride tomorrow, and you can tell me all about Singapore."

He smiled, and felt the claws of tension easing their grip. "Hong Kong, love!"

Welcome home.

Ten days passed before the official letter arrived at Hawks Hill Livery Stables. They were the longest ten days Ross had ever known. It was impossible to get used to his surroundings. Hawks Hill was always a ghostly presence, something which even the dull murmur of traffic or the whine of lorries in the night could not dispel.

Curiously enough, it was the same postman he remembered from past visits; good news and bad, he had known the Blackwood family for many years. He had brought the news of Ross's promotion to captain, and the announcement of the Colonel's death in Cyprus.

He was here now, watching Ross sign his register.

"Back to the Corps, then, Major. Don't give you much rest, does they? Seems like only yesterday you was down at the pub, before they pulled *that* down!"

Ross slit open the letter. He could sense Joanna loitering by the kitchen door, some cut flowers in one hand, an empty vase motionless in the other, as if she were holding her breath. Outside on the cobbles a solitary horse was being led to a loose box. The local milkman had just called, and was chatting up one of the girls.

A sane, everyday world. And the end of the line.

He reread the brief, almost matter-of-fact message a second time. One word stood out, the rank of full colonel, and the name of an office in a building of which he had never heard. Whitehall. The Ministry of Defence. *You are requested* . . . The rest seemed blurred.

"What is it, Ross? Please tell me."

He walked over to her and put his arms around her waist.

"A staff appointment. I'm not sure . . ." He did not continue.

She had put down the vase and was hugging him, the flowers draped over his shoulder. "You thought it was the axe, didn't you? After all you've done, whatever next!"

"I never realized until this moment how much it mattered, how much I cared. It was always there, you see? Then suddenly . . ."

"Staff job, eh? Not the cut an' thrust you've bin used to!"

They had both forgotten about the old postman.

She said something and closed the door, and Ross could hear him calling out to the milkman. It would be all over Alresford within the hour. He could feel the excitement running through him. Second lieutenant to major. Nothing changed. One step at a time. He stared at the official envelope. *But not the end of the line.*

He heard himself say, "I must acknowledge this. There's a special phone number, too."

She watched him. Sharing it, as she had done many times, before Cyprus.

"You old sod! I just heard!" Sue strode across the kitchen and shook a riding crop at him. "And I thought you were beginning to show some sense at long last!" She laughed aloud. "But give me a shout, and I'll drive you up to London in style."

Joanna smiled at them.

"In one piece too, I hope." She turned her back, and added quietly, "Come back here, Ross, whenever you can."

*

"You see?" Susanna Blackwood eased the wheel and braked to allow some pedestrians to use a zebra crossing. "Said I'd get you to your appointment on time. Just over the river, and bingo!"

It had certainly been a fast drive. Up early for a quick breakfast, Joanna already dressed and making sure he would forget nothing, the car out in the cobbled yard, the hood down, Sue making some notes in a pad which she was rarely without.

The stables had been awake, too. A group of women were being instructed by one of the grooms, horses watching from their boxes, tossing heads and munching titbits for the benefit of the first clients.

He had also met John, the manager of the stables, who had been working for Joanna for about a month. Not a young man; he was probably the same age as his employer. Straight-backed, an ex-soldier. Very formal when they had been introduced, his eyes partly hidden by a battered old trilby.

A strong handshake. "Served in the Blues, Major. About a hundred years ago!"

As he had climbed into the trembling Mercedes, Ross had seen his mother touch hands with the new manager. It was not by accident.

He had mentioned it to his sister.

She remarked crudely, "Wants to get his feet under the table, that's all!"

He watched her now. All that way, through the Hampshire countryside, by familiar routes and some unknown to him; they had stopped only once, somewhere outside Guildford. She had filled the tank at a garage, and made a phone call at the same time.

She had seen him looking at his watch and had said almost sharply, "Heaps of time, Ross! They can wait, surely?"

Was she always on guard against something? Getting too close, even with him? Her black jacket was in the tiny rear seat, her hair tied back severely with a piece of black ribbon. A red silk scarf was the only colour about her.

He adjusted his own jacket, a lightweight grey suit he had brought from Hong Kong. Here it was summer, but with the car roof down he was almost shivering.

He stared across the river at the Houses of Parliament and Big Ben: the tourists' London. Red double-decker buses, the familiar taxis . . . He looked at the old clock. Sue was right. *Heaps of time.*

She was saying, "Don't forget the address I gave you. I wrote the phone numbers down, too, just in case . . ." She banged the wheel with her fist. "Come *on*, then!"

Several Japanese tourists were being rounded up by their guide; one was taking a photograph of two children. She was on edge. Glad to be back, in her world.

She increased speed again. "I may be out late tonight. Just go to the address – I've told the porter to expect you." She took her eyes from the heavy traffic for a moment. "Take care of yourself, Ross. It's too bad we don't have more time." She looked away, as if she thought she had gone too far. Strangers.

A couple of minutes later she said, "That place over there is a studio. One of ours. I've done a few interviews there. A real hoot, some of them."

"You certainly know your way about."

She smiled. "Need to in this job. In more ways than one."

They pulled up beside a line of parking meters, all of which were labelled 'out of order'.

She sighed. "Security. Makes me sick!"

He got out of the car and straightened his jacket. Security . . . Just a few hours ago, when he had been putting his

141

suitcase in the boot, he had seen the small mirror fixed to the end of a piece of cane. He had asked her about it.

"Leave a nice-looking car unattended for any length of time in London these days, it's always a good idea to have a look underneath before you drive off. You never know what some maniac might have fixed there." She had shaken her head, perhaps at his naiveté. "It's another world, Ross."

"Sorry, miss. You can't park here." The figure in blue had appeared out of nowhere.

"O.K., officer." She turned her head so that Ross could kiss her cheek. "Good to have you around again." For only a few seconds, he could feel her sudden uncertainty, as if she wanted to share something, reach out for the first time. Instead, she puckered her lips into a kiss and drove away. She did not look back.

The policeman said, "Nice car, sir."

As if he had just heard her speak. *You never know what some maniac might have fixed there.*

He looked up at the Victorian building and checked the number; he could almost feel the policeman turning to observe as he switched on his radio. *A stranger, male, now entering Number Thirty-One.* He could feel a grin spreading across his face. The policeman was probably calling the local nick to find out what kind of sandwiches they had in the canteen.

The door opened before he could reach the bell, and he was confronted by a heavily built man dressed in a dark suit. Another figure, similar in build and dress, stood behind a counter. Provost, or security men, they might as well have been in uniform.

Instead he said, "Last time we met you was still a captain, when I was on a refresher course at Lympstone. You was the adjutant in that place. You got into a spot of bother because you rode a damn great horse into the officers' mess."

They shook hands, and Ross said, "The colonel gave me hell." They both grinned. "It was my birthday, although he didn't appreciate it!"

"I'll take you up, Major." He nodded to his companion and Ross saw him pick up a telephone.

Take it easy. One step at a time.

It was a tall building for one so old, and once in the lift he lost count of the floors. Bigger than the other one, but when he looked up he saw the open hatch, the wire cables shaking in the reflected light as if they were in need of an overhaul.

. . . Off Ice House Street, Hong Kong. Java House, gone now, all clean and shining, high and impersonal.

There was an old and stained mirror on one side of the lift. He knew his big companion was watching him, but careful not to show it. He saw his own reflection, the light-weight suit, slightly crushed after Sue's energetic driving. It seemed wrong to him that you rarely wore uniform these days unless you were on duty. *By the book.* As his sister had remarked, it was a different world. A girl so private, so self-contained. As if she was afraid of something.

The lift gave a violent jerk and the doors opened.

"Here we go, Major." He almost winked. "See you when it's over."

The doors slid shut and the lift began to descend.

A young man, also in a dark suit, was waiting to meet him.

"Major Blackwood? He'll not be long." He gestured to a solitary chair. "I'd fetch some tea, but . . ."

He had not introduced himself, but wore a plastic ID card on his label which said *A. Tucker, A.C.H.Q.* To further confuse any one, he was wearing an R.A.F. tie.

There was another door, and the occasional blare of a horn. London was never still . . . He walked to the window and looked down at the street, saw the pinprick of camera flashes and then the plumed helmets and horses of a troop of Household Cavalry.

Horse Guards. He thought of the man at Hawks Hill introduced only as John. *The Blues*. And Sue's curt dismissal, *wants to get his feet under the table*.

Was *she* never lonely?

He heard somebody laugh, or perhaps it was a cough. He faced the other door, surprised that he was so relaxed. He remembered one of Irwin's comments in a rare moment of confidence. *Not what you know, Ross, but who you know. Always keep that in mind.* Was that why he had pulled the trigger?

"The Colonel will see you now, sir."

Some one else was about to leave, and gestured with one hand as if to apologize.

"Sorry to keep you hanging about, old chap. It dragged on a bit."

It was like meeting somebody he knew, or had already met. He was probably used to it. Very tanned, those keen eyes with deep crows' feet at the corners, so often seen staring into the sun, or describing the character of the land in some wilderness or disaster area. Clive Tobin was never absent from the television screen for very long, always bringing some new calamity into the living rooms of Britain. Older than Ross had imagined, casually but, he guessed, expensively dressed in a gilt-buttoned blazer and grey slacks, the familiar spotted handkerchief flowing from the breast pocket. Unmistakable.

The door closed, but not before he had seen *A. Tucker A.C.H.Q.* rushing to open the other door for the departing celebrity. He was almost bowing.

Colonel Sir Aubrey Souter, Distinguished Service Order, was waiting behind a broad, polished desk, very upright, as if he were standing to attention. Again, it was like meeting some one familiar. Souter was well known, almost famous, in the Corps, but as far as he could recall Ross had only laid eyes on him two or three times, usually at some special parade, or perhaps at an inspection. A brief pause in the routine: this stern, gaunt face directly opposite you, eyebrows raised with the question. "What's your name, eh? Where're you from?" Then the scrutiny, and, "Good show!" On to the next stop, two or three further along. No doubt the same questions.

"Sit you down. Just a few points. Wanted to see you for myself." Souter sat and waited for Ross to occupy the chair opposite.

The room was nearly empty. There was only one other chair, with a minute table beside it, on which was an ashtray containing a cigarette, barely smoked and stubbed out. A window nearby had been partly opened. The sound of traffic again. The desk was bare but for a loose file of papers, pressed down by an ornate silver paperweight modelled on the badge of the United States Marine Corps, the Globe and Anchor with their motto scrawled around it. *Semper Fidelis,* always faithful. Sir Aubrey Souter was well-known for his interest in close co-operation between the two forces. Ross also noted that there was no ashtray on the desk, nor had Souter offered to shake his hand.

Like checking your defences. He had learned the hard way.

"I need experienced officers who can be relied upon under all conditions. Skill, initiative, just a bite of the apple." He had thinning grey hair, neatly trimmed, and partly covering a star-shaped scar above his left eyebrow. Close, no matter what it had been.

145

A little moustache, like De Lisle. But no other similarity.

A man used to getting his own way. Winning. He was now, among other things, a senior aide to the Combined Defence Staff. Next only to God. Almost.

He moved the paperweight to one side and opened the folder.

"You reorganized the Special Raiding Squadron when you took it over in Hong Kong. New boats, damn sight faster than the ones used by the Commies." He almost smiled. "Mustn't call them that now, eh? Illegal immigrants. For the moment, anyway." The smile had gone. "You saw action out there, and earlier when you were in Malaysia. What was that troublemaker called?"

"Richard Suan, sir." He watched the fingers lifting the next page. "He was never caught."

"Hmm." The page turned. "Probably never existed, or already dead." Then he said, "More and more work, fewer resources. Time moves on. New government. New prime minister. But who can say?"

Ross waited. The gaunt features were studying him. An old-fashioned face, his mother might have called it. Like some of those faded photographs in the study at Hawks Hill. The Somme, the Dardanelles, Jutland.

"You served with my nephew, right? Young Alan Piggott, same rank as you?" He made it sound like yesterday.

Sometimes it is.

"Yes, sir. I was there when . . ." But Souter held up his hand.

"I know." He stared at the window. "If it had been a war, a real war, I mean, that lad would have been awarded the Victoria Cross. Instead . . ."

He did not go on.

Ross recalled Steve Blackwood's words. They never

failed to bring the stark picture of Piggott's death back to centre stage.

"Piggott was terrified. Shit-scared, but he knew what had to be done. In my book, that's real courage."

Steve was still in the Corps, despite the wound he had suffered when he had blown the bridge. An instructor at Portland, the last time Ross had heard. Promoted to warrant officer, a W.O.2. Teaching others demolition and bomb disposal. *If you can't beat 'em, join 'em.* Houston had died, but he had not been forgotten; the 'gong' had been awarded. The Distinguished Conduct Medal. Very few had been handed out since World War Two, which was probably the reason Steve Blackwood was at Portland and not on the beach, like so many others.

It was as if Souter had been reading his mind.

"We are expected to achieve so much without the resources which are vital. I don't have to tell you that." He tapped the file. "I know your record, the family tradition. But with some of today's political minds, it's still not enough. I meet quite a few of them. They only see what they want to see. The Corps is expected to do everything, guard important sites, military or otherwise . . . We are now being told that the North Sea oil rigs will need our surveillance. I can see their point, of course. But if we get more reductions, who can say what might happen?" He looked at him directly. "You never married? Can't say I blame you."

"Never had the luck." Ross clenched his fist. It had come out too sharply. Angrily. Perhaps what Souter intended.

"Thought as much." Surprisingly, he smiled. It made him look like a different person. "Won't mention any names, but a chap I know fairly well on the Commons Defence Committee told me they're already planning more cuts for the next White Paper. That should go down well with some of the voters, the would-be tax savers." He moved the silver paperweight slightly. The file was closed. What had happened, decided him about something?

"They want to reduce the Royal Navy to little more than an anti-submarine force for the North Atlantic." He lifted one finger. "Don't get me wrong. I greatly admire our U.S. allies, but it doesn't mean I want the Stars and Stripes flying above the White Ensign! And the Corps will be under pressure, too. Again."

There was a quiet, almost gentle, tap on the door.

"Come!" Souter glanced at his watch. "God, as late as that!"

The door opened slightly, but Ross kept his eyes on the colonel. All the way from Hawks Hill, just to sit in this office and be interrogated. For what? *No longer required.*

Souter said, "I have another meeting to attend. In this job you sit on a very high ladder." He touched the star-shaped scar above his eyebrow. "So there's a long way to fall if you foul things up."

He thrust out his hand. "I was right. You're the one for the job."

He glared at the door. "All *right*, I'm coming!"

Ross was on his feet, the sensation of the handshake remaining like sandpaper on his palm.

"People want to know what we're doing, see it for themselves. It's risky, some might say, but worth it. *My ladder*, remember? My neck."

He walked toward the door, the file and the paperweight still on the desk.

He said, "I shall be in touch. Five days, probably. You know the drill by now."

Ross said, "May I ask what this is for, sir?"

Souter grunted.

"That chap you saw leaving the office. Tobin. *Clive*

Tobin. He's putting us in the spotlight. Can't say any more just now, eh?"

He paused with one hand on the door. "He's going across to Ulster. And you're going with him."

The door was closed. Even the traffic outside was silent.

Ulster. Like part of the dream, rolling back the years. The mean little street. The young marine and the barrel organ. One man's death, and he had never forgotten it. The marine had not even found time to be afraid. Or brave.

The door was open again, and a different man was putting the paperweight into a velvet bag.

Ross recalled De Lisle's concise summation of it all. *What we are. What we do.*

He heard the man remark, "Have the skin off my back if anything happened to this thing."

He thought of the face he had met at the door, only half an hour ago. The searching eyes. It had already been decided.

He said, "The Colonel's gone to another meeting."

"To the Dorchester, if I know him well enough!"

Ross glanced out of the window and saw several people with open umbrellas hurrying past the deserted parking meters. The pavements were shining with rain.

The man with the paperweight said politely, "No raincoat, sir?"

It was like a hand gripping his shoulder. He would get wet, and he had eaten nothing since he had left the stables. And yet he could smile.

"If you can't take a joke!"

The man grinned. "Shouldn't have joined, sir!"

The old lift was apparently out of order, or it had been delayed at another floor, so he made his way down by a chipped marble staircase. He neither met nor saw any one else until he reached the entrance lobby, as if the entire building were unoccupied but for that one, bare office.

There was another security man at the counter, who acknowledged him but said nothing. Out on the street it was still raining, and there was not a taxi in sight.

He strode away from Number Thirty-One, his mind lingering on the brief meeting and the even briefer closing remarks.

He wondered if there was any mention in Souter's intelligence pack that Major Ross Blackwood had once been intent on resigning from the Corps.

He felt the rain soaking through his suit and quickened his step. He no longer noticed that he was not even out of breath.

He knew what he had been dreading, and what it meant to him.

This was all he wanted. All he had.

"Taxi, guv?"

A new beginning.

CHAPTER NINE

Four days exactly after Ross's meeting with Colonel Sir Aubrey Souter, a messenger delivered the official summons to the door of Sue's flat. It was further confirmed by one of Souter's aides on the telephone. So it was on. His sister had been astonished when Ross had borrowed her ironing board and said he intended to press the one uniform he had brought with him from Hawks Hill. 'Official' meant just that. It was rare these days, except in naval ports or establishments where eager recruits would dodge traffic or cross a road simply to confront an officer so they could exchange salutes. In Plymouth on certain days, you could walk the length of a main road with one hand almost fixed to your beret or the peak of your cap.

This morning the sky was clear, and Ross had opened some of the windows as soon as his sister had departed, to do an interview in Woolwich, she had remarked vaguely. In the few days he had stayed here, they had grown no closer. Her home was a large, four-bedroomed flat in Chelsea, shabby but obviously expensive, and part of a block not far from the river; you could see the tall chimneys of Battersea power station in the distance.

One of the bedrooms had been converted into an office, with books, files and bundles of papers on the floor and everywhere else. A tax dodge, Sue had said. Untidy it certainly was, but he had the feeling that she knew exactly where to lay hands on the smallest scrap of information. While he had been staying here she had been away for most of each day, conducting interviews or at the magazine's main office in Fleet Street.

Maybe it was all his fault. Their lives had run on separate courses for too long. But he was interested, and he cared. Once or twice some one had telephoned the flat, but each time when he had answered the caller had hung up.

She had brushed it off with, "Probably Howard. He likes to stay in touch with all his slaves!"

'Howard' was Howard Ford, her boss. His magazine *Focus* was growing in popularity and had moved into other areas, including commercial television.

Ross hung the Lovat jacket across a hanger to join the trousers he had already pressed.

What M.O.A. could do better?

He walked to a window and felt the air warm across his face. By leaning over the sill, he could see the cars parked in line along the street. This block of flats had an underground car park, rare in this area. That, too, would be costly. So why did it trouble him so much? Sue was a grown woman, sister or not. She had been engaged once, but had called it off, although she had never divulged the reasons either to him or to their mother.

The second night here he had heard her return, slamming the door, sobbing and then shutting herself in her own room. He touched the object in his pocket; it only made him feel more helpless. He had found it when he had been setting up the ironing board, something catching the sunlight near the window, where Sue had dropped or thrown an old dressing gown.

A cuff-link, and not the kind any man would toss away. It was gold, and engraved with a lamb and star. The crest was common enough on pub signs, but the Lamb and Star was also the badge of a local regiment. It made no sense, or too much so.

He turned as the door bell cut through his thoughts.

Some one new in her life. A lover? Emotionally, she had both feet on the ground.

He opened the door, and said, "I'm so sorry. Did you ring before?"

There was a narrow window on the opposite side of the hallway, so that the sun was directly behind her, and her face was in shadow. She wore a pale, perhaps cream, safari suit open at the throat, and had one hand resting on a shoulder bag, relaxed, looking past him through the doorway.

She said, "I hope I'm not calling at an inconvenient time."

He said, "Sue's not here, I'm afraid. Can I do anything for you?"

He thought she would see the ironing board, the scattered items of clothing, the open suitcase. He added defensively, "I'm her brother."

She held out her hand. "I know. Ross, isn't it?"

He pulled the door wide. "That's me." A dry, firm hand, without pressure. A polite gesture.

She might have smiled. "Warwick. Sharon Warwick." She walked into the flat, glancing around. "Rude of me to drop in like this, unannounced. But I was coming this way." She half turned and looked at him directly. "I'm Clive Tobin's P.A. Thought it might help to meet you before tomorrow. You know what I mean."

"No secrets, then?"

She did not return his smile. "Waste too much time."

She walked into the main room and looked briefly at a wad of papers held together by an elastic band. "Still a mess, I see."

Ross looked around also, seeing it through her eyes.

"You know my sister well?"

"*Your sister* and I were once after the same job, I forget now which one!" She laughed, but it did not touch her eyes. There were blue, and in the stronger light Ross could see her hair, very short, and the colour of honey.

He said stupidly, "Have a chair . . . er, Miss Warwick."

She walked instead to the far window. Very easily, confident.

Over her shoulder she said, "Sharon will do, if you like."

She saw the uniform on its hanger and went straight to it.

"*Major* Blackwood." She touched the crown on one shoulder. "Full of surprises, this job. Like my lord and master, Mr. Tobin." She did not explain, but pointed at another door. "In that fridge she usually keeps some wine, chilled and ready for parched travellers." She tossed her head and ran her fingers through her hair. "She won't mind. You should know that."

I don't know her at all.

It seemed to take him an age to get the wine and find a corkscrew and some glasses. All the time he could feel the girl's presence, the relaxed aloofness, like a barrier.

He put a glass on the table beside her.

"Chilean," he said.

"It would be." She sipped the wine appreciatively. "Nice."

He looked at her hands. Well-shaped, like Sue's, the nails short and faintly coloured. She wore a jade ring on her right hand.

Then she said, "You're younger than I expected."

Ross covered his surprise, or hoped he did. He thought of Souter's well-thumbed file, the silver paperweight.

"It's all on the record."

She half smiled. "That's *not* what I said. No matter." She shook her hair again, and remarked, "Just had it cut. Can't do a damn thing with it now." She seemed almost relaxed.

"Have you worked with Clive Tobin long? What's he like?"

She took another sip, as if considering the question.

"He's a hard worker, makes high demands on every one, himself especially." She crossed her legs casually. "Everything has to be perfect."

"You have to travel a great deal?" There was a silence. "That was a stupid question!"

"It was." She put down the glass. "I'll be leading you into every session. But during each final take, you'll be talking directly to him. You've got a nice, easy manner. Keep it, no matter what."

She bobbed one foot up and down, frowning slightly, as if somewhere else.

She wore sandals, her feet and ankles bare. She would be quite tall in heels, he thought vaguely.

She said, "Ross . . . I can call you Ross?" She put the glass down gently. "Tell me, Ross. Have you ever killed any one?"

He gazed at her. She was unemotional. Cold. No, it went much deeper.

"Yes. Reaction, necessity, fear. It's not easy to put it into perspective." He thought of the bridge blowing up. One man falling but struggling on, the live grenade almost slipping from his bloodied fingers. "Sometimes it's simply us or them."

She stood up and reached for her bag. "I'll just use the loo, then I'll be off. Thanks for being so helpful. So frank. Something so often lacking in this sort of work."

"I'll call a taxi for you."

She shook her head. "A car brought me. It'll be waiting."

She crossed the room, the same easy walk he had first noticed. Without effort, like a dancer.

155

She held out her hand. "Tomorrow, then."

He wanted suddenly to grip the fingers, hold them against his mouth. She, and her 'lord and master', would have a good laugh at that.

He said, "I'll look forward to it." Like a green subaltern on heat. *What is the matter with me?*

He recalled that she was still there by the table and the half-empty glasses. She was looking at him, her eyes steady, searching.

She said, "I'll remember. Us or them."

Somewhere a tug hooted mournfully on the river. Like the old *Vigilant*, coming to the rescue.

The room was empty, the uniform still on the hanger, where she had touched it.

He wanted to laugh at himself. But it would not go away.

Colonel Sir Aubrey Souter did not conceal his relief when he greeted Ross in the foyer of the ministry building. It was not their original meeting place, but one of the older and grander palaces of Whitehall, now used by the Combined Chiefs of Staff.

The car Souter had sent for him had been delayed in a traffic jam, an accident of some kind; the driver had not stopped to inquire.

Souter said, "You are here to mingle, get the feel of things." He waved to somebody in the crowd of uniforms. "Officially, this is to greet one of the new senior officers." He grimaced. "A soldier, this time."

The room to which they had come would have been better described as a salon: gilt and pale blue, with vast paintings on the walls and busts by the ornamental fireplace, one of Admiral Jellicoe, the victor of Jutland, another of Field Marshal Montgomery of Alamein in the well-remembered beret with its two badges. On his previous, and only other, visit to this magnificent place, Ross had seen a bust of Mountbatten. It had been removed after his murder in Ireland. He could see no other relics or reminders of the Second World War, and, glancing at the others around him, he knew why. There were several foreign uniforms, French, German, and others he did not immediately recognize. The omission was clearly political.

The last time he had been near this room, he had been in charge of a guard of honour for some diplomatic nonentity; he could scarcely remember. He had been the junior officer at the time. He saw somebody wave to him, and returned the greeting; it could have been anybody. Now he was a major, and he was still the most junior officer in the place. The guest of honour, a major-general, was on his feet, being introduced by Souter; it was all very informal. The general thanked Souter and referred to him as 'my good friend'. That would not go unnoticed. Then he launched into his speech: peacekeeping, co-operation, mutual gain. Ross wondered if some of the foreign uniforms understood, especially when the general made a joke, and the others laughed. He saw Souter glance at the clock above the empty fireplace, although he was careful not to peer at his watch. On edge again about something. He looked toward the fine double doors, and saw two figures in white jackets waiting for the word to bring in the drinks.

But where was Clive Tobin? Maybe the weight of so much brass had scared him off. He thought of the girl's comment, *everything's got to be perfect.* The celebrity.

Souter had found time to point out a few faces in the crowd before the general had arrived. Civil servants, officials of the ministry, information and publicity. Ross had not realized there were so many. They, too, would be getting impatient.

In his mind he could see the girl in the safari suit, with

the honey-coloured hair and calm blue eyes. With Clive Tobin. Her lord and master . . . Even thinking about it made him feel foolish. Envious.

People were applauding, friends greeting friends, strangers feeling their way, doors opening, glasses clinking on trays.

Try as he might, he found it impossible to connect all this with the grim reality he had seen. Wading ashore on some unknown beach, hacking through a jungle, walking down some quiet street into a sniper's sights. Trying to uphold the rule of law, to defeat terrorism. He was angry, and anger was something to which he should be immune; it was not professional.

Tell me, Ross, have you ever killed any one?

As if she had spoken right here, beside him.

He swung round and saw the tall doors open again. Like making an entrance, right on cue, a blue velvet jacket that caught the overhead lights, and a matching bow tie. One hand partly raised, returning a greeting or acknowledging some one he knew. The same practised smile, unruffled, at ease, a face known to thousands. Souter was ploughing through the sea of uniforms like an icebreaker. The major-general had had his moment.

But Ross was looking at the girl beside Clive Tobin, in a long, dark green skirt which made her appear taller, and a simple sleeveless white blouse, her tanned arms unadorned but for the watch he had seen at the flat. Her hair was shining, alive.

Can't do a damn thing with it now. Was that only yesterday?

Souter was saying something. Relaxed now.

Tobin shook hands. "Glad you're joining the team." The famous smile again. "Hope you don't regret it!" He reached out and took her arm. "You've met the lovely Sharon, of course? She keeps the whole show on the road." He tightened his grip. "I couldn't survive without her."

A steward was offering a tray of glasses. Champagne.

Tobin laughed. "Not me – we're working tonight, aren't we?" But he took a glass and handed it to her.

A tall, grey-haired man in a crumpled suit stepped closer and said brightly, "Saw that programme you did on California – those awful fires. Brought it right home to me and my staff, I can tell you!"

Tobin nodded, a mask of gravity falling over his features. "Not something I shall easily forget, either."

He released his grip on the girl's arm and turned to speak with some one else.

Ross took a glass, but was looking at the fingerprints left on her skin.

She said, "What a gathering. If only the Devil could cast his net, what say you?"

Ross did not answer directly. Tobin's back was turned, and he was shaking hands with the major-general as if they were old friends.

"He must keep you very busy, Sharon."

"He does. It's hard to keep up with him some of the time."

Souter was looking at his watch, speaking to the major-general.

She said, "Just breaking the ice. It may not look like much to you, but Clive gets his lift-off from this kind of beginning."

She would make an excuse and leave soon. Ross asked, "What were the fires they were talking about?"

She smiled, for the first time. "No idea. But Clive doesn't like to admit a lapse in memory." The cool, direct eyes. "Do you?"

She was so close that her elbow was brushing his sleeve.

He imagined he could smell her perfume. He said, "I'll remember this, all right."

She staggered slightly and slopped some of her champagne on to her arm and skirt.

"These bloody high heels! I should have known."

Ross steadied her and pulled out his handkerchief to wipe it from her skin. The same place where Tobin had gripped her so possessively.

"This should do it. Sorry about the crush."

She reached over to take a fresh glass from a hovering steward, perhaps to give herself time.

"Don't even think about it." She sipped the champagne, but her eyes were averted. "I like you, Ross. And that's it. If you've got other ideas, we'll stop it right now."

Ross heard Tobin laugh at something, and said, "Because of him? Something between you? I just thought . . ."

"Then don't. It's not safe, for either of us."

Tobin was back, his eyes moving briefly between them.

"Sorry we didn't get much time to chat, Major . . . er, Ross. But we're almost there. Two or three days, and then we'll join you across the water, in 'English-occupied Ireland' as the boyos on the other side of the border call it." The smile vanished, as if it had been switched off. "I can see their point in some ways, of course. We wouldn't take too kindly to Irish soldiers with machine-guns patrolling Mayfair and Piccadilly, would we?"

She said, "We have to go now, Clive. Interview at the Ritz in half an hour."

Tobin spread his hands. "See? A real taskmaster, or is it mistress?" He waved to the room at large.

But all Ross saw was her expression: defiance, impatience, despair.

Tell Souter you don't want the job. To find somebody else.

It would not be difficult.

They were leaving now. She had her back turned, people were smiling, shaking hands, Tobin was writing something across a paper. His autograph, perhaps.

Then she did turn, and he saw that she was still holding his handkerchief against her bare arm.

Very deliberately, she tucked it inside her blouse.

He took another glass of champagne from a steward; he had forgotten how many he had had. That was not like him, either. The doors were closed; she had gone. He tried to contain his thoughts, make some sense out of them. He had only just met her; he knew absolutely nothing about her, her way of life, her background. To her, he was only part of the job. Soon forgotten.

So why should it matter, hurt so much?

He saw Souter beckoning to him. *But it does matter.*

Souter said cheerfully, "Went well, I thought. You and I are dining with the general." He almost nudged him. "*He's* paying, would you believe?"

Ross said, "Will this do any good, sir?"

Souter put down an empty glass. "We can but hope. Don't worry – just remember what I said. I'm the one on the ladder!" He became serious again. "Get on all right with Clive Tobin? Seemed pleased with things to me."

The major-general and his aide were saying their last farewells. Now dinner. When all he wanted . . . *What do I want?*

Souter said casually, "Saw you hitting it off with Tobin's P.A. He certainly can pick 'em."

"She been with him long?"

Souter was straightening his jacket, preparing himself.

"A year or so, I believe. They don't stay too long in that kind of work . . . Who can say? She went through a bad time, I heard. Husband was killed in an air crash. Still, she'll be safe enough with Clive."

Ross drew himself to attention as he was introduced. Souter was used to it. He would need to be.

But all he could think about was Tobin's grip on her arm, and her voice. *It's not safe, for either of us.*

There was a large car waiting at the main entrance, a uniformed driver with the doors already open. Military policemen, redcaps, were standing nearby.

The major-general was saying, "Knew your father, of course, fine man . . ."

Doors slammed and Ross did not hear the rest.

In a day or so he would be back where he belonged, and she would have forgotten their brief contact.

He thought of her hand, the plain jade ring. A reminder, so that she would never forget, no matter what.

The dinner, at the major-general's club in Park Lane, seemed to last forever. Their host had no difficulty keeping the conversation going, as it was mainly about himself, and his younger days when he had been a keen polo player. Souter seemed more than content to leave the field open.

Ross lost count of the various courses, apparently chosen with care well before the event, and all accompanied by the appropriate wines.

By the time it was finally finished they had the club dining room to themselves, and the few remaining waiters could barely stop yawning. There had been some sort of hint that they should move on to another late-night rendezvous, but there was only the official car, so Ross volunteered to make his own way by taxi.

It was easier said than done. There had been a film première at the Odeon in Leicester Square, and taxis were at a premium. Eventually he managed to flag one down and, feeling completely drained, he settled down and tried to consider his return to active duty in the future.

The taxi driver made a point of mentioning that Chelsea

was "a bit off my beat, guv'nor" and was taking him away from the more lucrative punters. "But seein' as you're in uniform . . ."

The street seemed darker than usual, and the electrically operated garage door was shut, so he did not know if Sue was back or not.

He heard the driver say, "Cheers, guv, thanks a lot!" and wondered what he had given him.

He groped for the spare key she had lent him. The porter was home and in bed by now. He was lucky.

He heard the taxi increasing speed and looked back across the street. He could see the tiny red light on one of the chimneys of the power station, and remembered the tug hooting. When she had been about to leave the flat. Yesterday. The day before, as it was now.

He stifled a yawn and turned back toward the flats.

It was like being punched. He was suddenly wide awake, his spine ice cold. Not fatigue, not imagination. He gauged the position of the window, and the floor. No mistake.

The flash of light. Then nothing. He counted seconds, then saw the light again. Moving this time: a torch. Like that other occasion, a lifetime ago. The staring eyes in the beam, the blade across his back.

A thief? Somebody who knew the flat was unoccupied? The thoughts meant nothing. He was at the door, the key in the lock. There was a dim light in the entrance hall, another above the lift. He saw the porter's telephone. Call the police? But he was already halfway up the narrow emergency staircase. *Suppose he's armed, or there's more than one of them?*

He separated the keys and slid his fingers around them, feeling the shapes as he ran his free hand over the door.

No sound. Nothing. He waited for his breathing to

steady, but there was no need. Reaction, necessity, fear. What he had said to her when she had been in the flat.

He eased the key into the lock, his body poised, balanced, without feeling it. The handle was turning, a change of air as the door moved very slowly under the pressure.

For a split second he imagined he had mistaken the direction, or the floor. The room was in total darkness. And not a sound. He breathed out very slowly. Then he saw it, a faint light moving again along the bottom of a door, where he had seen Sue hang her dressing gown.

Whatever it was, the intruder was taking his time.

Now the door was opening, some of the torchlight spilling around the edge, and hesitating over a pile of magazines. And then on a hand.

Ross could feel the ice on his spine, hear the voice of the instructor. *When surprise is all you've got, use it!*

He scarcely felt himself move. He sprawled across the man's body, his hands finding and gripping without hesitation, his knee coming forward. Like hitting something solid.

He heard a gasp of pain, and felt the immediate struggle.

"Keep still, you bastard!" He twisted an arm and heard another sharp cry.

He said, "*Easy*, now. We are going to stand up!" They lurched to their feet like two drunks, the door swinging against them. Ross reached out and found the light switch.

"Nice and easy now."

The light was almost blinding. He stared at the man whose arm was locked behind him. Grey hair, expensively cut, a tweed jacket, and the watch which was pinned under his grip was a gold Rolex Submariner. A strong body, but he had to be in his late fifties at least.

His reaction was equally surprising.

"Who the fucking hell are *you?*"

"I was going to ask you that."

Have you ever killed any one?

"I *own* this place." Then, accusingly, "You've got a key! She gave it to you!"

Ross released him.

"You must be Howard Ford."

"Of course I am!" Anger was replacing shock or fear. He was gazing at the uniform, rubbing his wrist with his other hand. "She said you'd be staying here for a few days. But I thought . . ."

"I'm her brother. I saw the torch. Thought somebody was breaking into the place."

Ford pushed some hair from his forehead and said abruptly, "I was looking for something. Not that I have to explain to *you* or any one else."

Ross saw the confidence returning, and, with it, anger. Like a court-martial, when the evidence becomes confused, and the accused goes on the attack.

I own this place. He remembered his sister's despair, her sobbing in the night. A strong girl, too strong in many ways.

No wonder the garage was closed. Ford had been intending to stay here for the night. For as long as he chose. Not a lover, just a casual relationship.

I should understand better than any one.

Ford stood in front of a mirror, touching his face gingerly with his fingertips.

"I shall leave now. Tomorrow I will expect . . ."

Ross said to his reflection, "I'll be gone. But don't take it out of my sister."

Ford had pulled a bunch of keys from his pocket.

"She is free to do as she wishes. If she is displeased with anything, she can tell *me*." He turned toward the door. "She's not a child. Can't you see that?" His confidence was growing, like something physical. "You, an officer, a major no less, should show some understanding, instead of jumping to conclusions!"

Ross made himself count the seconds. Like those other times.

He opened his palm and laid the cuff-link on the table.

"Not like the old regiment, Mr. Ford? Is this what you were looking for?"

The door was closed, but it seemed an age before he heard the lift begin to descend.

What would Sue say when she heard about it? She would know, whether Ford told her or not. She might lose her job because of it.

I wanted to hit him. Keep on hitting him.

He walked to a window and opened it, the night air cool on his face. *Then I would have lost mine.*

He picked up his green beret from the floor and touched the badge.

By Sea and Land.

So be it.

CHAPTER TEN

The khaki-painted Land Rover, with its familiar wire mesh protection and strips of armour, braked yet again to surmount the crude 'sleeping policemen', barriers which had been built to slow traffic. Ross Blackwood eased forward on the seat and ducked his head to peer at the nearest buildings. Shops, some old apartments, and a pub. It had been raining and the pavement was still wet, although above the serried rooftops he could see another patch of blue coming. He tried to memorize every detail. There was a checkpoint at the crossroads ahead. Sometimes it was manned, others not. The Land Rover rolled over another line of bricks and jerked down on to the road once more.

The outskirts of Londonderry. Ross heard the man beside him swear softly and say, "Don't make a meal of it! Take each one slowly."

The driver, another Royal Marine, almost shrugged. "Sir?" And his eyes moved briefly to the mirror, the owner of the voice and then Ross, the passenger. And that was what he felt like, most, if not all, of the time.

Over two weeks now. Not the 'two or three days' Clive Tobin had foreseen after that meeting. He winced as the rear wheels bounced across another obstacle.

He looked over at the pub, where a few people were standing with glasses in their hands, one teasing a ragged dog with a rolled newspaper. A couple of them might have glanced at the khaki vehicle and its four occupants, the green berets, and the Globe and Laurel insignia on either side, or perhaps at the sub-machine-gun lying across the knees of one of them.

No obvious resentment. If anything, there was only indifference.

That was probably only too true, he thought. Years since he had served in the province, but watching the passing scene it might have been yesterday. There were a few stark reminders: a boarded-up shop or gutted building, or some scarred and blackened patches on a roadway from burned-out car or petrol bomb.

He could feel his escort's eyes on him. Major Nick Fisher was a commando like himself, with only a few months' difference in age and service between them.

He was doing what he was told, and no more. Showing him the main centres of defence and, when necessary, attack. Where the commando patrols met or overlapped those of the army and the police. Road blocks. They were passing one now and it was manned, two grinning faces changing to stiff backs and salutes when officers were sighted.

Since his brief service here, he had noticed a lot of changes. Improvements, if they could be called that: anti-riot shields and CS gas grenades, flak jackets and night vision equipment to seek out the hit-and-run attacker who might otherwise slip past the most vigilant sentry or outpost.

No wonder they tried to keep each man's tour of duty to a minimum.

And the hostility was there, even when it was covert and often hard to recognize. The ordinary marine from the mainland had to get used to it, or go under.

A brick, or a petrol bomb, hurled without warning and usually from the back of a crowd, became an everyday possibility. It would bring no retaliation, other than the Corps' own brutal humour.

Some marines had been badly injured by potatoes used as missiles, each one carefully spiked with old razor blades. A very senior colour sergeant who had seen almost everything in the course of his service had said, "If I catches one of them brave bastards, I shall stick a couple of blades where they 'urt most, an' 'e'll not be able to ride 'is bike for a month or two without rememberin' it!"

One of the injured marines had apparently laughed about it.

But it was hardly what they had joined up for. Ross thought of a recruiting poster he had seen on his last visit to Plymouth. *Join the Royal Navy and see the World.* Some wag had printed underneath it, *Join the Royal Marines and see the Next!*

He turned to the other major and said, "I believe you're going on a bit of leave soon?"

Fisher came back from his thoughts.

"Next week. June – my wife – is going into hospital. Stomach trouble." He sighed. "She tells *me* not to worry. She's the one who does that." He gestured toward the street. "This place is doing it!"

They were passing a hospital, and Ross saw the driver turn his head to eye a couple of nurses waiting for a bus. He noticed that the building's ground floor windows were protected by wire netting. The nurses were both in uniform. Was that protection, too?

It never failed to remind him of Glynis, and the carefully worded letters he had written to various addresses gleaned from people she had known and worked with in Hong Kong. Some had been returned, *Not known at this address,* or simply, *Gone away*. Others had vanished. On his last assignment in Hong Kong, when he had visited the old sick quarters, some one had told him that Glynis had quit to take care of her husband, who had suffered a severe stroke. It had brought back the old memory, the golf clubs in the other bedroom. What Diamond had been doing when he was taken ill.

He thought of Souter in that bare office, with his U.S. Marine Corps paperweight.

You never married? Can't say I blame you.

The girl named Sharon had probably seen that in the file, too. And wondered, if she cared enough.

Perhaps Clive Tobin had had second thoughts about coming to Ulster after all. Not his scene. Going to somewhere more newsworthy, and more exciting. Following the sun. And she would be with him.

The driver said, "Looks like trouble, sir." He braked very slightly, and Ross saw the other marine move his sub-machine-gun closer to his waist.

A police car was parked at the roadside, and two officers of the R.U.C. were standing by another group outside yet another pub. One was making notes in his book; the other was watching a man sitting on the curbside, a bloodied handkerchief pressed to his nose while one of his companions was trying to tie a bandage around his wrist.

Ross noticed that the second police officer was leaning against a lamp post, head slightly turned, as if listening to something. Ross heard it: an ambulance was on its way. He had one hand resting casually on his open holster.

The driver said, "That's Jimmy Doyle, sir. Local bookie. Always a bit slow paying out the winnings, is Jimmy!" He chuckled. "He had it coming!"

This was one marine who knew the Londonderry beyond the barbed wire and the sandbags of company headquarters.

Major Fisher grunted, "Drive on." He dropped his voice. "Bet you're sorry you came, Ross."

At last the ice was breaking. Perhaps Fisher had thought he was being relieved. Sent home.

He would know about the regular communications from Colonel Souter's department. They made Ross different. An interloper.

Fisher was saying, "I heard we were getting a visit from that television chap, Clive Tobin. God knows what he'd make of this potmess."

They both laughed. So much for security.

The driver had been holding the intercom to his ear, watching the ambulance pass, lights flashing, perhaps on its way back to the hospital with the wired-up windows. Jimmy the bookie . . .

He said, "'Foxtrot', sir."

Major Fisher touched Ross's arm and smiled.

"Return to H.Q., Ross. It seems our V.I.P. has arrived after all!"

Ross thought of the hotel where Tobin and his party would be staying while they were in Londonderry. Used mostly by visiting government officials, possible targets, as Souter's aide had described them, it was built like a comfortable fortress. But a fortress all the same.

He saw an armoured car driving slowly in the opposite direction. The army: the next patrol sector. The headlights blinked, a fist poked through an open shutter and gave a thumbs-up. How would Tobin find an angle, a story to his taste? Surely he would not bring Sharon into this atmosphere of patent hostility?

Through the gates and barriers, and past the guardroom with its sentries and the duty officer, a young subaltern who looked as if he was not long out of school. Eager, and very aware of two majors in one car. Going through the formalities. Ross saw the shadow above one of the out-buildings, a hidden marksman. In case the ID or password was incorrect.

He wondered what the young subaltern thought about it.

"Major Blackwood, sir!" It was a corporal he had seen a few times on guard duty.

"What is it, Harwood?" He only remembered the name because he had had to write a lengthy piece about the naval commodore who had won the first sea battle of World War Two, when the German pocket battleship *Graf Spee* had been scuttled at Montevideo, rather than surrender. A less than significant affair when compared to the carnage which would follow, but Harwood had always stuck in his mind.

"Visitor to see you, sir. Asked for you personally. Cleared by security, of course, sir." He could have winked.

She was standing in the guardroom beside a long table, her back turned, replacing some things in her handbag.

Another corporal, much younger than the one called Harwood, was hovering on the far side of the room, obviously relieved as he said, "Major Blackwood, miss."

She faced him, and held out her hand. "You see, Ross, I couldn't stay away!"

She wore a two-piece suit in what he had heard Joanna describe as houndstooth tweed, with a dark green scarf knotted around her throat.

He said, "You look wonderful," and released her hand, having taken his time over it. Expecting her to raise the barrier. He knew the two corporals were watching with interest, and some one else, a defaulter of some sort, was peering through the bars in the cell block. It would soon be all over the company H.Q. And who could blame them? She looked stunning.

She said, "I just had my bag searched." She held up her hand again. "It's all right. I think he was more embarrassed than I was, poor lad." She bent over the bag for a minute and he saw a lock of hair fall across her forehead, as he remembered.

"Clive's at the hotel. I thought I'd call and see you before we go there. You're looking well . . ." She pretended to shiver. "God, it's like Fort Knox around here."

She was gazing at him in the direct way he had not forgotten. "I've been wondering how you were making out." The eyes moved around the guardroom, the harsh lights overhead reflecting on the honey-coloured hair. "The Bloody Hand of Ulster, and all that."

"I've thought about you, Sharon. Quite a lot."

For an instant, he saw the uncertainty. Like a warning. Then she reached into her bag and pulled out a little package. She held it out.

"A bit late, I'm afraid." He opened it; it was the handkerchief he had used to mop up the spilled champagne, beautifully pressed and tied with a piece of ribbon. "Just in case you couldn't lay your hands on another ironing board."

She zipped the bag shut and looked up briskly. "Shall we go? You can tell me what's been happening while we drive."

He took her arm and guided her toward the steps and the barbed wire.

There seemed to be far more people hanging around than when he had arrived. She was probably used to it. Took it for granted.

The same subaltern was on duty. She offered her hand to him; he hesitated, then lowered his head to kiss it. When he straightened up again his young face was pink with embarrassment and pleasure.

The car was waiting, a military police vehicle parked close behind it with the engine running.

Ross climbed into the car and sat beside her. The driver was another redcap.

"Seat belts, please, miss. And, er, sir."

She fastened the clip and placed her bag between them.

"Just to be on the safe side," she said.

The barrier was still there.

Early morning, and the sky was clear and drained of colour. It was Sunday.

Ross Blackwood had already lowered a nearside window and could hear the mutter of the engine, like an intrusion. Once a busy T-junction, with traffic lights to control the ebb and flow of daily life, nothing moved here now, and where there had been buildings, a few shops and some offices, there was open space. Only the shape and direction of the road could be identified on the map.

"Pull over and stop here. This should be about right."

He glanced at the driver, Corporal Dick Harwood. Only a few weeks, but it felt as if he had known him for years.

It was like that in the Corps. But he could never claim that he had got used to it.

When the engine stopped the silence and stillness were all the more intense. There were some carefully arranged piles of bricks and other debris left by the bulldozers until another day. Tomorrow. He opened the door and stretched his legs. One building remained, but was already partly demolished. It must have been stronger than the others. He looked at the bulldozer tracks across what had been a strip of parkland, perhaps with gardens where people had walked their dogs, or waited for friends or lovers. The ruin nearby had been a police station.

He glanced at his watch. Clive Tobin would be here soon. Right now, if he was as punctual as usual. What would he discover this time? He had been out and around with him every day for a week and he felt no closer to him. Sometimes abrupt and impatient, Tobin also had an indisputable ability to hit the nail on its metaphorical head in his search for background and truth. Without prejudice, without criticism. Once he had said, "In this work I have to be a neutral. I can't afford to be biased."

Harwood commented, "Some one's up an' about, sir. The God bosun, anyway!"

Ross heard the church bells and thought of the old photograph in the study, the foundation of which now lay somewhere buried under a new motorway. *Where no birds sing*.

"Here he comes, sir." Harwood swung out of the car and straightened his beret.

What did he think about all this, Ross wondered. A waste of time? A big name over here just to please the brass? *Roll on my twelve*.

It was the same minibus Tobin had been using since his arrival, with just enough room for his cameraman, picture editor and driver. No armed guards, nothing which might antagonize one faction or the other. But even Clive Tobin, an accepted celebrity, must be uneasy sometimes.

"Ah, Ross, on the ball as usual!"

He was wearing a black leather jacket with a pair of binoculars hanging around his neck, and dark sunglasses. When he removed them to stare around at the demolished site, he showed no sign of strain or tiredness.

"This the place?" He kicked at a loose stone. "They'll be throwing up new buildings everywhere once they can make a little peace for themselves." He kicked another stone. "Tell me about it."

Ross pointed at the remaining ruin.

"Police station. Came under mortar attack. Sparked off

175

the massive countermeasures about seven years ago. Operation Motorman, it was called. Over twenty thousand troops were used to clear the old no-go areas. Even the navy took part, and brought landing craft all the way up the River Foyle. Made things a lot easier to contain."

Tobin nodded. "Unless you lived here, of course." But he smiled. "You've done your research – that's good. I understand you were far away at the time. Far East, wasn't it?"

Ross heard the others climbing down from the bus. Sharon Warwick was not among them.

"You've done your research too, apparently."

The cameraman looked around and said, "Not much here, Clive."

Tobin waved his sunglasses. "Just a few shots, Mark. The usual. For openers."

The others moved away, glad to be doing something.

Ross said, "Sharon taking today off?"

"Hardly. I expect she's told you, I drive them all the way!" He looked at him keenly. "You like her, don't you? I can always tell, with people I care about." He was watching the camera crew now, but did not appear to see them. "She's a good girl. She puts up with a lot, especially from me!" His arm shot out. "No, Mark, more to the left, those trees, or what's left of them!" He nodded. "That's the ticket, man!"

He continued in the same unhurried tone as before. "I expect you know, her husband was killed in an air crash. Bloody fine photographer, too. Did a lot of work for me. It happened during the Palestine trouble. He was in a helicopter. Might have been an accident, but I think it was deliberate. The chopper was burned out, and the authorities, as they say, didn't want to know." He held up his binoculars. "They'd only been married a week when it happened. I blame myself sometimes. He wanted the job, and I wanted him. End of story. Or is it?"

"Ready, Clive!" The other man was holding a mirror. "Looks good!"

Tobin frowned.

"Not too sweaty, am I?"

"You'll look great."

Corporal Harwood muttered, "This lot aren't supposed to be here!"

It was another car, with military insignia on either door.

A sergeant leaned out of a window, and called, "Keep your party up here, will you, sir? Spot of bother just reported."

The car was already moving again. Ross asked, "Where is it?"

"Miles from here, sir. You'll be O.K. if you stay put." Calm, matter-of-fact, just obeying orders. He added, almost as an afterthought, "At the old market, Mahons Place." The car accelerated.

Ross turned, as the cameraman said, "What's up, Clive?"

Tobin was stooping to pick up the mirror from the road.

He said, "The market he mentioned," and for the first time he seemed unable to control his voice. "It's where she was going, I forget why. I didn't think . . ."

Ross seized Harwood's arm.

"Do you know it?" and almost pushed him against the car. "Then *move it!* Fast as you can!"

The car was lurching over scattered bricks before he could think. *Your duty is to keep with Clive Tobin.*

He felt the door jar against his elbow as Harwood swerved around a corner. A few terraced houses, an old man with a broom calling something and pointing as the car shot past.

He heard Harwood swear. Then, "Christ, I thought I'd missed the bloody street!" Another bend, and two policemen dropping a metal barricade and jumping clear. A blurred notice with an arrow. Mahons Place.

For a second he thought Harwood had driven into something solid, although they were still moving. But one of the windscreen wipers was missing and there was dust everywhere, like smoke. An explosion.

Harwood slammed on the brakes, hands pressed against the wheel, taking the strain as a whole length of timber flew across the bonnet as if it were paper blowing in the wind.

Ross was out of the car, fingers dragging at his pistol holster, eyes stinging with dust.

Harwood was coughing, but managed to call, "With you, Major!"

They were both running, the sound of their feet unusually loud and echoing. As if they were the only two people alive. He felt the gun in his hand, but did not recall drawing it; only his mind seemed to be reaching out ahead, preparing him.

An overturned vegetable barrow, its contents strewn across the road, some still rolling. Two figures, men or women he did not know, crouched in a doorway, perhaps at the back of a building in the adjoining street. The dust was clearing now, leaving the taste of charred wood on his lips.

A market. There was no sign of any activity. It was still early, but the church bells had been ringing. Nothing made sense any more.

Harwood's arm swung against him. "*There*, sir!" A low-roofed building with one wide entrance, like a garage or warehouse. The smoke was drifting from it. He thought he heard voices. Something came alive, moving beside an upended heap of empty milk crates, and croaked with fear as the pistol steadied a foot away from his face.

"Don't shoot! For God's sake!"

Harwood called, "Easy, matey! Stand very still, right?" The gun in his hands was steady, unwavering.

Ross wiped his mouth with the back of his hand. Harwood was not even slightly out of breath. *Neither am I.*

"What happened?"

The man was still crouching. "Down there, in the fish market. A bomb – some one havin' a go at the offices."

He was making no sense. Harwood said, "Sunday. Good time to blow a safe." He was nodding, excited. Sharing it.

Ross said, "We're going in." Harwood would follow. He did not have to be told.

A robbery. Not the IRA or any other faction. The army would be here at any second. Some one else . . . He could smell fish. Then he was running again.

The so-called fish market was suddenly ablaze with lights. Perhaps the explosion had blown the others, but it only made the scene more unreal: trolleys of fish waiting to be unloaded for display, scattered pieces of ice like broken glass in the hard glare, and in the far corner about a dozen people, mostly women, three with children. Some one was sobbing, close to hysteria.

All Ross saw was the man with the gun: he had two companions as far as he could see through the trapped smoke, one clinging to the other, his face bleeding, and obviously in great pain. A foul-up with the explosives. The 'bomb'. His mind snapped into place like a safety catch. Not professionals, then. These were the most dangerous kind.

He said, *"Drop the gun! Do it now!"*

"Says who!" The gun moved jerkily. "I'll take a couple with me, you bastard!"

A child began to scream. The gun wavered; his nerve was cracking. Somewhere, in another world, a whistle was blowing, car doors slamming.

Like sights hardening into focus. The gun moving toward the terrified child, but another figure was also there. That same two-piece suit, the honey-coloured hair, silver in the glaring lights, her arms around the child, hugging, soothing.

Ross walked toward them. Unhurriedly, or so it felt. Even his heart seemed to have stopped.

He said, "It's over! Drop it!"

The man swung toward him, the flash of the gun lighting his face, the shock as it fell from his hands.

Harwood strode past, the semi-automatic rifle barely smoking.

"Still!" But the other two were staring at him, already unable to move. The one with the bloodied face was looking at the figure sprawled across the melting ice. Even the children were quiet.

Ross walked toward her, thankful, ashamed, empty. It was beyond words or description.

The child was being prised away, he assumed by her mother, but she was staring back at Sharon, smiling and sobbing at the same time.

He said, "I'm sorry, Sharon. For this to happen . . . If only I'd known."

She had her arms around his waist. Not hugging, not moving. Taking deep breaths.

She said, "Ross. You could have been killed. Don't you know that?" She raised her head, and her face was only inches from his. "He'd already shot a security man." Her head jerked. "Out at the back." And her arms clasped him again, as if she could not release him.

The place was filling with uniforms, army, R.U.C., and figures in white coats, complaining harshly about "the damage done to our fish!" It was madness, and he wanted to laugh aloud. He saw Harwood on his knees beside the body of the man he had shot. There was an officer, too. He also wore a green beret.

He felt her hand covering his, and the pistol still gripped at his waist.

He said quietly, "I would have killed him," and tried to smile. "Does that tell you something?"

A policeman paused to touch his arm, and said, "Well done, sir. Some robbery – they fucked that one up, an' no mistake! Bloody safe was empty anyway, even I knew that!" He strode away, grinning.

She had not let go of his hand.

"How did you know, Ross?"

But the other green beret was here now. It was Major Fisher.

"You took a chance, Ross. I'd have had a ton of reports to write if anything had happened to *you*. That'd be all I'd need." There were flashes, brighter even than the overhead glare. "The goddamned press is here now, would you believe. I'll soon put a stop to that!"

Ross reached down to take her arm, but she shook her head.

"No. Hold me. I nearly died just now. I thought you'd be killed."

He could feel her shaking.

"That would make a perfect shot! But some people might not understand!"

It was Clive Tobin, laughing at them, hands on hips as if he were directing a film. Relaxed, not a hair out of place.

An hour; was that all? And he had seemed to be almost in a state of shock.

Fisher said, "You are not supposed to be here, Mr. Tobin."

"Oh, call me Clive, for God's sake, Major!" He pointed

to Ross. "Neither is *he*, remember? Just as well he was, in my book!"

Some of the others laughed.

Ross saw a stretcher going past. The security guard. His face was covered.

Harwood was passing and gave him a quick thumbs-up. The gunman was still alive, anyway.

Ross touched her hair very gently, surprised that his hand was so steady. He sensed Tobin turning to watch, and said over his shoulder, "I thought you said you were always neutral, Clive?"

Tobin shrugged. "Some days, more neutral than others."

Men and women were emerging now, venturing into the street, some pausing to stare at the cars and the uniforms or the debris left by the blast. Curiosity, rather than any show of emotion. They had gone beyond that.

Tobin looked at the sky. "Now, where were we? Back to the old crossroads, I think. So let's be moving, people, shall we?"

The professional had come to the rescue.

Harwood was reversing the car; a Range Rover was picking up some of Major Fisher's marines. A solitary R.U.C. officer held a telephone to his ear. Business as usual.

She walked with him into the pale sunlight, his hand on her arm, her eyes straight ahead.

She saw the car, Harwood's eyes in the driving mirror moving quickly away; she must have heard Tobin's voice calling to some one in the market.

Ross pressed her arm, waiting for her to pull away.

He said, "I want to see you again. Soon. It's the way I feel."

There were shouts and even some laughter as a flight of pigeons fluttered noisily over the newly erected stalls. One woman was pointing at them, pulling her daughter by the hand, trying to take her attention. But the child was gazing at Sharon, the tear stains still clear on her cheeks.

Sharon looked across at her and smiled. The child returned it.

She said simply, "I'd like that. We'll find time." She turned her face and looked at him. "We'll *make* time."

He got into the car, and saw the space left by the missing wiper. Had it been that close?

The car began to move, and he said, "Thanks, Dick. You did well. Bloody well."

Harwood settled back in his seat, letting the strain peel away.

"That's what it's all about, isn't it, sir?"

Ross could almost feel Harwood's relief. *It's what we do.*

He saw the minibus turning on to the main road, the blink of a flash bulb somewhere.

We'll make time. It was enough.

Ross Blackwood glanced around the room before sitting down by a table and placing his glass within easy reach. This part of the company H.Q. had been a school in more peaceful times, and still looked like it. When he had been invited to the junior N.C.O.s' mess for a drink, he had seen a blackboard on one of the walls. It was not difficult to see it as it had been.

He took out the letter and unfolded it. Just reading it brought it all back, except that it was still impossible to suppress the image of the old house, and accept that it had gone. Maybe on the next visit . . . He picked up the glass but it was almost empty; even the ice was melting. It was early evening, but the sun was still high outside, what he could see of it.

He began again. He could almost hear Joanna's voice. Her laugh.

As I told you, John has been such a great help around the stables, I could not have managed without him. Nothing ever seems to get him down. He remembered their meeting, the firm handshake, and his sister's comment. Getting his feet under the table . . . And why not? Joanna was strong, but she was human. And alone.

He twisted round in the chair. There was only one other occupant in the room, face covered by a newspaper, snoring gently. Beyond the door he could hear voices, music, the television. Perhaps a game of liar dice to pass away the time.

He looked at the clock above the sealed fireplace. It had been a short day for him; he had been with Tobin for less than two hours, watching his camera crew film a street scene from the top floor of the post office. Sharon had not been with them. Tobin had passed it off with his usual comment about being a slave driver. *She's typing up the final worksheet. Why she can never grow long fingernails!*

He thought about the shooting, Harwood bringing down the armed robber as if it were all part of some drill. The sobbing child. Sharon holding him, coming out of it. The moment of stress was past. Maybe the rest was a delusion.

And the 'rest' was not over. Major Fisher had tried to make light of it, but the hard fact remained. Ross had left his place of duty to dash off elsewhere. The army's job, or the R.U.C.'s; anybody's but his. Brigade would be informed, and a full report was no doubt already on Colonel Souter's desk.

What now? A reprimand or a change of posting? Another cheerless camp with young marines learning how to become commandos? And for what? To act as the world's policemen, until local need gave way to local hate?

He picked up the glass again and shook the chips of ice. *What's getting into me?* Even Nick Fisher was avoiding him. He would be off to England very soon, to see his wife in hospital, to build another diplomatic bridge.

A shadow moved across the table and Ross said, "All right, I *will* have another drink. To hell with it!"

The steward remained by the table.

"In the meantime, sir, there's a call for you. I can be getting you the same again while you're on the phone."

"Any idea who . . ."

He picked up the glass. "A lady, sir."

Calm, even formal. "I'm glad I caught you. I expect you were getting ready to go out and enjoy yourself."

He pressed the phone harder against his ear. There were voices in the background, not many. One, unmistakably, was Clive Tobin. "Are you O.K., Sharon? Nothing wrong, is there?"

"Fine. If you can't make it, just say so. I'll invent some excuse for you." She laughed. The background voices paused, but only for seconds. *Like some one else.*

"Of course I'll come. If you're sure you're up to it. I've been thinking about Sunday . . ."

He put the telephone down. It was dead.

He called, "Keep the drink till I get back!"

Tobin was probably preparing another sightseeing jaunt for tomorrow. Time meant nothing to him. He had an idea, and everybody jumped. She had sounded tense. Maybe she was still remembering Sunday, and who could blame her?

The same pink-faced subaltern was on duty when he reached the guardhouse. A schoolboy in a green beret. *Was I ever like that?*

"Is Corporal Harwood about?"

The subaltern stammered, "He's in the . . . gone to

185

the . . ." He gestured anxiously. "I'll have him piped at once!" He hurried to a telephone.

Ross calmed himself. His voice had been unnecessarily sharp. There was no point in taking it out on the kid, who had blushed after that chivalrous little gesture with Sharon's hand right here at this gate.

It was the first thing you learned. Never take it out of a subordinate who can't retaliate.

The one in question was back. "He's on his way, sir."

"I need the car. Otherwise . . ." He saw Harwood striding across the yard, his jaw moving busily to dispose of something he had been sampling in the NAAFI canteen.

"Sir?"

"I've got to meet Tobin. Sorry to disturb you again."

Harwood frowned.

"Car's out, sir. I only just heard myself."

The subaltern cut in, flushing, "It was Major Fisher, sir. In a big hurry . . . thought the car was free for the remainder of the day."

Harwood retorted as sharply as he dared, "It's all in orders, sir. The car is on stand-by until otherwise stated."

"I *know*." He looked at Ross, and shrugged helplessly. "Major Fisher's going on leave tomorrow, sir. He was only just told. He wanted to get something before the shops closed. I'm sorry, sir."

Ross touched his arm. "Something for his wife, I expect." He smiled. "Major Fisher *is* in command here, right?" He could feel the tension draining away. *For them. And for me.*

Harwood said, "I'll sign for another car, sir. Bit of an old banger, but I'll get you there."

He strode away, untroubled now that things had been sorted out: the same man who had acted so calmly, and had used his weapon without panic or hesitation.

It was certainly an old banger in appearance, but it started easily enough, and they were soon on their way, the barbed-wire barriers closing behind them, and Harwood confiding that the car was normally used for carrying officers' baggage or collecting films for the marines' cinema. Ross watched the evening sky above the passing houses, deep gold now, and cloudless. There were a few people on the streets, but little traffic. Harwood seemed quite at ease, and chatted about Londonderry and Belfast as he drove at a steady pace, one hand resting on his knee. He had served in Northern Ireland for almost a year and would be returning to Plymouth when his time was up. With luck, he would be promoted to sergeant when that happened.

Ross asked him about his service in the province.

He answered without hesitation. "A few nasty patches, sir. But on the whole, more laughs than tears."

It would make a good memorial, he thought.

Harwood was saying, "Might even be gettin' hitched if I get my tapes."

He put his free hand on the wheel, and added, "Spoke too soon, sir." So quietly said. It could have been a cat running across the road in front of the car. "Trouble of some sort." He slid his arm over the back of his seat and Ross saw the gleam of metal as he dragged his rifle beside him.

Blue police lights flashing above a diversion sign, a few uniformed figures standing around, a screen of some kind like part of a tent. Some cars parked beyond the barricade.

Harwood said, "I know another way to the hotel. Once we get the all clear . . ." He opened the window as two constables walked up to the car.

One peered at the docket behind the windscreen; the other looked at Ross's uniform and rank.

"Been a shootin', sir. We're waitin' for the forensic boys

to arrive. My lads will pass you through. No need to delay you."

They began to move forward again. In the meantime it seemed to have become darker, the near side of the street in deep shadow.

The car stopped, not with a jerk, but almost as if Harwood had been prepared for it.

More police immediately moved toward them.

"Drive on! There's nothing you can do!"

Harwood remained motionless.

"It's our car, sir."

Ross could see it in the failing light. Shattered windows, one door hanging open, the side pockmarked with holes, naked steel through the khaki paint. The corpse was slumped half in and half out of the front seat. As if he had been about to park or drive away.

Not just a few shots, but a volley. There was blood everywhere, like black paint in the shadows. Point-blank range.

A police torch played across some fragments of broken glass in the road, where it must have fallen when the door swung open. And Ross could smell it. Unreal, brutal. Perfume. Fisher's present for his wife who was in hospital, waiting for him.

The right car. The wrong victim.

"Drive on, Dick."

It would have been me.

CHAPTER ELEVEN

The boatshed was huge, like an aircraft hangar, and covered land and water in equal proportions. There were ramps and slipways for some of the larger craft, with tackles dangling from overhead rails. The screech of somebody using a high-speed drill was deafening.

Ross Blackwood watched some marines clambering into a grey-painted launch, a sergeant barking out instructions as it was secured alongside a jetty. Two police boats lay nearby, swaying in the shallows as another vessel surged past. He glanced toward the entrance, a rectangle of sunlight, and saw Corporal Harwood standing beside the Land Rover, wiping the windscreen with a leather, perhaps to pass the time, or to take his mind off the previous vehicle, the car nobody mentioned. As if it had never happened.

There were plenty of smaller boats either propped up on the land, or bobbing together on the water. Sailing dinghies, too, used by local service clubs, or possibly owned by people stationed here. Clive Tobin and his little team were down by the main jetty, although it was difficult to imagine what he was finding to film or describe in yet another recording.

Tobin had mentioned the shooting only briefly, and asked him if he had known Major Fisher well. The same Corps, the same rank. Beyond that . . . Even the facts were scanty. A witness had told the police that a youth on a motorcycle had pulled up beside Fisher's car and fired some sort of automatic pistol at point-blank range as Fisher had been about to step into the road. To pick up a newspaper from a nearby stand, another had suggested. A careless moment, his mind no doubt occupied with details of the next day, going home to see his wife.

Ross clenched his fist inside his pocket. You often thought about yourself, what you would do if this or that happened. You never thought about what it would do to others.

He had received a direct order to stand by and supervise Tobin's security, and assist the adjutant until Fisher's replacement arrived. It made him feel more helpless than ever.

Like the night when it had happened, when they had seen the car riddled with bullets, the blood and the perfume. He had called the hotel and to his surprise had been put through directly to Tobin.

I understand, old chap. Matter of duty, eh? I'll call you tomorrow.

He had had the strange feeling that Tobin already knew what had happened. Accepted it. His world. His life.

He heard footsteps, and Harwood speaking to some one. Somehow he knew it was Sharon.

He turned and saw her walking down the concrete slope from the entrance. A pale windcheater and matching slacks, a green scarf tied over her hair, making a patch of colour.

"I was told you were down here." She joined him and looked at the marines who were still working on their boat. She had her hands in her pockets, and kept them there. Very erect, tense, one lock of hair rebelliously curling beneath the headscarf. "Is Clive *still* at it? I see I'll have to drag him

190

away again." It was without scorn or bitterness. "I sometimes wonder where he gets his energy." Then she faced him, and the composure was a lie. "Are you all right, Ross?" She hurried on, as if she expected him to interrupt. "I've been so worried, ever since I heard . . . I tried to ring you, but nobody wanted to tell me anything." She turned her head as the marines laughed at some unheard joke. It seemed to give her time. "I saw the pictures of the car. *Your* car. It made me realize something. That you can't always be on the outside, an onlooker. It's not just something you see on the television, and switch off when it becomes too cruel . . . too close."

He reached out to hold her arm but she dragged it away.

"It could have been you." She gestured at the men in the launch. "Or any of them."

He took her arm, and this time she did not resist. "It shouldn't happen, but it does. That's why we're here, for what it's worth." He slipped his arm through hers. "Walk with me. Just us. Just two people."

They moved along the jetty, their reflections following on the oily water.

She said, "The one who was killed." He heard the hesitation. "He was at the market that day, wasn't he?"

"Yes." He felt her turn to look at him. "I never really got to know him well, beyond the line of duty. That's probably the best thing about it."

"It's *not* the best thing. He was married. Clive told me." She had pulled one hand out of her pocket and was gripping his now, like that moment in the market, the frightened children and Harwood with his rifle. And Fisher.

He said, "You and Clive must be pretty close . . ." He got no further.

"Close? Not in that way. He's been like an anchor for me, a lifeline, but the only real love of his life is Clive

191

Tobin." She said it without malice. "When Larry was killed he saved my sanity."

Larry. The first time she had mentioned his name. Like an intrusion, a betrayal.

He heard voices, Tobin's easy laugh, and felt her fingers tighten around his wrist.

She said, "He hasn't told me yet." Again the hesitation. Uncertainty. "But I think we're going back to London." Her hand was still, and then, as if unconsciously, it moved a little on his skin. "Probably soon. If that happens, what will *you* do?"

It was like a door slamming in his face. What had he expected? But the moments remained fixed in his mind, vignettes caught in time. The room full of uniforms. Speeches. Handshakes. Dabbing champagne from her arm. This arm . . .

"Back to general duty, I guess. Maybe the Far East. Listen . . . I want to see you again. To belong . . ." He broke off. "I'm not doing very well, am I?"

"You hardly know me."

"I want to."

She looked along the jetty, one of the cameraman's lights reflecting like a pinpoint in her eyes. Somewhere a voice of authority was shouting orders, boots stamping, like another world. But it was not another world.

She looked at him in that unflinching, direct way.

"Suppose . . ."

"There will always be *that* word, Sharon."

She moved to the edge of the jetty and said nothing.

Ross saw the reflected glow of a cigarette in the water and guessed Harwood was waiting by the Land Rover. Watching them, maybe thinking of his own girl, whom he intended to marry when he got the three 'tapes' on his sleeve. This would make a good yarn in the NAAFI . . .

He knew it would not go that far.

He felt a new sense of urgency, something beyond his control; nor did he want to control it. There had been too much of that.

"Don't just leave, Sharon, not without telling me. There's so much I want to say, to share with you."

"Have you got another handkerchief, Ross?" When he took it out, she almost snatched it from his hand, and held it to her eyes. "Now look what you've done." But a shadow of the smile remained. "I will tell you, as soon as I hear something. How could I just walk away?"

He heard Harwood call, "He's on the jetty, chum!"

Loud enough to let him know he was about to be needed, and to warn him. He had heard Tobin too, coming this way, with an edge in his voice as he called after one of his team.

Her eyes moved to the marine as he stamped to attention and saluted, a message pad at the ready. Ross's world . . .

Ross folded the paper, and thought he heard Harwood slam the Land Rover's door.

She asked, "What is it?" Chin lifted slightly. Prepared.

"There's a bit of a flap on. I'll have an escort to take you and Clive back to the hotel. I'll ring when I know something."

"What's all this about 'the hotel'?" Tobin was climbing up some steps to join them. "Who says we're going back there?"

"I do. You've finished here, anyway."

Tobin nodded slowly. "If you say so, *Major* Blackwood." Then, "I wish I had you on camera right now, as you really are. The professional fighting man behind the quiet formality. I wondered how soon it would appear." He swung on his heel and shouted, "Show's over, lads! Mount up!"

He paused to kick a stone into the water below the jetty.

193

"I just hope you don't regret this. Either of you."

Then he walked toward the sunlight, pausing just long enough to speak with a workman unloading paint cans from a barrow. It was timed, like part of a script. Or perhaps Ross was seeing the real person for the first time.

He said, "I didn't want it like this. With you, of all people." He saw her move, felt her hand on his arm, turning him toward the water, her voice quite calm, steady.

"Remember? 'Walk with me. Just two people.'"

She faced him again, and pulled his hands to her waist, pressing them against her. "Hold me, Ross." The handkerchief fell to the ground, unheeded. "Take care. For both of us." The smile would not come. "Go now, Ross. Don't look back."

She kissed him quickly. A touch of skin, her hair, a last contact.

He saw Harwood climb down beside the Land Rover, one glove half pulled on to his hand, as if he were unwilling to move. To break into something. It seemed to take forever to reach him. The way back . . .

He was leaving her. It was all in his mind. It had never even begun.

Harwood said tentatively, "Back to H.Q., sir?"

"The adjutant's office."

He gripped the door and turned around to stare back at the jetty.

A few marines were still working in or near the boats, and the same sergeant was busy with a mobile telephone. The big boatshed could have been empty but for the two of them.

She had not moved, and was looking along the jetty directly at him. Waiting. Knowing.

Then, very slowly, she lifted one hand and, he thought, touched her heart, and held the hand to her mouth, as if blowing him a kiss. Even when she was gone, and the jetty deserted again, she was still there.

He spoke her name aloud, or thought he did.

It was enough.

A sergeant opened the office door for him. "The adjutant knows you're here, sir. He'll be along directly."

Ross thanked him, but did not know him by name, and the fact made him feel still more like an intruder.

He heard the door close behind him; he could guess what most of them were thinking. He walked across the polished floor; even that was different. How could a place have changed so much?

This office had been the head teacher's room, or maybe the school secretary's. Beyond the shuttered windows there should have been children's voices, or the whistles of authority. Now all he could hear was an occasional shouted command, and the stamp of a squad drilling.

He paused by the desk, and, after a moment, touched it. It had been cleaned and dusted, the drawers emptied except for a message tray. Two framed photographs remained: a young woman in a flowered dress, smiling and waving on a beach somewhere. The other was of a small girl in some sort of uniform, a Brownie, he thought. A paper knife with an initialled handle, and a box of pills. The ordinary detritus of a man's life: it was little enough to mark his death.

He sat in the desk chair and looked at the book shelves, empty but for a few military volumes. He had been in this situation before. It had never failed to move or unsettle him.

Fisher's successor was already listed. He had been serving in Germany, and was probably on his way. But you were not supposed to notice, or to care. You were above those negative emotions.

He rubbed his eyes, and tried to put his mind in order.

Hard to believe that only an hour had passed since he had been driven from the boatshed, had seen her touch her heart and then blow him a kiss. A girl he scarcely knew, would never know, so where could it lead?

The door opened cautiously and the same sergeant came into the office, his boots loud on the bare boards.

"Brought you some char, sir. Pity it's not something stronger."

He saw the question in Ross's eyes and said, "Salter, sir. I was with you a couple of years ago, in Norway."

It was coming back to him. "You were a corporal then. Captain Marsh's unit."

"Right, sir." He clattered a spoon on the saucer. "The adjutant is here, sir."

He had only encountered him a few times since he had arrived in Ulster. Captain David Seabrook, as he knew from experience, would have been Fisher's strong right hand, in regular consultation on all aspects of the company routine from training to discipline, with a ready eye for those due or suitable for promotion. Or a good kick up the backside, as one N.C.O. had remarked.

In his late twenties, with a keen, alert face which made him appear younger, Seabrook was the sort of Royal Marine who would always manage to look like a recruiting poster, smartly turned out even in combat rig and smeared with camouflage.

He stood directly opposite the desk, leaning slightly forward as if ready to hurry away on another pressing mission. He had a quizzical smile, which Ross had noticed before when he was listening to some subordinate, as if his mind was occupied elsewhere.

Ross stood up and they shook hands across the empty desk. Even the message tray with the framed photographs had vanished. The sergeant who had once served with him in Norway, learning to ski with the professionals, had performed some sleight-of-hand in removing it.

Seabrook said, "Sorry to drag you back like this, sir. It was top secret. No ifs or buts."

Ross sat down again and saw the keen eyes flick to the chair for a split second. Thinking, perhaps, that he would be sitting here, acting in command until Fisher's replacement arrived. Or even promoted to acting-major ahead of his time. The next step; the sort of thing that happened to others. *It happened to me.*

"You did the right thing. Clive Tobin and his team will be finished here soon. But security is paramount."

Seabrook said, "It seems that another active group has been reported here in Derry, or moving this way. We're doing all we can – even Brigade accepts that. I don't see what else we can do without more information."

Ross heard a gust of laughter from outside the building, quelled immediately by one of the N.C.O.s. Like the boatshed this morning, the marines with the launch. Joking with each other, not a care in the world. *Just roll on my time and let's get back home.* Until the next crisis. He could hear her voice. *It could have been you.* She had pointed to those same marines. *Or any of them.*

"Never ease up, David." He saw him blink, perhaps at the use of his name. "We are dealing with a skilled and dedicated enemy. Many of them truly believe in their cause. To think otherwise is asking for disaster. It will fall to others to create a solution fair and acceptable to all sides." He shrugged. "Until that blissful day, it is up to our people here. No compromise." Like a warning. *Don't look back.* But he could remember the other major, Houston. Any one on the other end of a gun was the enemy, pure and simple.

He saw Seabrook's right hand curl into a fist, pressed against the seam of his trousers. Resentment?

"If any one has been criticizing me, sir, I think I have a right to know." No anger, no change of expression.

Ross leaned back in the chair.

"I went to the boatshed this morning, as instructed."

"I know, sir. I sent word ahead."

"Neither I nor my driver was challenged or asked for any identification. Likewise, when we left."

"I told the messenger . . ."

Ross shook his head. "He was not questioned, either." He slapped his hand on the desk. "I *know* they all probably know each other. Familiarity, maybe? Like the car taken by Major Fisher the night he was killed. Somebody knew. And he paid for it."

He was on his feet, although he did not recall standing up. "The lads can think what they like. *New broom throwing his weight around* . . . I know. I've been there. But too many have been killed or crippled because of apathy. So let's do it." He paused. "And let's do it together, right?"

He thought of the car again. Harwood had told him he always took a different route whenever possible.

Seabrook said, "I'll pass the word, sir. I have a few ideas of my own, too."

"Good." The first bridge. "I'll be seeing the intelligence people this evening."

Seabrook nodded. "Eight bells, sir."

"I'd like you to come with me, all right?"

"Anything I can do, sir . . ." He looked away; his fist was still pressed against his leg.

A solitary telephone shattered the stillness.

Seabrook snatched it up without hesitation. The desk and the telephone which might have been his own immediate step to promotion.

"Yes?"

He turned on his heels, like a dancer. "Very well. Then do it." He put down the phone and said, "Security have just reported an explosion. A small device, it seems. The Bomb Squad are dealing." He faced him, very composed, Ross thought afterwards. "At the boatshed, sir."

"Where, exactly?" Quietly said, but it was as if he had yelled it at the top of his voice.

This time Seabrook did reveal surprise.

"The second ramp, sir."

Ross strode past him to force open the window. A group of marines were already gathered around the guardroom entrance. They had heard. It was always like that; security could do nothing about it. The 'family'.

But all he could see was the jetty, and the long ramp where they had been working on the launch. Where Tobin and his crew had been shooting. And where she had been standing as she had waved to him.

"Any one injured?"

Seabrook was still gazing at him, as if he were a stranger.

"A workman, sir. Civilian. Still alive, I think."

"Find out. Then get a car. We're going down there."

He half listened to Seabrook's voice behind him, clipped, impersonal, and saw a van parked by the guard-room, the engine ticking over as armed marines climbed into it. Foot patrols on their way to some local checkpoint. He heard the security barrier being hauled aside. Routine. You could probably set your watch by it.

He felt the window; the glass was warm, although no sun was visible. He saw a couple of marines waving to the departing van. *See you later, chum.* No wonder young, untried recruits found it impossible to accept this kind of duty. Surrounded by ordinary, law-abiding people, trying to make their various ways in life. Who watched the same sporting events on television and avoided political bombast. And then, without warning . . . He snapped the window shut and heard Seabrook say, "Transport ready, sir."

Ross glanced around the office. They were trained and instructed in the recognition of an enemy. Usually in puffs of smoke as missiles found their mark, or dropped from hovering helicopters. The vague outline in a telescopic sight, or suddenly taking human form and flesh, when you could almost feel his breath. But always the enemy.

Outside the office he saw the tray lying on top of a packing case, the two framed photographs waiting to be sent back to England with the other remains of Fisher's life. The smiling face. Her name was June, he remembered. The perfume on the road.

Perhaps Seabrook was right. War in any guise should never become personal.

At another window some two miles from the Royal Marines' temporary headquarters, Sharon Warwick was watching two of the hotel staff loading waste into a truck. From the sound of it, it consisted mostly of empty bottles. It was a square, inner courtyard, and on the far side some of the rooms, the larger ones, were partly shielded by balconies. Plants at intervals broke up the severity of the building, 'Fort Amazon' as it was jokingly called by both staff and guests.

Security was everywhere and obvious, and she wondered what ordinary people travelling on business thought about it. Surely nobody in his right mind would book into the Hotel Amazon for pleasure.

She turned and looked around the room. Clean, functional, and dull. There was a telephone, but it took time and patience to call any one.

She walked across the room and pressed her forehead

against the other window. She could see part of the street, a man selling flowers at a tiny stall. He had doubtless been vetted, unless he was one of the protectors.

Don't keep going over it.

Clive had called her, and told her about the explosion at the same gaunt boatshed where she had been with Ross. She formed his name with her lips, giving herself time, teasing herself for her foolishness. How could it happen? Where could she see any future? She was thirty-two years old, with a good job; you could hardly call it a profession. Why throw it all away?

She thought of Clive's voice on the telephone. Level, concerned, but nothing over the top. A touch of mystery; that was Clive all over. She still did not know when to take him completely seriously, except when he was talking about his work. To Clive Tobin the celebrity, the work was everything.

She had no need to look at her watch. Six hours had passed since she had watched him drive away with the stocky marine, the corporal, whose eyes missed very little.

A 'device', was the euphemism for it. She sat on the big double bed. A bomb, large or small, casual or intentional. *And we were there.* How did Clive really feel about it, she wondered. He had seen danger at close hand a good many times, in France during some industrial upheaval, the Far East, and more recently in the U.S.A., when some madman had taken a shot at him during the course of a live interview. And later in the Middle East, Israel, then Palestine, where Larry's helicopter had crashed. Brought down deliberately . . . She turned her wrist and looked at the watch, his last gift to her. She could remember her first assignments after his death. She had taken his photograph with her, everywhere she had gone. A comfort, but no protection against those with more intimate association in mind. She thought of the flat in Chelsea, where she had gone deliberately to meet Ross before this tour had begun. Another coincidence. The flat was often used by Sue Blackwood, Ross's sister. She twisted the watch around her wrist. And she worked for the infamous Howard Ford, of *Focus* and other interests. She pictured the flat again, the misty shapes of the power station chimneys across the Thames. One session there with Howard Ford had been sufficient. As Clive had later remarked, a man with more hands than scruples.

Sue Blackwood would get nothing but trouble if she was having an affair with him. She turned the watch to her inner wrist again. So brief a memory of marriage. A dream and a fantasy, but always a protection. *More hands than scruples.* What some people thought about her relationship with Clive. Gripping her arm, kissing her in public. But he respected her, just as she respected him, the other Clive Tobin who walked alone.

What was Ross doing now? Right now? Talking with his fellow marines, perhaps? She imagined him down at the boatshed, inspecting the situation, damage, pain, injury or worse. He never seemed to reveal any doubt, any fear.

She tried to recall Clive's plans for this evening. She had made a list. She needed to.

Suppose . . . And Ross's response. *There will always be that word.*

In that scruffy flat in Chelsea, the ironing board, his uniform hanging on a door. Suppose . . . She looked around the room again. Two pictures on the walls, sailing boats and a sunny beach. A notice telling her what to do in case of fire. She pressed her hand on the bed. Maybe she felt things differently after all these months. Larry would always be there, no matter what. But even now . . . She started as the telephone buzzed. Clive had probably changed his mind.

Thought of another guest to invite, or something else for the menu.

She did not know what she said, or how it sounded. Maybe because she had been thinking about him at that very moment. As if he had been reading her thoughts.

"I'm glad I caught you, Sharon. Reminded me of what you said when we got here. It bloody well is like Fort Knox!"

She heard the inflection in his voice, like a smile; she had first noticed it when . . . She pressed the receiver under her hair. There could be some one tapping the line right now.

"Just wanted to put your mind at rest. Not to worry. I'm going to try and see you tomorrow. I'm not sure yet." He broke off, then, "I just wanted to hear you. Make sure."

She said quietly, "You *will* be careful, Ross." There was a click on the line. "I want to see you, soon if you can make it." She touched her breast. Like this morning. She imagined she could feel her heart beating, and wanted to laugh. Or cry.

Somewhere far away she heard the shrill sirens, some unknown emergency. Police, fire, ambulance: normal enough in a sane world. But to hear it now was like being gripped by something beyond control. Other people endured it, because they had no alternative. But it was always there. She had been sitting in the minibus with Clive on their way to another location, and had stopped at some traffic lights. She had heard music, and had seen a band of uniformed musicians sitting on stools, playing popular hits to entertain the locals. She had watched the feet tapping, people stopping to listen and smile. It could have been anywhere. The musicians were either soldiers or Royal Marines, she could not be sure; it had been such a brief interlude. But she could remember the tune, being pounded out in true military fashion. "Jesus Christ, Superstar".

"Are you there, Sharon?"

She made an attempt to steady her voice. All she could remember now was that each of the musicians had been wearing a flak jacket. Like a warning. The reality.

She pressed the phone harder against her ear, until it hurt. She could hear his breathing. Feel his hands around her waist, where she had put them.

"Hold me, Ross." She heard him say something, and repeated, "Hold me."

She did not recall putting down the phone.

She looked around the dreary room again, almost expecting a rebuff.

Aloud she said, "I want you."

Suppose was silent.

CHAPTER TWELVE

Ross felt a hand on his arm, and tensed as the voice murmured, *"Wait."* A pause; he must have been no more than a foot away, but he was invisible. Not even a shadow. "We wait for the all clear."

Another voice said, "For Christ's sake!"

It was midnight, or a little later. Ross waited for his mind and body to relax. Kill the tension. At the intelligence briefing it had looked straightforward enough. Two streets being demolished to make way for new shops and a bus garage. A face-lift, much needed in this part of Londonderry. Near the river. You could feel it. Smell it. He shivered despite the combat jacket and sweater beneath. He knew the reason. Not the hour, or the dampness of the river.

There was no point in asking questions or moaning about it. The guide was hand-picked, an undercover policeman who knew the ground, the whole area, like the back of his hand.

He thought of his other companion, Lieutenant Peter Hamlyn, a commando from Special Operations. They had met for the first time at the briefing. He shifted his shoulders beneath the jacket and the weight of his holster. Maps, street plans, photographs. And names. It was as important as that.

Hamlyn was no newcomer. Probably in his late twenties,

solid and broad-shouldered, so that at first glance he appeared shorter than he really was. Up from the ranks, tough and confident. He and his party had arrived two days earlier, after a stopover in Belfast. *Acting on information received.* The decision had been made.

They had driven part of the way, then changed to an unmarked van that stank of fresh paint. There had been just that fleeting, timed moment, lasting only seconds, when the switch was made. Harwood had twisted round from the wheel, his hand hard, gripping Ross's. Looking back, Ross recalled that Harwood had even managed to remove his glove, which was rare for him.

"Keep your head down, sir! Fingers crossed!" Then he was gone.

After all this time, he should be used to it. He was not.

On the first part of the journey Lieutenant Hamlyn had said little, feeling his way, testing the mettle or otherwise of the man beside him, whose behaviour might determine the margin between life and death.

Like Major Fisher. Ross bit his lip. No, not like Fisher at all.

He imagined the adjutant, Seabrook, alerted, and prepared for any unforeseen complications. But he had the feeling that the eventual arrival of the new commanding officer still took precedence in Seabrook's mind. *Was I like that?*

He heard a gate being dragged open, the security fence surrounding most of the area slated for demolition and redevelopment. The sound of feet, too, colliding with fallen brickwork or ballast. In the complete stillness it was like an avalanche.

Whispers, some one stifling a cough, and the smell of tobacco smoke. They had arrived.

"This way. Keep close. Mind the steps." It was not just dark, he thought. It was black.

He moved forward. Funny the things that crossed your mind at times like these. Like Hamlyn's words when they had been about to leave in the Land Rover.

"At least there'll be one face you'll know. Name, too." Clearing the way. No room for friction.

It was Steve Blackwood, now a sergeant-major, a W.O.2 and explosives expert. Fate or coincidence, it was good to know he had won his own battle. One doctor had insisted that the bullet would have killed most men on impact.

He wondered what Hamlyn thought about it, if he thought at all. Two Blackwoods in one small team. But he had served long enough to know the full story; it was hard to keep a secret in this regiment.

More scattered bricks and then some scaffolding, a ladder leading nowhere, pointing at the sky.

Friday night, Saturday morning. If the facts were accurate, it would be tomorrow. Sunday, like that moment in the market when the thieves had blown the safe. And then the screams and the guns and the terrified children. And Sharon . . .

"Stop here." The scraping sound of a heavy curtain, canvas, he thought; the tiny blink of a torch. And more steps.

He felt Hamlyn close behind him.

"Are you O.K., Peter?"

Hamlyn thought about it. *First names. No bullshit.* He said softly, "I could use a pint!"

This had been a pub. He remembered hearing the details. Rooms, stairways, doors. His foot found another step. It must be the cellar. The heavy curtain was down and he heard some one fastening it, or poking it into place.

The voice said, *"Now."*

The lights were small and hand-held, but after the total darkness it was like Earls Court.

Crouching and standing, there were no more than a dozen figures here. But as he waited for his eyes to become accustomed to the light, Ross thought the old cellar was packed, shoulder to shoulder.

Like all those other times, the same feeling, almost the same faces, the tension and uncertainty melting away. Hamlyn was speaking in the same matter-of-fact voice, while the figures, now individuals under the hard light, crowded closer, eyes on Ross, who was a total stranger to most of them.

One of them strode out of the shadows, face split in a grin.

"The old firm again!"

Ross gripped him by the shoulders and shook him gently. "Steve, you old bugger! I feel better already!"

"Yeah. The bad penny will always be ready to pop up."

Everybody seemed to be talking at once. Hamlyn stood slightly apart, and Ross thought he saw him smile with relief or satisfaction.

His cousin looked much the same, he thought. The lines at the corners of his mouth were deeper, and his hair showed streaks of grey beneath the beret; hardly surprising for one who had at least twice nearly died in combat. In two or three years, he would be forty. In the Corps they said that after that it was time to roll over, or be promoted.

Ross said, "Sit down if you can find a place." He looked around, taking his time, trying to see each face and assess the man behind it. He could see the remains of the pub cellar. Circular stains on the walls where barrels had been hoisted on racks for the beer to settle before being tapped, or connected to the bars on the next floor; a few crushed

Guinness tins. Some sort of toilet, too; the door was hanging open and he could see the scribbled graffiti even from where he was standing. Like pubs everywhere. *It's useless standing on this seat/ 'Cause Chatham crabs jump sixteen feet!* Or the ubiquitous *You would think by all this wit/ that Shakespeare once came here to shit.*

He cleared his throat. A handful of marines, all volunteers. Trained, chased, and tested to the hilt. And for what? Others made the decisions. But they were left to carry out the actual deeds, whatever the final outcome.

Like all those who had gone over the top in Flanders in that other war, or the individual sniper in Burma and Malaysia crouching in some rice paddy or jungle; choice did not enter into it.

"You've all seen the local map and sketch-plan?" Some nodded; a couple smiled. Wondering perhaps about the man, the officer, in whose hands they were placing their lives. Most of them would know the surname, but he had seen the surprise when he and Steve had hugged each other. They might bear the same name, but rank was usually an unbreachable barrier in the Corps.

"Information tells us that explosives will be brought ashore from the river early Sunday morning. Mines, detonators, and very likely some weapons, mortars and that type of thing. Not a big cargo," he looked around at the intent faces, "but deadly in the wrong hands."

He had said enough. These men had trained, lived and worked together long enough to act as a team or as individuals. No ranks or badges.

"Sunday or not, there may be civilians in the area." He touched his own holster. "They are not the enemy."

Hamlyn took over, calling out a few names, adding a detail here and there about vantage points and concealment. He saw Steve Blackwood watching him, perhaps remembering that other time when a young officer had overcome his fear to take the lead, and die.

Now, all they had to do was wait.

Steve Blackwood switched off the battery-powered razor and rubbed his hand around his chin. It would never match a proper blade and hot water, but it was better than starting the day like a scruff. *Starting the day.* He did not need to peer at his watch. It was four in the morning. He eased his legs to take away the stiffness, and put his mind in order.

Saturday had been endless, taking turns on watch, peering through the camouflaged hides, keeping out of sight in case somebody was poking around, or walking his dog, being suspicious of everything. He listened to rain dripping from one of the canvas awnings. It had poured for most of the previous day, and much of the night. Rain was the best policeman, they said. They could have it.

When people saw the marines on parade or walking in the street, they probably thought that the green beret went with the uniform. He moved again to ease the pain in his back: the reminder. If you wore the green beret, you had bloody well earned it.

It was still quiet in the pub cellar, and he wondered if there was any tea left in the thermos flasks. His mouth was dry; too many cigarettes, although he had tried to ration them.

He heard somebody move, the sound of metal, a voice lowered to a whisper. Two of them chatting to pass the time.

Waiting . . . He had known this same mixture of impatience and uncertainty so many times that he had lost count.

But you could never show it. The sergeant-major, a

warrant officer as in all three services, stood firmly between the brass and the other ranks. Looking back, he was surprised that he had become used to his promotion so quickly. Some of his friends in the sergeants' mess had made a point of shouting, "Sir!" just to catch him out. It seemed a long time ago.

Now there was another sound. The *snip*, *snip*, *snip* of somebody checking the cocking lever on his semi-automatic rifle. He did not need to; it had already been tested. Just to make certain . . . That must be Jock Marsh, a crack shot. He had even competed for the Blackwood Trophy. He felt his mouth crease in a smile. You could never get away from that name in the Corps.

He turned his thoughts back to the job at hand. Why he and the others were in this partially demolished pub, at the back of nowhere. Maybe the rain had put paid to the operation. Or some informer had talked too loudly.

The plans, the photographs, might be hot air. It happened often enough.

He heard some one flushing the toilet; it was about the only thing that still worked here, but not for much longer, by the look and stench of it.

And after this? Another year, two at the most, and he would be out of the Corps. On the beach. He was lucky to have made it this far. But for his service, and the coveted D.C.M., what might he have done? And now there was Mary. During that last explosives course at Portland he had met her, working in a chemist's shop in Weymouth. He had been in uniform and they had started to talk. Her husband had been a Royal, but had deserted her for another woman. It was surprising that she had even wanted to speak to another of the Globe and Laurel mob.

He had not told her about his work with explosives.
But I will. Next time I see her.

"Want some char, sir?" A hunched shape came out of the shadows.

He took the mug, lukewarm.

"Magic," he said, and then, "Time, is it?"

The marine slithered down beside down. "Be light soon." His teeth were white in the gloom, and faintly chattering. "Glad to be doin' somethin'."

Twenty-one years old. What kind of future could he expect? *Cut, cut, cut,* all the bloody politicians could think about. If there was another war, who would carry the can?

He pushed it to the back of his mind. Today was important. He thought about the photographs, the mug shots they had all been shown. Hamlyn had made sure that everybody got a good description, too. Barry Fallon from Sligo. An old hand at the game, who had done time in England, but got off with a short sentence on some technical point in the defence. It had still been a murder, whatever they said. And Jack McGee from Armagh, who had begun life right here in Derry.

But how good was the information?

He said, "I'd better call the Major." He thought, *not that he'll need it.*

He recalled their meeting in this stinking cellar. No pretence, no airs and graces. Probably surprised the hell out of some of the others. Especially the ones who knew it all.

He had often wondered how Ross Blackwood had felt about the loss of the old house, all because of some bloody new motorway that had to go through, demolishing history. He thought of the solicitor's letter, the money which had been sent to him, without strings; his rightful share, it had been explained. Not the lawyers' doing, he was sure of that, but the man's, the officer who had become his friend, and who had raised the roof until his medal had come through. Not a fortune, but if Mary agreed to marry him they would not have to exist on a warrant officer's pension.

He knew Ross was wide awake, watching him in the faint glow of a solitary police lamp.

"All set?"

"Yeah. It's a wonder this place isn't flooded out!"

"Have a sip of this." It was a hip flask. "Officers' perks!"

Brandy, Scotch; it went down so well he could not be sure which it had been. But he was aware of the warning. Ross was not so calm as the face he showed to others.

These same men had listened to his quiet words when he had arrived. Even the hard cases had been impressed. And the lieutenant, Hamlyn. A good enough officer from what he had seen and heard, but a man who would come down on you like a ton of bricks if you failed to measure up.

He wondered if Ross still thought about that other young lieutenant. Mister *follow-my-example*. Blondie.

Obeying orders. And dying in terror. The greatest kind of courage.

"Good stuff."

Ross was on his feet, checking his pockets, his watch, his holster and ammunition, automatically. Like the drill.

"It'll take a while to occupy positions, Steve. We'll stand-to in fifteen minutes." He half turned as the toilet cistern rattled again, and grinned. "Not before time, by the sound of it!"

Steve watched him. Hong Kong, Malaysia, Singapore. He could remember the woman in Hong Kong, older than Ross in more ways than one. The pompous husband who played golf whenever he could. *And I'm still here. The lucky one.*

The lights were coming on. Time to move, let the eyes adjust to the dawn, when it came.

213

He followed Ross out of the canvas shelter, feeling the way. Accepting it.

It was now.

Lieutenant Peter Hamlyn raised himself on his toes to peer over yet another stack of new, plastic-wrapped bricks. Everything was wet, and there were puddles like lakes in the open sites where buildings had once stood. He wore grubby white overalls over his combat rig, and his beret was wedged through his belt. Just in case there were other eyes on the move. There were two night watchmen, sealed in a little hut with the telephone. And the undercover policeman. A weekend they would all remember, no matter what happened.

He moved on, using some fallen planks to cross over another muddy pool. It was deeper than he thought, but he made himself stand still as water soaked over his boot and into his sock. He looked at a wedge of concrete, pale in the dawn. New foundations. He pictured the map in his mind, noting distances and bearings, moved again, and saw the gleam of the river. Like a sliver of metal.

It was still cold, but the sky seemed clearer, offering a jagged horizon for the first time. Buildings, windows like empty eyes, shapeless lumps of timber and metal: a hive of activity on any working day, but now still, dead, only the river making it a lie.

He heard a soft footstep over his left shoulder. Sergeant Ken Norris, known behind his back as 'Smiler', because he very rarely did.

He had only been made up from corporal a few months ago. He was good at his work, but not an easy man to know.

He climbed carefully on to some ballast and stared toward the river. No bends here; it was almost like a canal.

And it *was* brighter, pale smudges of cloud where there

had been total darkness. He imagined his marines in their various hides, waiting and on edge, cursing the brains who had got them into this godforsaken place. Grubby, unshaven, except for the W.O.2, the other Blackwood.

He thought of the man in command of this unlikely operation. Part of the legend. Several well-known families had made their mark in the Royal Marines. Unlike himself: he was a first-generation marine. Both his parents were teachers at a local school. They had accepted his decision to enlist, but no more than that . . .

A tiny movement. He froze, his hand on steel. Ready.

But it was the last lookout. Their crack shot, Jock Marsh, from Glasgow, with an accent like a chainsaw. Narrow dark features and very bright eyes, like black stones, as he had heard one of the others comment. He was chewing gum. On parade it was entirely different. Today, he looked like something from a gangster movie.

"Quiet?"

Marsh shrugged. "Saw a police boat twenty minutes back."

"Are you sure?"

Marsh tapped his waterproof cape, where his breast pocket would be.

"Checked the number." He smiled, chewing busily. *One up on you, Jimmy!*

Hamlyn turned his cuff. His watch must have stopped, surely . . .

Marsh said, "Early bird, sir." Instantly alert, the unseen semi-automatic rifle taking shape under his stained cape.

Very quiet, but steady. *Put-put-put*, a small engine, maybe only an outboard.

There was to be a sailing regatta this morning. But not up as far as this. The police boat would have seen and checked, as a matter of course. Hamlyn calmed himself. There would

215

be a tug, and some barges. The only time they had to shift some garbage, and more building material. It was all in the brief. Nothing must interfere with the regatta. He turned his head slightly. Not close, very faint, but strangely moving. Church bells.

Marsh moved the gum to the other side of his mouth and scowled. "That's *all* we need!"

Hamlyn ignored him, watching the slow-moving boat, taking on shape and personality as it passed two overloaded barges moored nearby. No wonder they needed a tug; one of them was so filled with rubbish and debris that it might have been aground. He groped for his binoculars, which were wedged under the overalls. A quick glance at the sky, brightening slowly, the far side of the river still faceless and in darkness. Two gulls, cruising on motionless wings, no doubt searching for food. But holding the light like still-life.

He pressed against the bricks and levelled his glasses. Somebody's pride and joy, but not very beautiful. About thirty feet long, probably an old naval craft, like a cutter, sold off in their hundreds after the war. Conversions, they were termed by professional sailors. A low cabin roof, and two masts with half furled sails, a bright club burgee fluttering from the truck, a tattered ensign down aft. No headroom between decks. He focused on a solitary figure standing in the cockpit, presumably at the wheel. Bright red jersey, dark hair tied or plaited down her back. He almost smiled. Who cared about headroom with a companion like that? The smaller the better.

He heard Marsh mutter, "All right for some!"

Now there was somebody else. A man, climbing into the cockpit from the cabin. It was funny to think that this boat had probably been used for teaching seamanship to new recruits in those far-off days. Double-banked oars pulling up and down, with an instructor marching between the new boys, calling the stroke, with a few harsh words to hurry things along.

The man wore a sailing smock and was staring at the shore. Hamlyn did not move; it felt as if he was looking directly at him, which was impossible.

He was saying something and he saw the girl reach out, and the immediate change in the engine sound. The boat was turning slightly, slowing down, and the man in the blue smock was moving across the deck, holding a backstay to steady himself.

Marsh said dourly, "What's he up to? There's fu—" He checked himself. "There's nothing here!"

Hamlyn moved the glasses slightly. Another barge, half hidden by the partly demolished brickwork, filled with rubbish like the others. He remembered searching it in the darkness. It stank, too.

What was he doing? Stepping off the boat to relieve himself? The local authorities were getting very pusser about boat owners using the river instead of their cramped chemical toilets as directed.

Closer now, the boat still turning, making for the barge. He could see the girl more clearly too, leaning over slightly to gauge the distance. Her face was tanned. Used to boats. Her companion waved his arm, and he had picked up a rope fender, ready for the impact, if any.

Why else would they stop here?

"Tell the major." Blackwood would think he was round the bend. What did it matter anyway? Suppose this boat was the means to the end? But the picture would not form. He repeated, "Move it!"

He trained the glasses again. The girl was standing on something, peering across the bows. The engine had stopped, and he could see the bubbles in the water, catching

217

a light which had not been there before. Another quick glance. Still no sun, but a window was shining somewhere. It would be soon now.

The man jumped on to the barge's side deck, using the fender to take the contact, hauling a line after him to make fast. He looked back and called something. The girl did not move, or smile.

A hand on the shoulder. "Something up, Peter?" Calm. Even. No impatience or annoyance. Not like some.

"This boat alongside. What's the point?" He sounded sharper than he intended.

Ross replied, "Saw it a bit earlier. Bound for the regatta, I thought." He had trained his own glasses on the barge, but Hamlyn did not feel him move.

"He can see the boundary fence, and will know what's going on here. There's enough barbed wire to scare off the Red Army. It's their boat right enough. They can lay hands on everything without looking."

It was like hearing him thinking aloud. Hamlyn said, "They couldn't carry much of a cargo in that, sir."

Ross looked again. The girl had stepped down into the forepart of the cockpit by the cabin door. He saw her fully before she turned away again. Hamlyn was right. No room. No speed, either.

But more than that. The girl's face. She was worried. He touched Hamlyn's arm again. "Pass the word, Peter. Stand fast, but it's a go." He held his arm and added quietly, "That girl is scared out of her wits."

He saw the question in his eyes. "A try-on, just to see if it's safe to go ahead."

He heard Hamlyn move away. *Probably thinks I have too much imagination. Maybe he's right.* Pleasure craft came and went every day here. And it was regatta time. And it was Sunday.

Perhaps the plan had fallen through. Or some one had grassed, or had just been unable to keep his mouth shut. The explosives and weapons might have been smuggled to an entirely different location. There were a million *ifs* and *ors* filling his brain.

But the long-haired girl in the bright red jersey remained. He knew terror well enough to recognize it.

He tensed, and held his breath. Another man had climbed on deck and was preparing to jump across to the barge. A big, athletic figure dressed in a sort of track suit, and deck shoes. Ross levelled the glasses with extra care. He could see sunlight on the water. No time to take chances. But the face was fixed in his mind. Square, tight-mouthed. Thinning hair; not one of the faces he had studied. *But I will know it again.*

He was standing beside the man in the sailing smock, almost touching him, saying something and peering at his watch. Looking at the demolition site. *At me.*

He knew Hamlyn was coming back, the sergeant called Norris close behind him.

Afterwards he remembered that Hamlyn had his mouth open, an unspoken question hanging in mid-air. It was an explosion, somehow muffled, and far away. A sensation more than anything dangerous; you could barely feel it. He looked up and across the nearest wire fence. But the birds had heard it well enough. More gulls, slivers of white, scattered like feathers in the sunlight.

Timed to the minute. Every police car and ambulance would already be racing to the scene of the latest incident.

Hamlyn made as if to move. Ross said, "Stay!" Quietly, but it was as if he had shouted it. "It'll be soon now!"

He saw Hamlyn flinch, caught off guard by the sound. Like a champagne bottle being clumsily uncorked. Their eyes met. Or a pistol fitted with a silencer.

When they looked again, the burly figure in the track suit and deck shoes was still standing on the barge. Alone.

Hamlyn gasped, "Jesus Christ, he killed him! Just like that! Can't we . . ."

Ross kept his eyes on the barge and the boat alongside. Hamlyn was shocked, unable to accept what had happened. *That I'm doing nothing about it.* He stared at the figure on the barge, turning now, pulling out a pack of cigarettes. Unreal, as if he had imagined it. And what about the girl?

His fingers were suddenly dragging at his holster, his mind rebelling against every warning. "I'll get the bastard!" But he did not move, could not. He stared at Hamlyn's hand gripping his wrist, pressing it down, his eyes half closed in concentration or despair.

He whispered, "They're *coming*." Then he twisted round and stared fully at him. "It *must* be them!"

Ross tried to calm himself; every fibre of instinct was fighting his will.

Hamlyn said sharply, "What we're here for, sir!"

Only then did Ross hear it. Another craft approaching, faster and more powerful. A work boat of some kind, a company name and number painted along one side of the squat wheelhouse. Men too, half a dozen, maybe more below deck, some looking at the land, others crouching with grapnels. In another world Ross could hear sirens, but no louder than the church bells. *Timed to the minute.* It seemed to mock him.

He attempted to sharpen his senses, shut out everything else. The marines were in position. It was too late to change anything. If they slipped up now, they would lose everything. And a man had been murdered. Butchered.

There were two crates, wrapped in canvas with rope handles at regular intervals so they could be easily carried. Like coffins. Not heavy; the explosives were smaller and lighter than most. His mind fought against it: the details and the diagrams, the new menace from a reputable arms dealer. Two of the men were carrying long cases like golf bags. Mortars, which had already made their mark against police stations and other soft targets.

He glanced at Hamlyn, who must have been thinking the same. Patriots or terrorists, others were making money from them, no matter who died as a result.

The 'coffins' were on the barge. A few steps to the shore, and then the final journey past the wire barriers. Transport? More armed men waiting for the next, and last, signal?

Ross stood up and jumped on to the bricks, the sun suddenly in his eyes like the lights in the beer cellar. For an instant nobody moved or spoke. *Frozen.* As if he was completely alone.

Then Steve's voice, harshly, on the loud-hailer most of them had thought would never be used.

"Stand still! Stay exactly where you are! We are the Royal Marines!"

He heard the one called Marsh, somewhere to his left, mutter, "Go on, make my day!"

Figures dashed past and down the slope toward the water, sun on the stubbled faces, the green berets, the glint of weapons.

Somebody must have made a run for it. There was a scuffle, and the thud of a heavy blow. A man sprawled into the shallows, gasping, perhaps only just realizing what had happened. A marine walked toward him. Ready. And maybe, despite all the training, eager to fire.

More shouts, glass breaking, something splashing in the water alongside. A gun, an identity, who would care?

Ross seized the wire guardrail and leaped on to the boat which had initiated the action. It was pale green in the strengthening light, the hull showing the scars and knocks of a long life. He peered into the cabin where a man sat, back against a locker, hands on his head as he stared at the marine who had just searched him, the muzzle of an automatic inches from his mouth.

He did not look at Ross, but said, "The girl's all right, sir. She's spewing up in the heads right now." He was watching his prisoner. "She keeps asking about her friend."

Ross thought of the clenched fist he had seen protruding from the muck and rubbish in the barge. Like a last plea, or a curse.

"You're doing fine, Burgess. Keep it up." He saw the question still on the young marine's face and was glad he had remembered his name. "If this one tries anything, let him have it!"

Voices called to one another, a hand reached out here and there to slap a friend in passing. More than any words. Hamlyn was shouting something, wiping his face with the back of his wrist. Some one else called, "One of 'em in the wheelhouse, sir!" and there were insults or obscenities, too muffled to distinguish.

Ross climbed on to the other boat. One of the canvas coffins was still there, and he saw Steve peering across at him, giving him a thumbs-up.

No more resistance. Nothing. Just empty faces staring at the marines and their trained weapons. All it needed . . .

The wheelhouse was rough and ready, clothing and personal gear lying everywhere. The boat had been stolen, too. Another story.

"Watch out!"

He swung round, aware only of the figure beside some hanging oilskins. Where he must have been hiding when the loud-hailer shattered the silence.

Not a face, but a photograph. It made no sense.

Movement, too, and the sound of breaking glass, and maybe a shot.

The sun had gone. And he was falling. Like a tunnel, darker and darker.

Then nothing.

CHAPTER THIRTEEN

He sat quite still, deliberately so, his palms pressed on the arms of the chair, his feet flat on the floor, his heartbeat and his breathing regular.

It will take time. How often had he heard that? Or was that all part of the unreality?

He gazed across the room, moving his head without pain. If he closed his eyes it would all come back. The hands, groping, tapping, squeezing. *It will take time.*

Hours, weeks, yet sometimes it seemed like yesterday. Now. Other memories. White jackets, patient and sometimes anxious voices. More pain, then sliding away. Like swimming underwater. Or dying.

Vague memories of being driven somewhere, in a vehicle so well sprung that it was like being in a boat of some kind. Ironic, that . . . An ambulance. Another hospital. More pain. Somehow trying to hold on. Keep a grip. *It will take time.*

Then the first steps, with an orderly holding his arm. A wild sense of triumph after crossing this room unaided.

Visitors too, vague and unrecognizable. When he had felt only their pity. Uniforms and voices; he should have known them.

He turned his head carefully and looked at the other wall. A uniform hung from a rack, neatly arranged, a green beret on the top. It would be a new one. The other one, once they had cut him out of it, must have been a bit of a mess.

He pressed his back against the chair. He could face it. Accept it. This was now. The smart Lovat uniform was not an illusion. Major Ross Blackwood was here.

He was surprised that he could remain so calm. It was real. The rest was the nightmare.

He saw the flowers on a table. Sharon had brought them whenever she came to visit him. And all those other times when she had been prevented from seeing him, even from holding his hand. And on that first clear visit, which had seemed like a reunion in its quiet intensity. Sometimes he had fallen asleep, fatigue, drugs, he was never certain of anything, except of the strength she had given him.

Even now, after his steady improvement, it was impossible to accept the tricks his mind had played on him. From despair to absurdity. Like the moment when he had realized that the figure at the bedside was his mother, Joanna. Holding his hand, very still. All he had been able to grasp was that she had somehow reached him in an instant, as if by crossing the road from Hawks Hill. And another time, when he had since learned his condition had been critical, she had been beside him again, one hand on his face, exactly like the day when he had been knocked off his new bicycle on his way to school. He had been wanting to explain that it was an accident, nobody's fault, so that she would not worry about it. She had been crying then, too.

He had seen her sitting with Sharon. Were they friends now, or rivals? Joanna had stayed in a hotel near the hospital. Now she was back in her house beside the stables. She must have dreaded it. Reminded all the time of her husband's death, and the brutal formality of the telegram. *It is with deep regret that I have to inform you . . .*

Even his sister had managed to get in touch with him by

telephone from some obscure location in Scotland where she had been covering a story for *Focus*. She was still with Howard Ford. Perhaps for his own reasons, Ford had kept the news of her brother's confrontation with death from her until the crisis had passed.

Perhaps. Maybe. Like a puzzle which might never be solved.

He still wondered how Sharon had managed to remain in Londonderry at such short notice. She had been about to leave for London when the world had exploded.

And later, the official visits. Major Fisher's successor, a grave-eyed officer who kept his conversation to a minimum. Captain Seabrook, alert and cheerful; 'relieved' might have been a better description. And Corporal Harwood, another firm handshake which he remembered so well from that last time he had seen him.

He looked at the uniform again. Today, this afternoon, he would put it on, and resume his identity. He allowed his mind to explore it, confront it. He had nearly died. There were times when he had believed he *was* dead. Blurred faces, the soundless explosion. The pain. He had pieced it together deliberately, sharpening the edges, pushing the shadows aside, like those last moments in the pub cellar, and amongst the bricks and scaffolding. The pistol with its silencer, and the girl who had lost her man in a callous murder.

But the ambush had been a success, and they had not lost a single life. Even Colonel Sir Aubrey Souter had sent his congratulations. Ross found he could smile again, and it felt like life returning. Souter would have been just as correct in sending his condolences.

So what now? Back to England, to face possible discharge. *Unfit for active duty*, no matter what the medical gurus said.

"Are you ready to make a start, Major?"

It was the duty sister, fresh and very clean in her uniform. She had, apparently, been here when they had brought him in. She had probably forgotten that, shut it from her thoughts. Had to, in her work.

He recalled when she had first spoken to him, changing his dressings, telling him he had called her 'Glynis'.

He said, "Yes, I'm ready. I can't thank you enough, but you must have been told that many times."

She looked at him. "From you, it means something. After what you did." She shook her head. "I hope they remember when all this insanity is over and done with."

And she was Irish.

She was leaving. "Your car will be here soon. If you need anything else . . ." She was gone.

Ross glanced at the neat pile of clothing. He was going to the same high-security hotel as Clive Tobin's team had occupied, 'Fort Amazon'. It might be the last time he met Sharon before he was ordered back to England, and she continued with her contract wherever events dictated. He felt some of his resolve crumble. It took more than a uniform . . .

It will take time. Mocking him.

He touched his side, feeling one of the scars. Cheated because he could recall so little. The face, full of hatred, changing to a mask of agony, the one he had imagined was a photograph even as the blast had smashed him down. And the other twisted scar now on his chest, where his binoculars had been shattered by a splinter, and had saved his life. He pulled on the clean shirt and saw himself in the wall mirror, the scars and the uncertainty.

Then we'll make time.

Leaving the hospital was harder than he had expected. It was a large, busy establishment which he had seen a few times when being driven past it, but no closer. Behind him he could imagine the room, the same room which had taken so long to show its personality. The bed changed, the fresh flowers taken away, the military policeman gone from the passageway. Maybe a new occupant already installed.

The last part was different again. The staff nurse smiling, but dabbing her eyes when he had said good-bye. The sister he had called Glynis, turning her cheek to receive a kiss. Enough; there were no words at all.

And the surgeon who had hurried from somewhere to shake his hand: the man who had done most of the repair work. Only a blurred image above a white mask, until today. All smiles. Mere pleasure or professional surprise, who could say?

And other vignettes. A couple leaving, pausing to look back at the curved stairway, as if unwilling to abandon some last hope. The woman in tears, the man gripping her around the shoulders. No words needed there, either.

Then, signing some sort of register, a porter watching him do it. *Seen it all.*

A few visitors, some turning as the uniform passed. He felt himself straighten his back, the chill running through him. Like hearing the orderly again, the taskmaster, urging him to take those first steps across that same room. And again.

His transport was waiting by the main entrance, not a Land Rover this time, but a staff car. Harwood was standing by the open door, throwing up a salute that would have done credit to an admiral's guard, but unable to control a great grin of pleasure.

Lieutenant Peter Hamlyn was here too, although Ross had heard that all of the original section had returned to England some days before, including Steve Blackwood, who had visited him several times in hospital. Probably

228

sick and tired of all the official reports and interviews. *You'd think we were the bloody villains.*

Hamlyn said, "Good to see you, sir." They shook hands, and again Ross felt eyes watching them.

As Harwood put a suitcase in the car boot, Ross saw several other bags already stowed, his own belongings from the H.Q. on the other side of town. So it was final. They were sending him home. No speeches or boozy farewells. For him, it was over.

The car moved away from the entrance, as an ambulance was about to enter. Perhaps that same room . . .

Hamlyn said, "Just wanted to see you before we were split up. To say thanks, as much as anything. I thought I knew most of it." He almost shrugged. "That day on the river changed a hell of a lot. Not just for me, either. The other side of things, which we so rarely see . . . then suddenly you're bang in the middle of something you'll never find in any drill book!"

Ross glanced at him. Quick-thinking, reliable: only once had he given way, when he had seen an unarmed man gunned down, and his killer turning from the wind to light a cigarette. Like the young marine who had been so concerned for the girl, sobbing for her friend or lover, who had been killed without pity or remorse.

Steve had told him that the same girl had been seen outside the police station where the prisoners had been taken, screaming and damning the marines for what had happened. As if they were the culprits. Leaked information, or a double betrayal; the truth would remain buried forever in the official records.

Hamlyn said abruptly, "I'd like to be considered for active duty, sir." He turned in the seat and met Ross's eyes directly. "When you need a good, hard-working gun dog!"

Harwood braked carefully as a woman pushing a pram crossed the road in front of the car.

He had knocked around in every kind of unit, both ashore and afloat. Good men, bad men, cheats and liars, they all fell into line in the Corps, or they went under.

And the same went for the officers. He lifted his hand casually to the woman with the pram. Especially the officers.

That was what Lieutenant Hamlyn was trying to say now, in the back of the car. He glanced at the driving mirror and his grin was even wider. In the canteen he would never hear the last of it. *What? Give up your chance of a sergeant's tapes, for a bloody officer?*

Ross turned to look across at a police box, two soldiers chatting with the occupants. He thought he recognized the street. It seemed so long ago. Like the sky and the weather, dull and overcast. All changed. A momentary panic flickered through him, and then, once more, acceptance. Like the face he had seen at the moment of the explosion, the features he had studied in the mug shots. A lifetime ago. Or the terrified girl who had lost everything, and might never know why.

He reached over and gripped Hamlyn's wrist roughly, and released it.

"I'll not forget, Peter."

Or that you just helped keep me sane.

The car had stopped.

Harwood opened his door. "Fort Amazon, sir." The grin had gone. "I'll get the porter."

They stood side by side on the front steps. The hardest moment: there was suddenly nothing left to say.

Hamlyn said, "I'm on my way tomorrow, sir. Steady and slow. No first class air travel this time!"

The bags had disappeared. Harwood was standing beside the car. More handshakes.

Hamlyn said brightly, "We'll meet again." *Like the song.*

Some one spoke behind them. The moment was past.

"Welcome to the Amazon, sir. Proud to have you with us." The manager, it had to be, in a smart grey suit, almost bowing as an unseen hand opened one of the tall, polished doors. "Your room is ready for you. Anything you need . . ."

Ross half turned, the warmth of the hotel foyer on his cheek, the damp air of the street clinging like a reminder.

The staff car had already merged with the other traffic.

There were a few people in the foyer; one man was waving a piece of paper at a member of the desk staff, probably his bill, but he seemed to be making little impression. A newspaper lay on a chair by a rack of greeting and postcards, the headline in bold print. BOMB DISCOVERED AT AIRPORT. SUSPECT ARRESTED. It did not seem to reach him; it was something that could have happened anywhere, on any day of the week.

The manager was saying, "Difficult times to be sure, sir, and that's the truth!"

Ross did not hear him. She was standing by some lift doors, as if she had just come down. Motionless, like that moment in the boatshed, as if there was nobody else here. Her hair, shining in the overhead lights, her lips slightly parted and one hand to her throat, like a glove.

Afterwards he could not remember who had moved first. She was standing, holding his arms, at a distance, as if she could not believe it had really happened.

Then she was pressed against him, her voice so close that it was like that last time, on the telephone, before he had gone to that near-fatal rendezvous.

"Ross. Hold me." Her eyes were closed. "Hold me!"

The manager stood aside, smiling. His carefully

prepared little speech could wait. This was more important, a far cry from the headlines; and it was good to see.

A man sitting in a comfortable armchair by some phone booths closed the book which had been lying open in his lap. He was a big, ruddy individual in a creased tweed suit, who could have been a farmer up from the country. Or a policeman. He reached inside his coat and switched on a tiny radio, and murmured, "He's here, sir." And then, "Yes, all correct." He watched the two figures opposite him and switched off the radio. *Lucky sod. In more ways than one.*

They walked slowly toward the lifts. One was open, a page-boy guarding it, his eye on the manager.

One of the hotel porters stepped from behind a desk and sketched a salute with his fingers to his forehead. He smiled faintly, and Ross recognized the medal ribbons, from his father's war, among them the Atlantic Star. Like another hand reaching out.

He had not released her arm. It was real. She was here.

She said, "I wanted to see you walk in." She hesitated. "I should have told you. Clive is here, too. He wants to have a word. I'm sorry . . ."

He said, "*You're* here. That's all I care about now."

And it was true. Only the shadows remained.

Clive Tobin poured more champagne and waited for the froth to settle.

"As you know, Ross, I'm off back to London tomorrow. The programme, such as it is, is finished." He looked over at Sharon, who was sitting in one of the matching chairs. "In spite of my P.A. being here in Derry just when I needed her, eh, Sharon?"

She said quietly, "I wanted to be here, Clive. You know that."

He smiled. "Insisted, wouldn't you say?"

Ross took one of the glasses. Tobin had not refilled his own. Off to another function to complete his tour. He was wearing a dress shirt, and Ross had noticed the dinner jacket and bow tie tossed carelessly over a chair by the desk. Always so casual and at ease, but he could not resist the little waspish comment about Sharon's determination to remain here. In case she could help, she had said. She would never know how much she had done just that.

"I must say, Ross, you came through your ordeal remarkably well. I'll make sure that certain boffins at home take some note of it." He shook his head, and the famous smile was gone. "There has to be a political solution in the end to settle all this violence in the province. Expunging the hatred will take rather longer, I think." The smile flashed again. "Until that day, my friend, men like you must and will maintain the rule of law. I shall take that as my lead line."

A telephone rang somewhere. "Be back in a second." He went to another door and closed it behind him.

Ross said, "Did he give you a hard time?"

She smiled, and it was like a cloud lifting. "His bark is usually worse than his bite. But to Clive, the job comes first. I could live with that, until . . ." She looked down at her hands. "You know what I mean. I never thought I would ever feel that way again." She raised her head, and her eyes were clear, direct. "Your mother was wonderful. We didn't talk very much, but she made me feel as if I belonged, d'you know what I mean?"

"Joanna went through bad times when the Colonel was killed. She's strong. You must get her to tell you her own story some time. During the war . . . Wonder what Clive would make of that?"

She said, "I love the way you laugh. I kept thinking of it, hearing it . . . Now you're here. I'm so happy."

Tobin came back from the other room. "That was our pal Shylock, calling from Paris. Reversed the charges, cheeky devil." He looked from one to the other. "Slight change of plans. Earlier flight tomorrow. Makes sense." As if he were ticking off the points on his fingers. "Two days in London, then across the Channel. The NATO squabble has come up again. They want me to do some interviews." Then to Sharon, "You'll need some warm clothes. You know how these things can drag on. 'At last the story can be told etcetera, etcetera'."

She said, "How early?" Like stones dropping in a pool.

"Ten a.m." He picked up the bow tie. "Better get cracking!"

She stood up, turning her back on Ross. "I'll talk to the front desk. The car . . ."

Tobin said, "She never forgets a thing." He was regarding his reflection in one of the windows, pulling and knotting the bow without effort. "Can't stand these new-fangled made-up ties, can you? Like a lot of . . ." He swung round and stared at him. "I'm *pleased* for you. Both of you, if it comes off. But I need her until the job is wrapped up. Same as you, in some ways, eh?" He was very calm, contained; and it was not an act. "Just don't fool about, Ross. She's been through enough." Abruptly, he seemed to relax. "Christ knows how I'll get another P.A. as good as Sharon."

Ross recalled the hospital room. The flowers, which were always fresh. And all that time she had been waiting, either here, dealing with Tobin's backlog of enquiries, or at the hospital, as close as she could be.

He said, "I hope I was some use during the tour. I'll be watching out for the end product on TV."

Tobin said, very seriously, "More than you'll ever know,

234

my friend. I learned a lot. I'd never admit that to any one, of course."

Ross stood and touched his chest, suddenly aware of the dressings. There were three, to minimize any irritation.

Sharon would be landing in London while he was on his way to Plymouth. The aftermath. More interviews and statements. Some leave 'to get over it', and then what?

He would write to her, call her whenever he could. Maybe see her before too long. *I can't go on without her.*

Tobin had put on his dinner jacket and had turned to face him again, and for an instant Ross thought he had spoken aloud.

But he said simply, "See you around." Another handshake. Perhaps the first genuine emotion he had shown. "Keep the flag flying, Ross. Some one's got to!"

She came into the room, but looked only at Ross, like a question.

"Car's here, Clive. The driver's name is Patrick."

He said lightly, "Well, it would be, wouldn't it, dear?" and flashed the famous smile again. In control. "On with the show!"

The door closed and she crossed the room to put her arms around his neck. There were no words. It was like coming back to life. On the far side of the room the television was still switched on, but the sound was off. Athletics, football, it could have been anything.

Somewhere, outside, Ross heard some one putting down a tray, tapping discreetly on a door.

The windows were already dark. He shivered, and felt her tense.

"Did I hurt you?" He touched her hair, pulled her closer, and shook his head. "I was so scared." Then she looked at him, with the expression he had never forgotten. "Oh, Ross, we're *here*!"

"Is your room as grand as this one?"

She moved away, but did not lose contact with her eyes as she reached out to switch off the television.

Then she gripped his hand, her voice soft, determined.

"Come on. I'll show you."

The aircraft touched down at Plymouth airport exactly at noon. There were only four other passengers, two army officers and a couple of dockyard officials who had been on some exchange visit to Ulster. The plane was small, twin-engined, and noisy, for which Ross had been grateful. He did not feel like talking to any one, let alone shouting over the engines.

He would go to Stonehouse Barracks and make his report, and from there to Hawks Hill for a few days, or until he received fresh instructions. He could not even force himself to consider what those might be: the possibility of dismissal was like the ground falling from under his feet.

Captain Seabrook had collected him from the hotel, his appearance timed to the minute. Probably eager to discharge another responsibility. He had even waited to see him on to the plane, in case something delayed his departure.

Ross knew he was being unfair, but knowing it did not help.

He kept seeing her, hearing her voice even above the monotonous drone of the engines.

Don't watch me leave, Ross. Promise me. I'd crack up.

But he did. Peering down into the street, waiting while a car had pulled up, a military police truck in close company. A few flash bulbs, Tobin in an unbuttoned camelhair coat, a bright scarf draped flamboyantly around his neck. Smiling and waving, although there was no audience. But it would look good in the photos.

Then Sharon, in dark green, her hair so pale against the dull pavement. The hair he had felt against his face, and his skin. Her mouth, and her hands. He could feel the pain in his chest and shoulder now. But then, when all caution and all doubt had melted away, he had known only passion, and fulfilment.

She must have sensed it. Had sensed it. Even as she had released some one's hand she had turned and looked up at the hotel windows. *At me.*

On the aircraft he had closed his eyes and tried to hold on, to relive it. Her concern that he might be injured, perhaps her own fear of what she was doing. It all faded, passed away, like a squall at sea. And memories, like photographs. The curve of her back, the skin silver in some light from the street; the feel of her suddenly pressing against him, holding him, wanting him.

And dawn. The parting. So much to say. No time, even for tears.

Somebody said, "Lady waitin' for you, sir."

The other hurrying figures fell away. It was Joanna. They hugged, and he heard himself say, "I didn't know. I didn't expect . . ."

"That I'd be here?" She shook him gently. "You *are* a nut, if you thought I'd let you arrive like some rookie on his first leave!"

She touched his cheek with her fingers. Like part of a dream. "There now. I've left tears on your face!" She was serious suddenly. "I know what you said on the phone. Stonehouse Barracks, then down to Hawks Hill for as long as they'll allow. I've booked a couple of rooms at the Post House on the Hoe, so you can take a breather before we drive down." She was smiling now, tears forgotten. Radiant. "And I want you to tell me all about Sharon."

"You got on well."

"Better than that . . . You love her, don't you, Ross?" Then she frowned. "*Hell*. Here comes the regiment!"

It was in fact a young Royal Marine, smartly turned out and carrying some car keys.

"Major Blackwood, sir?" He almost saluted. "I'm the Commandant's driver. I'm to take you to Stonehouse." There were two more marines by the barrier, standing beside a baggage trolley. He sensed that it was not all straightforward, and added hesitantly, "The lady can ride with you, sir."

Ross looked at her. "I wasn't expecting this. Will you come?"

She glanced at the marines, but did not seem to see them.

"For old times' sake, Ross?"

He took her arm and squeezed it. She was wearing the familiar diamond brooch, fashioned like the badge on his green beret.

"No, Joanna. For *me*, if you like."

She touched the brooch, and the gesture seemed both unconscious and reminiscent.

"For him, too." She seemed to come to a decision. "I don't suppose the old place has changed much." It said everything.

Then, with something very like relief, the young marine led the way to his car.

She climbed in, and was looking at the crest on the windscreen.

Ross said, "How's John?"

She looked at him, and took his hand.

"You don't mind too much, do you?"

He smiled. "I'm glad. For both of you."

He touched his chest, and she said quietly, "Does it hurt?"

"Only when I laugh!"

"Very funny. You've had a long day, Ross. When we get to the hotel you can put your feet up and . . ." She leaned forward. "What's the hold-up? We're almost there, too."

Ross felt her fingers tighten. She remembered. The wall, the tower . . .

He said, "Oh, shit. There's some sort of ceremony going on. Can you get round it, driver?"

The marine said, "Won't take long, sir." He revved the engine slightly to show that he was unconcerned.

Ross saw another car, already parked, the driver standing beside it. Like Harwood, he thought. What would *he* do next?

He tensed, seeing a full guard of Royal Marines, white helmets, fixed bayonets, a lieutenant with sword drawn. The regular tramp of boots. Like other times, especially here. *What we are. What we do.*

The other car mounted a senior officer's plate. He tried to calm down, release the tension. *What a time to choose.*

"Sorry about this, Joanna."

The guard had halted, clicked round to face the road. Some spectators had gathered, although ceremony was common enough here, in Drake's seaport.

But there were always cameras ready and waiting.

Joanna said quietly, "Here he is, Ross. The great man himself."

It was Colonel Souter. Away from that bare office in Whitehall, with its paperweight on a polished desk. Straight-backed, the gaunt features he remembered so well. When he had met Tobin. He clenched his fist. And Sharon . . .

The driver was getting out, standing beside the door. At attention.

She said, "He's coming over to *us*, Ross."

Ross climbed out on to the road, and held her hand to assist her.

As if from another world, a voice was calling, *"Guard of honour! Pre-sent arms!"*

Pale sunlight touched the bayonets, boots stamped down as one.

Colonel Souter saluted, with a faint smile, like something shared.

"It's for *you*, Major Blackwood. Welcome back."

1982

DARING

CHAPTER FOURTEEN

"If you'll take a seat, Major Blackwood, Sir Aubrey knows you're here. He's been expecting you." He did not glance at the clock on the wall, but he might as well have done so. Even his voice implied, *what took you so long?*

Ross looked around. There was no chair, except for one which was piled with large envelopes awaiting collection.

He walked to a window and stood staring down at the street. Number Thirty-One: the same entrance, identity check and telephone calls. All that time ago. Months . . . He ran his hand over his hair. It felt like yesterday.

He caught sight of his reflection in the glass. He had not even had time to change into a more presentable rig. *Scruffy.*

Poole, in Dorset, was at a rough guess about a hundred and twenty miles from this building; and he had felt every yard of it.

It was almost noon. He saw a taxi waiting by the curb, perhaps hoping for a fare, then a policeman gliding out of a doorway and moving him on. Security . . . that word. At least nothing here had changed.

But I have.

He had made a couple of phone calls en route to London. It had been hard to get much sense out of anybody, but bad news always made a fast passage. They had driven through some market town and he had seen it chalked on the blackboard beside a news-stand. TOP ROYAL MARINE MURDERED BY TERRORISTS. Not in one of the trouble spots in the Middle East, or even in Northern Ireland; it had happened here in London. The newspapers had been mistaken about one thing: the senior officer, Lieutenant-General Sir Steuart Pringle, had survived. But he had been seriously injured.

The Commandant-General of the Royal Marines, at his own home. How could it have been allowed to happen?

Many civilians believed the bombings and shootings were on the wane. Would they never get the true picture?

"If you will come this way, sir." The young man in the crumpled suit was back. Ross followed him past yet more doors, flickering screens, telephones, and somebody dictating, or rehearsing what he was going to say. They were passing that same door now, and in his mind he saw Clive Tobin, pausing with the famous smile. It was sometimes difficult to believe that it had ever happened. Tobin had been back and forth to France, and apparently Germany as well, several times since their last meeting in Londonderry: Sharon had told him as much as she could during their conversations. Distance, always distance. Testing both of them. But if anything . . .

"Here, sir."

The office was exactly as he remembered it. Bare, as if nobody ever stopped here for long.

Colonel Sir Aubrey Souter was on his feet behind the desk, erect, and facing the door. A button of his tunic was unfastened and his tie was loose, as if he had been pulling at it. He looked, uncharacteristically, worn out. Without effort, Ross could recall him at the entrance to Stonehouse Barracks, the genuine pleasure he had not tried to hide when he had been parading his guard of honour to welcome him back. This was like seeing some one else.

"Sit you down, Ross. Sorry to drag you up here like this." He gave a shrug; even that seemed an effort. "Place is a madhouse at the moment."

The same U.S.M.C. paperweight, and one loose file of papers.

"I hear you've been doing well at Poole with the Special Boat Squadron. Knew you'd fit in after your stop-and-search experiences in Hong Kong." He scowled. "To say nothing of Ulster!"

Ross sat upright in the hard chair. Even after all these months, it could still catch him unaware. The scars were always ready to remind him. Warn him.

"All been said before – don't need to hash it all over again. But we're being called on more and more to provide cover – protection, if you like – when we're still being cut down at every opportunity. The boat sections you've been putting through their paces will most likely be used to watch over the new oil rigs, stuck out in the North Sea or some other godforsaken place." He banged his fist on the table. "Instead of doing the job they joined for!"

A telephone rang noisily. Souter ignored it. Moments later it rang again in an adjoining office.

He said, "I'll need you up here for a bit. There's a new face joining the A.C.H.Q. team. Parsons, Roger Parsons. Know him?"

"I think so. Way back . . . he was a captain when I last bumped into him."

"Well, don't *bump* into him next time. He's a half-colonel now." He paused. "On the way up the ladder, right?"

Ross smiled. "Right." No stronger warning was needed. And it mattered. Souter trusted him.

"Small, hard-hitting units, men well trained and capable

of working alongside bigger and more conventional forces." He flicked the papers on his desk. "Or going it entirely alone, like the team sent over to Londonderry to stamp on that explosives run." He looked up sharply. "The lieutenant, Peter Hamlyn. Good choice?" He did not wait for a reply. "Thought as much," and he smiled unexpectedly, like some one else looking out of the gaunt features. "Wants to serve with you again, if he gets the offer!"

The smile vanished as abruptly as it had appeared: some one was rapping on the door. This time it was a uniform, a colour sergeant with a rugged face and brush-like moustache.

"I thought I told you . . ." Then he relaxed a little, and said, "This is Sergeant Pike. He really runs this place when I'm not around!"

The man grinned. "Good to see you again, Major Blackwood."

Ross remembered the face. The one who had reminded him of the time he had ridden a horse into the mess for a bet, or as part of a celebration. How could he forget? Trafalgar Day, and also his birthday, something he had never been allowed to ignore since the day he had first donned a uniform.

The sergeant said cheerfully, "Thought you might 'ave forgotten, sir." He thrust out his watch without looking at it. "Sun's well over the yardarm, sir."

Souter seemed to unwind, as if a burden had slipped from his shoulders.

"Right you are, Pike," and to Ross, "Horse's Neck suit you?" As usual, he did not expect an answer. Pike strode to a cupboard and was soon busy with some glasses.

Souter said suddenly, "I think I have to congratulate you, Ross. I'm told you might be getting married after all this time. No escape, you see!" He watched the sergeant topping up the brandy with ginger ale. "Easy, man – don't drown it."

Then he said, "Good luck to you, anyway. Tobin let it out of the bag. I met the girl myself a couple of times . . . too good for you, if you ask me. Doesn't know what she's in for!"

Ross sipped the drink slowly. Souter was merely passing the time of day before telling him the real reason for this summons. He would never guess how near the truth he had come. Phone calls, often interrupted because Tobin needed her for something urgent. It was always that. Hanging on to each precious moment while the world passed them by, or so it seemed. One night together, and two brief meetings at airports. And always saying good-bye. *Doesn't know what she's in for.* Did any of them? He could still remember Houston, the broken-nosed major who had died on a beach in Malaysia he had known only as a map reference. And Blondie Piggott, Souter's nephew, more afraid of showing fear than of fear itself, who had died at the hands of an enemy most people had long forgotten. And Fisher, who had been killed in error. *It should have been me.* He could feel the scars on his body, but knew if he touched them Souter would see, and perhaps have doubts about him.

The door closed and the faithful Pike had gone.

Outside, the sky was heavy, and it was raining; he could see drops falling from the eaves opposite. And in three days' time it would be Trafalgar Day.

He thought of the scrawled announcement by the newsstand; he had not even noticed the name of the town through which they were driving. The Commandant-General had perhaps been considering that date, too; some ceremony or speech would have been scheduled. He was lucky to be alive. Luckier than many others.

Souter was saying, "Want you back here for a week or two, Ross. I've fixed it with Poole. That chap . . . forget his name . . . he can cope without you breathing down his neck for a bit." He tapped his empty glass on the desk. "Forester, that's it. Like that writer I used to read."

Ross waited. Souter never forgot names; he never seemed to forget anything.

"I want you to put Parsons in the picture. He's new to this side of things. Might get the wrong idea about Special Operations. You're the one to lead him into it. You've done it – you know it, right? I don't want some clever bastard giving him wrong ideas, some desk-warrior, if you get my drift." He leaned right back in his chair and regarded him steadily. "Watch your step." He laughed, but it did not reach his eyes. "For all our sakes, eh?"

He looked briefly at his watch. "Sorry I've gone on about it, but it's important. And so is what I'm trying to do in this establishment." Feet moved noisily beyond the door and Souter got to his feet.

"Be here Thursday. My staff will fix you up with a place to stay." He grimaced. "Hide, rather!"

The door was open; somebody handed Souter his cap, another picked up the paperweight. The room would soon be bare again.

Souter paused and looked at the window. "What a day. I hope our Nel had better weather before Trafalgar!" Then he turned back. "Set the date yet, Ross?"

"We're getting there, sir."

"Do it. Don't wait. Send me an invitation, if you can stand it!"

Doors slammed, and some one called, "Car's here, Sir Aubrey!"

Pike, the colour sergeant, probably one of the few people who had Souter's complete trust, was back.

Ross tugged at his tunic. There was a lot to do, his gear to be sent for . . . He could no more face another drive back to Dorset, with more explanations, than he could understand why Souter had insisted on his coming here for this conversation. It was as if he had needed to know something, be convinced of something.

"I'm just leaving."

Pike touched the back of a chair. "Thought you might be wantin' to call some one, sir." It could almost be said that he winked. "Privately."

"From here?"

Pike pulled a drawer open in the lower part of the desk. "'Ere, sir. Special line." He pressed a button. "The Colonel likes to keep 'imself to 'imself sometimes."

Ross sat down once more. He was wasting his time. Or hers.

Pike was closing the door.

"Call me when you leave, sir."

Ross pulled out his pocket book. There was no sound, not even of voices. The traffic seemed to have stopped, too.

The same group of numbers. He knew them by heart; there was no need to go through them again. He confronted it, suddenly nervous, almost shy. Afraid he might tarnish something, or ruin it altogether.

He dialled slowly, his free hand clenched into a fist on the desk. He saw that Souter had left his papers behind, and that he had pencilled something next to several vague jottings, the sketch of a sailing vessel and the words, *England Expects!*

He realized that she had answered, and he said, "Sharon, it's me."

"I was just going out. I heard the phone ringing." A pause, and he thought he could hear her breathing. "Are you all right, Ross? You don't usually call me at this time of day. Tell me."

"I'm here, in London. At Number Thirty-One." He watched the drawer and the secret instrument, expecting the metallic click, or the voice. *This is a restricted line. It is forbidden . . .*

Her voice, closer. Anxious. "Ross, are you sure everything's all right?"

"I'm here for a few days, I think. I'm sorry. I'm a bit mixed up." He was speaking too fast, but he could not help it. "I've got to send for some things. I didn't know, you see." He unclenched his fist very slowly, watching it, as if it belonged to some one else.

She said quietly, "I know what you mean. I understand." She might have stifled a cough, or a sob. "Just write this down. Then call a taxi." She repeated the address more slowly. "We can arrange things from here. I'll be waiting, Ross. It's about twenty minutes away by taxi. Oh, this is *wonderful.*"

She was crying now, and he said, "Are you sure, Sharon?" A tiny red light had started to flicker by the telephone rest, Souter's private warning, perhaps. "I love you!"

The line went dead; even the traffic beyond the window had started again.

He stared at the address scribbled in his pocket book. Twenty minutes away. It could have been on the moon.

He looked around the empty room, and knew it was a moment he would never forget. Or want to.

He called, "I'm leaving now. Thank you!"

But the colour sergeant named Pike was already downstairs at the main entrance, and so was a taxi.

"Thought you was in a 'urry, sir." He was trying to hide a grin now. "Otherwise I'd 'ave found you an 'orse!"

Ross touched his arm. "No wonder the Colonel leaves you to run this place!"

One of the doormen sauntered across to watch Ross climb into the taxi.

"What's so special about him, then?"

Pike glanced at him. An ex-soldier, with a few medal ribbons on his uniform to show for it. But what would a pongo understand about the Corps?

"I'd watch yer step, mate." He tapped the side of his nose. "I've 'eard 'e's on the way to th' top!"

He turned to see the taxi drive off, and smiled to himself.

One of us, he thought.

The taxi pulled up and stopped, the engine ticking over with that indescribable sound only London cabs seemed to make. He had taken taxis almost everywhere else in the world, but only here was that familiar sound, part of memory.

It was a quiet street, and the houses were large, probably Victorian, most of them converted into flats or large apartments. As the cabby summed it up, "For them what can scrape up the asking price!"

South of the Thames, and twenty minutes from Whitehall. Exactly.

The cabby was saying, "Number Two – that'll be upstairs, left 'and side." He watched Ross take out his wallet. "Tough luck about that officer who nearly caught it yesterday. Dropped a few fares around that address in me time, I can tell you. One of your lot, too." He peered at the uniform. "Don't know what the bloody world is comin' to!" The notes disappeared into his gloved hand. "Thanks, squire. You're a sport!"

Ross waved an acknowledgment and turned toward the building. The taxi was already out of sight, and he felt suddenly at a loss. Dazed. Yesterday . . . Was it only that? And this morning he had been down in Dorset, handing over to his second-in-command, Captain Forester. *Like that writer I used to read.* He gripped his small case more firmly. It was Souter's fault: brandy and not much ginger ale. He had not eaten today, except the half bar of chocolate he had shared with his marine driver. *I should have waited. Done something.*

He heard a window open and looked up.

"I'm here! Come straight up!" She was waving, her hair shining against the old bricks. "This is lovely!"

A man walking his dog turned to look up, and smiled at them. Somebody else called, "Very nice, too!"

Ross saw and heard neither of them.

He was standing there, looking up, a few drops of rain touching his face, and then the next moment, or so it seemed, he was in the doorway, holding her away from him, his hands on her shoulders, long enough to see her, to look and only look, unable to find the words.

Then she was pressed against him, and somewhere a door was closing behind them.

"I'm such a mess . . ." He was vaguely aware of the room, some letters on an antique table waiting to be opened or posted. Music coming from somewhere; the smell of coffee.

She was holding him, very tightly. "When I heard the phone I was outside. I nearly kept going." She was kissing him, her hair against his eyes, his mouth. "I could have missed you!"

He said again, "I'm such a mess."

She was trying not to laugh. Or cry. "I've got a nice ironing board, darling!"

She looked down, and he could not see her expression.

"How long, Ross?"

"Three days." He felt her trembling as he touched her. "I want you."

Then she raised her head, and her eyes were filling her face.

"And I want you. Let's not waste a minute of it!"

A whistle shrilled yet again. Most of the marines had lost count of the times it had urged them on to yet another first-degree exercise. Fit though they were, some of them were ready to drop. And it was raining heavily, the trampled ground more like a bog than ever.

One of the warrant officers yelled, "Stand easy, sir?" He swore under his breath. He already knew the response.

Lieutenant-Colonel Roger Parsons waved his hand. "Once again, Mr. Todd! They're like a lot of old men this morning! *Move it!*"

Ross Blackwood wiped his face with a sodden handker-chief, and looked at the crude pontoon bridge which had been thrown together across a fast-moving stream, faster than ever now in the torrential downpour. He heard Parsons calling out to one of the 'umpires' in his quiet, curt voice. He was not even out of breath, although he had kept pace with everybody else. Ross was impressed by the miles they had travelled, days of it at first, then weeks. Boatwork and field exercises, from Portland Bill to Lympstone, from Dartmoor to Poole; communications, a must with Parsons, and weapon handling under all conditions, at any time of day and in every sort of weather.

Roger F. Parsons . . . Ross had checked him out in the List. The 'F' stood for Francis, but he guessed that almost every marine in this commando unit had a very different suggestion.

Souter had been emphatic. "He'll want to see every aspect of Special Operations. So show him. Keep with him

253

all the way." He had added forcefully, "And that's an order, from the top."

Did that mean that Souter was looking over his own shoulder? Maybe his own place on the ladder was no longer secure.

All this time, living almost shoulder to shoulder, and still Ross did not know him. Parsons was slim, neat, and obviously very fit, with a watchful, intelligent face and deepset, questioning eyes. Ross had felt himself under scrutiny from the beginning, and had tried not to resent it. If Parsons mentioned some incident from his past service, in Northern Ireland for instance, Ross had the feeling that his response was being recorded somewhere, as if he were being tested. Parsons had a free hand at the moment; that was all there was to it. He felt the rain exploring his neck. But you did not have to like it.

He should be used to it, more so than most of the marines around him. He was thirty-seven years old, as of Trafalgar Day. It had been their last day together. He had reported to A.C.H.Q. as ordered, and Sharon had left for Paris on some errand for Clive Tobin. She had been holding him in a tight embrace, with a car waiting to take her to Heathrow. Again.

"I'll be free after this job, Ross."

Three days together. And then, suddenly, there was no time left, even to find the right words. Was there ever any time?

They had been up to the West End, and together they had chosen the ring. She had let him put it on her finger before that last night together.

Ross heard one of the marines guffaw. Wet, mud-stained and bedraggled, and they could still manage a laugh. What had somebody said about his service in Ulster? *More laughs than tears.* That said it all.

And after this?

He thought of her hands in his, the ring flashing in the solitary light beside the bed.

"What about Easter?" She had rolled over, her stomach muscles tightening as he touched her again. "A new start?"

Easter. It would be perfect, no matter what the next appointment proved to be.

Souter had said, "The young blood in our commando units needs somebody who's seen and done it the hard way. It could be a step up the ladder, if I have any say in the matter." The 'ladder' was always in the background.

"Time to get moving again." Parsons did not consult his watch; he seemed to have an inbuilt system of time-keeping. "We'll do that exercise once more. Tell the section leaders I want it done from the signal to *go*. And no moaning and dragging of feet this time."

He did not point, but seemed to indicate with his chin. "That lieutenant, Hamlyn, isn't it? Seems a cut above the others." It was a question.

Ross smiled. "He's good, sir. Keen to stay with this company."

"Looks up to you. No bad thing, up to a point."

They both turned as the senior warrant officer, one of the 'umpires', shouted, "What? Call yourself a man? Look at *me*, lad. *I'm* a man! See the difference?"

Ross thought of Pike, the Colonel's right-hand man. It was good to know that a few of the old Royals were still in harness.

Parsons remarked, "A word in some one's direction, I think."

He changed tack just as swiftly. "I understand that you were closely involved with the Clive Tobin documentary? Quite good in parts, I thought."

It was another question.

Ross watched the marines falling into squads and

sections, their camouflaged combat gear soaked with mud. Like the pictures in the museum at Portsmouth. His mind seemed to hesitate. Or on the walls at Hawks Hill . . . The faces did not seem very different. Trafalgar, or 'where no birds sing'; only the uniforms had changed.

"Leadership is part of it. Trust carries all the weight."

Parsons gave him a thin smile.

"Muskets to rockets. But you have a point. In the end it's obeying the right orders, at the right time."

Ross saw Lieutenant Hamlyn saying something to his sergeant. He would never forget that moment by the river in Londonderry, when a civilian had been gunned down in cold blood. There were two sides to obeying orders, but rarely time to make a choice.

He thought of Steve, the other Blackwood. They had met again during the assault exercises at Portland Bill, and Ross had also met the girl Steve was going to marry. All the legal complications caused by her husband's desertion had been cleared up, and they were getting married as soon as possible: "full steam ahead", as Steve had put it. Very different, and yet so right for each other. Ross did not know if she knew about his work with explosives.

"*Right! In position!* Mr. Hamlyn, *you* are in command. All the other officers have been killed!"

Ross saw a young marine grin and murmur something ripely sarcastic to his mate.

Only the uniforms had changed.

In early December the combined manoeuvres were finally called to a halt, and there was more speculation about Christmas leave than the verdict on their many exercises ashore and afloat. It was hard to know what Lieutenant-Colonel Roger Parsons thought of the results. Satisfied or bored, he gave very little away.

Once he had remarked, after a particularly gruelling cliff-scaling effort, "They hate my guts. So it must be working!"

They had been given some makeshift living quarters, once again on the fringe of Dartmoor, where they had been working with and alongside some crack S.A.S. troops, rivals who were always attempting to display their superiority. Nobody could accuse Parsons of sparing himself at the expense of others. Even at the end of a long, hard day Ross had seen him on the telephone to one section or another, demanding, pleading, sometimes threatening, to obtain what he required for his various schemes.

On the last night before Parsons was due to leave for London, he asked Ross to join him in his temporary quarters, an old Nissen hut left over from the war, and boasting battered furniture and some cartoons drawn by past occupants, insulting, funny and, occasionally, strangely sad. Luggage was strewn across the floor, and Parsons' greatcoat lay over a chair, a sheaf of scribbled notes beside it. Ross had wondered why he had not left earlier, or delayed his departure until he had had a good night's sleep. His driver would have plenty to moan about: it would be a long haul to London, especially on some of the local roads.

"Just thought I'd put you in the picture." Parsons jerked his chin at a canvas chair. "Not worked you too hard, have I?"

Ross felt himself tense. Would the past never leave him? He had been asked to drop in on the P.M.O., "a routine check-up, old chap". They often said that. And the scars always looked so much worse under the probing medical lights. Bringing back the same memory. Parsons had said nothing in so many words. His casual remark was enough.

He said, "I hope it's all been useful."

There was music coming from a cassette player in a corner by some camp beds, a pure, woman's voice. Opera, somehow familiar.

Parsons bent over and switched it off. He said mildly, "New tape. My wife sent it to me. I'm not sure . . ." He did not finish it.

The merest glimpse of the man behind the authority, and the driving impatience.

He said, "I'm glad you're on stand by for the leave period. Never had time to have a good punt around Poole, but I suppose . . ." He looked at Ross directly. "You're getting married, I hear. Maybe she could come and see you?"

"Afraid not, sir. She's still working for Clive Tobin. Not for much longer, though."

Parsons snapped his fingers. "Of course. *That's* how I heard about it." Again the steady appraisal. "Clive Tobin." He half smiled. "Still sweating on getting his knighthood!" A slight shrug. "Well, why not, I suppose, when you see the list of runners. Does make you wonder sometimes."

Ross heard feet clumping along a boardwalk outside the hut, some one catching his boot on a loose plank. The whole place was falling apart. *Cutting down.*

Parsons repeated, "Glad you're on stand by. Need somebody who knows the problems, who'll spot 'em immediately." He swung round and clenched his fist. "Logistics – the clue to the obstacle, and the cure. How much, and how many can you move if and when it's needed! There are far too many people still living in the past, who have learned absolutely nothing from it. Pearl Harbor, Korea, Vietnam – the same minds, the same bland solutions!"

He stepped over a suitcase and dragged open a cupboard door.

"Logistics. Top of the list. Mine, anyway!"

He came back with a bottle of Scotch and two glasses.

"Neat, I'm afraid. I don't trust the tap water in this museum."

Ross said nothing. It was a rare moment, and oddly precious: to speak would have ruined it.

They clinked glasses. But for one, semi-official occasion, he had never seen Parsons drink anything stronger than a single glass of wine.

He said slowly, "Here's to you and your Sharon. That's right, isn't it?" and sipped, his eyes thoughtful. As if he were testing it. Or himself.

The Scotch was full and fierce. Souter would approve.

"Thanks, sir. I'll pass it on when I next speak to her."

Parsons had not heard him.

"Some one told me you've chosen Easter for the wedding. Can't remember who it was."

Ross said, "We thought it would be a good time. There are things to arrange, invitations . . . but you'll know that better than we do."

Parsons put down the glass. It was empty.

"Yes. It takes a lot of care. A lot of planning. So easy for people to get hurt, people you love . . ." He seemed to be meditating aloud. "I believe what we are doing is very important. Perhaps vital. For us, and for the future."

Ross stood up. There were voices outside. Perhaps the car had arrived.

"You'll find me ready enough." Like a flashback to school, all that time ago. *Romeo and Juliet. You shall find me apt enough to that, sir, an you will give me occasion . . .* The drawn rapiers shining under the stage lighting.

Parsons held out his hand, and said without a smile, "I'm banking on it, Ross."

It was the first time he had used his name.

CHAPTER FIFTEEN

The nightmare was surging to a terrible climax. Worse than before; or was it always the same? Vivid flashes of light, and the roar of drums, like the sea smashing into the foot of a cliff.

Faces, distorted and never still, revolving, shouting, but the voices were quelled by the din. Like dying, unable to breathe.

Ross fell on his side, his chest heaving. Now the impossible climax. Utter silence, as if his breath had in fact stopped.

He pulled a pillow from his head. The telephone shattered the silence and he snatched it; his hand brushed something, and he heard a glass fall to the floor beside the bed. He saw his watch glowing in the dark. Four in the morning.

It was all coming back to him: the party. The drive from Weymouth. Hedges looming out of the night, the car swerving, whoever it was at the wheel swearing, but, mercifully, slowing down.

"Yes?" He cleared his throat and tried again. "Blackwood." He propped himself on his elbow. He was half-dressed, but still wearing his tie.

"Hamlyn, sir." Very calm, and possibly relieved. "Sorry to disturb you at this hour."

The mist in his head was clearing. Hamlyn was the duty officer. He had spoken to him before the car had taken him to Weymouth. Too late for the actual ceremony at a registry office in the town hall, as Steve and his girl had wanted it.

He said, "I'm listening."

"Signal, sir. Priority. A.C.H.Q."

Ross had both feet on the floor now, although he had not felt himself move; the floor was cold, and he could hear wind shaking a door somewhere. Like the roadside hedges in the car headlights, wild spectres. *Something's happened.*

Hamlyn said, "Operation Lazarus. Execute."

Ross reached for his watch. "Well done, Peter. Verified?"

"Done, sir." He *was* relieved.

What a time to choose. Parsons' name would be well and truly vilified at this hour. A full state of readiness for the whole company. Another bomb attack somewhere? A border dispute getting out of control? It was what they had been trained to expect. He swallowed, knowing that his immediate concern had been for Sharon, in Paris or not. He could hear marching feet, the clink of metal. *If you can't take a joke* . . . He fumbled around before he found the right switch. He was still not used to Poole, nor would he be at this rate.

The phone rang again. This time it was his second-in-command, Captain Forester, wide awake, clipped and formal.

"All sections closed up, sir. One man missing. Marine Osborne. Duty boat alongside." All in the same breath.

Ross peered at his watch. Fifteen minutes.

"Tell them that was well done."

Forester sounded as if he was grinning.

"Osborne has just turned up, sir. I'll deal with *him*."

How many other units were being alerted, he wondered.

And for what? Like the little boy who cried "Wolf!" once too often; if some idiot on the staff kept getting ideas . . . It happened.

The telephone once more: Forester. "It's Lieutenant-Colonel Parsons, sir." No grins this time.

"Put him through."

Forester answered quietly, "He's *here*, sir. In the guardroom."

Parsons came straight to the point, as if nothing about the situation was different.

"I was on my way here to see you in any case. Thought it might be a good moment to find out what 'Lazarus' could do in a real emergency. Pity to waste it." A pause. "Are you there?"

"Where else would I be?" He was gripping the telephone so hard that he could feel the bones in his fingers aching. "Fifteen minutes, sir!"

"I made it sixteen, but no matter. I've told them to stand down now."

Ross tried to contain his anger. Of all the stupid, irresponsible . . .

Parsons said, "There's a flap on. I want to put you in the picture."

Ross heard a sudden outburst of shouting, the sharper voices of authority, and then eventual silence. Parsons was less popular than ever.

He said, "If it's not urgent . . ."

Parsons interrupted coldly, "Well, I think it is. I'm coming over. Some fresh coffee won't come amiss. And don't tell the galley it's for me, right?" The phone slammed down.

He was astonished when he saw him that Parsons managed to appear so fresh, despite the hour and his journey from London.

He strode across the room and stood beside a window, the curtain slightly folded as if he were watching the sky. It was even colder outside, the papers had been hinting at snow, and yet Parsons was without his greatcoat, and there was rain on his shoulders as if he had been walking somewhere. Unable to keep still.

He said, "I was at a meeting, two meetings, in fact. Took up most of the day. They told me it was hard to get a car and driver 'at that time'. God, you'd think this was *Dad's Army*, not the Corps!"

Ross sat on the arm of a chair, consciously relaxing himself. Preparing. He was angry. He could accept that. But there was something different this time. Parsons seemed to exist in a world quite apart from the life around him. Reasonable one moment, impatient and intolerant the next.

He had turned away from the window, his hair shining in the overhead light.

"Whatever the politicians say in Parliament, or in the press, our chiefs of staff just seem to lap it up. Don't want any trouble . . . nothing must upset the daily routine." His eyes flashed. "*Or* Christmas leave, can you believe that?"

An orderly tapped on the door and padded between them with a tray of coffee.

"Thanks, Cooper." Ross waited for the door to close. "If you tell me what's happened, sir . . ."

Parsons stalked to the table and poured two cups of black coffee without answering.

Then he said, "You always seem to know their names, and remember them. I've never had the knack, I'm afraid. Not that it . . ."

"I think it does matter, sir."

Parsons smiled, for the first time. "*All that they can call their own* – isn't that what Nelson said once?"

263

He sipped the coffee. "Not bad. Not bad at all. They must like you."

Ross watched in silence. The coffee was scalding, and yet Parsons had not appeared to notice.

"There's been a big debate going on in the House of Lords. More defence cuts. What it would mean. How much it will save. The morning papers will have it in large print. The latest one to come under fire is H.M.S. *Endurance*, our ice patrol ship." He broke off. "You know her?"

"The *Red Plum*, they used to call her. Her garish paint used to make her stand out against the ice. I did a few days aboard her, way back – we were testing some new life-saving gear for use in Arctic conditions." He waited; it was not what Parsons had been expecting. "I heard they wanted to scrap her, or sell her. Has it been decided?"

Parsons said, "The Defence Secretary, no less, wants to get rid of the old lady. After all she's done, is doing, to support our interests in the South Atlantic and Antarctic waters. She also acts as survey ship when working with the British Antarctic Survey team. But you know this, of course." He was pouring himself another cup of coffee. His hand was quite steady. And yet . . .

"A few days ago an Argentinian supply ship put into Leith Harbour, the old whaling station in South Georgia. A so-called trade mission to sort out the scrap prospects there."

"I remember the old 'catchers'. The trade was pretty run down even then. I suppose the Falklands can do with the business these days, even scrap metal?"

Parsons said, "The visiting ship was a naval auxiliary. Visitors are supposed to request permission from the Governor's representative in South Georgia. This one did not. In fact, they landed a working party to have a look at the junk lying around. The ship departed, without asking for any kind of permit, and left the working party behind on the island. An official protest was lodged with the Argentine government in Buenos Aires, but was not followed up by our people in Whitehall. The next move was the plan to get rid of *Endurance*. Bit of a coincidence, wouldn't you say?"

Ross remembered the bitter cold, the stark landscapes of arctic blue, and ice. A long, long way from Dorset. And now, in a few words, it was right here.

He heard a vehicle stopping out in the darkness, the sound of milk bottles, and some one whistling.

Parsons said, "Argentina has been on the boil for years. Political unrest, reprisals, all those things nobody wants to hear or know in Whitehall. They've had their eye on the Falklands for ages, never stopped since the last confrontation. *Now*, perhaps, somebody thinks we're too busy making cuts to notice, even to care."

"What's the general view?"

"There isn't one." Parsons stood up and walked to the centre of the room. "Colonel Souter agrees with me. But only in theory." He regarded Ross coolly. "He's more concerned with his immediate prospects. I suppose we all get like that eventually." He clapped his hands together. "But *not yet, not me!*"

Experience, instinct; how to define it? Like turning a corner, something completely different. Not some hole-in-the-wall experience. The booby trap, the sniper, the hidden bomb with just minutes to clear the building.

Ross knew very little about the Argentine armed forces, except that many of their ships were originally British, including their one and only aircraft carrier. If things were half as bad as Parsons believed, one would be enough. Especially with the 'Red Plum' in a breaker's yard.

He said, "So Operation Lazarus is a warm-up?"

Parsons sat down, as if a wire had been pulled. "Something like that. I'm seeing Colonel Souter again, day after tomorrow. Staff meeting. A couple of big noises from M.o.D. will be there, too." He suppressed a yawn. "At least we might save *Endurance*. That would be a start."

He was at the window again the next minute, the curtain turned back once more. This time the edge was grey, not black.

He turned and faced Ross.

"You haven't said much. Didn't give you much of an opportunity, did I? For or against, now's the time to say. I care, but I'll not hold it against you. Tell me, and it stops right here."

Ross heard a faint scraping sound over the tannoy system. At any moment the morning bugle would wake the birds, and the people who lived nearby. Even though it was only a taped Reveille.

He thought of Souter's despair. *More cuts . . .*

Their eyes met. Later, he might regret it. But then . . .

He said, "I'll still be ready, sir."

"Never doubted it." Parsons patted his pockets as if he was searching for something. Or momentarily at a loss. "Probably all blow over."

Long after the fake bugle call, his words seemed to hang in the air.

Sharon stood by the window and looked beyond the rooftops opposite to the power station chimneys on the other side of the Thames, sharp and clear in the sunlight. She had forgotten that the street here was so narrow; without curtains, it seemed she could reach out and touch the houses facing her.

She could hear Sue Blackwood slamming drawers in

another room. A last look, to make sure she was leaving nothing behind.

Sharon had only been back from Paris for twenty-four hours. It felt as if she had been away for years. She half turned. The apartment had been stripped bare. Packing cases awaiting collection, a bin full of screwed-up papers, an old calendar tossed on the top. The whole place looked alien. Waiting for them to go . . .

They had had lunch at a small Italian restaurant Sue had suggested, just around the corner, as everything seemed to be in Chelsea. It had been a busy, noisy place, a good choice; it had given them both time. Sue, the sister of the man she loved, until now had been a stranger.

The apartment had been sold. Even the *Focus* letter rack had vanished. Sue had said, in the midst of packing another suitcase, "They say it's going to be made into two flats. Property is like gold in this district."

She came into the room, flicking dust from one sleeve. "That about wraps it up!" She suddenly seized Sharon's hand and raised it to a shaft of sunlight, and held it so that the ring caught the light, as she had done in the restaurant, when she had lowered her head and kissed it. A few people had watched; one of the Italian waiters had beamed with pleasure and confusion.

"I'm so glad. For both of you."

Sharon took her arm. Just for a moment, she had seen Ross in the smile.

"What will you do now?"

Sue tossed some hair out of her eyes, in a characteristic, extravagant little gesture.

"Oh, it was never mine, as well you know, but it's gone, and my job's gone too. Not much of a Christmas present, is it?"

"What did your mother have to say about that?"

Sue was gazing around the room. "Joanna? I think she's quite glad." She took some keys out of her pocket and smiled. Ross again . . . "At least the car's paid for, that's something!"

She had told Sharon about Howard Ford during lunch.

"He's joined up with some other chap, or rather, his wife did. She's the one who holds the purse-strings."

"I heard about that when I got back to London." Sharon had seen the surprise in her face. "You know what it's like in our work – the old bush telegraph. Nothing's a secret for long!" She had waited for a lull in the conversation and clatter of crockery. "Clive told me about it. He's got a job for you, Sue, if you want it."

Sue had tossed it off carelessly. "Ross knew a good thing when he found you!" But she had been close to tears, something Sharon suspected was very rare. And it meant something had changed between them, perhaps from that moment. Sue had tried to hide it, and had called abruptly to one of the waiters, "Luigi! More wine! Another celebration!"

That was then. They walked slowly through the empty apartment. And here, where a bed had stood, Sharon felt her hesitation. Memories. Regrets.

Sue said, "What will you do for Christmas? Will you and Ross . . ." She saw the quick shake of the head. "Come down to Hawks Hill, then. It will be good for both of us. *All* of us."

"I spoke to Ross as soon as I got back. He's tied up, but we'll try to see each other." She twisted the ring around her finger unconsciously.

She felt Sue squeeze her arm. "You'll have to get used to that, now you've joined ranks with the Royals. You know what they call it. The family!"

Sharon said, "Take a last look around, Sue. Then we can go over to my place. Make a few arrangements."

Ross's sister had not heard her; she was looking at the room, and across into those adjoining, as if she were seeing something else. And there was the same door, where his uniform had been hanging. *Suppose I had never come here that day?*

She thought of his voice on the telephone. In England again, but so far away.

Sue said, "Ross nearly quit the Royal Marines, you know. You could almost feel the walls of Hawks Hill start to shake!"

"He told me. I was very touched that he could talk about it. We had only just met."

They left the room together, and Sue locked the door behind them. The same worn carpet. This was how she would remember it.

Sue was saying over her shoulder, "Fixed up the wedding yet?"

She was glad she could not see her face. "Long way off yet, worse luck. Invitations and dates. My mother will want to come over for it. I called her, long distance."

Sue did not turn.

"Come over?"

So much others did not know or share. But they would.

"Adelaide. She went to Australia a few years ago for a holiday and decided to stay. It's a long story. I'll tell you all about it some day."

The front door now, where a workman was already putting up a builder's notice board. So soon.

The garage was open, as she had seen it when the taxi had dropped her here. It was empty but for one car, a pale cream Mercedes 280SL. *At least the car's paid for.*

And Clive had made the job offer. She wanted to stop, right now, and go back into the deserted apartment. Hold on to something . . . the past. But she kept hearing Clive's voice. Perhaps she knew him too well, or believed she did. It had only been a casual remark, Clive just being himself. She should know . . .

But it would not go away.

Sue was putting the last bag into the boot. The car was very dusty, and some one had written with his finger on the side, WASH ME.

"Well, I'll be damn glad to get away from the Smoke for a bit!" She looked back. "You coming, love?"

Sharon said, "Yes," absently. It had been about the wedding. Clive had remarked, "Easter? Very romantic!" Then quickly, or looking back, it seemed so, "Could be a busy time for Ross's commandos. Manoeuvres, and all that sort of thing."

Her own voice. "Have you heard something?"

He was being vague now, the other Clive. Non-committal; smoothing it over.

"Just talk, darling. But it would be such a shame to do all that work and lay out all that cash, if you should have to postpone it."

Was that all?

Sue had opened the passenger door for her. "You'll have to show me the way!" She was laughing, glad to be out of it now, on the move.

Sharon slid in and reached for the seat belt.

Ross had told her about this car. She lowered her head to look up at the windows, the one where she had been standing.

Could be a busy time for Ross's commandos.

Maybe it was only something to say. But Clive knew a lot of people, and heard whispers and rumours that later made the headlines.

As if he was trying to prepare her. Warn her.

She felt Ross's sister pat her thigh companionably.

"Don't worry, Sharon, we all go through it. Life can be crappy sometimes."

She watched the house backing away, the workman turning to watch the sports car drive off.

And suddenly, she was afraid.

Lieutenant Peter Hamlyn stood on the edge of a makeshift jetty and watched the working party of seamen and marines crowding around a tea fanny, the arrival of which had brought things to a halt. It was hard to tell how much had changed or been achieved since his last inspection: fresh grey paint gleaming in the hard sunlight, piles of wood shavings littering the deck or floating in puddles left by yesterday's rain. Difficult to picture the final result, or even feel any excitement at the prospect.

This was one of three powerful-looking launches which had been berthed in Poole while a transformation was carried out. Many of the more senior men had been complaining about it, not directly to Hamlyn, but always loudly enough for him to overhear.

Small craft were being hired, commandeered or borrowed to ease the strain on naval building programmes, and this particular vessel had been intended for the protection of maritime oil rigs. In the near future, due to the threat of terrorist attacks, marine commandos would be required to carry out patrols alongside the drilling mechanics to ensure that possible targets were always under surveillance.

The government would do anything, it seemed, rather than provide funds for suitable, purpose-built vessels, designed and laid down by people who had been supplying the Royal Navy and marines since sail had given way to steam. Hamlyn had endured plenty of wry humour on the subject, particularly the one about the NAAFI manager who always locked and immobilized his canteen supply launch whenever he was called elsewhere, otherwise he feared he might find it painted grey and flying the White Ensign by the time he got back.

Once the greatest navy in the world, they said. Now it was reduced to anything that could be begged, commandeered or hired. Exaggerated, maybe, but privately Hamlyn was in full agreement.

He had seen several vessels similar to this one already in use in Northern Ireland, as well as the Middle East. But it took more than a lick of paint to turn it into a weapon of war. If only they could get away from the never-ending drills and stand bys. He could feel the men's resentment and discontent for himself, but requests for transfer to other units, plus the growing list of names at the defaulters' table, told the full story.

He heard some one shouting names, checking them against the inevitable list. Sergeant Ken Norris, nicknamed 'Smiler' because he never did. Always on the ball; one of the most reliable faces in the company. Marine Jock Marsh, the crack shot who had demonstrated his skills in Londonderry. Another voice: Sergeant Dick Harwood. Tough, popular, no-nonsense. Hamlyn had been surprised that Harwood had taken his third 'tape' rather than remain a corporal after he had married. That was another story. But his loyalty to Ross Blackwood was something else, personal and very private.

Harwood had a ready wit, and knew exactly how far he could go with it. Hamlyn had welcomed him to the company, and remarked how well and fit he was looking after his tour in Ulster.

Harwood had clasped his hands across his belt and grinned.

"Gave up drivin' officers about every day, sir! I was gettin' as porky as they were!"

He glanced at his watch. The afternoon was free, provided some senior officer did not drop in with another crackpot scheme to start everybody dripping. And Captain Toby Forester would be doing his rounds soon. He never seemed to get bored or impatient. But with Forester, how could you tell?

He stamped his feet; he had not noticed how cold he had become. So near the sea, the keen wind making a lie of the sunlight.

He had gone over it so many times, but it made no difference. It had happened before Christmas, with all the flap about stand bys and Operation Lazarus, if that wasn't enough. *Keep them on their toes. Drive them, if you have to. Remember, the first line in defence and the springboard for attack!*

It was easy to say. Easier still to lay the blame.

He had even thought it was quite funny at the beginning. It wasn't funny any more.

It had all started with a game of tennis. There were two large undercover courts just outside the temporary base. He could hear Forester saying it, as if it were yesterday.

"We'll make up a foursome, what d' you say? No time to get bored or browned off!"

Two young women. One was Forester's sister, a tall, rather ungainly player, but deceptively fast on her feet. Hamlyn could not even remember her name. And the other one was Lois, slim, dark, vivacious. So full of life. The sort of girl . . . He tried to close his mind. Slam the door. But it was already too late. He had known it would happen, right from the first hint, the first touch and response. She was Forester's wife.

Then why? He knew the score, and had been close enough once or twice. Mess parties, the aftermath. Maybe the risk had always been part of it; the temptation. If he

273

stopped to think about it, he wondered if it was because he was a little older than most of his companions. *Up through the ranks.* More experienced. She had remarked on it once, asked him if he worried about it. That her husband was two years younger than his 'lovely lieutenant'.

So easy to deny, to pretend. He should have stopped it there and then.

Next year, if everything continued in his favour, promotion was at the gate.

He had done well, and had learned a lot, not least that it didn't come on a plate. When it came down to it, the Old Pals' Act carried far more weight than Queen's Regulations and Standing Orders put together.

I saw it coming, old boy. Or, *what can you expect?*

But he had wanted her. He still did.

He heard Harwood telling some one to get a move on. *Get the bloody job over an' done with.*

He was here now, his eyes moving across the working party and the empty tea mugs.

"Nearly finished, sir." Then, "Great news about Major Blackwood namin' the day. Just right for each other. It comes to all of us in the end, the lucky ones, I mean!"

He strode away, already consulting his list and calling another name. Hamlyn breathed out slowly. A hint? A friendly warning? Even his mind was playing tricks on him.

"That looks more like it, Peter!" It was Forester, and he had not even seen him coming. "This boat and that other one in the moorings have got to be ready to move in two days' time. Devonport, to await collection. All they've told me so far." He covered a yawn with his fist. "I suppose we'll be the last to know, as usual."

"I'll have them ready, sir."

"Never doubted it. Seems a long time since Christmas

. . . they're already taking bets on Easter leave. Maybe we'll draw the right straw this time."

What would he do if he knew what had happened? Would happen again if she so much as crooked her little finger?

Like that time, sitting in the back of the car, when Forester had been at the wheel with the passenger seat full of Christmas gifts for the local hospital. She had pulled his hand on to her knee, held it there, and had even laughed about something that had happened that day. And all the time, watching him, moving his hand suggestively, nearer and nearer . . .

Forester swung round and said, "Lieutenant-Colonel Parsons. I can tell *you*, Peter. I'm not happy about him." He hesitated, as if testing himself, or perhaps gauging Hamlyn's silence. "He's going to the top, and fast. Too fast for my liking. You have to tread on a lot of people to rise so quickly. Say what you like, it puts a nasty taste in the mouth."

Hamlyn looked down at the launch alongside. The frank description of Parsons had taken him completely aback. Always correct where duty and routine were concerned, but Forester had never shown any concern or interest in personalities, not senior ones, anyway.

He said cautiously, "He's a go-getter. Not a bad thing at this stage of affairs in the armed forces, I'd have thought." It gave him time to recover. "Major Blackwood seems to get along with him."

"Hmm. You're an admirer of Ross Blackwood, I can see that."

Hamlyn thought of the girl in Derry, weeping for her man. The same girl outside the police station, cursing the marines as if they had killed him. *Maybe we did.* He heard himself answer, "I trust him, sir. It was why I came to this unit."

"Good. Good show." Forester turned away. "Come over for a drink this evening." He waved to somebody, his driver, perhaps. "I'd like that. So would Lois."

Hamlyn was still standing on the makeshift jetty when the car drove away.

Leave it. Walk away right now. While you can.

He thought he heard Sergeant Harwood blowing his whistle. It was time to dismiss, until tomorrow, and that damned launch which never seemed to be any different. He should have a quick word with Harwood, check what still needed doing. But he did not move.

She would be there. Ready to tease him, excite him, in Forester's very presence. He was not naive enough to think that she had not done it before, and she would do it again with some one else after they were moved apart.

Even the thought of that aroused him.

He looked down at the launch. It was deserted.

Tomorrow could wait.

CHAPTER SIXTEEN

Ross Blackwood nodded to the shadowy figure who had guided him to this place and indicated a chair by an empty table. He had lost count of the doors and stairways and, finally, a fast-moving lift, but remained conscious of urgency and privilege. No 'what took you so long?' this time. Even his identity had been only casually checked. As unreal as this place, a subterranean world beneath a busy street of double-decker buses and grid-locked, homebound traffic, people hurrying to Underground stations, and shops crammed with chocolate Easter eggs, rabbits and Disney-like, fluffy chickens.

He looked around the cellar, or vault; a 'Tactical War Room', some one had called it. The ceiling was curved to withstand blast from bomb or rocket, and perhaps was one of many, a relic from the war when London had known what it was like to live under bombardment.

Down here it was silent, timeless. Heavy traffic moving overhead, and yet not a vibration or a sound. Like being suspended in space. He felt warm air on his cheek. Or being buried . . .

He leaned forward slightly. There was another level immediately below, only partly lit, but he could see several huge map tables, covered with sheets, and more hanging charts beyond.

He saw his reflection in a glass screen. That was another curiosity. He seemed to be the only person here in uniform. Like an intruder.

And yet the other, more familiar building could not be more than ten minutes' walk away.

He was surprised that he was not tired. Unlike the last time when he had been driven directly from Poole: the glaring headlines, the haste. He felt his mouth lift in a smile. Parsons and all his schemes . . . Well, they had done their part. And for what?

Some one coughed, and more lights came on, as if it were a prearranged signal.

It was Colonel Souter, hand outstretched, his shadow leaning ahead of his body against the stark background.

"Good to see you, Ross! Sorry about the cloak of secrecy!"

For an instant Ross thought he was referring to his own appearance. He could not recall the last time, if ever, he had seen Souter in anything but uniform. Now, in a smart dark grey suit, gleaming white shirt and Royal Marines tie, he might have been mistaken for some successful businessman, or perhaps one of those so confident politicians who appeared regularly on TV or in the press.

"Everything going well at Poole? That's good." As usual, he had not waited for a response. He gestured toward the map tables, one of which had been uncovered, although Ross had not seen anybody on the lower level. "Things are moving, Ross. Wanted to put you in the frame, so to speak. I feel I owe it to you. I got you mixed up with Clive Tobin's various escapades, and, my God, you almost bought it. I blame myself for that."

More lights spread across the nearest table, and an immense map of the Falkland Islands. A man's head and shoulders threw a small shadow across one corner: another of Souter's invisible army.

Souter said, "It's still on, although from the common sense you glean in certain quarters you'd think it was all in the bloody mind!"

Ross had studied all the available information which had been sent to him, or imparted by Parsons between various combat exercises. The Argentines had landed workers in South Georgia to sort out and value the scrap in and around the old whaling station. They had not requested permission, and despite the messages dispatched by the Falklands' governor to Whitehall no action had been taken, and no official complaint lodged. In the House of Commons and in the Lords, the question of H.M.S. *Endurance* had been raised again, several times. To be sold or to be scrapped? One minister had suggested that as things stood, *Endurance*'s continuing presence in the South Atlantic might be a liability, or interpreted as a provocation.

Endurance had landed her own small contingent of Royal Marines in South Georgia. That, too, had brought criticism from politicians on both sides of the House.

Souter said, "Do nothing, and that's wrong. Show even a hint of displeasure and you're branded a warmonger!"

He sat down heavily and stared at the map below him.

"We've had another meeting. Intelligence people – you name it. All you get is wait-and-see. What bloody strategy is that?" He grunted with obvious disapproval. "Parsons is in the thick of it too, but you know that. The army and the R.A.F. are all on Easter leave, or soon will be, and our lot aren't much better."

Ross watched the anger, the crushing, aging despair. Like somebody else. Recalling the guard of honour, Souter's personal welcome back to England, to life. It was hard to see him as that same man.

Souter looked at him keenly. "You get on with Parsons?"

"We don't always agree, sir. But then, I don't always go along with your ideas, even though I might not dare to say as much."

He saw the makings of a smile. Not much, but it was more like the Souter of old.

"Takes me back, Ross. Takes me back. Your father . . . it could be him sitting there." The moment passed. "I still think I'm right. Weeks, months, who knows? I don't trust these Argentines. A cover-up, a show of power elsewhere, and they think the world will ignore the very real troubles they've created in their own damned back yard!"

He reached out and opened a drawer.

"Private report. Thought you should have it. Might come in handy if the going gets rough. You and your team are still on stand by." There was the faintest suggestion of a smile. "'Lazarus'."

Ross took it. It was written in Souter's sloping, recognizable hand. He knew what was coming; perhaps he had guessed it from the start.

"I'm leaving, Ross. Going to Washington, then on to the U.S. Marine Corps. A bit of open co-operation . . . it makes sense. Good sense, the way things are heading."

Ross watched him, hating it, thinking of the bare office. The U.S.M.C. paperweight would be gone, too.

Souter said, "Be ready, Ross. It's coming soon. Sooner than most people believe." He tapped his forehead. "Closed minds! As that old sod Harold Macmillan said, 'They never had it so good!'" He stood up abruptly. "At a price, but they don't remember that."

They walked together, Souter leading, to a door Ross had not noticed before. Souter glanced back; the map was suddenly in darkness.

He said, "Parsons will be all right. Bit ahead of his time, maybe." He gripped his elbow. "Just watch out for *yourself.*" The hand moved gently on his arm. "Sorry about delaying your wedding."

More stairs, and another lift.

He felt a gust of cold air, and heard the increasing rumble of traffic.

Somehow he knew they would not meet again.

He would tell Sharon, share it with her. He looked down as if he expected to see her hand on his arm, the ring, a promise and a future. No matter what . . .

He turned to speak, or to reply. But he was alone.

Sergeant Dick Harwood paused outside the door marked 'Guardroom' and looked over at one of the cars nearby, recognizing its number, something he had taught himself to do when he had been driving around Ulster. Faces might change; numbers did not. It looked as if the stroppy half-colonel Parsons was back. No peace for the wicked, his father used to say.

There was a full-length mirror outside the guardroom. Above it was printed in large letters, GOING ASHORE? THEN *LOOK* THE PART!

He grinned at himself. Uniform right, nothing unbuttoned, green beret at the correct angle. His eyes lingered on the three stripes on his sleeve. Those, he was still not used to. Corporal to sergeant was perhaps the biggest step a marine could take. It made him feel different. He *was* different. He even felt taller.

It seemed so quiet, not like the usual bustle, the constant comings and goings of their local headquarters. He had heard that this had once been a holiday camp, then a sailing club. It was hard to believe.

He looked at the main gate and the marine on picket

duty. The only difference there was that he was wearing a sidearm on his belt. *For the emergency.* He pushed open the door. If the sentry had time to draw his pistol, it wouldn't help much if there was a vehicle filled with explosives and a time fuse on the doormat.

A corporal looked up from the table.

"You're wanted over at the officers' mess, Sarge. Just got the call."

"Never been much of a hand at mind-readin', Todd. Do I have to guess?"

He was still learning, feeling his way, and getting there.

Todd was a good enough corporal, but he took chances if he could. *It takes one to know one.*

Todd answered smartly enough, " 'Tenant-Colonel Parsons. The major's not back yet." It sounded like a warning. Todd might make sergeant himself one day.

Harwood left the guardroom and headed for the officers' mess building on the far side of the square, where parades, when required, were mustered. He glanced at the mirror critically once more as he passed. Parsons seemed to be on top line where his work was concerned, but he was not above handing out a bottle if he thought some one needed it. He had heard him having a go at one marine for letting his hair grow too long. The sort of blast you might expect from a green subaltern on his first posting.

He smiled to himself. Hair just right. Not over the collar, and not too short like some brand-new rookie, or one of the hard cases just out of the glasshouse.

There was nobody around. Not even a defaulter doing some extra work. Everybody was already away on Easter leave, at home with their families, or on holiday abroad. No wonder the marines of the Special Operations units were fed up about it.

He thought of the launches he had been helping to

convert for active service. A couple of Bofors guns, and a few strips of plastic armour: a bit like Derry and Belfast. *Too little, too late.* Two boats had already been moved to Devonport; a third would follow shortly. After that, probably back to Stonehouse Barracks . . . But he never got bored. There was never time. This was the only life he knew or wanted. And he had almost got engaged. He breathed out loudly. *Almost.* It could keep for a little longer.

One of the messmen saw him coming.

"End room, Sarge. The Boss-Man wants to see you!"

"Any one else?"

"Cap'n Forester. Looks as if 'e needs some back-up."

Harwood said nothing. But he always listened; there was not much that the messmen missed. Casual conversations at table, anger, humour, depression, nothing got past the men who were merely part of the background. He waited while the messman went ahead to tell the 'Boss-Man' he was here.

This was the first time he had served under Forester. Always very calm, never gave off much. But an officer who missed very little.

He glanced at a letter rack by the porter's lobby, and saw a letter slightly apart from the rest, for Lieutenant Hamlyn, his immediate superior. A good man to have around if you were in a jam, or you were really up against it. Those in his unit seemed to like him, and Harwood had noticed from the beginning that nobody took liberties with him. Or, if they did, they soon learned to watch out for themselves.

He considered the other side of Hamlyn. He took risks, and he was taking a big one now, if he was hoping for promotion. There were not too many secrets in 'the family', and he had heard that Hamlyn was all set to get his third pip.

So why would he hazard everything by playing around

with Forester's wife? Maybe it wasn't obvious to most people, or not yet, anyway. But a sergeant was in the middle, neither one thing nor the other, and the sergeant often saw what others missed. Until . . .

"This way, Sarge."

Lieutenant-Colonel Parsons was standing by a mock fireplace, facing the door. He was hardly ever seen sitting down. And even those who hated his guts had to admit he could keep up with the toughest marine on any of the exercises they had endured since he had first appeared amongst them.

This was a wooden building like all the others, very similar to the sergeants' mess eighty yards away. A picture of the Queen at one end of the room; some group photographs at the other.

Forester said, "That third launch will be moved tomorrow, Sergeant. Have you got the working parties lined up?"

Harwood said, "Yes, sir." It sounded like *of course*.

He thought Forester looked worried. That was unusual.

Parsons said abruptly, "There have been a few changes. The first two boats are to be put aboard the fleet transport *Manxman*, and it will save time if the same working parties are used."

Harwood waited, expecting Forester to intervene. He felt the tension, and trod warily.

"Tomorrow, sir?"

Parsons glanced coolly at him. "You are the duty N.C.O., I believe?" He did not wait for an answer. "I mean now!"

The same messman entered with a tray and a silver teapot.

Parsons said, "Good show. You could die of thirst in this place!"

Harwood saw the messman give him a look. *Watch your step.*

Forester stared at the cup of tea which had been placed at his side.

"Major Blackwood will be back very shortly. He wants all N.C.O.s here in an hour. Put the word about. I want *everybody*, no absentees, right?"

Harwood said, "Right," and cleared his throat. "Has the balloon gone up, sir?"

Forester turned blank eyes on him, surprised, or angered into silence. Parsons banged his cup into the saucer.

"Well, why not? You're a part of it, Sergeant." He was smiling. " 'Lazarus' has risen again. It is a full emergency. For *us*, in any case."

That would be something to make them all sit up in the sergeants' mess. *And I said to the Boss-Man . . .*

He saw another messman come in with a telephone, and plug it into a wall socket. Forester had a file of papers open on his lap, and was staring at them, but his eyes were not moving.

Parsons took the telephone, and covered the mouthpiece. "Don't hang about. Get more men if you need them. That's an order." He turned his back. "From *me*!"

Harwood left the room, still grappling with what he had seen and heard. Piece by piece, as if he was describing it. All those faces, some he had known on and off over the years; it was like that in the Royals. Others just walked into your life, and after that it was up to you. You laughed it off, or you hit back.

He saw the duty corporal running to meet him. It was no longer a secret. A full emergency. Soon the whole place would be jumping.

He did not know why, but he was glad the waiting was over. And that he was a part of it.

Reeves, the W.O.2, the senior and also oldest marine stationed at Poole, drew his heels soundlessly together and reported, "All present, sir. Sarn't Harwood on special duty." Big, heavily built, and known as 'Tosh', but only behind his back, he was an impressive figure. He had barely raised his voice, and yet it was as if he had crashed his boots and shouted at the top of his powerful lungs. One of the old school: he did not need to do either. He was in charge.

Ross Blackwood walked to the edge of the low platform and looked at the waiting faces. It had taken longer than expected to get here. A truck overturned in the road, angry exchanges, unmoved police taking notes. Some one sobbing.

He lifted his hand.

"Sit down, please. You've been hanging about long enough." He felt the tension slipping away, the resentment also. This had to be close, personal. It had to be right.

Captain Forester and a lieutenant he scarcely knew were by the wall. Parsons was still around, but out of sight. His mind repeated it. *It has to be right.*

Faces with names; others he knew only by sight or caught in some aspect of memory. All part of it. Young, some very young, but all individuals.

'Tosh' Reeves might be remembering when the Royal Marines were very different. As one old instructor had said, *So long as you can salute smartly an' shoot straight, you'll do for me!*

Now, even the inner strength of the commando was changing. Acting as one, or standing together, each man was a separate unit. Professionals. Sergeants and corporals. It was no longer enough merely to obey orders, and die.

"You've all been following the news about events in the South Atlantic, and in the Falklands. You have been on stand by, and you have probably used and heard more curses and gained more cuts and bruises than even Mr. Reeves knew existed!"

A few smiles; the lieutenant was leaning over to answer or ask Forester a question.

"There have been more reports, *verified* reports, about Argentine ship movements. These are not something you can hide. And the official reason is that the Argentine navy is on a combined anti-submarine exercise. I am informed that most of the naval berths and moorings are empty. So, if it *is* only an exercise, it will certainly prove a damned expensive one."

He had their full attention; they were very quiet now, and he saw one man turning to say something to another behind him, exchange nods. A grin, too.

"Most of our armed forces are on leave. I could hear you lot moaning about it from the main road!" There were some laughs. He saw the sergeant known as Smiler prod his companion's arm, perhaps to ask him something. The other man nodded, very definitely.

"The situation is officially unchanged. A watching brief, you might call it."

He thought of her voice on the telephone. "I *knew*, Ross. I had a feeling. I want you to know. I understand. I love you. I'll wait to hear . . ." The rest had been lost. What must she really think?

"For us, things have been upgraded. Tomorrow the first sections will be moved to Plymouth, Devonport, where you will embark aboard a transport." He looked along the faces, wishing he could reach each one individually. This was a technique, an interpersonal skill, which could never be gained by training. They never told you . . . "As of now, we are at combat readiness." He must have been making some gesture; he let his arms fall to his sides. "People will be proud of you." He wanted to smile, or offer something profound, some sentiment they would remember, but all that came was, "As I am."

He walked from the platform, leaving behind a silence so intense that he could have been back in the underground War Room.

They were all on their feet, not at attention, but turning to watch him leave.

One voice shattered the stillness.

"Good on you, Major! We're on our way!"

The tension seemed to snap. They were stamping and cheering, and he felt some one reach out to touch his arm as he passed.

He did not remember finding the door, the escape. He was glad only that they could not see his face.

Captain Toby Forester leaned over a guardrail and peered along the full length of the ship. Like most of the Royal Marines, especially commandos, his sea experience had been limited to small warships, frigates or the mixed collection of launches and patrol vessels of the Special Boat Squadron, where you knew every face and could relay an order without even raising your voice.

The Royal Fleet Auxiliary *Manxman* was huge by comparison. Built along the lines of a freighter, and used for carrying every kind of equipment, fuel and stores for the fleet at large, she was almost overwhelming.

The two launches were dwarfed, side by side on the main deck. Above and around them derricks hovered like storks, ready to hoist and then lower them alongside under almost any conditions. One of *Manxman*'s officers had said, "We'll put 'em where you want 'em. After that it'll be your problem!" Like the ship's stocky, bearded captain, he had seen and moved just about everything.

To them, the commandos and their kit were just another cargo.

It was almost done. N.C.O.s had reported their sections allotted to messing areas, muster points for any emergency, and places where they could exercise or drill as events dictated. Devonport was next to and a part of Plymouth itself, although local people insisted there was a distinct, if invisible, barrier between them.

To the marines, Plymouth was a part of their own particular world, and Forester had seen several of them looking wistfully at the land, maybe thinking of risking a run ashore, despite rigid orders to the contrary.

A long day: Forester could hardly remember a busier one since the so-called emergency. Ever since Parsons had burst into their lives.

He was up on the massive bridge right now. Studying the ship's navigational aids, "getting the feel of things", as he put it. Maybe if the emergency proved to be a false one Parsons would be sent elsewhere, to make some one else's life a misery.

Forester moved along the rail, if only to avoid some seamen who were hoisting yet another crate of stores from one of the carefully marked hatchways.

It was getting dark. He shivered. Darker than usual. He could see a procession of headlights passing between two blocks of buildings. People going home for the long week-end. Or maybe, like most of the armed services, heading away on holiday. No wonder he had heard some of the marines complaining about it. 'If you can't take a joke' did not carry much weight at the moment aboard the *Manxman*.

He thought suddenly of Blackwood, and his address to the N.C.O.s. He had not bragged or boasted; he had simply talked. Shared it. Forester always felt that he had the measure of his men when he was called upon to speak about company matters and daily routine. If you went beyond that, you could so easily make a fool of yourself if you stepped over the line. Keep your distance, and your self-respect remained intact.

He heard voices below him and saw Hamlyn with a corporal, studying a sheet of paper and ticking off one of the items. The corporal laughed, and Forester saw him touch the lieutenant's arm. "You owe me a tot for finding that one, sir!"

That sort of familiarity disturbed him. When he had been a young subaltern he had found himself in hot water with his commanding officer because one of his marines had let him down. He had trusted him, and had got the rocket because of it.

Hamlyn seemed to cope with it. Outwardly easygoing, but never casual. He knew where to draw the line.

He turned toward the dockyard again. It was darker still, and some lighted windows were coming to life by the road. Probably a pub. There would not be much business this evening. Everybody was on leave.

He thought about Lois, considered what she might be doing. Maybe visiting the people she knew at the tennis club. They had been married less than three years, and he still noticed the looks they got when they were together. She could turn anybody's head . . . He could guess what some of the glances implied. In a strange way, it excited him. Something he always remembered when they were alone together.

She had seemed keen on Peter Hamlyn from the beginning, teasing him, even scolding him when they played tennis; and he seemed to enjoy it. Who wouldn't?

He still did not know what had made him do it. She had been writing a letter a few days ago when he had arrived at their rented flat near the Poole H.Q. He had seen her cover it, so it was something private. It was only later that he began to question it. And then later, when he had seen an envelope in the porter's lobby, for Hamlyn. The address had been typed, and yet . . . He still could not understand what had made him suspicious, but he had pulled the letter from the rack to examine it. If any one had seen him, it would have been hard to explain, and now he almost wished he had left it alone. He had not recognized the envelope but her perfume had left no room for doubt; it was the same musky, sensual smell she had sometimes sprayed on letters to him. He saw her vividly now in his mind. The way she laughed and moved, and touched her lower lip with her tongue.

I must have been blind. Stupid.

He swung round; there was some one right beside him. "*Yes?* What is it?"

He hardly recognized his own voice.

"From Major Blackwood, sir. Would you join him on the upper bridge." He was pointing into the shadows.

"I *know* where it is, man!" He wanted to reach out, apologize. It was not like him; he never lost control. But the messenger had gone, and was probably even now letting off steam about it. *Forester's got the jitters.* Or worse.

He forced himself to walk unhurriedly toward the bridge superstructure, taking his time, allowing his mind to settle. Some one was testing the starboard navigation light, *on – off – on – off*, like a huge green eye. As if the ship was preparing to get under way.

But all he could think about was Lois. What might have caused this . . . this thing to happen. Beyond imagination and belief.

Something close by gave a metallic shudder, a small generator or a piece of hoisting tackle. In his blurred mind, it seemed as if the entire ship was coming alive. Leaving.

There had never been any rift or misunderstanding in their marriage. People had remarked on it. Friends envied them.

Only once, that he could remember, there had been something trivial, when Lois had had a bit too much to drink, and he had warned her about it. There had been no anger that he could recall, but her words were suddenly as fresh as if she had just spoken them aloud.

Say and do what you like, Toby. But don't you ever take me for granted.

And now, it was too late.

Ross Blackwood paused on the bridge wing and stared into the surrounding darkness. After the contained world of the chart room it seemed noisy and almost hostile, with pellets of spray hitting his borrowed oilskin, thrown up from *Manxman*'s invisible bows. He could feel the ship trembling to the regular thrust of the screws, as if *Manxman* were glad to be moving, free of the land, now that the uncertainty and frustration were over.

Things had happened quickly. During the forenoon watch today, Friday, the signal had been received, and everything had changed. It infuriated him to think that those in authority had delayed until the very last moment, ignoring the inevitable, until it was too late to prevent it.

In the early hours of the morning Special Forces of the Argentine army and navy had landed in the Falklands, over a thousand troops sweeping into the capital, Stanley, with armoured vehicles in support.

He looked abeam and saw some tiny lights blinking through the darkness. Navigation buoys, the last links with the land. The ship was moving fast, despite her size and bulk; the captain had mentioned eighteen knots, and you could feel it. Down Channel, and leaving the Lizard astern, into the deep and heavy water of the Atlantic itself. You could feel that, too.

The captain seemed quite unruffled by the sudden demand for action; his ship had been made ready for sea in no time. Ross had been on the bridge when *Manxman* had moved into open water. A few people waving from the dockyard; and he had seen the last mail go ashore. There had been less than he expected. Perhaps the marines, irrespective of age or service, were like the ship, tired of waiting and eager to get on with it. And some had probably thought they would hear it was another false alarm when eventually they reached their first stop. It only added to the sense of unreality. Time and distance: a challenge even to the most experienced sailor. Ascension Island was their first landfall, over three and a half thousand miles away, where they would rendezvous with other ships. Ross could imagine the nightmare this was for operational and signals staff: thousands of men and women to be recalled from leave, many of whom would be out of the country, blissfully unaware of the crisis until the truth burst in upon them. Ships with depleted crews, aircraft standing down for Easter, utter confusion until some one took overall command. A war footing. In the midst of peace, it was almost incredible.

It would take a week, maybe more, to reach Ascension. What then? So much for the 'anti-submarine manoeuvres'. The Argentine chiefs of staff must be laughing their heads off.

He had been around the ship and spoken to as many of the marines as he could at such short notice. There was a certain grim determination, and a measure of bitterness as well. *Some one should have known! Done something!*

Ross felt much the same; but the sentiment had to stop right there.

Parsons had been outwardly unmoved by the sudden call for action. He had stayed most of the time on the bridge, ready to deal with any relevant signal the moment it was decoded.

"Keep them all on their toes. Don't let 'em get stale before we even reach the first hurdle, eh? It's not going to be a walk-over, no matter what the 'experts' have to say about it!"

Ross went down to his cabin and decided to go through his notes yet again. Parsons was right about keeping occupied. Empty days meant boredom, and even the most reliable marine could come apart waiting . . . always waiting.

He opened his old pocket book; he could not remember how long it had been with him. Bits of dried leaf used as markers, from the jungle in Malaysia. Grains of sand caught in the binding. Scribbled telephone numbers, Londonderry and Belfast. Her name beside them. He could remember so well, waiting at the hotel. He smiled a little. Fort Amazon . . .

The small photo she had found for him that last day. One Larry had taken of her in a swimsuit on location somewhere. He felt only sadness, not envy. But how could he expect her to put up with this sort of life?

He watched an empty cup vibrating beside the notebook, and could imagine the great shafts driving the screws, thrusting into the Atlantic, the land sliding away, lingering in the radar for a little longer.

There was a gentle tap at the door. It was Forester. Like Parsons, he had seemed unruffled by the call to arms, but he had always managed to contain his emotions. He seemed a trifle strained, but nothing unusual.

He was glancing around the cabin, probably without seeing it.

"Thought you might care to come along for a drink, sir."

Ross stood up. He liked Forester, but he was not an easy man to know, 'beyond the wrapping', as he had heard Harwood say of some one.

"Sure, why not? Been on your rounds?"

"Yes, sir." But he was staring at the photograph, Sharon in her swimsuit, legs lean and tanned against the sand. "They're all settled down, as far as I can judge."

Ross put the photo back into his notebook. *Relax. Have that drink, and take it off your back.*

Very soon, everything would change. He thought of the major with the battered face and broken nose. All that time ago. It felt like last week. *You think you know it all. Can handle any damn thing that crops up. Part of the job. Then one day, everybody's looking to you. You're the only one who can deal with it. Know your people, Ross. Don't rely on your rank or popularity when the cards are stacked against you.*

He remembered Forester's eyes on the photo. He was married; Ross had met his wife a couple of times. He heard Harwood's voice again. *Nice bit of stuff. But likes to put it around a bit.* Some one else, then, but was that the problem?

If they had to fight, they were expected to win. It was what they had all been taught to believe. The green beret: something special, something to be proud of.

"A drink it is, Toby. We'll get the others to join us."

He turned toward the door, but not before he had seen the shutters come down. Like Houston's warning, all those years ago.

Know your people.

But that was then. This was now.

CHAPTER SEVENTEEN

The Royal Fleet Auxiliary *Manxman* arrived at Ascension Island in the South Atlantic half a day ahead of schedule, despite heavy weather and strong winds for much of the passage. There was no time to get used to the island; within three days of frantic activity the order was received to weigh and proceed. Any belief, or hope, that the operation had gone off at half-cock came to an end.

Ross Blackwood was on the same bridge wing when *Manxman* got under way again. It was something he would never forget; an experience exciting, after all the uncertainty and rumour, and also very moving.

Ascension was a hump of volcanic rock jutting out of an empty sea; the island of St. Helena was its closest neighbour, seven hundred miles away. The mountain, which had appeared on radar before anything else, was surprisingly green and lush, and must have been an answer to many a seaman's prayer in the days of sail.

There were so many ships assembled that it was hard to believe such a fleet had been gathered in so short a time: Fleet Auxiliaries, freighters, and tankers. Two frigates also made a welcome appearance. The queen of the fleet was the liner S.S. *Canberra*, a household name, and well known on the major cruising routes.

Canberra's decks were lined with khaki figures, waving

and cheering as *Manxman* passed slowly abeam.

Ross had gone over the details of transfers and cross-loading: Royal Marine commandos, the S.A.S., and men of the Parachute Regiment, the toughest fighting force he could imagine. Even the hardest critics had changed their tune.

If anything, the mood of this Special Operations company was anger, an unspoken desire to hit back. The day after leaving Plymouth they had received the signal which had changed everything. Argentine forces had extended their invasion to the big island of South Georgia, where their first unofficial landing parties had gone ashore, and, despite protests by the Governor, had remained. There had always been a small garrison of Royal Marines in Stanley, a token force of some thirty-seven men. They had put up a stiff resistance when the initial attack had been launched, but had been ordered by the Governor to surrender to the invaders to avoid civilian casualties. They had little choice, three dozen marines against an army of Argentine Special Forces. There was also a detachment of marines in South Georgia, which had been landed earlier from their own ship, H.M.S. *Endurance.* The one-sided battle was settled after two and a half hours' fighting, during which the marines had managed to shoot down an enemy helicopter and damage a corvette with small arms fire.

From that moment the campaign had become personal, a matter of pride, and of revenge.

He watched the lines of troops and marines on *Canberra*'s upper decks; there were more tiny figures clinging to stays and lifeboats, cheering and shouting, their voices suddenly drowned by *Manxman*'s booming response.

From the first definite news of an Argentine invasion, it

had taken only twenty-four hours to send warships heading south. A token force. He found that he had raised his arm and was waving at the ill-matched armada with all the rest. Lieutenant-Colonel Parsons had been in conference with the other senior officers. On his return to *Manxman* he had been sharp and in an ill humour.

He had been outnumbered and outranked, something quite new to Parsons. Unless he had already forgotten what it was like.

"I want all officers in the chart room. Fifteen minutes."

He glanced at some marines who were waving at one of the anchored ships.

"What are those fools doing? Get some of that muddle cleared up, if they need work to do!"

Ross said, "Senior N.C.O.s too, sir?"

Parsons snapped, "Do I have to repeat myself?" and his mood changed instantly. "Forget that, Ross. Didn't mean to take it out of you. Too many voices – I thought my brain would burst!"

Ross looked down involuntarily as Parsons gripped his wrist.

"The S.A.S. will do *this*! The Paras will do *that*! Don't they realize that the real brain is at Northwood? *It* will decide!"

Ross thought of the underground War Room, the last time he had seen Souter. It was nothing compared with Northwood, or H.M.S. *Warrior*, its official title. A massive underground complex outside London, in the suburbs, and unofficially known as The Hole. The First Sea Lord would be there with his huge operational staff. He had probably taken command when the first indication of Argentine intentions had been brought to his notice. He had not missed much; otherwise this strange fleet would not be here at Ascension, might never have left harbour.

Parsons knew that side of operations better than most. But this was the sharp end. Something very different.

He said curtly, "The first prime target is South Georgia itself, where the whole thing started. Except that nobody would believe it, not *then*, anyway." He calmed himself with an almost physical effort. "It was a good choice. It's eight hundred miles from the main Falklands group. Gives them more scope for manoeuvre, or compromise."

Ross recalled the bundles of tough winter clothing which had been brought aboard almost as soon as *Manxman* had dropped anchor. Flown directly from England. The weather and conditions would be terrible, a real challenge even to the hard men. Perhaps 'Lazarus' made some sense after all.

The 'muddle' to which Parsons had referred was still scattered across the foredeck, scrambling nets, hoisting gear, and more canned stores. *No going back. You are on your way.* Most of the marines had probably never heard of South Georgia. Unlike the ones who had surrendered there.

Parsons faced him, his eyes very steady.

"Ours will be, largely, an individual role. Specialist work for true specialists. Paving the way for the brute force." He did not smile. "I have to be with the overall command. I am next senior in the land forces, so I will be able to keep an eye on *your* involvement, you can be sure of that!"

They walked together to the outer wing. *Manxman* was heading into open water, the wind across their faces like ice, tightening the skin.

"Pity we couldn't have waited a bit longer for the rest of our chaps. They're on their way, but by the time they catch us up it may be all over. Part of history. Just leaving the tab for the taxpayer, as usual."

Ross was silent, examining his own feelings. If anything, there was only a sense of relief. The decisions would be his, right or wrong. What he had lived and trained for. He licked his lips; they were very dry. And it was not due to the icy wind.

He thought of the old house. The portrait of the Colonel, and his mother's words on that last day. *Your father would be so proud of you.*

After all this time, he still felt that he had never really known him. Maybe that was the measure of strength. Keeping at a distance. Keeping them merely faces, without doubts or fears. Or love?

Parsons said, "Had a letter from my wife, just before we shoved off. She's having a child. Quite a surprise. Funny time to tell me!"

"Congratulations. Something to look forward to."

Parsons looked at his watch. "Fifteen minutes, then." He turned and gazed at him once more. "Well, so long as it's a boy. That's not too much to ask, surely?"

Ross wrenched open the chart room door and stepped into its comparative warmth. He looked back, and saw Parsons standing by the ladder, facing the sea and the wind, his body moving evenly with the deck.

A man you would never truly know, even if he allowed it.

It was the first time he had ever felt sorry for him. Perhaps because he was completely alone.

Lieutenant Peter Hamlyn seized a stanchion to retain his balance as the hull dipped and lifted violently through yet another trough. It was pitch dark, and he had lost all sense of time or direction. Maybe he had been too long aboard *Manxman*'s massive bulk, which had ridden the wind and sea more comfortably. Or maybe it was simply tension, checking and rechecking each detail.

He kept telling himself that he should be used to it: all

those drills and exercises in small boats should have done the trick. He felt his mouth crack into a smile. He had felt a wave of seasickness within minutes of casting off from the towing vessel. At least he had managed to find some humour in it.

All the windows of the launch's squat wheelhouse were fully lowered, so that the sounds of the sea and the mutter of the twin diesels seemed deafening. Surely some one would hear or see them? He gripped the stanchion as the deck fell beneath him. Even through his thick glove the metal felt like ice.

Occasionally he saw a splash of white as water lifted above the side deck like ghosts, before pattering into the wheelhouse. He should be used to this too, he thought. All the hours they had scrambled through this same launch, and that was when it had been lying with its twin on *Manxman*'s spacious foredeck.

He had studied the charts and the close-action maps until he thought he would know every cove, bay and glacier by sight.

Suppose it was no longer a secret? Weapons already trained, sights set on the target. *Us*. They had gone over it again and again. *What happens if?* Day after day during the long haul from Plymouth, they had thought of little else.

They had even joked about it. He could feel some of the others standing and lurching around him. Dark shapes, not even shadows. And yet he felt that he could see each man, recognize an expression or habit. Sergeant 'Smiler' Norris, watchful, taciturn, never in a flap, always there when you needed him. Marine Jock Marsh, who had been checking his ammunition and weapons almost up to the moment of climbing down into the launch. Nobody could question his skill and accuracy with any kind of weapon, automatic or otherwise. But you could see it in his face; like that day on the river in Londonderry. He enjoyed it. Beside him, in complete contrast, Marine Frank Burgess, who had also been there and had served in several trouble spots before. Hamlyn could still remember his concern for the girl, sobbing for her dead lover.

And Marine 'Ginger' Leach, a hard case if ever there was one. Always in a fight, or causing one. Even now he had a deep scar on his cheek after a punch-up with some soldiers in a pub. S.A.S. men; he should have known better. He had been promoted to corporal twice, and had been busted each time. Forester had made it clear that he would not get another offer.

Maybe Leach was watching or listening to the two soldiers who were positioned each side of the helmsman, the three of them swaying and bowing as if in some ritual dance. They were both S.A.S., and had been brought out to *Manxman* as key players in the operation. Hamlyn touched his chin, still smooth from a last shave before he had changed into his combat gear. All these men had probably done likewise. It was no use asking why; you might be dead before you needed another shave. It was their way. You could hardly say that about the two S.A.S. men who were to be their guides for the first leg of this attack.

He tested the word in his mind. An attack. It was no longer an operation, on paper, or in some one's head at Northwood, 'the hole'. They looked the part, dirty and unwashed, their combat gear stained and torn. And unshaven.

As one marine had muttered, "Wouldn't care to meet those guys on a dark night!" He doubted if it would deter Ginger Leach next time. If there was one.

They had lived on South Georgia for days, watching and reconnoitring Argentine positions and defences. Now they were going back. Volunteers. A different face to the same conflict.

He heard another voice: Lieutenant Colin Ash, from Aberdeen. A good all-rounder, he must have taken to his first ever commando training like a duck to water. Climb, swim or march for miles in full kit, he seemed tireless. Always ready to answer questions or demonstrate something difficult to one of the new faces. Captain Forester did not seem to approve, but then, you were never quite sure with the captain. He stiffened as Forester's voice reached him above the boat and sea noises.

That was the strange part. Smart, reliable, unswerving when there was a job to be carried out. Again he felt his stomach muscles tighten against his belt. Like this morning. *Now.*

Guilt, then? He had tried not to let it get to him. A couple of times he had caught Forester staring at him. Or was that, too, part of it?

That afternoon would not go away. He could still see the room. There had even been a framed photograph of them together on a chest of drawers near the bed. Next door there had been children playing in the garden. Home from school, a sound he knew so well.

She had deliberately drawn the curtains, and then with that slow, provocative smile, had turned the photograph face down.

They had kissed, like the last time. No, not like the last time. It was like nothing he had known. She had pretended to fight him off, but had kissed him again and again, then she had fallen back on the bed and watched him, opening her legs. *Come on, Peter. Take me. Rape me.*

There would be some one else now. It was how she got her kicks.

He would put her out of his mind. He heard the louder

sound of sea against the land. It could have been his own heart beating. He could not forget her. Or want to.

He heard the chink of metal. Somebody had not taped his loose gear properly. He squeezed his eyes tightly shut.

They had arrived. Tromsø Cove, probably named by one of those long-gone Norwegian whalers. And there was no shooting. They were going in. The second launch would be waiting to follow, or stand away if the worst happened. He pictured Blackwood; he would be out there watching, listening. *He would not run.*

"All set, Peter?" So calm. He could have been discussing the cricket score.

"Yes, sir." He looked through the open screen. Still dark, but it was land. "I'll check the others."

"Do that, will you." He turned away as the engines took on a lower note, but louder as the land reached out on either side.

Forester climbed up to join the helmsman, and added, "Just watch your step."

It was no longer a secret.

Sergeant Dick Harwood winced and bit hard on his upturned collar as the hull shuddered against his hip. The launch had either touched bottom or scraped against a wreck of some kind. It could be just about anything. Somebody had dropped a weapon and he heard one of the marines cursing him for his sloppiness. Lucky the safety catch was on, whatever it was; they seemed to be making enough noise without a burst of gunfire. And there was another sound, some kind of pump. They might as well have a bugler playing *Wakey Wakey* and make a proper job of it.

He wiped his face with a sleeve as wet and cold as everything else. He could hear the sea: movement all around, like steering into a trap. Tromsø Cove looked small enough on the map, as if it had been hacked into the coast by a giant axe. You could feel the land, and the spray like heavy rain.

He reached down to test the lashings on their cargo. Explosives, packed and ready to use, if or when they reached their target. One stray bullet in this lot and they would go up, not down.

It all depended on surprise. Blow up the target and fall back. It would open the way for the main attack by commando and S.A.S. units, covered by gunfire from two frigates. He wiped his eyes again. Provided they could find their way through this appalling weather.

But first, the target: powerful recoilless guns, said to be 105mm, which would make short work of any landing attempt, and the frigates too, if they came into these restricted waters.

He could not see the low wheelhouse but imagined the major there with another S.A.S. guide and the helmsman, who must be wondering what miracle he would be asked to perform next. Some one touched his knee: no words. Like a warning. It was Lieutenant 'Daisy' May. Harwood had his own golden rule where most officers were concerned, especially junior ones. And especially now that he had three tapes on his sleeve. Let the officer prove himself first, and not the other way round.

Unlike most of the others, May was still a stranger and had been training with anti-tank launchers for much of the time. With a youthful, polished face, he did not need to shave yet. *He walks in a strong wind, to blow the fluff away!* But he took life very seriously indeed. Perhaps it was his defence.

"Coming in now, Sergeant. Have your sections ready to land, port side. There is a small gully . . ." one hand moved

305

vaguely toward the land, and an unbroken line of surf. "Single file after that."

"Looks as if we'll get our feet wet again."

May might have shrugged. "Better than around the headland. The glacier would be ten times worse, believe me!"

Harwood smiled. It was as if the lieutenant had already been over the ground before.

The hull gave another lurch, and a voice exclaimed, "Oh, *shit*!"

May snapped, "Take that man's name!"

Nobody answered.

He said abruptly, "Of course, you've known Major Blackwood for some while. Ulster, wasn't it? Mr. Hamlyn mentioned it. I . . ."

The rest was lost in another surge of water over the side. More curses.

Harwood thought about it. May was a fully trained commando, otherwise he would not be here. But there was always a first time. His own had been in Cyprus during the troubles there. He had been on foot patrol, with a sergeant called Arthur; he could not remember his full name. A shotgun in an alley, just like that. Arthur had died in his arms, coughing blood. He had not even had time to get off a shot at the killer.

It would be different now. But the first time . . . that was something else.

'Daisy' May was young, and it showed. Like his formality: *Major* this and *Mister* that.

He said, "If you get in a tight corner, there's none better."

It was a start. He had not even offered May a 'sir'.

Then May remarked, almost sadly, "Not much use for anti-tank launchers here."

Harwood heard the marines moving into position. He could not see it, but the picture was there. A last word, a grin, a thumbs-up or a joke. Being close to a mate or a particular oppo. Like a pattern. You needed it.

He turned back toward May; he could see the youthful oval of his face now against the dark backdrop. It was May who needed it now.

"We didn't know that the Argies would have a sub or two here, either. We'll take it a step at a time, right, sir?"

May was still looking at him. "Thanks." One word, but Harwood was satisfied. It was enough.

He said, "If I say *down*, sir, fast as you like, see?"

The launch grated over another ridge, and the engines stopped.

Harwood shouted, "Go, lads, *go!*"

They were all scrambling and wading through swirling water, weapons held high, some of them wheezing like old men as the cold took a ruthless grip.

Harwood almost fell but regained his feet, his mind snatching at essentials and shouted commands. Ammunition, clips in position, commando knife within reach for instant use. His hand groped around his streaming waterproof. Two days' rations, always a joke with the lads. But not now.

He punched a man's shoulder. "Move it, Thomas! Jump about!"

He could almost hear his thoughts. *Bloody sergeants, why don't they shove it?*

They were on hard, slippery ground, and the launch was lost in the gloom. It might have sunk, for all they knew.

Nothing mattered now but to keep going. Harwood bared his teeth. Even the air tasted different.

They were in the gully. Funny how you knew, even though you had never seen it, except on that bloody map.

They were keeping together, boots hammering and

splashing, as if something ruthless and impersonal were driving them.

Harwood saw a flicker of light, perhaps a reflection from the ice they had been discussing. Then the sound of a shot, and another, or an echo.

Some one cried out and fell.

Keep going. Don't look back.

They had reached the end of the gully. As if a curtain had been dragged away, here was the sky, and the hint of water beyond. Harsh and metallic, the air freezing your lungs. But still running, running.

There were more shots, but they were here at that first pencilled cross. A building, like a large shack, red with rust and buckled with age. Near the old whaling station. It had to be.

Blackwood's voice then, some one else repeating his orders, as they had done so many times. Sunshine or snow, sand or jungle, who cared? Harwood fell on his stomach, holding his breath, blinking to clear his vision, one glove dangling while he trained his semi-automatic rifle.

Don't fail me now, chummy. It was ice-cold, too. But ready.

Ross Blackwood dropped on to one knee, snow or freezing rain half blinding him while he peered from side to side to recover his bearings. He could see the nearest marines in his section spread out on either side, not as individuals any more, but part of the attack. Just pausing for a few seconds was enough. Like hearing something or some one screaming a warning, or feeling the bullet hitting you like a steel fist.

It should have been lighter, something to offer a hint of position. Fragments of ice bounced over his shoulders, like broken glass. He covered his face with his wrist, gripping the rifle with his free hand. It flashed through his mind. *Officers should not be distinguished from their men by uniform or weapon.* How many had died to drive that lesson home? He looked up, astonished that he could remember such trivial instruction, and he saw it. The ridge, which he was just beginning to believe had eluded him, or that he was leading the others on the wrong bearing. The ridge, like a pile of crude steps, outlined in ice against the sky. Beyond it, a steep slope, then a drop into the sea . . .

He waved his arm and started to run again. Something hissed through the air, a stray shot, or aimed at him, but it meant nothing.

Others were running, the pain and weariness falling away; time and distance had ceased to have any meaning.

He saw another figure crouched nearby, and signalled with his fist. Corporal Tasker knew what to do. A blurred shape, and yet Ross could recognize him. Just promoted; a Londoner with a good singing voice. His father was a Billingsgate fish porter. Pity he could not see him now . . . He loped forward again. Dangerous to allow your mind to play games.

It *was* getting lighter. When daylight came, it would be sudden. If they mistook the direction now, they would be laid bare and helpless, like insects on a fly-paper. *Now or never.* He heaved himself up and ran to the first ledge of rock.

If he were both blind and deaf, he would have known it was the sea. In his mind's eye he saw the chart again, and the folded map now squeezed inside his jacket. A pencilled cross. Not even that.

He forced his brain to steady, deal only with *here* and *now*.

He began to scramble forward once more. There was a similar ridge on his right. Invisible as yet, but he could *see*

309

it. Any well-sited guns would play hell with men trying to land, and could easily drive off the two promised frigates. He waited for his breathing to slow. Forester's marines would be fanned out below and behind. To offer supporting fire, or to cover the retreat if the worst happened. Retreat? Where to? One launch damaged or sunk, and the other could be anywhere.

He moved forward again, his knees scraping on rock or ice, against which the protective clothing seemed useless. He could feel the pain in his chest, the crooked scars left by bullet and shattered binoculars. So long ago. The hospital, her shadow beside the bed. Always the pain . . .

He flung out his arm and thought he heard a clasp or buckle clink against the ground.

Harwood was here somewhere, keeping an eye on the young subaltern. Without letting him know it, of course.

He took another deep breath and raised himself very slowly, giving his eyes time to discover and determine.

The map no longer mattered. It was more like a giant photograph, unreal in the grey-blue light.

He levelled his binoculars, new, and still warm from his body. King Edward Point, well to the left, and there was the abandoned whaling station at Grytviken. It could have been anything, but it would soon show itself. Where all this had started. He moved the glasses very carefully. The light was stronger here. Like a camera lens focusing. He could see the outline of the cemetery, and the perfect landmark, the tiny, white-painted church. Nothing moved, not even the water; close inland, it was almost black. Solid.

He moved his head. His neck felt stiff, raw.

All in position. *How do I know that?* They were there. There was no more shooting. An accident? Some one trying to sound the alarm? They might never find out. Now.

He looked at the stretch of level ground: a narrow road,

maybe only a track leading from the whaling station. Sheltered by the other ridge, a few buildings and some pale shapes faintly outlined against the sea. For a moment he felt something like shock. Panic. This was the camp of the British Antarctic Survey Party, those hardy and dedicated souls who had done so much for the welfare and improvement of the islands, and who had been the first people to be suspicious of the Argentine 'scrap metal merchants'.

He tried again, the glasses moving very slowly. The pale shapes sharpened in the lenses. White, probably coated with frozen snow. He remembered reading about it somewhere. Inflatable life rafts had been brought to the Falklands, to South Georgia, to be tested in the worst possible conditions before being issued to those ships which were stationed here year round. They had proved useless, and they looked out of place in the B.A.S. camp. They would, however, be perfect camouflage for the target. *Our reason for being here.* The 105mm guns. If not, there was nothing else that fitted the intelligence analysis.

"All set, sir."

It was time. If there were no guns, the main attack would go ahead, and they would have died for nothing. But if the guns were in position, they had no choice.

He did not need to look to know it was Harwood. He groped for the rifle, and felt Harwood's eyes on him. They would both remember this. Given the chance.

Captain Forester and his men would be in position also. Explosives team, lookouts in line with the little white church. Hamlyn and Smiler Norris, perhaps thinking of Londonderry, and that other dawn by the river. All their faces . . .

Only one could give the order.

He stood up, and felt the life returning to his legs.

"Let's take a walk, shall we?"

Strange to be walking on flat ground after the hard slog from Tromsø Cove. Only another blurred memory now. It seemed bigger, longer, than it had appeared from the ridge, although Ross knew the distance to the very feet and yards. The silence was almost the worst part, just their boots and the scrape of frozen combat gear. They had reached a dip in the land, so that the nearest buildings looked half buried in slush, and the little church was marked only by its steeple, like a dark fin against the sea beyond.

He looked quickly to his left, and saw the nearest marines stretched out in an uneven line. A trick of vision or nerves: they all seemed to be moving faster, driven on by the silence and the inevitable.

Forester's men would be moving too, in small groups, covering each other and ready to offer support. Always reliable, never needed telling twice, although initiative might be another matter.

It was hard to imagine the size or scope of the eventual landing force, ships, launches, men and guns. South Georgia was the first step back. He looked to his right and saw Harwood lift his fist.

Parsons would be out there somewhere, alone despite the numbers all around him. Glad or resentful that over-all command was in another man's hands? Impossible to tell.

It was as if he had heard his voice. Seen his expression, or lack of it. *She's having a child.* Not *we.*

Ross felt the ground rising more unevenly. Slippery here. A few feet, but it felt as if they were climbing out of a valley.

The crack of gunfire was sudden, impartial, as if it were somewhere else, distant. But the slap and thud of bullets was real and direct.

He waved his arm but they were running again, zig-zagging and gathering speed as the church took shape, and a square building which had been so far away was right here, beside the road.

The sharper rattle of automatic fire ripped the morning. Forester's men were on the flank, and Ross could hear the shots cracking through and against some of the rust-streaked buildings, and saw feathers of ice being torn from the road, back and forth with hardly a break. He heard some one yell a command and knew that the explosives team were ready, taking full advantage of covering fire. Another voice was shouting at somebody to keep down. Almost shrill in the bitter air: it was young May, in charge and up there with his team.

Ross flung himself against a snow-covered hump. It could have been anything, but he heard bullets hitting it, to no avail.

There was less firing now, and he saw two marines charge past, one calling to the other, then one of their rifles slid over a patch of ice and the leading marine skidded to a halt, turning back to stare at his companion, who had been flung on his back by the power of the shot. He called again, the words torn from his mouth, then blotted out by a retaliatory burst of automatic fire.

There was nothing any one could do. So much blood, obscenely scarlet against the piled snow.

Ross was on his feet, and across the road. The sky above King Edward Point was clear and empty, but without comfort for the running, stumbling figures. He tasted smoke, the smell of rapid-firing weapons, heard men shouting, to one another or at the unseen enemy.

A figure suddenly appeared from a narrow gap between two buildings. Ross saw the gun jerk up and level, the face above it like a mask. Unreal.

Some one else was kicking a broken door out of his way, as if nothing else mattered. It was Harwood.

Ross yelled, "Dick! *Get down!*"

The other figure swung round. Young, wild-eyed, wearing a uniform of some kind. Ross had no time to think or consider. Even the weapon in his hands seemed beyond his control.

The other man shouted something, his mouth a black hole, his arms clawing at the air as the gun came alive.

Harwood stood very still, looking down at the blood-soaked uniform, the eyes now tightly shut at the moment of impact.

Then he walked past the corpse and gripped Ross's shoulder.

"Thanks. Near thing that time!"

Ross dragged out a fresh magazine. "Not your turn yet!"

He looked at the dead face. Perhaps he had been trying to surrender. *Did he even know what he was doing in this place?* And he thought of the dying marine, his friend arrested by the abrupt impartiality of death. *Did he?*

There were two sharp explosions. The charges had been blown. He wanted to laugh. *And I never even saw the guns we came to destroy!*

He saw Hamlyn and several of his men coming around the side of the building, weapons levelled and ready. One of the marines saw them standing by the corpse, and called, "'Ow much longer?" It did not seem to matter what they saw or did, so long as they kept together.

Was it that simple?

More shouts and sporadic firing, bullets whining in all directions, glass shattering, rust blowing like red sand from a nearby roof. He saw a marine turn and staring up at the nearest building, his semi-automatic rifle wavering as the first sunlight lanced over the water.

314

Ross heard a shot and saw the marine stagger, pivoting round before he hit the road. But the picture was wrong, and the front of the building seemed to be falling away, no sound or explosion offering warning or explanation.

Harwood was here, but, like the building, at the wrong angle. As if he was above him. It was madness. *Not now. Not now.* He wanted to call out, to tell some one . . . And then the pain came, and he heard a voice crying out. Somehow he knew it was his own.

Then there was oblivion.

Lieutenant Peter Hamlyn was standing on a collapsed boardwalk beside one of the buildings. It had been a store of some kind, and was now a wreck like everything else. He saw a white silhouette through the drifting smoke. Except for the church.

He peered at his watch. It was badly scratched, but still functioning: his parents had given it to him when he had got his first pip, at his eventual commissioning.

Three hours. Was that all it had taken?

Smoke everywhere, and he could see the long muzzles of the guns they had come to the ends of the earth to destroy. They would never fire a shot in anger. He coughed, and took the cigarette from his mouth. Two bodies lay by the wall, covered by blankets and a strip of canvas. One was the marine who had been killed by a high-velocity bullet. A sniper, or a stray shot? They would never know.

He heard the intermittent bang of gunfire and exhaled slowly: the main attack was under way. The frigates, probably close inshore now that the hidden guns had been rendered useless. A few armed marines were standing farther along the roadway. He saw the prisoners standing or squatting in groups, a few still carrying makeshift white flags of surrender. If they had put up a real fight and delayed the marines a little longer, their roles might have been reversed.

Men fighting, falling wounded. Some dying, but not many. He relit the cigarette and looked at one of the covered corpses. He was good with names usually, and he could remember this young marine's face without difficulty. But the name was gone. One of Colin Ash's section. He had not known that he had saved Ross Blackwood's life. The high-velocity bullet had punched right through him. His body had taken the full impact.

He could remember Harwood's face; he was unlikely to ever forget it, or his voice. A man who had seen and done as much as any of them, suddenly stricken.

The bastards have done for the Major!

No wonder. There had been blood everywhere. If Blackwood had been dead, those white flags would not have afforded their prisoners much protection.

Some one said, "They're comin' now, sir."

Hamlyn straightened his back. He felt as if he had been on his feet for a month. He had not realized that there were others standing close by, part of it. Sharing it.

They brought the stretcher out into the cold sunlight and propped it carefully on some empty ammunition boxes.

Harwood was here too, strained and still on edge.

Hamlyn said, "Is he O.K.?"

Harwood looked at him, and the shadow of a smile crossed his face.

"Didn't know you smoked, sir. Fitness, an' all that?"

Hamlyn gazed down at Ross Blackwood's face.

"I didn't." He cleared his throat. "Don't see what they get out of it!"

He reached down to the stretcher, but withdrew the hand. "Is he really going to be O.K.?"

Harwood nodded. Even that was an effort.

"Bloody miracle. Opened the wound he got in Derry."
Their eyes met. "When he was with you. But for young
Bishop gettin' in the way, well, who can say?"

Hamlyn glanced at the other bundle. *Bishop*. That was
his name. The lads had often pulled his leg about it. He said
in a quiet voice, "God, I'm so glad."

Ross Blackwood heard, or thought he heard, most of it.
Like coming out of a fog. The pain was there, but held at
bay. He was drugged and nauseated, but he could remember everything. Almost everything . . . He had even heard
the gunfire. Now there was another sound, a coughing roar.
Getting louder, nearer. His mind responded this time.

"Helicopters?"

Harwood leaned over him.

"From the frigates, sir. One of their choppers is taking
you out of this dump."

He was not just smiling now. The grin was filling his
wind-burned face.

Ross stared at the sky.

"Leaving?" It sounded like a protest.

"Yeah. You'll be fine after a patch-up an' a spot of leaf
at 'ome!"

Hamlyn saw a corporal running to signal the helicopter
pilot, and shaded Ross's eyes against the dust being
churned up by the flashing blades.

But Ross was looking at the Union flag, which had been
hoisted on a makeshift mast where the defenders had
displayed a huge white sheet. He murmured, "Good
thinking. He'll need to know the wind direction for a safe
landing," and smiled, beginning to drift on morphine. "*In
this dump.*"

The medics were running toward them now, through the
slush and rust. Harwood said, "We did it for *you*, Major
Blackwood."

Then, surprisingly, he stood back, and saluted.
The helicopter was even noisier when it started to lift off.
But Harwood was saying, "And for *her*!"

Badge of Glory

Douglas Reeman

It was an age of Empire, an age of contrast, and an age of dramatic change – and one which would determine the destinies of nations as well as of men.

Captain Philip Blackwood of the Royal Marines rejoins his ship, HMS *Audacious*, in the August of 1850, anxious to get back into action. Per Mare – Per Terram is the Marines' motto. In the torturous heat of Africa, where they are sent to stamp out the remaining strongholds of slavery, and later, in the bitter war of the Crimea, Philip Blackwood and his men learn to obey it without question.

This is the first novel in the Blackwood saga, spanning 150 years in the history of a great seafaring family and the tradition in which they served.

arrow books

Dust on the Sea

Douglas Reeman

It is 1943, and Captain Mike Blackwood, Royal Marine Commando, is a survivor. Young, toughened and tried in the hellish crucible of Burma, he labours, sometimes faltering, beneath the weight of tradition, the glorious heritage of his family, and the burden of his own self-doubt.

For Blackwood, the horizon is not the lip of the trench seen by men of the Corps in the previous war, but the ramp of a landing craft smashing down into the sea, and the fire of the enemy on a Sicilian beach.

Here, tradition is not enough, and Mike Blackwood must find within himself qualities of leadership which will inspire those Royal Marines who are once again the first to land, and among the first to die.

This is the fourth novel in the Blackwood saga, spanning 150 years in the history of a great seafaring family and the tradition in which they served.

arrow books

First to Land

Douglas Reeman

1899, China. The Mandarins are becoming troublesome again and there are rumours that attacks will soon begin on British trade missions and legations. Captain David Blackwood of the Royal Marines, received a VC in the bloody battle for Benin, Africa but is now being packed off to this apparent backwater.

But there are plenty of troubles in store for Blackwood in the shape of an errant nephew and a beautiful German Countess who insists he personally escort her up river on a small steamer into the heart of the country. China is a sleeping tiger that will soon awake when the Boxer Rebellion erupts into bloody war in 1900. True to their motto, the Royal Marines are the first to land – and the last to leave.

This is the second novel in the Blackwood saga, spanning 150 years in the history of a great seafaring family and the tradition in which they served.

arrow books

In Danger's Hour

Douglas Reeman

Aged only 28, Ian Ransome was already a veteran of warfare. Captain of the fleet minesweeper HMS *Rob Roy*, he daily faced the ever-present risk of death – from the air or the sea – in waters strewn with lethal mines.

But the summer of 1944 is on the horizon. As the allies prepare for D-Day, Ransome must steer *Rob Roy* towards her most dangerous mission yet: a deadly challenge that will test captain and crewman alike to the limits of endurance – and beyond . . .

In Danger's Hour is the electrifying bestseller by the master storyteller of the sea, Douglas Reeman. Full of human drama, suspense and unforgettable battle scenes, it tells the story of the unsung heroes of the navy's 'little ships' who fought in one of the most dangerous areas of war.

arrow books

Path of the Storm

Douglas Reeman

The old submarine-chaser USS *Hibiscus*, re-fitting in a Hong Kong dockyard before being handed over to the Nationalist Chinese, is suddenly ordered to the desolate island group of Payenhau.

For Captain Mark Gunnar – driven by the memory of his torture at the hands of Viet Cong guerrillas – the new command is a chance to even the score against a ruthless, unrelenting enemy.

But Payenhau is very different from his expectations, and as the weather worsens a crisis develops that Gunnar must face alone.

arrow books

Surface With Daring

Douglas Reeman

Hiding, lying in wait on the sea bed, is *EX 16*, one of the most important ships in the Royal Navy. She's not much to look at, and she's only 54 feet long, with no defensive armament. But her four-man crew knows that the outcome of the war could depend on this midget submarine.

Seaton, her commander, understands what his men face. There is the boredom, the discomfort, the jealousy and bickering; and already they have confronted enormous dangers on desperate raids into Norway. Now, poised for the attack on a secret Nazi rocket installation, Seaton must hold his crew together for the hell that awaits them . . .

arrow books

The Last Raider

Douglas Reeman

It is December 1917. Germany opens the final, bitter round of the war with a new and deadly weapon in the struggle for the seas – the Vulcan sails from Kiel Harbour.

To all appearances she is a harmless merchant vessel. But her peaceful lines conceal a merciless firepower; guns, mines and torpedoes that can be brought into play instantly.

The Vulcan is a commerce raider. And under crack commander Felix von Steiger her mission is to bring chaos to the seaways.

Torpedo Run

Douglas Reeman

It was in 1943. On the Black Sea, the Russians were fighting a desperate battle to regain control. But the Russians' one real weakness was on the water: whatever they did, the Germans did it better, and the daring hit-and-run tactics of the E-boats plagued them. At last the British agreed to send them a small flotilla of motor torpedo boats under the command of John Devane.

Devane has been in the Navy since the outbreak of war. More than a veteran, he was a survivor – and the two rarely went together in the savage war of MTBs. Given command at short notice, Devane soon learnt that, even against the vast and raging background of the Eastern Front, war could still be a personal duel between individuals.

arrow books

Twelve Seconds to Live

Douglas Reeman

The mine is an impartial killer, and a lethal challenge to any volunteer in the Special Countermeasures of the Royal Navy.

They are brave, lonely men with something to prove or nothing left to lose. Lieutenant-Commander David Masters, haunted by a split second glimpse of the mine that destroyed his first and only command, H.M. Submarine *Tornado*, now defuses 'the beast' on land and teaches the same deadly science to others who too often die in the attempt.

Lieutenant Chris Foley, minelaying off an enemy coast in ML366, rolls on an uneasy sea with a release bracket sheared and a lie mine jammed, and hears the menacing growl of approaching E-boats.

And Sub-Lieutenant Michael Lincoln, hailed as a hero, dreads exposure as a coward even more than the unexpected booby-trap, or the gentle whirr of the activated fuse marking the last twelve seconds of his life.

arrow books

Order further Douglas Reeman titles
from your local bookshop, or have them delivered direct to your door by Bookpost

	Title	ISBN	Price
☐	Battlecruiser	0 09 943987 5	£6.99
☐	First to land	0 09 942410 X	£6.99
☐	Go in and Sink!	0 09 909760 5	£5.99
☐	In Danger's Hour	0 09 946238 9	£6.99
☐	The Last Raider	0 09 905580 5	£6.99
☐	Path of the Storm	0 09 907070 7	£5.99
☐	Rendezvous – South Atlantic	0 09 907820 1	£5.99
☐	Strike from the Sea	0 09 918780 9	£5.99
☐	Surface With Daring	0 09 914550 5	£6.99
☐	Badge of Glory	0 09 932100 9	£6.99
☐	Dust on the Sea	0 09 942167 4	£6.99
☐	Deep Silence	0 09 907860 0	£5.99
☐	The Destroyers	0 09 911610 3	£5.99
☐	Dive in the Sun	0 09 907050 2	£5.99
☐	For Valour	0 09 928062 0	£6.99
☐	High Water	0 09 907900 3	£5.99
☐	The Horizon	0 09 948443 9	£6.99
☐	Hostile Shore	0 09 907880 5	£6.99
☐	Last Raider	0 09 905580 5	£5.99
☐	A Prayer for the Ship	0 09 907890 2	£6.99
☐	The Pride and the Anguish	0 09 907940 2	£5.99
☐	Send a Gunboat	0 09 907060 X	£5.99
☐	A Ship Must Die	0 09 922600 6	£5.99
☐	To Risks Unknown	0 09 905570 8	£6.99
☐	Torpedo Run	0 09 928380 8	£5.99
☐	The Volunteers	0 09 945960 7	£6.99
☐	Winged Escort	0 09 913380 6	£5.99
☐	With Blood and Iron	0 09 906270 4	£5.99
☐	Twelve Seconds to Live	0 09 941487 2	£6.99

Free post and packing
Overseas customers allow £2 per paperback

Phone: 01624 677237

Post: Random House Books
c/o Bookpost, PO Box 29, Douglas, Isle of Man IM99 1BQ

Fax: 01624 670923

email: bookshop@enterprise.net

Cheques (payable to Bookpost) and credit cards accepted

Prices and availability subject to change without notice.
Allow 28 days for delivery.
When placing your order, please state if you do not wish to receive any additional information.

www.randomhouse.co.uk/arrowbooks